W9-AAE-215

3 1804 00210 2901

Damage Noted Prior to Checkout
Markings_____ Liquid_____ Binding_____
Broken Case_____ Torn/Loose Pages_____
Stains _____ Other_____
Date/Initials _____

WITHDRAWN

DATE DUE

S

FE

FIRESIDE

SUSAN WIGGS

*F*IRESIDE

ACORN PUBLIC LIBRARY
15624 S. CENTRAL AVE.
OAK FOREST, IL 60452

MIRA®

ISBN-13: 978-1-60751-608-8

FIRESIDE

Copyright © 2009 by Susan Wiggs.

All rights reserved. Except for use in any review, the reproduction or
utilization of this work in whole or in part in any form by any electronic,
mechanical or other means, now known or hereafter invented, including
xerography, photocopying and recording, or in any information storage or
retrieval system, is forbidden without the written permission of the publisher,
MIRA Books, 225 Duncan Mill Road, Don Mills, Ontario, Canada M3B 3K9.

This is a work of fiction. Names, characters, places and incidents are
either the product of the author's imagination or are used fictitiously, and
any resemblance to actual persons, living or dead, business establishments,
events or locales is entirely coincidental.

MIRA and the Star Colophon are trademarks used under license and registered
in Australia, New Zealand, Philippines, United States Patent and Trademark
Office and in other countries.

Printed In U.S.A.

This book is for my friend Lois, with love.

ACKNOWLEDGMENTS

Thanks to my own personal brain trust—
Anjali Banerjee, Carol Cassella, Sheila Roberts,
Suzanne Selfors, Elsa Watson, Kate Breslin,
Lois Faye Dyer, Rose Marie Harris, Patty Jough-Haan,
Susan Plunkett and Krysteen Seelen—
wonderful writers and even better friends.

Thanks to Mr. David Boyle, president and co-owner
of the New Haven County Cutters, for information
regarding Independent Baseball and the
Can-Am League.

Thanks also to Margaret O'Neill Marbury and
Adam Wilson of MIRA Books, Meg Ruley and
Annelise Robey of the Jane Rotrosen Agency,
for invaluable advice and input. Thanks to my publisher
and readers for supporting the Lakeshore Chronicles
and for coming back to Avalon again and again.

With every word I write, I'm grateful to my family—
the reason for everything.

Dear Reader,

There are many ways to make a family, and that's really the essence of the LAKESHORE CHRONICLES books. As each story ends, a new one unfolds. The one element they all have in common is the key ingredient that makes everything hold together—love. I deeply appreciate the readers who have been so supportive of these books.

Later this year, Christmas comes to Avalon in a new hardcover novel. In *Lakeshore Christmas,* bad-boy rocker Eddie Haven teams up with Maureen Davenport, the town librarian, to direct the annual Christmas pageant. Please look for *Lakeshore Christmas* in bookstores in October 2009.

Happy reading,

Susan Wiggs

One

LaGuardia Airport
Concourse C
Gate 21

The dark glasses didn't hide a thing, not really. When people saw someone in dark glasses on a cloudy day in the middle of winter, they assumed the wearer was hiding the fact that she'd been drinking, crying or fighting.

Or all of the above.

Under any number of circumstances, Kimberly van Dorn enjoyed being the center of attention. Last night, when she'd donned her couture gown with its scandalous slit up the side, turning heads had been the whole idea. She'd had no idea the evening would implode the way it had. How could she?

Now, at the end of a soul-flattening red-eye flight, she kept her shades on as the plane touched down and taxied to the Jetway. Coach. She never flew coach. Last night, however, first class had been sold out, personal comfort had taken a back seat to expediency, and she'd found herself in seat 29-E in the middle of the middle section of the plane, wedged between strangers. Sometimes the need to get away was more powerful than the need for legroom. Although her stiff legs this morning might argue that point.

Who the hell had designed coach class, anyway? She was convinced she had the imprint of her seatmate's ear on her shoulder. After his fourth beer, he kept falling asleep, his head lolling onto her. What was worse than a man with a lolling head?

A man with a lolling head and beer breath, she thought grimly, trying to shake off the torturous transcontinental night. But the memories lingered like the ache in her legs— the lolling guy with a snoring problem, and, on her other side, an impossibly chatty older gentleman, who talked for hours about his insomnia. And his bursitis. And his lousy son-in-law, his fondness for fried sweet potatoes and his dislike of the Jude Law movie Kim was pretending to watch in hopes of getting him to shut up.

No wonder she never flew coach. Yet the nightmare flight was not the worst thing that had happened to her lately. Far from it.

She stood in the aisle, waiting for the twenty-eight rows ahead of her to deplane. The process seemed endless as people rummaged in the overhead bins, gathering their things while talking on mobile phones.

She took out her phone, thumb hovering over the power button. She really ought to call her mother, let her know she was coming home. Not now, though, she thought, putting the phone away. She was too exhausted to make any sense. Besides, for all she knew, the thing had one of those tracking features, and she didn't feel like being tracked.

Now that she'd arrived, she wasn't in such a big hurry. In fact, she was utterly unprepared to face a dreary midwinter morning in New York. Ignoring the stares of other passengers, she tried to act as though traveling in an evening gown was a routine occurrence for her, and hoped people would just assume she was a victim of lost luggage.

If only it could be that simple.

Shuffling along the narrow aisle of the coach section, she definitely *felt* like a victim. In more ways than one.

She left behind a scattering of sequins in the aisle. There was a reason clothes like this were designated as "evening wear." The silk charmeuse dress, encrusted with sequins, was meant to be worn in the romantic semidarkness of a candlelit private club or southern California garden, lit by tiki torches. Not in the broad, unforgiving daylight of a Saturday morning.

It was funny, she thought, how even a couture gown from Shantung on Rodeo Drive managed to look tawdry in the morning light. Especially when combined with a side slit, bare legs and peep-toe spike heels with a crisscross ankle strap. Only last night, every detail had whispered *class*. Now her outfit screamed *hooker*. No wonder she was getting funny looks.

But last night, in the middle of everything, Kim hadn't been thinking about the morning. She'd just been thinking about getting away. It seemed as though a million years had passed since then, since she'd dressed so carefully, so filled with hope and optimism. Lloyd Johnson, star of the Lakers and the biggest client of the PR firm she worked for, was at the pinnacle of his career. More importantly for Kimberly, he'd found his dream house in Manhattan Beach. They planned to live there together. It was supposed to be her night, a moment of triumph, maybe even a life-changing occasion if Lloyd had decided to pop the question. Well, it had been life-changing, just not in the way she'd anticipated. She had sunk everything she had into her career as a sports publicist. And overnight, that had crumbled. She was Jerry Maguire without the triumphant ending.

She finally reached the front of the aircraft, murmuring a thank-you to the flight attendants as she passed. It wasn't their fault the flight had been so miserable, and they'd been up all night, too. Then, just as she stepped onto the Jetway, the security doors opened and a ground-crew guy in a jumpsuit and earphones blew in on a gust of frigid wind.

The arctic air slapped her like a physical assault, tearing at the silk dress and skimming over her bare legs. She gasped aloud and gathered a fringed wrap—the only outerwear she had—around her bare shoulders, clutching it in one fist, her jewel-encrusted peacock evening bag in the other.

Sweet, merciful Lord. She had forgotten this—the East Coast cold that simply had no rival anywhere in California. She grabbed her long red hair but was too late. It had already been blown into a terrifying bouffant, and she was fairly sure she'd lost an earring. Lovely.

Holding her head high, she emerged from the Jetway and entered the terminal, walking at a normal, unhurried pace, though she wanted to collapse. The red-soled Louboutins with their three-inch heels, which had looked so fabulous with the single-shoulder sheath, now felt hideous on her feet.

Silently cursing the couture shoes and clutching the silk wrap around her, she scanned the concourse for an open shop to buy something to wear on the last leg of the trip, to the town of Avalon up in the Catskills, where her mother now lived. Last night, there had been no time to grab anything, even if she *had* been thinking straight. She'd made the flight with moments to spare.

To her dismay, all the kiosks and shops along the way were still closed; never had she craved a pair of flip-flops and an I ♥ NY T-shirt more. It was a long walk to the commuter concourse, especially in these heels.

She passed people in warm winter clothes, probably heading up to the mountains for a weekend of fun. She pretended not to notice the looks of speculation, the comments whispered behind snugly gloved hands. Ordinarily, other people's opinions were her first concern. But not today. She was too tired to care what people were saying about her.

Across the way stood a guy, leaning with his foot propped against the wall, staring at her. Okay, so a lot of guys were staring at her, since she was dressed like an escapee from a Hooters convention. He was easily six foot five and had long hair, and he wore cargo pants and an army surplus parka with wolf fur around the hood.

She was an idiot for not being able to ignore him. Men were her downfall; she should know better. And—please, Lord, no—with a leisurely air, he pushed away from the wall and seemed to be ambling toward her. Kim had never been much of a student of literature, but as he advanced on her, she found herself remembering a phrase coined by Dorothy Parker—*What fresh hell is this?*

More quickly than was prudent in the skinny heels, she

headed for the moving walkway, wishing it could be a magic carpet, whisking her away from her troubles. She stepped aboard—and felt one of her heels sink down between the grooves of the walkway. Gritting her teeth, she tried to tug her foot free. As she did so, the other heel sank into another groove.

And just when she thought the day could not get any worse, it did.

Two

Bo Crutcher sized up the redhead in the high heels at the gate across the way. She'd arrived on the red-eye from L.A. He was waiting for a different arrival, a red-eye from Houston. The sign over the gate was flashing *Delayed.*

The L.A. redhead was exactly his type—tall and slender, amazing hair and big tits, slutty clothes. He loved that in a woman. She was glaring daggers at him, but since he had time to kill, he welcomed any distraction. She was all of Bo's favorite things in one package—tequila shots and Dreamsicles, Stanley Clarke riffs and the most perfect throw of a baseball, the one that could never be touched by any batter ever born. She had one of the world's perfect asses and a face like a goddess in a Renaissance painting. Unforgettable.

At the moment, he had no business checking her out, but she was hard to ignore. He studied her the way an art afficionado might check out a painting of Botticelli's *Venus.* Bo had never understood how an artist could sit there and paint a picture of a naked woman. How the hell could the guy concentrate in the presence of a nude model?

As though attuned to his inappropriate thoughts, the redhead sped toward the moving sidewalk in the middle of the concourse, her heels clicking with disapproval.

And Bo was left to remember his purpose. This was not the way he had planned to spend his weekend. He should be home, sleeping off a big night at the Hilltop Tavern. Torres had fought Bledsoe in the match of the year, and Bo had ponied up a thousand bucks for a satellite feed to the bar. He'd anticipated staying up late, drawing beer after beer for the patrons and friends, cheering for the underdog on the 60-inch plasma screen that had put the bar in debt and drawn the wrath of his boss, Maggie Lynn. It was shaping up to be a damn fine night, any way you looked at it.

Except it hadn't gone that way. His plans fell apart when he checked his voice mail, receiving the most unexpected phone call of his life. At that point, he'd been obliged to drop everything and drive as fast as he dared from Avalon, deep in the Catskills, down to New York City in order to meet the flight from Houston.

Now, standing at Gate 22-C in the terminal, he was sweating bullets made of grade-A panic. And he had another half hour to kill. He glanced around, focused again on the redhead, now gliding away on the automatic sidewalk. She seemed to be having a little trouble with her shoes, though. She was bent over, apparently trying to unbuckle the straps.

Realizing she was stuck, he hurried over, stepped aboard the walkway and sprinted to her side. "You look like you could use a hand, ma'am," he said.

She continued struggling with the strap of her high heel. Not one but both heels appeared to be stuck. He looked around wildly for a moment, seeking an emergency switch. Seeing nothing, he bent down, put his hand around one of her ankles and yanked her foot free. She gave a yelp of surprise and panic.

"Get away from me," she said. "I mean it, back off—"

"In a minute." The other shoe wouldn't give, and they'd nearly reached the end of the walkway. She was risking serious injury now. He gave her foot a final tug, freeing it with a lurch and the distinct sound of tearing fabric. He grabbed her to keep her from falling, lifting her off her feet as he strode to the end of the walkway. He stepped off, with his arms full of pissed-off redhead. He set her down and backed off, holding up his hands with palms out to show her he meant no harm.

He should have known better than to expect gratitude. Should have let her fall on her ass or get sucked through the conveyer belt like a cartoon character. Still, he couldn't help but notice she had a face like a goddess in a museum sculpture. He wondered what color her eyes were behind the sunglasses.

Then he spotted her small, fancy handbag on the floor and stooped to pick it up, a fresh chance at chivalry.

"Ma'am." With a small flourish, he handed her the bag. "Nice peacock," he said. "She has no peer, that Judith Leiber."

The comment seemed to further disorient her. It always surprised women when he showed off his knowledge of designers. Some assumed he was queer. What it really meant was that he loved women and studied their likes and dislikes with the thoroughness of a cultural anthropologist.

The redhead snatched the purse from him.

"Can I buy you a drink?" He nodded toward a bar across the way, open for business and plenty busy despite the ungodly hour.

She stared at him as if he had frogs coming out of his mouth. "Certainly not."

"Just thought I'd ask." He kept his smile in place. Sometimes they played hard to get to make sure he meant business. "Rough night?"

A small, tight smile curved her very pretty mouth. "I'm sorry," she said, "but clearly you've mistaken me for someone else." She spoke with a precise, prep-school diction he found sexy. "Someone who has the slightest bit of interest in talking to you." With that, she turned and left, the torn seam of her dress offering him a glimpse of long, slender leg.

"You're welcome," he muttered, staring at her ass as she walked away.

Strike one, he thought. It was for the best, anyway. He wasn't here for flirting. He had a busy day ahead of him.

After the redhead disappeared at the end of the concourse, he was forced to deal with the reality of being here. He paced back and forth, eyeing the gate like a gladiator awaiting an onslaught of hungry lions. The thick gray door was still firmly closed. He'd already annoyed the gate agent by flashing his security pass and asking four different times when the flight would arrive.

He glanced at the clock. Still twenty minutes to go.

The busy bar was crammed with people, sipping coffee or bloody Marys while talking on cell phones, checking their e-mail or reading the paper. Damn. Didn't anyone just sit around and drink anymore? When did people decide that it was necessary to be busy all the time, even when you were sitting there, nursing a cold one?

Bo's mouth watered at the idea of a tall beer, crisp and cold from the tap. Hell, there was time. He could just grab a quick one and be back to the gate in a few minutes.

He watched a line of people boarding a flight to Fort Lauderdale and felt a twinge of envy. Yeah, Fort Lauderdale would be good right about now. Without even thinking about it, he ambled toward the bar at an unhurried gait. Hell, fifteen minutes was more than enough time to scull a beer. A morning eye-opener. He'd just park himself at the bar opposite the cash register. That was where to stand to get the best service. His many years as a bartender had taught him that. Every time the bartender went to the register, he'd see the customer's face in the mirror. A guarantee of faster service. He'd just step up to the bar and—

"Taylor Jane Purvis, you come back here!" shouted an angry voice.

A very small, laughing dynamo whirled past Bo, heading for the moving sidewalk that had nearly swallowed the redhead. The dynamo was a little girl with a mop of yellow ringlets. She had outmaneuvered her mother, who was burdened with about nine pieces of luggage. The little kid jumped on the sidewalk and ran. With the added speed of the moving walkway, she easily outpaced her harried mother. The woman looked as if she was about to lose it.

Bo hesitated, thinking about the redhead. He'd already been accused of being a perv once today. But the kid was getting farther away from her mother. He left his spot at the bar and strode to the moving walkway, easily catching up with the little kid. He reached over the side and plucked the child from the stream of pedestrians like a carnival prize. The startled kid's feet kept pedaling away.

"Are you Taylor Jane?" he asked, holding her up at eye level.

Dumbfounded, she nodded.

"Well, your mama is looking for you," he said.

The girl got over her surprise. She let out a scream, and kicked him in a vulnerable area.

Bo taught the kid a new vocabulary word as he set her down and backed away, palms out, regarding her like a stick of dynamite.

The girl's mother rushed forward and snatched her hand. "Taylor Jane!" she said, then turned to Bo, her eyes filled with terror. "You stay away from my child, or I'll call security."

"Yeah, whatever." He didn't bother explaining that he'd only been trying to help. He just wanted to get the hell away from Taylor Jane. He'd never been good with kids, anyway.

Strike two. The little incident ended up costing him that beer. A flight had let out, and the bar was now three deep with thirsty customers.

He returned to Gate 22-C just as the uniformed agent was opening the security door. Redcaps were lining up with wheelchairs and electric carts. Bo felt himself tense up, and all his senses sprang to awareness with the kind of hyper vigilance he felt when he pitched in a ball game. Every detail came into sharp focus—a guy striding past, a guitar case lightly bumping his back. The bright clack of a woman's high heels on the gleaming floor. The scent of pot smoke wafting incongruously from the overcoat of a passing businessman. The staccato cadence of two skycaps' conversation in Spanish. Everything bombarded him in that moment, and a burst of adrenaline gave him one final warning.

Escape was still an option here. There was still time to walk away, to disappear. It wouldn't be the first time he had done something like that.

He scanned the gates, noting flights bound for Raleigh/Durham, Nashville, Oklahoma City... The flight to New Orleans was boarding, the sign flashing Final Call. One quick transaction and he could buy a seat. *Go,* he urged himself. *Do it now.* No one would blame him, surely. Any guy in his right mind would leave things up to people who were equipped to deal with the situation.

He approached the counter with the flight to New Orleans. The gate agent, a heavyset iron-haired guy hacking away at a keyboard, looked up. "May I help you?"

Bo cleared his throat. "Are there any seats left on this flight?"

The agent nodded. "Always room for more in the Big Easy."

Bo grabbed the wallet from his back pocket. As he flipped it open, an old receipt and a coin fell out. He stooped and picked up the coin. It was ancient, embossed with a triangle symbol. It was a token they gave out at those meetings held in church basements, when you swore you'd stayed sober a whole year. It sure as hell hadn't been earned by Bo. Who wanted to go a whole freaking year without a drink? Certainly not him. It was hard enough lasting an entire baseball season. He kept the coin because it was old, because it came from a time, a place and a person he didn't know, but to whom he was intimately connected.

"Sir?" the gate agent prompted. "Is there something you need?"

Bo studied the coin in his hand. *Service, unity, recovery.* "Guess not," he said quietly, and his fingers closed into a fist around the token. He started walking back to Gate 22-C. A waiting skycap held a radio, which crackled as he fiddled with the tuner.

In his head, Bo heard the distant roar of a crowd, sounding like the ocean through the whorls of a seashell held to his ear. An announcement blared over the stadium's PA system—*Ladies and gentlemen, it's a sellout crowd tonight at Yankee Stadium. And here's our starting pitcher for the home team, stepping up to the mound. This has to be the toughest and most triumphant walk of his career, folks. I would think, at this moment, that mound is the loneliest place on earth. He's one and one to Tony Valducci. Now he's ready: Fastball, high, ball two. You can't blame the guy for pushing it, with so much at stake. An All-American out of Texas City, Crutcher was considered to be an early-round draft pick straight out of high school...but the draft came and went. It took another thirteen years and a mother lode of luck, but here he is at last. He's proof positive that sometimes, age is just a number. It is his time to shine....*

Bo nearly bumped into the skycap. He shook off the fantasy and focused on the gate. Passengers from the Houston flight were coming through the door in a steady stream—businesspeople were already talking on their cell phones, couples and lone travelers were heading toward the baggage claim, exhausted-looking parents emerged with cranky, tousle-headed kids. The emptying of the plane seemed to take forever.

So long that Bo began to have his doubts. Had he written down the flight number correctly? Was he completely wrong about the time, the airline, the day? Was this some freakish, horrible mistake?

He was about to approach the gate agent when an elderly couple shuffled off the plane. Skycaps helped them to an electric cart. Finally, a flight attendant with wispy hair and weary eyes emerged from the Jetway with someone behind her. The attendant went to the podium, handing over a clipboard. The last passenger walked off, toting a battered carry-on suitcase repaired with duct tape and a backpack clanking with gear, and wearing a Yankees baseball cap, which had been a Christmas gift from Bo. A clear pouch on a string, with a card that read Unaccompanied Minor, dangled around his neck.

Strike three. *Yeeee're out.*

Bo stepped forward, assumed his best posture. "AJ?" he said to the boy he'd never laid eyes on before. "It's me, Bo Crutcher. Your dad."

Three

Kim hobbled through the airport to the commuter-plane concourse. The dress, torn to within a few inches of decency, flapped around her chilled, bare legs. She hoped to catch a flight on a private carrier upstate, thus avoiding a trek into the city and a long and lurching train ride. In this, at least, fate was on her side. Pegasus Air had a seat available on a flight to Kingston that was leaving within the hour. She didn't dare look at the charge slip of her credit card, but scribbled her signature and headed for the waiting area. Within minutes, the flight was called and the small cluster of passengers lined up to board the plane.

The route to the commuter aircraft was a long outdoor walkway with a canvas awning, currently being whipped into a frenzy by an icy, sideways wind. She was beyond exhausted, beyond feeling conspicuous in her evening wear. That didn't, however, protect her from feeling the pure, freezing torment of the cold, lashing about her ankles and legs. Small rivers of snow eddied underfoot, chasing her to the truck-mounted stairway leading up to the dual-prop Bombardier.

She dozed during the short, bumpy flight north to the snow-clad hills of Ulster County, and jolted awake when the plane slammed down on the foreshortened runway. Blinking at the flat, gray winter scene outside the window, a fresh wave of misgivings nudged at her. Walking out on last night's party and going straight to the airport, leaving behind a successful career, a crappy boyfriend and all her belongings, might not have been the best idea she'd ever had. Quite possibly, heading directly from the L.A. disaster to the small town where her widowed mother now lived was a bit extreme.

Still. Sometimes a girl simply had to respect her instincts, and every instinct last night had urged her to flee. Quite often, her impulses had proven to be wrong; she'd get a head full of steam over something, only to discover things weren't so bad, after all. This time, she acknowledged, was different. Because beneath the shock and panic, the humiliation and disappointment, something else emerged—determination.

She would get through this.

Squaring her shoulders, she endured the arctic crossing of the open-air tarmac and headed into the waiting room of the tiny airport. Here was something Kim was good at— appearing calm. To the point where she actually was calm. No one would guess that she was on the verge of screaming.

The waiting room was a drafty, cavernous aluminum building that became a virtual wind tunnel every time the door opened. She set her jeweled clutch on a vacant counter. The evening bag had been a Christmas gift from Lloyd, and was worth thousands of dollars. But when she peered inside, all she could see was how small it was, how empty. It contained her remaining diamond chandelier earring, a gift from the hockey player she'd dated before Lloyd. She wouldn't miss wearing the earrings, since they were heavy and uncomfortable. There was a lipstick and a tube of concealer, one credit card, a platinum American Express. Her driver's license and a wad of cash she'd withdrawn from an ATM at the airport, charging it to the American Express. This would likely incur an exorbitant fee but she couldn't worry about that. Not now. She had more immediate worries.

Gritting her teeth, she took out her phone, balking as she had earlier. Turning on the phone meant acknowledging what had happened last night. Well, ignoring the phone was not going to make her troubles go away. She set her jaw and hit the power button. As expected, there was a full queue of missed calls. She scrolled through them but didn't listen to the messages. She knew they would be a string of rants from Lloyd and, no doubt, Lloyd's manager, his various coaches and teammates, his parents. Good lord, the man was thirty years old and didn't even take a piss without getting input from his parents.

She definitely wouldn't miss that aspect of him. She wouldn't miss *any* aspect of him, not even his money, his status, his looks or reputation. None of those were worth her heart. Or her self-respect.

As she glared at the tiny screen, it gave her a low-battery warning and then went blank. All the better, she thought. Except she really did need to make a call.

She looked around for a pay phone. The only one in range was a phone booth about fifty yards across the frozen tundra of the parking lot. Please, no, she thought, approaching the counter. "Excuse me," she said to the girl working there. "Is there a pay phone indoors? My cell phone died."

"Local call?" the girl asked, eyeing Kim's outfit.

"Yes."

The counter girl indicated a phone on the wall, surrounded by scribbled-on Post-it notes. "Help yourself."

Kim watched her own fingers punch the numbers as though they belonged to someone else. To her horror, she was shaking uncontrollably. She could barely connect her fingers with the correct number. After a couple of false starts, she finally got it right.

"Fairfield House."

Kim frowned, momentarily disoriented. "Mom?"

"Kimberly," her mother chirped. "Good morning, dear. How are you?"

Trust me, you do not want to know.

"You're up early," her mother continued.

"I'm not there," said Kim. "I mean, I'm not in L.A. I came home on the red-eye."

"You're in New York?"

"I'm at the county airport, Mom."

There was a beat of hesitation, weighted with doubt. "Well, for heaven's sake. I had no idea you planned to fly out from L.A."

"Can you come and pick me up?" To her dismay, Kim's throat burned and her eyes smarted. Fatigue, she told herself. She was tired, that was all.

"I was just cleaning up after breakfast."

Screw breakfast, Kim wanted to scream. "Mom, please. I'm really tired."

"Of course. I'll be there in a jiff."

Kim wondered how long a "jiff" was. Her mom was always saying things like "in a jiff." It used to drive Kim's father crazy. He always thought colloquialisms were so déclassé.

"Wait, can you bring a spare coat and some snow boots?" she asked hurriedly. But it was too late. Her mother had already hung up. She wondered what her father would think of her current getup. No, she didn't wonder. She knew. The form-fitting gown would earn his skepticism at best, but more likely disapproval, her father's default mode.

I wish we'd had time to forgive one another, Dad, she thought.

She pulled her thoughts away from him, telling herself not to go there, not in her current state of mind. One day, she would get to work on making peace with the past, but not this morning. This morning, it was all she could do to keep from turning into a sequined Popsicle in the waiting room. She found a bench to sit on in the terminal, and started nodding off like a wino.

She jerked herself awake and glanced at the clock. It would probably take her mother another ten minutes to get here. Ten more minutes. How many things could happen in ten minutes? That was about how long it took to send a flower delivery. Or to write an e-mail.

Or break up with a boyfriend. Or quit a job. These ten minutes, Kim thought, right here, right now, were the start of forever.

The notion made her sit up straighter. Right here, right now, she could pick a new path for her life. Leave the past behind and move ahead. People did it all the time, didn't they? Why couldn't she do the same?

Her mother had made a new start in Avalon, Kim reminded herself. It could be done. After the death of her husband, Penelope Fairfield van Dorn had moved to the small mountain town to live in the house where she had grown up. Kim had visited only one other time, two summers ago. Penelope claimed she preferred to meet her daughter in the city, having lunch and strolling the Upper East Side neighborhood where Kim had grown up. Penelope was certain Kim would find Avalon too uneventful and boring.

Penelope was endearingly dazzled by Kim's work, her friends, her way of life. Just a few weeks ago at Christmas, they'd rendezvoused with Lloyd's family in Palm Springs. Penelope had adored Lloyd, and vice versa—or so it had seemed to Kim. But after last night, she wasn't sure she knew Lloyd Johnson at all. She did, however, know enough now to realize she never wanted to see him again. Ever.

The waiting room rang with emptiness. The girl at the counter and a couple of workers stood around, sipping coffee and acting as though they weren't sneaking glances at Kim. On an ordinary workday, Kim might be having coffee and gossiping, too. In her line of work, gossip was more than just a way to fill the silence. Sometimes it was a mortal enemy, to be fought off like the bubonic plague. Other times, it was a means to an end, a way to get a client attention. Kim had used gossip like a power tool. She wondered what people would be saying back in L.A., at her old firm.

She just lost it, right in the middle of the party.
He always had a mean streak in him.

*Then again, who knew she had that kind of fight in her?
And the breakup was so public....*

People at the firm had no idea what had happened after the public part of the breakup. Lloyd had followed her to the hotel parking lot and—

Agitation drove Kim to her feet. By now, her toes were numb, so the shoes didn't bother her so much. She went to the ladies' room and removed the dark glasses. As a resident of Southern California, she was never without a pair of shades. This was the first time she'd used them for such a purpose, however.

Taking out the concealer, she touched up her makeup. It was a top-of-the-line product, used by professional makeup artists to cover up even the most glaring flaws. And really, this was just an extension of what she did so well in her career. She was a master of the cover-up, though usually on her clients' behalf, not her own.

Satisfied that she looked perfectly fine, she returned to the waiting room and stood at the window, willing her mother to get here but at the same time, worrying about the road conditions. Upstate New York winters were not for the faint at heart. SUVs and cars lumbered and skidded along the state road in a steady progression. She didn't know what kind of car her mother was driving these days. Was it a cautious little hybrid? A shiny Volkswagen bug?

It was funny, not knowing, yet oddly diverting to guess.

A safety-conscious Volvo? An economy-minded Chevrolet or a practical import? Perhaps it was the Cadillac that was approaching like a glossy beetle. Kim had no idea. It was startling—and a little disturbing—for her to realize how much she didn't know about her mother's life these days.

Since Kim's father had died, her mom had gone through a radical transformation. Initially, she had been all but destroyed by the devastation and loneliness of her loss. The physical signs of grief had been starkly drawn on Penelope's face, deepening its lines into creases of hurt and worry.

Yet the old adage about the healing power of time was true. Her mother improved as the weeks and then months passed. Penelope was still quick to say she missed her husband, but her smile was even quicker, and her natural exuberance emerged, evident in her voice and demeanor. How did that happen? Kim wondered. How did you get over a loss like that? How did you say goodbye to someone you'd loved for more than thirty years?

She really wanted to know, because she wasn't doing so hot herself, and she and Lloyd had only been together two years.

When the daisy-yellow-and-white PT Cruiser turned off the roadway into the terminal parking lot and pulled haphazardly close to the curb, she leaned closer to the chilly window glass. Even before she could see the driver's face, she somehow knew it would be her mother.

On the side of the car was a magnetic sign that read, Fairfield House—Your Home Away from Home.

Kim could not begin to assimilate the significance of that. At the moment, she was too tired to do anything but step out to the curb and let her mother's arms enfold her. Grains of salted ice slipped into Kim's peep-toe shoes. She winced and an involuntary sound came from her, part gasp, part sob. The reality of what had happened last night nearly sent her to her knees.

"Sweetheart, what's the matter?" Her mother pulled back to look up at her.

Kimberly teetered on the verge of falling apart, right then and there, on the crusty, salt-strewn sidewalk in front of the terminal. At the same time, she gazed at her mother's soft, kindly, clueless face and made a snap decision. *Not now.*

"It's been a long night, that's all. I'm sorry I didn't call first," she said. "I didn't… This was an unplanned trip."

"Well. This is simply a marvelous surprise." Her mother wore an expression that seemed determinedly cheerful, yet concern shone in her eyes. "And look at you, in your evening clothes. You'll catch your death. Where is your luggage? Did the airline lose your bags?"

"Let's just go home, Mom." Weariness swamped Kim like a rogue wave she couldn't escape. "It's freezing out here."

"Say no more," Penelope announced, bustling around to the driver's seat. Kim got in, the hem of her dress dragging in the dirty slush. She yanked it into the car after her and slammed the door shut.

The tires spun as the car skated away from the curb, reminding Kim that her mother was not the world's greatest driver. When Kim's father was alive, they'd lived in the city and Penelope had hardly driven at all, and never in the snow. Now she had moved upstate and was learning to live her life without a husband, and that included driving. Penelope's adjustment to it was proof that she had reserves of inner strength Kim had never guessed at. Leaning anxiously forward, Penelope nosed the car out of the airport and headed north and west, into the Catskills Wilderness, where the road narrowed to a two-lane salted track.

"I've left Lloyd," Kim said, her voice calm and flat. "I

quit my job. I'm— Watch the road, Mom." A semi came at them, hogging most of the roadway.

"Yes. Of course." The car drifted to the right. The semi's tires spat slush across the windshield, but Penelope appeared unperturbed, simply flipping on the wipers. "Leaving Lloyd? Dear, I don't understand. I had no idea you were having problems."

As she settled in and buckled her seat belt, Kim realized the story was too long and complicated and her brain too fried with fatigue and trouble to explain everything, so she went with the digest version.

"We had a huge falling-out at a party last night," she said. "Double whammy—he both dumped me and fired me. It got...kind of loud and ugly, so I went straight to the airport with only the clothes on my back, and this little evening bag." She touched her sunglasses, but decided to leave them on.

"It's a lovely bag," her mother commented, glancing over.

Kim flashed on the wolf-fur guy in the airport, handing it to her. How had he known it was a Judith Leiber? Was he gay? Judging by the way he'd hit on her, no. "Lloyd gave it to me for Christmas," she told her mother.

"I bet you could sell it on eBay." Her mother turned up the car's heater.

Kim savored the hot air blasting from the vents. "Anyway, sorry I didn't call first. I wasn't really thinking clearly."

"And now? Regrets?" her mother asked gently.

"No. Not yet, anyway. So here I am."

"For good?"

"For the time being." Kim knew she was in a state of shock. She had suffered a trauma. She'd been the victim

of a very public attack. For all she knew, her breakup could
be playing on YouTube right this moment.

People did recover from things like this. She'd lived in
L.A. long enough to see people suffer career meltdown,
only to rise again. These things happened. People got over
them. She would get over this. But she just couldn't imagine how.

"This move is permanent, Mom," she heard herself say,
and realized the decision had been made somewhere in the
sky over the midwest. Maybe she hadn't even been fully
conscious of making it but now spoken aloud, it sounded
like the only good decision she'd made in a long time. "The
firm will let me go first thing Monday morning."

"Nonsense. You've been the best publicist on the West
Coast, and I'm sure everyone at your firm knows that."

"Mom. It's Lloyd Johnson. Of the Lakers. Biggest client
who ever walked through the doors of the Will Ketcham
Group. It's their business to give him everything he demands. If he wanted the walls of the office painted plaid,
it would be done the next day. Firing me is no bigger deal
than changing bottled-water vendors."

"Wouldn't they opt to keep you on, just not working
with Lloyd?"

"Not a chance. If their most important client wants me
gone—and believe me, he does—then I'm gone. I'm a
good publicist, but I'm not irreplaceable. Not in their eyes,
anyway." *Or Lloyd's.*

"Well. In that case, it's their loss. They've done themselves out of an enormously talented publicist."

Kim attempted a smile. "Thanks, Mom. I wish everyone
in my life was as loyal as you."

"What about all your things?" her mother asked.

"My stuff's in storage, remember? I told you about that." Just before Christmas, she had given up her apartment. "Lloyd and I were staying at the Heritage Arms in Century City while he house hunted. The plan was to move in together. I thought everything would be wonderful. Am I terminally stupid?"

"No. Just a romantic at heart."

Was she? Romantic? Kim pondered the suggestion. She'd always considered herself a savvy businesswoman. Yet there was some truth in her mother's statement. Because not quite hidden beneath Kim's façade was a heart that believed in foolish things, like falling in love and staying that way forever, trusting the secrets of your soul to your best friend and lover. Like planning a future based on faith alone rather than expecting promises and guarantees.

So much for her romantic heart.

"Mom," she said, "I am so done with athletes."

"Sweetheart, you'll never be done with athletes. They're your passion."

"Ha," said Kimberly. "They're not all alike. But it's been so long since I've had a client who wasn't a complete ass—er, jerk—"

"You can say *asshole,* dear."

For the first time since last night's debacle, Kim felt the stirrings of a smile. "Mom."

"Sometimes there's simply no polite way to put it."

Kim studied her French manicure. "When I first started out, I loved it. I worked with boys who needed me. Lately all I've been doing is concocting lies and spin to cover up for clients who can't behave. I've started to hate what I do. I persuade the media and fans that being good at a sport is a free pass for bad behavior. It wasn't what I signed up for, and I'm tired of it."

"Oh, now that's unfortunate."

"What's that supposed to mean?"

Her mother didn't answer as she turned onto the street where she lived. King Street was a wide, stately boulevard divided by swaths of tall maple and chestnut trees. Well over a hundred years old, the grand homes had been built by railroad barons, bankers and shipping magnates of a bygone era. Each house was a masterpiece of gilded age splendor, surrounded by fences of wrought iron or stone. Nowadays, some of them belonged to people who were obsessed with preserving them. Others had fallen into disrepair, and a few—like Fairfield House—had been in the same family for generations.

Penelope navigated down a long, fence-lined lane and steered the car into the driveway, causing the back end to fishtail around the curve.

Kim regarded the house, one of the largest and best-known historic properties in town, with her mouth agape. "Mom?"

"I've made some changes around the place," her mother said.

"I can see that." It was not the stately house-at-the-end-of-the-lane she remembered from her girlhood.

"Isn't it wonderful, dear? We finished painting it at the end of summer. I meant to send you pictures, but I haven't quite figured out how to send them in e-mail. What do you think?"

There were no words. The actual structure had not

changed. The vast grounds, though currently blanketed in record amounts of snow, did not appear much different, either, except that some of the larger shrubberies appeared to have been sculpted into topiary shapes.

The house itself was a different story. The Fairfield House Kim remembered, the one where her grandparents had lived, had been an understated white with neat black trim. Now it was painted with colors not found in nature. With colors not found anywhere except maybe on Barbie's dream house, or in a bottle of Pepto-Bismol.

Kim blinked, but the image didn't go away. She couldn't take her eyes off the garishly painted house. The house, with its rotunda, turrets and gables, stood out like a wedding cake frosted in DayGlo colors. The carriage house and garden gazebo also wore shades of lavender and fuchsia, stark against the white snow.

Maybe it was an undercoat. Sometimes the primer coat came in weird colors, didn't it? "Sorry, Mom, did you say you'd *finished* painting it?"

"Yes, finally. It took the Hornets all summer." Her mother parked under the elaborate porte cochère that arched above the driveway at the side entrance. The gleaming coral trim was offset by lime sherbet, with sky blue on the domed roof of the arch.

"The Hornets painted the house," Kim echoed.

"Indeed, they did. The players are always in need of work, after all. And a fine job they did, too."

The Hornets were Avalon's very own baseball team, a professional club affiliated with the Can-Am League. The entire community had embraced the team when it had arrived a few years before, transforming the sleepy lakeside hamlet into a legitimate baseball town. The fact that the league operated on a tight budget meant that local boosters were vital. Families offered jobs, room and board, and sometimes even moral support to the players.

"Mom, isn't there some neighborhood covenant against bright colors?"

"Certainly not," Penelope said. "Or if there is, no one's ever told me about it."

Kim entered the house. The dizzying kaleidoscope of colors was not limited to the outside. The walls of the entryway, and the curved stairway sweeping up through the center of the house, were all as crayon bright as the outside.

Her mother hung her coat in the hall closet. "The colors are a bit over the top, don't you think?"

"A bit."

"I simply thought, if I'm going to go crazy with color, I should go big."

Kim summoned up a smile. "Words to live by."

"To be perfectly honest, it was a matter of economics," her mother said. "These are discontinued colors, so the paint cost me next to nothing. I simply used a little of this, a little of that…and I encouraged the painters to be creative."

There were probably worse color schemes than those created by baseball players, but at the moment, Kim couldn't think of any.

"Speaking of going big, are you sure you're done with Lloyd?" her mother asked.

That, of course, was Kim's chief function—to make Lloyd and all her clients seem nice. Personable. Worthy of their insanely huge salaries. Sometimes she did her job so well, it became impossible to separate the media-trained persona from the real man. Maybe that was why she hadn't seen the incident with Lloyd coming. She'd started to believe the hype she herself had created.

"Kimberly?" Her mother's voice startled her.

"Absolutely," she said. "This is for good." In that instant, she felt a dull blow of shock, an echo of last night, and she began to tremble.

"You're as white as a ghost." Her mother took her arm, making her sit on the hall bench. "Do you need something?"

The words sounded as though they'd been shouted down a tube. Kim reminded herself that the humiliating, horrifying, confusing incident was behind her now. She often told clients with injuries to move past the pain, focus on the healing. Time to take her own advice.

"I'll be all right," she told her mother in a voice that was soft, but firm. Then she gingerly removed her dark glasses, set them aside and used the corner of her shawl to gently wipe off the makeup.

Her mother stared, cycling fast from horror to fury. Penelope van Dorn was not the sort to anger easily, but when she did, it was as swift as a sudden fire. "Dear God. How long has this been going on?"

Kim hung her head. "Mom. I'm an idiot, but not that big an idiot. I had no idea he was capable of hitting anyone. Then last night, we had this terrible fight about something stupid, and it escalated." She swallowed a wave of nausea, remembering the gawking crowd at the reception, and her walking out, Lloyd following her to the parking lot. His fist didn't seem like a human appendage at all, but a weapon of blunt trauma. It had come out of nowhere, powered by anger.

There was one thing about Kim. She was a quick study. She was gone before he even remembered to straighten his tie.

Her mother's eyes filled with tears. "Kimberly, I'm so sorry."

"I know, Mom. Don't worry. He's history," Kim said firmly.

"You must press charges."

"I thought about that. But I won't do it. Given who he is, I'd never stand a chance. I'd have to relive the whole thing and for what? Nothing would happen to him."

"But—"

"Please, Mom, don't pity me or call the authorities. I want to pretend Lloyd Johnson never happened. This is the best way—coming here. Starting over."

Then her mother's arms were around her, at once soft and sturdy, and Kim was engulfed by a faint, ineffable element she hadn't realized she'd been missing so much. It was the mom smell, and when she shut her eyes and inhaled, an old, sweet sense of security bloomed inside her. Yet it was a piercing sweetness, breaking ever so gently through her pain and shock. Sobs came from deep within her, erupting against the pillowy shoulder of her mother. They sat together, her mother stroking her hair and making soothing sounds until Kim felt empty—and cleansed.

Her mother gave her a wad of Kleenex to wipe her face. Kim blotted at her eyes. "I'll be all right. I've had worse injuries playing sports."

"But being hurt by someone you love and trust strikes deeper than any injury." Her mother spoke softly, with a conviction that worried Kim.

"Mom?"

"Let's get you settled," her mother said, her manner suddenly brisk.

Kim followed her mother past the front parlor—apple green—to the main vestibule—pumpkin.

"You'll be in the same room where you used to stay when you visited your grandparents as a little girl. Won't that be nice? I've kept it virtually the same. You've even got a few things to wear, in the closet, so you can get comfortable. You don't look as if you've gained a pound since high school."

Living in L.A., Kim hadn't dared gain an ounce. And still, as a size six, she had felt like a linebacker next to most other women out there. She liked how comfortable her mother seemed in her own skin here.

In this huge, quiet house filled with so many childhood memories, Kim entered the world of her past. The second-story hallway made a T in the center; to the right lay Kimberly's domain. As the only grandchild, she'd had the wing all to herself.

"What's that face?" her mother asked.

"I'm not making a face."

"Yes, you are. You're making the defeated face," her mother insisted.

"Well, look at me. I'm supposed to have a fabulous life. Instead, I'm moving back in with my mother." She paused. "Assuming that's all right with you."

"All right? It's going to be exactly what we both need. I'm sure of it. Think of this as coming full circle. It's going to be wonderful, you'll see."

What's going to be wonderful? Kim wanted to know, but she didn't ask.

"I'll run you a bath. That'll be just the thing," her mother said, bustling into the adjacent bathroom.

"A bath would be heavenly," Kim agreed.

Hearing the rusty groan of the plumbing, she set down her bag, dropped the silk wrap on the end of the bed and finally—dear heaven, *finally*—took off her shoes. She spent a few minutes poking around the room, reacquainting herself with things she thought she'd forgotten—the collection of memorabilia from Camp Kioga, a rustic summer camp at the far northern end of Willow Lake. Kim had gone to camp there as a child, and as a teenager she'd worked as a counselor. Her ties to the small town were tenuous, but vivid memories stood out. Each summer she'd spent at Camp Kioga had been a magical string of endless golden days on Willow Lake, a world apart from the Upper Manhattan life she lived the rest of the year. Those ten weeks of summer had loomed large every year, shaping her as definitively as her expensive Manhattan prep school had attempted to do. The painted oar, autographed by all the girls in her cabin, brought back a rush of memories of ghost stories and giggles. The row of trophies on a shelf had belonged to a girl who was good at sports.

She took down a gray hooded sweatshirt with the camp logo, left over from her seventeenth summer, and put it on. The oversized shirt hung down to midthigh. The soft fabric warmed her, evoking secret memories of that distant time. She hadn't known it back then, but that had been the summer that had defined the direction her life would take. She shut her eyes, thinking about how intense everything had seemed that summer, how everything had mattered so much. She had been filled with idealism, picturing a fabuous life for herself. A life she thought she'd had—until last night.

The gabled window offered a view of the mountains beyond the town. As a little girl visiting her grandparents, she used to curl up in the window seat and gaze outside, imagining that her future life lay somewhere beyond the horizon. As indeed it had, for a while. Now, as her mother pointed out, she'd come full circle.

Her evening gown fell to the floor in an expensive shimmer of sequins and silk. The strapless bra had been engineered for performance, not comfort, and she peeled it off with a sigh of relief. She had nothing on her bottom half. With a gown as clingy as the one she'd worn last night, a girl had to go commando.

"Are the towels in the linen closet?" she called to her mother.

"That's right, dear." Her mother said something else, but the drum of running water drowned it out.

Kim walked down the hall toward the linen closet.

A strange man in a trench coat stood there, staring straight at her. He was older, with iron-gray hair and a tough-guy demeanor—and he had absolutely no business being in her mother's house.

Panic rolled up her spine, culminating in a scream. At the same moment, she clutched the sweatshirt tighter around her and desperately stretched the hem downward.

"Aw, jeez, hey, didn't mean to startle you," the man said.

Kim tried not to hyperventilate. "Stay back," she said in a quiet, she hoped calming voice. Mom, she thought. She had to keep him away from her mother. Kim usually had mace or pepper spray on her, but of course last night, her purse-size aerosol had been confiscated by the TSA. "The valuables are downstairs," she said. "Take whatever you want. Just…leave." She gestured at the stairs, keenly aware that every movement gave him a peep show.

The intruder turned out his hands, palms up. "You must be Kimberly," he said. "Penny talks about you all the time."

Penny? The housebreaker had a nickname for her mother?

Kim's heart constricted when her mother came out into the hall, an expectant look on her face. "I thought I heard voices out here— Oh."

"If you lay a hand on either of us," Kim warned, "I'll hurt you, I swear, I will." She did know self-defense, though she didn't relish the idea of performing the moves nearly naked.

Her mother gave a laugh. "Dear, this is Mr. Carminucci."

"Dino," he said. "Call me Dino."

He smiled, which made him resemble that Italian crooner, Tony Somebody. Bennett. Tony Bennett. Kim felt so disoriented she could barely say a word. Caught up in the surreal moment, she offered a halfhearted smile while trying to make sense of his presence here, in the second-story hallway of her mother's house. He really did look a lot like Tony Bennett, right down to the warm brown eyes and iron-gray waves of hair. He was gazing at Kim's mother as though he might burst into song at any moment. *Penny.* No one called her mother Penny.

"Dino is one of our guests," her mother said easily. "You'll meet everyone else at dinner."

Guests? Everyone else? Kim didn't bother hiding her confusion. "Um, it was nice to meet you, but…" She let her voice trail off and gestured vaguely toward her room. She thought about the sign on the car. Suspicion reared up in her.

"Kimberly just arrived for a nice stay," her mother explained to the stranger. "She came in from L.A. on the red-eye."

"Then I imagine you must be ready for a rest, Kimberley. See you later, ladies." Whistling lightly, he headed for the stairs.

Kim grabbed her mother's hand and pulled her back into the bedroom. "We need to talk."

Penelope's smile was tinged with irony. "Indeed, we do. I've thought the same thing for the past, oh, fifteen years."

Ouch. Well, maybe now they would finally get the chance.

"I drew you a nice warm bubble bath," Penelope continued. "We can have our talk while you bathe."

Kim was too tired to do anything but surrender. Within minutes, she was in the adjoining bathroom in the deep, claw-footed tub, surrounded by a froth of lavender-scented bubbles. It felt so comforting that her eyes filled with tears. She quickly blinked them away.

Seated on a vanity stool nearby, her mother regarded her fondly. "It's nice to have you home, Kimberly."

"If it's so nice to have me home, why haven't you invited me to visit since Grandma's funeral?" That had been two summers ago, Kim realized. It had been a time of terrible loss for Penelope, the loss of her mother coming so soon after her husband's death.

"I always thought you'd prefer meeting in the city, or having me come out to Los Angeles. I imagined you'd find Avalon terribly boring compared to life in the big city."

"Mom."

"And, all right, I didn't think you'd be supportive of my enterprise."

"Your enterprise. The 'guests,' you mean."

"Well, yes."

"How many people are you talking about, Mom?"

"Currently, I have three visitors. Dino owns the pizza parlor in town, and he's in the process of remodeling his home, so he's staying temporarily. Mr. Bagwell normally goes south for the winter, but this year, he's staying in Avalon and needed a place to live. Then there's Daphne McDaniel—oh, she's just delightful. I can't wait for you to meet her. And there's room for more. We just finished refurbishing the third-floor suite. I hope to find a guest for that one very soon."

"Mom, what's going on? Why do you have a bunch of strangers living here? Were you that lonely? I wish you'd said something—"

"They're not strangers. They're guests. Paying guests. And believe me, they are no substitute for my daughter."

"You should've said something to me." She winced with guilt as she thought of the visits with her mother in the aftermath of her father's death. They had rendezvoused in Southern California, Manhattan, Florida. It had never occurred to Kimberly that her mother wanted her to come here. To come home.

"My life has changed a lot since your father passed away," her mother explained.

Kim thought of Dino Carminucci. "I'd say so, Mom."

"I obtained a business license and started this right after Labor Day."

"This…?"

"My enterprise. Fairfield House."

Kim's head felt light. She wasn't sure it was from the hot

water, exhaustion or sheer confusion. "I had a long night, Mom, so forgive me if I'm a bit slow on the uptake. Are you saying you've turned this place into a boardinghouse?"

"Indeed, I have." She spoke as casually as she might have about getting her nails done. "And actually, it's in keeping with family tradition. My great-grandfather, Jerome Fairfield, built this place with the fortune he made in textiles. At the time, it was the grandest mansion in town. Then, like so many others, he lost everything in the crash of '29 and never quite recovered. He and his wife took in boarders. It was the only way to keep the house out of the hands of his creditors."

Kim had never heard that bit of family history before.

"So truly," Penelope concluded, "you could say it's in my blood."

Kim was speechless, taking in the news the way she would if her mother had said, "I've taken up bungee jumping." Or, "I've become a nudist."

When she found her voice, Kim asked, "And you were going to tell me this...when?"

"To be honest, I've been putting it off as long as possible. I knew you wouldn't be pleased."

"There's an understatement. Taking in strangers, Mom? For money? Are you crazy?"

Her mother stood up and placed a stack of fresh towels on the vanity stool. "Say what you will, Kimberly, but I'm not the one wearing an evening gown and spike heels on a cross-country flight."

"This is not crazy," Kim said defensively. "This is a crisis, Mom. My own personal crisis."

Her mother smiled. "Then you came to the right place."

"So this boardinghouse—it's a home for people in crisis?"

"Not by designation, no. People in transition, though. They seem to find their way here, to Fairfield House." She spoke with a curious pride.

Kimberly studied her mother's mild, sweet face as though regarding a stranger. Did she even know this woman anymore? Had she ever? Penelope Fairfield van Dorn had been born and raised in Avalon, and was a card-carrying member of the town's old guard—the elite upper class, her roots going back to the days when the Roosevelts and Vanderbilts used to keep summer places in the mountains. Yet while most people grew more stuffy and more pretentious as they aged, widowhood had the opposite effect on Kim's mother. Kim's father had never liked this little Catskills village, even though it was his wife's hometown. Daddy had always preferred the city, pulsing with the noise of commerce. But Mom claimed her heart had never left here, and she seemed happy enough to live in the house where she'd grown up. Even as a child, Kim had observed that her mother used to be happy here in a way that eluded her in the big city. This was the only place she'd seemed truly relaxed and at ease.

And finally, Kim came to understand why the house of her girlhood was so important to Mom and why keeping it meant everything to her.

Kim found jeans, a T-shirt and a pair of thick socks lying on the bed beside the sweatshirt. Her old—ancient— clothes were not too small for her, but the fit was different. Not quite comfortable. The clothes, however, were the least of her problems.

She towel-dried her hair, reapplied her makeup and, after checking out the hallway to make sure the coast was clear, headed downstairs to the kitchen, which was blessedly warm. She took a seat and curled her hands around a thick china mug of her mother's hot chocolate.

The kitchen gleamed with a coat of tomato-red paint, the trim a garish shade of yellow. Kim watched her mother wiping down the stove and sink, and dark thoughts crossed her mind—clinical depression, early-onset Alzheimer's, a rare form of dementia...

"Mom—"

"It was the only way I could see to keep the house," her mother said, replying to the question even before it was voiced.

"I thought you owned the house free and clear after Grandma died."

"I did. I do. But then I needed money, so I agreed to an ill-considered equity loan. I'm afraid it was a rather bad decision on my part."

It felt strange, talking with her mother about finances. Kim's father used to handle the money exclusively, and she and Penelope never heard a word about it. "How bad?" Kim asked. "Are you saying you can't afford to live here without taking in boarders?"

"I'm saying I can't afford to live at all without doing something," her mother said, her voice quiet and resigned.

"This is crazy, Mom. What happened? We had everything. Dad earned a ton of money." Kim studied her mother's face, wondering why she suddenly felt like a stranger. "Didn't he?"

Penelope paused, set down her cloth and took a seat at

the table. "Kimberly, perhaps I was wrong to keep this from you, but I didn't want you to fret about it. I knew you'd worry if I explained my new circumstances."

"Worry?" Kim said. "You think?"

"No need to be sarcastic, dear. We've both kept our secrets."

"I'm sorry. What part of 'my boyfriend gave me a black eye' is the secret part?"

"Oh, Kimberly. I'm the one who should be sorry."

"Just level with me, Mom. I'm a big girl. I can take it."

"Well, the truth is, your father left behind a great deal of debt."

That simply didn't compute. They hadn't lived like a family in debt.

"I don't get it," Kim said.

Her mother smiled, but without amusement. "I had some notion of preserving your memory of your father, but I suppose that was naive of me."

"I don't understand. Did he have some secret life you only discovered after he was gone?"

Penelope folded her hands on the table. "In fact, he did, in a way. When he was alive, he never said a word about his debts. I had no idea and to this day, I still don't quite understand. He invested in a number of hedge funds that were called in, and had to mortgage and remortgage all our property. It's not that I didn't love your father," she said. "I did. Very much. We enjoyed life and I had no idea how much we were living beyond our means. Sometimes I think that's what killed your father. The stress of it. The strain of pretending."

"I never knew." Kim shut her eyes, trying to conjure a

picture of her father, always so distinguished and reserved. The two of them had always had a turbulent relationship. This only made him seem more distant, as though she'd never even known him at all.

"In settling his affairs, it all came to light," said her mother. "I've had to take measures in order to cover his liabilities. I had to…liquidate some things."

The quaver in her voice caused Kim to feel a clutch of apprehension. "What things, Mom?"

"Well…everything."

Everything. That was inconceivable. They had a home in Manhattan and a weekend place on Long Island and a condo in Boca Raton. There was an extensive stock portfolio. Wasn't there?

"Are you sure?" she asked.

"That was what I asked the lawyer and the probate judge. There was a subprime second mortgage on the apartment, about to balloon to twelve percent. The house in Montauk and the condo in Largo were in foreclosure. Our equities and savings were nonexistent. I own this house free and clear, because my parents left it to me, but that's the extent of it."

"Mom, I'm so sorry. I had no idea." She felt betrayed now by two men she'd trusted, two men she thought she knew.

"Nor did I."

"Are you sure? While Dad was alive, you had no idea?"

Her mother's smile was tinged with bitterness. "None. I feel so foolish for keeping myself in the dark about our finances."

"You weren't foolish, Mom," Kim said. "You had every reason to trust him. But…are you sure taking in boarders is the answer?"

"Believe me, I left no stone unturned. But, Kim, just think of it. I majored in women's studies a hundred years ago. I've never had a career and I have no marketable skills. I had to do something desperate or I would have fallen in arrears and been forced to sell Fairfield House."

"I can't believe Dad left you like this. How could you not have known?"

"Because," she said, getting up from the table, "I didn't realize I should have been looking."

"You should have told me sooner."

"Yes. It just seemed so cruel, though, to burden you with this. It was bad enough your father died so suddenly. I didn't want to add this to your grief."

"What about *your* grief?"

"I beat it into submission with anger and resentment," Penelope said simply.

Kim wasn't quite sure whether or not her mother was joking. After all she'd heard this morning, she wasn't sure of anything.

"Richard was a master of deception, of making people see what he wanted them to see."

That was true, Kim reflected. Everyone, across the board, had the same opinion of Richard van Dorn—that he was a refined and monied individual. In Manhattan, they had lived in the "right" area and she had gone to the "right" schools. They'd taken luxurious vacations, and her parents had hosted and attended the sort of parties and events that were written about in the society columns the next day. Her parents belonged to exclusive clubs, took part in charity fund-raisers. How had he managed to hide the fact that he'd run them into a world of debt?

How her father would have hated this, she thought. He would have despised the idea of his wife taking in tenants, opening her home to paying strangers. Maybe he should have thought about that before driving himself into debt and then dying and leaving all the humiliation and heartache to his wife, who never did anything but believe in him. Except her mother did not appear to be humiliated. Rather than spiraling into despair like a latter-day Jane Austen character, Penelope van Dorn had embraced the new project.

Racing in a taxi to the airport last night, Kim had hoped to find a sense of peace and security, home with her mother. Instead, she'd found a house filled with strangers and painted all the mad colors of the rainbow. She realized she had a lot to learn about her father. At the moment, however, she could barely think straight.

Now that she understood the financial fiasco that had necessitated her mother's move, Kim wondered if Penelope was only pretending to like it here. Pretending that turning her home into a boardinghouse was some kind of delightful, quirky adventure.

Finally, in the dead of winter, Kim could fully appreciate how radically her mother's life had changed two summers ago, when she lost her husband. The contrast between her Manhattan lifestyle and the winter wilderness of upstate was sharply pronounced. Yet it struck Kim that she didn't know her mother very well. She had never bothered to look beneath the surface of Penelope Fairfield van Dorn. Instead, she'd taken her at face value, the way the rest of the world did.

If she accomplished nothing else here, Kim thought, at

least she could remedy that. She would help her mother sort out her finances. Now Kim understood the reason why Penelope had not urged her to visit. Her mother hadn't wanted to burden her with the knowledge of her true circumstances. Hadn't wanted to poison a daughter's memories of her father with something so inconvenient as the truth.

Things happened for a reason. Kim would do whatever it took to help her mother. If this meant moving to a tiny mountain town and rolling up her sleeves, so be it. This was hardly the life Kim had planned for herself, but her own goals and plans and hard work had led to a dead end. She'd been driven by a need to impress her father, burnishing his reputation by making a name for herself. In a way, that was exactly what she did for her clients—made them look good. Clearly there was a flaw in that strategy.

She wasn't likely to find the answer to her dreams here, but maybe coming here would yield something more precious—the chance to reconnect with her mother. To give back to the one person who had given Kim unconditional love. And maybe, if Kim was very lucky, to figure out a direction that didn't lead to disaster.

Four

There were some papers for Bo to sign before the airline could officially release its unaccompanied minor.

"See you around, AJ," said the flight attendant, handing Bo duplicate copies of the paperwork. She was a pretty woman in her dark uniform and sweater, and in a different situation, Bo might flirt with her, offer to buy her a drink—which he now needed worse than ever.

She offered a smile that somehow hinted she might be open to such an offer. In general, women tended to like him. Now was hardly the time for flirting, though. "He did great," she reported. "You must be very proud of your son."

Bo nodded, but didn't know what to say to that. What the hell was there to say? Twelve years the kid had been on this earth, his flesh and blood, walking around, and this was Bo's first time to see him. He had no clue what AJ thought; the boy was regarding Bo like a stranger or, at most, a distant relative.

Which pretty much described Bo to a T—distant. Relative. It was completely screwed up.

And none of it—nada, zippo—was the kid's fault. So Bo offered his most disarming smile to the flight attendant and said, "Yes, ma'am. I sure am proud."

A gate agent double-checked the paperwork in AJ's neck tag. Then she handed Bo a receipt, like a claim check for a rental car. "All set," the agent said. "Have a nice day. Thanks for flying with us."

Bo nodded again and stuffed the receipt in his pocket. "Baggage claim's this way," he said, indicating the sign.

They started walking, keeping a wide gap between them, like the strangers they were. Naturally, Bo couldn't help checking him out. AJ was small. Like, really small. Bo didn't know how big a twelve-year-old was supposed to be, but he was pretty sure AJ was puny.

As they passed a trash can, the kid took the tag from around his neck and dropped it in the garbage.

"Hey, I sure wish we were meeting under different circumstances," Bo said to him. He didn't know what the hell else to say.

No response. Maybe the kid was in shock, or something. If so, it was understandable. This was probably the scariest day of the boy's life.

Bo played Yolanda's phone call over and over in his head. That she'd called him at all was unprecedented. Over the years, she had called him only a few other times—to tell him of AJ's birth, to advise him she was marrying some guy named Bruno, and—just last year—to let him know she was getting a divorce.

For reasons of his own, Bo had been more than willing to abide by her wishes, to keep his checkbook open and his mouth shut. He didn't know diddly squat about being someone's father, but he sure as hell knew how to give money away.

And then yesterday…the urgent call that didn't leave him a choice. "Thank God, you answered," she'd said in a voice he barely remembered.

"Yolanda?"

"I'm in trouble, Bo. There was a raid at work. I'm at the Houston Processing Center of the INS."

"The INS." It took a second for him to realize what she was talking about. Then it came to him—Immigration and Naturalization Service—and he felt a sick curl of apprehension in his gut. "Hell, Yolanda, what does that have to do with you?"

"There's no time to explain," she said. "I'm not supposed to be making any calls, but I'm desperate, Bo. I've been detained."

He wasn't quite sure what that meant, but he knew it was nothing good. "What, like a foreigner? I thought you said you grew up in the U.S."

"I did. They say I'm undocumented, and I have nothing to prove otherwise."

He winced, hearing her voice shake. There was nothing quite so compelling to Bo as the sound of a woman whose heart was breaking. Truth be told, he couldn't remember a hell of a lot about Yolanda Martinez—but he remembered what was important. That she had a tender heart and beautiful eyes. That they had been each other's first love. That she'd been the first to teach him that love alone couldn't save a person from hurt.

"What do you mean, 'prove otherwise'?" he'd demanded. "Nobody ever asked me to prove I'm a U.S.

citizen." Even as he said the words, he knew he was being willfully ignorant. People didn't ask light-haired, blue-eyed Anglos if they were citizens. Such inquiries were reserved for people with dark skin and Hispanic surnames...like Yolanda Martinez. "Okay," he'd told her, "then just clear it up for them. Show them whatever paperwork they need and everything will be fine."

"I don't have anything to show them. Don't you remember, Bo? They way we ended things... The way my parents were?" She reminded him that she was the only child of ultra-conservative parents. Having a baby at age seventeen had strained her relationship with them, and the years had only increased the distance. Her father had died a while back, and her mother had returned to Nuevo Laredo, her Mexican hometown, just across the Rio Grande from Texas.

Yolanda had no time to explain much more about the situation, but suddenly Bo was part of it. Although he felt sorry for her, he also felt himself suppressing a surge of anger at her, hiding it from AJ. The kid had enough troubles without being told his mother had screwed up. The last thing Bo wanted to do was lower the boy's opinion of Yolanda.

Rounded up en masse with undocumented employees at the factory where she worked, Yolanda claimed she had no one other than Bo to turn to. "I'm being sent to a detention center," she'd said in a voice strained by terror and dread. "AJ's at school..." She related the rest in a furtive, terrified tone. The armed raid had begun without a breath of warning. Seventy undocumented workers had been rounded up for deportation. Many of these workers' American-born children would be left alone, to be lost in the foster system or fobbed off on relatives, most of whom were undocumented, as well.

AJ had no one, Yolanda had explained between sobs. He was an only child, and she was a single mother. All her trusted friends and relatives had already been detained or deported. With no one else to look after him, AJ would be sent to foster care and lost.

Bo had felt a sick lurch of panic. He didn't want the kid thrown to the wolves, but hell. He and Yolanda had been in high school when she'd gotten pregnant. Their lives were completely separate; the only tenuous tie had been the flow of Bo's money into an escrow account set up a dozen years ago. Now, all these years later, that tenuous tie was made flesh and blood: AJ needed Bo.

He'd ponied up for a ticket; the only flight he could get last-minute was a red-eye routed through Chicago, making the journey an all-night ordeal. Mrs. Alvarez, a teacher's aide at AJ's school, had helped him. She'd dug up his birth certificate and put him on the plane.

It had been a hell of a night for the kid.

Bo took out his phone. "I need to call Mrs. Alvarez. I promised to let her know as soon as your flight got in. We'll see if there's any word on your mom."

Finally, a flash of interest sparked in the boy's eyes. He offered a quick nod. They kept walking as Bo scrolled to her number and hit Send, dialing a woman he'd never met, but whose semihysterical phone call had thrown his life into chaos.

"Mrs. Alvarez?" he said when she picked up. "AJ's with me. He just got in."

"Thank you for calling. Is he all right?"

"Seems to be." He glanced at the dark-eyed stranger. "Quiet, though."

"AJ? That's not like him."

"Any word on Yolanda?" Bo felt the boy looking at him.

"None. I've spent hours trying to get answers, but it's impossible. The bureaucracy is absolutely incredible. The INS and the detention center are closed for the weekend. Nobody knows what's happening. We're lucky she managed to call you before they in-processed her at the detention center."

The sinister terminology made him shudder. "Yeah, lucky. Okay. Well, keep me posted."

"Of course. Can I speak to AJ?"

"Sure." Bo handed him the phone.

AJ's face sharpened as he took it. "Where's my mom?" he asked. His voice was different from what Bo had expected—and then he realized he hadn't known what to expect. Not this, though. Not this boyish rasp of emotion as AJ lowered his head and asked, "Is she okay?"

Then he was quiet for a minute, his face solemn. It was the face of a stranger. Bo had trouble wrapping his mind around the idea that this was his kid. He tried to pick out some resemblance, some point of reference that would somehow make sense of all this. But there was nothing. The Yankees cap and Windbreaker, maybe. Bo had sent them in his annual Christmas box to AJ. The fact that the kid was wearing them had to mean something, Bo told himself.

Right, he thought. It didn't mean shit. Years ago, when Bo had asked to see AJ, Yolanda had claimed that if Bo showed up in AJ's life, it would only confuse the boy.

Now that he'd met AJ face-to-face, Bo knew that was a

total crock. This kid, with his keen, guarded eyes, was not the type to be confused by anything.

AJ handed over the phone. Did all kids have such soft eyes, such thick lashes? Did it always hurt to watch a kid's chin tremble as he fought against tears? He didn't want to tell AJ that he'd talked to both the teacher and teacher's aide at length already. He had been desperate for this not to be happening, and not just because it was inconvenient for him. It was because this sudden upheaval was so brutally cruel to the boy. Bo felt guilty about his earlier impulse to bolt. He would never do that to this kid. It had simply been his default fight-or-flight reaction to the unexpected.

For AJ's sake, Bo kept mum about his conversation with the teacher. Mrs. Jackson had taken a bleak view of Yolanda's prospects for getting out of her predicament. "It happens a lot down here," she explained. "More than people realize. Long-time workers are detained and then summarily deported. And no one seems to worry that much about the kids. School-age children are allowed to go with their parents, but quite often, the parents don't want that. I'm quite certain Ms. Martinez doesn't want that for AJ."

"So what happens to kids whose parents don't bring them along?"

"They go to relatives if there are any, or into foster care if there aren't. Some of them—too many of them—fall through the cracks."

"What's that supposed to mean?"

"They…the system loses track of them. They've been found living in cars or on the street, sometimes in abandoned apartments."

"And how often do the parents get to come back for their kids?" Bo had asked her.

There was a long hesitation, so long he thought he'd lost her. "Mrs. Jackson?"

"I've never seen it."

Bo didn't think AJ needed to hear any of that. He put the phone away, saying, "Try not to worry. We'll figure out how to fix this thing with your mother."

The kid didn't say anything, but Bo was sure he could feel doubt radiating from AJ's every pore.

"It'll be all right."

"You don't know that. You don't know anything about me."

"True, but right at this moment, I'm all you've got." Bo watched the boy's face change. "Sorry, that came out wrong. I intend to help you, AJ. That's all I mean. I'm real sorry your mother never told you anything good about me."

"She never told me *anything* about you," the boy said.

Bo was stunned. "She didn't explain where the monthly checks came from? The stuff I sent for your birthday and every Christmas?"

The kid shook his head. "I never knew about any checks. The gifts…we didn't talk about those, either. She just handed them over."

Bo tamped back a fresh burn of anger at Yolanda. There were lots of times when writing that check meant skipping meals or dodging the rent, but he never let her down. He figured it was the least he could do, since she was raising their child. It never occurred to him that Yolanda wouldn't explain where the gifts came from. He gritted his teeth against saying what he really thought. "Maybe she didn't tell you more because she wanted you to feel like you belonged to Bruno."

"I belong to my mom. Not to Bruno *or* you."

"When did you find out…about me?" Bo asked.

"When my dad—when Bruno left. I thought we'd handle it like other families, you know? You get to visit the parent who left. But Bruno, he didn't want it that way. He said I couldn't visit because I don't belong to him."

What a jackass, thought Bo.

And AJ had been left to deal with the reality that his father came in the form of a monthly obligation instead of a flesh-and-blood guy. Bo wondered if the boy would ever regard him as someone who cared, who would keep him safe and dedicate himself to helping Yolanda. And, yeah, there was probably some pride involved. He wasn't the jerk Yolanda had painted, and now he had a chance to show his boy the truth.

"Tell you what. You've got a home with me for as long as you need it. And I'm going to help your mom. The smartest lawyer in the world just happens to be married to my best friend, Noah," Bo explained. "Swear to God, I'm not exaggerating. Sophie's an expert in international law."

"My mom needs an immigration lawyer," AJ said, the term sounding disconcertingly adult as it rolled off his tongue. "Is your friend an immigration lawyer?"

"Sophie's the best possible person to help," Bo replied. "I told her what happened, and she's already working with lawyers she knows in Texas, trying to figure out what's going on down there."

Sophie had warned him the situation might get complicated. She said this "temporary" detention might last for a while.

Bo didn't see how the government could keep a hard-working single mother away from her own kid. It didn't just feel wrong, but inhuman.

They reached the baggage-claim area, and Bo found the carousel that corresponded to AJ's flight. The conveyor belt was already disgorging pieces of luggage, the occasional box bound with bailing wire, a car seat, a set of snow skis.

"Let me know when you see your bag," Bo said.

The boy watched the conveyer belt, then glanced at the duct-taped suitcase he toted behind him. "It's right here," he said.

Bo frowned. "You mean you don't have any luggage?"

"Only this." He indicated the carry-on bag and his back-pack.

"Then what are we standing around here for?"

AJ just looked at him.

Damn. There was something that drew him to this kid. This solemn, very unkidlike kid. And it wasn't just DNA.

"Is this the first time you've ever flown in an air-plane?" Bo asked.

"First time I've ever flown in anything."

At last, a glimmer of humor. "Well, hell. This is where the checked luggage comes out. And since you don't have any, we're done here." Bo grabbed the carry-on and led the way to the parking lot. As they stepped through the auto-matic doors, the outside air assaulted them with bone-cutting January cold. The cindery reek of jet fuel and diesel exhaust bloomed in thick puffs from the shuttle buses.

AJ seemed dazed. He hunched up his shoulders and

stuffed his hands in his pockets. Bo stopped walking and lifted the suitcase. "Hey, you got an extra coat in here?"

The kid shook his head, plucking the nylon fabric of the Yankees Windbreaker. It flapped thinly against his skinny arms and shoulders. "This is all I got."

Great.

"It was hot in Houston," AJ added.

Now that, Bo could understand. Once in a blue moon, a cold spell might hit the Gulf Coast in a fistlike front known as a Blue Norther. Usually, it was plenty warm down there, and often muggy. Growing up, Bo hadn't owned a coat, either, except for his varsity letterman's jacket, purchased by someone from the high-school booster club; no way could he have afforded it himself. Now, that thing had been a work of art—smooth black boiled wool, sleeves of butter-soft cream-colored leather.

He peeled off his olive-drab parka, handed it to AJ. "Put this on."

"I don't need your coat."

"Yeah, well, I don't need you catching cold on top of everything else, so put it on." A knifelike gust of wind sliced across the multilevel lot.

"People don't catch cold from being cold," AJ objected. "That's an old wives' tale."

"Just put on the damned coat. It's a long walk to the car."

The boy hesitated, but then put on the parka. Bo couldn't quite conceal his relief. He didn't know what he would have done if the kid had defied him. Bo was a bartender. A ballplayer. Not a dad.

He got his key out of his pocket. The key fob still felt strange in his hand. He pressed the smooth, round button and the low-slung BMW Z4 roadster winked a greeting at him. He pressed another button and the trunk released. Carlisle, the sports agent who popped up at exactly the right time, had put the precontract deal together. Bo remembered standing in the cold November rain, just staring at the thing. A BMW Z4. *Convertible.*

Never in a million years did he think he'd own such a car. But life was funny like that. Everything could change on the turn of a dime. In a heartbeat. In the time it takes to pick up the phone. Just as he was getting his shot, he found himself in charge of a kid.

"Here's our ride," he said, inviting AJ to put his stuff in the trunk.

The kid complied without comment, though Bo could tell he was checking out the car.

It had been one of the first things he'd bought when, last November, a single phone call had rocked his world. Years after Bo Crutcher had hung up his dreams of a major-league baseball career, he'd gone—same as he did every year—to tryouts. The difference this time was that the Yankees finally wanted to do business. Bo knew he was well past the age most players started in the major leagues. He knew he was a long shot. But at last, against all odds, he was getting a shot. Sure, they only wanted to acquire him for a midseason trade; it was a strategy move on the part of the Yankees, but he intended to make the most of whatever time he had with the club. It would be a hell of a thing to earn his spot on the forty-man roster and on the pitching staff. His competition was a hell of a lot younger, but none of them wanted this more.

He had planned to spend the entire winter getting ready

for his big break. Life, however, seemed to be making other plans for him.

"All set?" he asked the boy.

"Smells like smoke," he said.

"I've been known to enjoy the occasional cigar," Bo said. "In the off-season."

"Carcinogens don't take any time off."

Bo felt like telling the kid he was being a pain in the ass, but he kept his mouth shut. He knew why AJ was being a pain in the ass. He was acting this way because he was scared shitless, uncertain of his future and worried about the only person in his life who meant anything to him—his mother. And he was pissed, no doubt, about being sent to a dad he'd never met.

There was a shitload of things to talk about, but Bo figured he'd hold off, let the kid adjust to this bizarre and unexpected situation. Only yesterday, AJ had gone to school as if it was any other day. He had no idea that when school let out, his mother would be gone and he would be bundled aboard a plane bound for a place he'd never been, to a person he'd never met before.

The engine sprang to life with a growl. Bo navigated his way out of the parking lot, paid the booth attendant, then headed for the airport exit.

The last of the cold night lingered, and heavy clouds held back the dawn. AJ didn't say anything, just shifted in his seat and glared straight ahead, his profile clean and angry in the yellow glow of the freeway lights.

"Look, I'm sorry this is happening," Bo said. "I'm doing my best to fix it as quick as I can."

"I don't see why I can't just go where my mom is," AJ said.

"Because she wants what's best for you, and going to a—" He broke off, not liking the sound of *detention center.* "Going where she is won't help her, or you. I didn't ask her to call me, AJ, but...I'm glad she did." Bo couldn't figure out if he was lying or not. Sure, he'd always wanted to meet AJ. But he wasn't certain of his own motivation—curiosity? Ego trip? Or did he really care about this boy?

AJ shifted in his seat. Before long, the shifting became a squirm.

"Something the matter?" asked Bo.

"I gotta take a leak." The kid sounded sheepish.

And you couldn't have taken care of this back at the airport? Bo clenched his jaw. He stopped himself from asking it aloud.

"I'll find a place to stop." Within a few miles, he spotted a Friendly's sign poking up into the gray day. The place was open, surrounded by a few semis and travel trailers. They got out, and discovered the air was even colder here, outside the city. Bo hated the cold. He usually tried to spend winters training in Texas or Florida, someplace warm. If the Yankees deal worked out, he'd be headed to Tampa soon enough for training and exhibition games.

The restaurant smelled like pure heaven—frying oil and fresh coffee. Bo waited in the foyer while AJ went to the men's room. Behind the hostess stand, a young woman checked him out. Bo acted as if he didn't notice, but he stood up a little straighter. The fleeting moment reminded him that he hadn't had a girlfriend in a long time. It was easy enough to get dates, but harder to keep them.

AJ returned, sniffing the air like a coonhound on the

scent. His eyes shone with a stark, naked hunger, and his face looked pale and drawn.

"You all right?" Bo asked.

"Fine." AJ's hair gleamed at the temples, as if he'd slicked it back with water.

For some reason, Bo was touched by the hasty attempt at grooming. "When was the last time you had something to eat?"

A shrug.

"Did they feed you on the plane?"

"Yeah."

Bo had his hand on the door. Something made him hesitate, and he turned back. "What?" he asked. "What did you eat on the plane?"

"A snack."

"You mean like a little packet of peanuts and a Coke?"

"Yeah, only I had a Sprite."

"This way," Bo said, heading to the hostess stand. He offered the hostess another smile. "You got a table for two, darlin'?"

"I sure do." She took two glossy, oversized menus from beneath the podium. "This way. Your server will be right with you."

Despite the undercurrent of flirting with the waitress, Bo was irritated. "You should've told me you were hungry," he said. "I'm not a mind reader."

AJ regarded him solemnly across the table. "I don't know what you are. I don't know you at all."

"I'm your father, that's what I am. And it's not my fault you don't know me. It's not your fault, either."

"Sure, let's blame Mom for everything," AJ said.

All right, so this was going to be an emotional minefield. Bo was bad at blindly feeling out someone's vulnerable areas, particularly with a boy who was a stranger. An angry, resentful stranger.

"I'm not looking to blame anybody," he said, trying for a kindly, reasonable tone. Wasn't that how you talked to a kid? With kindness? "Your mother isn't to blame for anything, AJ. She made the best choices she knew how to make under the circumstances. I respect her for that."

The boy stared at the menu, his face expressionless.

"Sorry I sounded pissed. I'm mad at myself, okay?" Bo continued. "Not at you. I'm new to this—to being in charge of a kid. I should have asked if you were hungry, or if you needed the restroom, but it didn't occur to me. I'm not a subtle guy, AJ, and I'm not real smart about a lot of things. Sometimes you're going to have to speak up, spell out for me what you need. Can you do that?"

"I guess."

"Good." He picked up the carafe the hostess had left at the table. "Coffee?"

"I'm a kid. I don't drink coffee."

What Bo knew about kids would not fill the stoneware mug in front of him. "Well then, take a look at the menu and order anything you want."

The waitress came, and AJ asked for a blueberry muffin and a glass of milk.

"Oh, you gotta do better than that," Bo said. "I mean it, AJ. Anything."

The kid packed away food as if he was hollow inside. A stack of pancakes, steak and eggs, a ham sandwich, a vanilla milkshake. Watching him eat, Bo felt oddly gratified. He didn't know why. There was something primal about feeding the boy, watching him fill himself up like a tanker taking on fuel. If he ate like this all the time, maybe he'd grow.

Bo had a club sandwich and coffee, wishing it was a beer. As he paid the tab, he felt AJ's eyes on him.

"What? You need something else? Dessert?"

"No, just…thanks." The kid's gaze shifted to an array of pies in a revolving lighted display case.

"We'll take that, too," Bo told the waitress. "The apple pie."

"Two pieces?"

"Nah. The whole pie, to go."

Once they were back on the road, Bo felt downright talkative, thanks to the coffee. "So what'd you think of your first airplane ride?" he asked AJ.

"It was okay, I guess."

"You know, I was even older than you when I first took a plane flight. Summer before my senior year of high school. I made the same flight you just did—Houston to New York. It was for an all-star baseball team that brought together kids from all over the country. We got a chance to work with a coach named Carminucci. Dino Carminucci. He had a big career with the Yankees for a while. He's retired now, but manages the Hornets these days, which is the reason I ended up in Avalon a few years back." He paused, trying to figure out if AJ was interested in talking.

The boy kept his eyes straight ahead on the gray horizon.

"The Hornets," Bo explained, "that's my team in the Can-Am League. It's Independent League Baseball. Totally separate from major league. I've spent my entire career in the Independent Leagues. Never thought that would change. It might, though. If everything goes the right way this winter, that'll change." He sneaked another look at the kid. AJ clearly didn't give a hoot about any of this and, honestly, Bo didn't blame him.

"Sorry," he muttered. "Just strumming my lips. You're probably tired from your trip."

AJ nodded but didn't say anything. However, Bo's remark made the silence seem less awkward. He relaxed, resting his wrist at the top of the steering wheel, and watching the road. He remembered that first airplane flight as though it were yesterday. He'd been a boy on fire. Not literally, of course, although at seventeen, that was the way he felt, all the time, like a struck match. With no supervision at home and nothing to keep him from exploding, he was into anything that would give him an adrenaline rush—swimming in the long, deep rice wells west of town, skateboarding through parking garages, having bottle-rocket wars with his friends, racing hot rods along the spillways and bayous of Houston—an accident waiting to happen.

He wasn't looking for trouble. It was just that life excited him, though not always in a good way. That particular summer, he was on fire because he was pissed at his mom, who was broke again and had to give up her place in the Wagon Wheel Mobile Home Court. Sometimes when that happened—which it did on a regular basis—Bo went to stay with his big brother, Stoney. But that year, Stoney, just out of high school, was working on a rig offshore and couldn't take him. Nor could he bail their mother out of debt. Generally speaking, Stoney was just as foolish as she was about money, and just as broke.

With his mom drifting around the Gulf Coast and his brother out on a rig, Bo had been looking at yet another summer in foster care. However, it turned out his baseball coach, Mr. Landry Holmes, had other plans for him. Holmes had played college ball in Florida with a guy named Dino Carminucci. They'd stayed in touch ever since. Holmes ended up coaching in Texas, and Carminucci became a scout for the Yankees. Coach Holmes had made all the arrangements for Bo to take part in the all-star program, somehow coming up with airfare and pocket money. Coaches were like that, all hooked into some vast, invisible network. The scheme was supposed to keep Bo out of trouble, and to give his one-and-only talent a chance to do him some good, so maybe he wouldn't end up like his mom and Stoney, drifting aimlessly.

Bo had been on fire about girls that summer, too, an affliction that had first struck him in the eighth grade when he'd sat behind Martha Dolittle in social studies, watching her every fluttery, girly move. If there was a scale to measure craziness about girls, on a scale of one to ten, Bo would register about a ninety-nine. He'd been in love with Yolanda Martinez the summer before their senior year of high school, and they'd had a huge fight about him going north for baseball. She thought he was abandoning her, but he claimed that if he did well enough, he might get a scholarship to college, which would mean he actually had a shot at a future.

He had been the best damn ballplayer ever to wear the uniform of the Texas City Stings, and that was no brag, just

fact. And finally, thank you, Jesus, finally he'd been tagged
for one of the most elite baseball programs in the country,
where he'd be training with the top high school players in
the sport and, more importantly, in full view of talent scouts.

He hadn't slept a wink on the flight to New York City.
Sure, he'd been tired, and the trip seemed endless, but he
hadn't wanted to miss a single second of the experience of
flying in an airplane. All his life he used to watch planes
flying overhead, silver flashes in the smoggy sky above
Texas City, and he'd imagine being aboard, flying beyond
the murky pollution to a place where the skies were clear
and the air sweet. He didn't much care where the plane was
headed. *Away* was good enough for him, even if it meant
leaving Yolanda, whom he hadn't managed to sweet-talk
into bed—yet.

Flying was everything he wanted it to be. When the
gate agent saw his height, she gave him an exit row seat
with lots of legroom, and all he had to do was say he was
willing to help out in case of an emergency. Which was a
complete joke, because in an emergency, he'd be yelling
his head off like everybody else, but he knew better than
to point that out. He'd brought along a copy of the training
camp's prospects report—a detailed scouting writeup
about each player—and a book called *The Celestine
Prophecy.* It was one of the biggest hits of the '90s, promi-
nently displayed everywhere—particularly the airport. He
was a fast reader and it was a short book, so he finished it
between periods of simply staring out the window.

The guy in *The Celestine Prophecy* was on the trail of
some kind of ancient manuscript, and he kept having these
spiritual insights, like discovering it was divine to be a

vegetarian and that a guy needed to know his own personal mission. It wasn't much of a book, but Bo saw a handful of other people on the plane reading it, so he kept plugging away, waiting for it to get more interesting. Mostly, though, he kept watching out the window. It looked like a dreamland out there. Sometimes all he could see was an eternity of cotton-candy clouds. This was what heaven looked like in every movie he'd ever seen about heaven. The weather cleared at certain points and he found himself looking down at the world. The green landscape was veined by the silvery twists of rivers and streams, and crisscrossed by roads. Everything looked so tiny and neat, it was surreal, almost. Like flying over a map of the world.

The guy next to Bo was a been-there-done-that kind of businessman. However, when the flight attendants came with a cart laden with meal trays, Bo couldn't contain himself. He'd been dying of hunger and here they were, bringing him hot food. It was a meal fit for a king—a piece of meat molded into the shape of a football, with gravy on a bed of rice, chunks of green beans on the side. A little salad in its own container with an even tinier container of salad dressing. A dinner roll and a chocolate brownie. Bo looked out the window again. This *was* heaven.

He all but inhaled the tray of food and downed a carton of milk. The businessman next to him glanced over. "Would you like my entree?" he asked. "I haven't touched it."

"Sure, that'd be great," Bo said. "Thanks."

The guy handed over his foil-wrapped mystery meat and the dinner roll, too. That seemed to break the ice, because the guy asked, "Is this your first trip to New York?"

Bo nodded. "First trip to anywhere, now that you mention it." Other than team trips for games, the farthest he'd been from home was New Orleans. Last summer, he and Stoney had driven half the night to the Big Easy, because they wanted to get laid. The evening hadn't really worked out, though, because Stoney—never known for his smarts—couldn't manage to convince anyone they were over twenty-one. When they finally found a club with a bouncer who looked the other way, it turned out that the phenomenally gorgeous, sexy pole dancers in skintight sequined costumes were *guys*. Bo still got the willies, remembering that night. They couldn't get out of there fast enough.

"Where are you staying?" the guy asked.

Bo handed him the brochure about the all-star program. It was a glossy pamphlet with pictures of lakes and forests that stayed cool even at the height of summer's fury. "The program's invitation only," he told the businessman, "run by a guy who has connections to the Yankees organization."

"You don't say." The guy sipped his coffee. "You must be pretty good."

"I guess I'll find out this summer." At that moment, Bo had considered himself the luckiest guy in the world. He still remembered the heady feeling that anything was possible. It was the feeling he got every time he stood on the mound, his fingertips playing over the laces of the ball. Baseball had always been his passion and his salvation, even when injuries, bad timing and bad luck ruined his chances in the draft, year after year. He never gave up, though, never stopped trying, even when he was over thirty and had earned a nickname in the league—"Bad Luck Crutch." When some brutish rookie asked him why he kept showing up, Bo had learned to grin and say, "I figure I need to be here when my luck comes around."

And indeed, a decade late, that was exactly what had happened. Last fall, his luck had come back, triggered by a phone call from Gus Carlisle, a sports agent. There was a spot on the Yankees' pitching staff. They were interested in pre-contract talks. Bo had been invited to the Rookie Development program this winter, and if things progressed, he'd be included in spring training and exhibition games.

Suddenly, Bo felt very close to that boy on fire. "You a baseball fan?" he asked AJ. Maybe the kid was ready to talk.

"Not really."

Great. "Not even the Astros?"

"I don't really follow them. Or any team. Or any player, either."

"Well, hell." Bo drummed his fingers on the steering wheel. "What do you like to do?" He fiddled with the radio dial. "How about music? You like music? I play in a band in Avalon. We're not that good but we have quite a time together. One of us is good—a guy named Eddie Haven."

Bo was no virtuoso, but ever since high school, he'd played in a variety of garage bands. In the movies, a band was like a second family, but in real life, that was never the case. Every band he'd played in was as dysfunctional as his own family, if not more. Except the group he was with now, which was more about drinking beer and male bonding than about making music. The group consisted of Bo on bass and his best friend, Noah, on drums, and a local cop named Rayburn Tolley on keyboards. The real talent of the group was Eddie, on lead guitar and vocals.

A long silence stretched out. It was always a surprise to

Bo when he met someone who wasn't a baseball fan. More surprising when they didn't have a favorite band—or song. He glanced over at AJ, then did a double take. The weak, cold light of winter flowed over his face. He held one curled fist tucked up under his chin, and he appeared to be fast asleep.

"Oh, you are scintillating, Crutch, that's what you are," Bo murmured. "Purely scintillating."

Bo had to remind himself to watch the road. It was irresistible, sneaking glances at that sleeping face. Was there a resemblance? Some indelible stamp that branded this boy his? Bo couldn't tell. He drove the rest of the way to Avalon listening to Stanley Clarke and Jaco Pastorius on the Z4's state-of-the-art MP3 player.

For Bo, music was never just background noise. It was a place he went in his head, like a sanctuary. Home base, where he was safe. This was something he'd invented when he was a kid, left alone in a noisy trailer park in Texas City. The air smelled of burning petroleum products from the refineries, and the sky was always a dull amber color, even at night, because the refinery never slept. Bo's mother and brother were gone most of the time, and he'd found that music was a way to fill the dark corners of the house and drown out the sounds of the neighbors fighting, dogs barking, trucks and motorcycles coming and going.

When he was about twelve years old, his brother, Stoney, gave him an electric bass and an amp. The instrument was hot, of course; everything of value Stoney brought home was hot. Bo hadn't objected, though. Sure, stealing was wrong, but Stoney was good at it, and he only ripped off people who owed him money.

Bo had taught himself to play by ear.

Bo glanced over at AJ, wondering if the kid liked music. Hell, he wondered if AJ liked anything. This boy, who carried around half of Bo's DNA, was a complete stranger to him. Bo harbored no romantic notion that just because they were blood relations, they were going to find some deep connection and form a meaningful, life-long bond.

Bo's own father had disabused him of that notion. Wiley Crutcher had married Bo's mother, Trudy, and stuck with her only long enough to give her a name that sounded like a prosthetic device, and two large, athletic boys. Wiley had left when Bo was a baby. Bo's only memory of the man came from an encounter that occurred when Bo was in grade school. Wiley had shown up for a Little League game; Bo had no idea why. Bo's mother had introduced them before the game.

"This him?" Wiley had asked.

"Yes. This is Bo. Bo, this here's your daddy."

Bo remembered feeling those eyes, checking him out. Wiley Crutcher had taken a sip from a bottle in a bag; he'd wiped his mouth with the back of his hand and said, "Dudn't look like much."

"Oh, he's a real good ballplayer. Wait till you see."

"Yeah?" Wiley had tossed him a coin. It had a triangle and some words on it. "Here you go, kid. For luck."

Some guys' dads gave them bikes and baseball mitts for presents. Bo got a one-time visit and this coin. His father hadn't stuck around, but the coin brought Bo luck. That was something, at least. Bo had pitched his first shutout that day. His team and his coach were overjoyed, but when the game ended, his father was already gone. He went to get some beer, Bo's mother explained, and he never came back.

So now, when Bo regarded this boy, this stranger-son he'd picked up at the airport like a piece of lost luggage, he did not fool himself into believing that the tenderness that touched his heart as he watched the boy eat and sleep was anything but pity. This boy's mother had been rounded up at the factory where she'd worked for ten years, put in detention to await deportation. No wonder the kid was freaked.

Sophie would fix this, Bo reassured himself. Maybe even over the weekend; she was that good when it came to matters of law. So, really, there was no point in getting attached to the kid. AJ would be back with his mama in no time.

A few hours later, they rolled into Avalon, a town that, to Bo and most outsiders, looked too pretty to be real. Clustered around the southern end of Willow Lake, it was a town forgotten by time, where the seasons changed but the landscape didn't. Currently the lake was frozen over, a vast white expanse of hell, as far as Bo was concerned. He preferred to stay inside where the real men were, shooting pool and drinking beer.

When it came to winter sports, Bo figured he'd rather have a root canal. He was a summer guy, through and through. He'd grown up with the sticky-hot sun of the Texas Gulf Coast beating down on him. It wasn't his choice to live in the tundra. Initially, he'd moved to Avalon because it was the only place that would have him, pitching for the Hornets. Now he was entrenched, awaiting a once-in-a-lifetime opportunity that was not yet quite real.

The main part of town had a railway station with a few

daily trains south to Grand Central Station in New York City and to Albany and points north. The town square had a courthouse, shops and restaurants that catered to tourists year round. Radiating from the main square were quaint streets of homes, schools and churches. They passed the Apple Tree Inn, a high-end restaurant where you took your date if you wanted to impress her, thus increasing your chances of getting laid. The Avalon Meadows Country Club was the place where the local nobs sipped martinis and traded travelogues.

And then there was the Hilltop Tavern. It had been Bo's home away from home since he'd moved to town. It belonged to Maggie Lynn O'Toole, who had to buy out her ex in their divorce settlement. The bar, located in a historic brick building at the top of Oak Hill, had started life during Prohibition as a speakeasy. Through the years, it had gone through many transformations and was now the most popular watering hole in town.

Bo lived in a studio apartment tucked into a corner of the building over the taproom. AJ didn't wake up when Bo pulled into the nearly empty parking lot at the back of the old brick walk-up, and stopped the car. Damn, now what? He hated to wake the kid after the night he'd had. God knew, sleep was a better place for the boy than being awake and fretting about his mother. But they couldn't stay in the car all day.

"Yo, AJ, we're here," Bo said.

The boy didn't respond.

Bo made plenty of noise getting out of the car and retrieving the bags from the trunk. He took the bags upstairs, hurried back down to check on AJ. He went around to the passenger side and opened the door. "Hey, we're here," he said again. "Come on upstairs and you can get some sleep."

AJ was already getting some sleep. A fresh gust of arctic air caused him to shudder, but he didn't wake up. Bo considered giving the boy a nudge, then decided it would be cruel to wake him from a sound sleep into a strange, cold world of worry. He reached into the car and released the seat belt. Bending low in a supremely awkward stance, he snaked one arm behind AJ and the other under his knees, and lifted him up.

The kid stayed sound asleep. Amazing. Also amazing—for the first time in his life, Bo was holding his son. Twelve years too late, AJ was in his arms, a deadweight. He was small, but not that small. Bo staggered a little, getting his balance on the icy surface of the parking lot. Damn. He could blow out a knee like this. And that would blow everything for him.

He moved slowly, carefully, waiting to feel some kind of connection to the bundle of humanity. Maybe now that he was touching the boy, it would happen.

Music pulsed from the taproom, interspersed with laughter and conversation. The afternoon crowd wasn't too rowdy, but now Bo heard it with new ears. He instinctively hunched his shoulders as if to protect the kid from the intrusive noise. "Let's get you inside, my buddy," he murmured, and headed for the door.

The carpet on the stairs and in the hallway was grungy from winter boots; Bo had never noticed that before. He resolved to talk to Maggie Lynn about replacing it. Inside the apartment, he lowered AJ to the sagging sofa that occupied one wall, under a Rolling Rock Beer clock. The boy still didn't awaken, just sighed lightly, drew his knees up and turned his back.

Bo grabbed a pillow from his bed and pulled off the comforter, tucking it around the boy. Then Bo pulled the blinds and stood still for a few minutes, totally at a loss. Now what?

He'd never noticed before how small the apartment was, how cluttered. He listened to the noise of the tavern below. Was it always that loud? That obnoxious? Suddenly it bugged the shit out of him. He went to the fridge, grabbed a beer. The bottle gave a hiss of relief when he opened it.

He sat for a long time, sipping the beer and reflecting on his own childhood. He'd had a single mother, too. They'd lived in all kinds of places, none of them anything special. Where he hung his hat had never mattered much to him until now. Having the boy here made Bo flinchingly aware of the small, shabby digs. He knew for a fact he didn't ever want to embarrass this boy, didn't ever want AJ to feel ashamed of who he was or where he lived. Bo had been through that, and the vivid memories haunted him still.

Bo could afford a new place now. He just hadn't gotten around to it.

Studying the kid, he wondered what the hell he was going to do. He thought about Coach Landry Holmes, the man who had taken him under his wing when he was about AJ's age. Coach Holmes was, in many respects, more of a parent to Bo than Trudy Crutcher had ever been. Holmes had first spotted Bo playing sandlot baseball, pitching to kids on a field polluted with refuse that blew like tumbleweeds across the dying grass. They used old Circle K bags for bases and kept score with a stick in the clay-heavy earth.

Holmes had seen the strength and promise in that

twelve-year-old's pitching arm, and he'd made Bo his project. When Trudy got behind on her bills and the boys had to go into foster care, it was Coach Holmes and his wife, Emmaline, who took the youngsters home and fed them, made them do their homework and get their hair cut and go to church. The Holmeses attended their sports practices and games with more reliable frequency than Trudy ever did. That had been just fine with Bo, because whenever his mom showed up somewhere, she always created a stir. She wore her hair teased up high, and her shirt cut low. Looks like hers were impossible to ignore.

Yet despite the kindness of Landry and Emmaline Holmes, Bo felt completely unprepared to be a father. It was probably also why he felt so strangely disassociated. He vacillated between the urge to flee and take no part in this, and the opposing urge to protect this boy at all costs. He'd coasted for years, sending child support even when he couldn't afford to, because it made him feel like he was doing his part without requiring an emotional investment from him. Yet now, out of the blue, here was a kid in desperate need. And Bo could no longer turn his back on his responsibility, could no longer write a check to make it go away. Well, actually he could, but even he wasn't that big a jerk.

AJ was young, and undersized for his age. But his presence here was huge. He was the proverbial elephant in the room. What a mess, Bo thought.

"I'll do the best I can, kid," he muttered to the boy.

Five

Kim thought she'd sleep for a week once her head touched the pillow, but little demons of worry prodded her awake at the crack of dawn. She lay motionless in a room that was both familiar and strange to her. The last time she'd slept in this bed had been years ago, yet the memories that haunted the shadowy corners and the folds of the drapes were as fresh as last night's dream. This had been her heart's home as a child, a place of clarity and peace. Her grandparents' house, where she was the adored only grandchild, had always been filled with magic for her.

When she was small, she hadn't understood why she loved visiting Avalon so much. As she got older, she realized it was because here, she was accepted for herself, unweighted by expectations and unbound by restrictions. According to her father, her Fairfield grandparents spoiled her.

Kim hated that word, *spoiled.* She hated the fact that her father had described her as spoiled and, years later, so did most of the men she'd dated, including Lloyd Johnson. *"Spoiled"* implied something irredeemable, past saving.

Something smelly that should be sealed up tight and kicked to the curb.

She exhaled slowly, sitting up in bed and holding the quilt under her chin. Maybe she *was* spoiled. Maybe someone should kick her to the curb.

Come to think of it, that was exactly what Lloyd had done. She tugged her mind away from him. The truth was, she was sick of thinking about him. She was sick of her*self.* Sick of her problems, her dilemma, her life. Stewing about it was simply depressing and got her nowhere.

She darted a suspicious look at her cell phone. Its battery was dead and would not be revived until she bought a replacement charger and plugged it in. She was in no hurry to do so, knowing she'd discover a world of unpleasant voice mails. Maybe she'd simply get rid of the phone for good, start fresh with a new one. Did people do that? Did they dump their dead phones, never bothering to retrieve the messages? She found the notion deeply appealing. Maybe there was an invisible cloud of unheard messages hovering out there in the digital ether somewhere, never to reach their intended recipients.

The sound of antique plumbing groaned in the walls of the old house, reminding Kim that she was far from alone. In addition to Mr. Dino Carminucci, there were two other houseguests, and the house had room for two more on the top floor. She could barely get her mind around her mother's surprise "project." Unbelievable. Her mother ran a boardinghouse. Kim hadn't even known people still did such a thing.

She wondered what her grandparents would think of Penelope's enterprise. She turned in bed, resting her cheek on her elbow as she studied an old photograph of Grandpa and Grandma Fairfield. It was a studio portrait from the mid-'70s, the colors fading but the smiles as bright as the day it was taken.

"I wish you were here," she whispered to them. Both had died too young; her grandmother had succumbed to cancer a year and a half ago. Since it was in the summer, Lloyd had come along for the funeral. Foolishly, she'd thought he would be a comfort to her. Instead, he'd insisted on staying at the Inn at Willow Lake instead of with Kim's mother, claiming he didn't want to impose. What Kim should have realized back then was how selfish Lloyd was, and how foolish she'd been to let him create distance between her and her mother.

"I'm back now," she said to the memory of her grandparents. "I just hope I'm not too late."

Closing her eyes, she sank into memories of the past. She always thought her love of sports had come from her grandfather. He'd been a huge fan and he didn't discriminate; he loved all kinds of sports. As his sole grandchild, Kim became his favorite companion at games, both professional and amateur. She loved the excitement of the crowd and the elemental struggle of the contest, whether it was on a baseball diamond, basketball court or hockey rink. Mostly, she'd loved the feeling of sharing the experience with her grandfather, who adored her.

When she was twelve, he visited her in the city and gave her season tickets to the Mets, promising her a winning season. The next day, he had kissed her goodbye and gone home. There was no way she could have known she'd never see him again.

The chances of a golfer being killed by lightning were one in a million. The thing no one thought about was that one fatality. For him, the odds were overwhelming.

People said it was a blessing that her grandfather had died doing something he loved, and that it was a blessing to go instantly, feeling no pain, no fear. Just a quick cosmic wink, and no more Grandpa. Kim understood that they were only trying to make her feel better. She even tried to accept the blessing explanation. But for the life of her, she couldn't buy into the concept.

After that, she used to beg her father to take her to games, but he was always too busy. She went on her own, taking the bus or subway to Shea Stadium or Madison Square Garden. Going to a game made her feel closer to her grandfather, even when she was on her own. Caught up in the high excitement of the contest, she missed him just a tiny bit less. Sometimes it even made the terrible ache of loss ease up, if only for a few minutes.

Lying there, remembering, she made a vow. Her love of sports was a gift from her grandfather, and there was no way she'd let Lloyd Johnson or anyone take it away.

It was tempting to turn her back on the light trickling in through the bedroom window, to pull the covers over her head and fall asleep. For days or months. Forever.

Unfortunately, every time she shut her eyes, she caught herself thinking about the night in L.A. Intellectually, she knew the problem was Lloyd, not her. Yet when she replayed the scene over and over in her head, she kept wondering if she might have done something differently, if she could have said the right thing, maybe the disaster would have been averted. As soon as she felt her thoughts heading in that direction, she gave herself a mental shake. She was not to blame for Lloyd's ego and his nasty temper.

"All righty, then," she said, flinging back the quilt. She caught a glimpse of her long red hair in the mirror over the dresser. Yikes. "On that note, we'll get up and see what the day brings."

She went downstairs to find a stranger in the kitchen, with the countertop TV playing cartoons. Well, not exactly a stranger. One of her mother's boarders, Daphne McDaniel. Kim would have to get used to seeing strangers around the house.

"Wow, that takes me back," said Daphne, turning down the volume as she eyed Kim's Camp Kioga sweatshirt. "Coffee?"

"Thanks." Kim accepted the steaming mug and took a grateful sip. She was wearing the ancient jeans and camp hoodie, thick socks and Crocs her mother had given her yesterday. Prior to coming downstairs, she'd hastily washed the sleep from her face and pulled her long red hair into a ponytail. "These clothes are left over from…a hundred years ago. That's what it feels like, anyway. I, um, traveled light, coming here." All her worldly possessions were in L.A., most of them in a storage unit off Manhattan Beach Boulevard. She'd given up her apartment in order to be with Lloyd. She would have everything shipped to her eventually, but she didn't want to think about that just now.

She had a funny urge to unload on Daphne, although they'd only just met. A girl needed her girlfriends. In her world—former world—friends and enemies blended together and morphed from one role to the other. There was even a word for it—frenemies. You couldn't always trust them. It struck Kim that she didn't have many friends. There were coworkers, sure. But there was no one she could point to and say, this is my friend. She hoped Daphne would turn out to be more genuine.

"I'm going to need to run into town to grab a few things," she said.

"Try Zuzu's Petals in the town square. Best shop there is."

Kim used to shop in boutiques haunted by movie stars in floppy hats, and women with more money than common sense. She now counted herself a member of that group and vowed to change. "Thanks. Did you go to Camp Kioga when you were younger?"

Daphne laughed, but not with humor. "Honey, I was never younger. FYI, I'm having my childhood now, because I missed it the first time around."

Kim stirred a partial packet of Splenda into the coffee. She sneaked a peek at Daphne, who was sitting on a bar stool at the kitchen island, eating FrankenBerry cereal from a bright yellow bowl. With daring facial piercings and pink-streaked hair, she looked like a punk rocker. In contrast to Kim's buffed-and-polished L.A. friends, Daphne was refreshing—quirky, but genuine.

Daphne fished a clear plastic packet out of her cereal bowl. *"Yes,"* she said. "I got the prize. I love when I get the prize."

Given the type of cereal she was eating, she wasn't likely to have much competition.

She wiped the toy on a napkin. "Troll doll," she said, holding it up like a tiny trophy. "God, I *love* these things."

Kim touched her hair, feeling an uneasy kinship with the

troll. Then she lifted her coffee mug in salute. "Here's to enjoying your childhood."

"On the weekends, at least."

"What do you do during the week?" She pictured Daphne working at a roller rink or surfing the Internet, bookmarking anime sites.

"I work in a local law office. It's up over the bookstore in town. It's okay. I prefer Saturdays, though. Back-to-back *Looney Tunes,* you know?"

Kim offered a bright smile. "My fave. So, a law office?"

"Parkington, Waltham & Shepherd. A full-service firm. I'm the receptionist and office manager." Daphne lifted the bowl to her mouth and took a sip, leaving a milk mustache. "So, really, you can relax. Your mom's not running a group home for wackos here. The tenants are just regular folks, who happen to want to live simply."

"I'm relaxed," Kim protested.

"Nah, I saw your face when your mom introduced us. You were worried I'd turn out to be a one-woman freak show," Daphne said easily. "Most people do, when they first meet me. Trust me, I'm totally normal. Just—like I said—having a late childhood. In my family, I was the eldest of five siblings. My mom got sick and my dad took off, so I ended up raising my brothers and sisters. I did a lousy job, too, seeing as I was all of eleven years old when it started. That's why I never want to have kids. Heck, I don't even want to have a place of my own."

"Because you missed out on your childhood?"

"Yeah." Daphne took her bowl and spoon to the sink, and grabbed a pitcher of orange juice. "I decided to have my childhood now, and that means living here, where I don't need to worry about adult responsibilities. Those responsibilities include, but are not limited to, property taxes, utility bills, meal preparation and long-term commitments."

Kim stared at her for a few seconds. She studied the black wool leggings, the snug leather skirt and Doc Martens, the black manicure. Daphne just looked so comfortable, being herself.

"Good plan," she said. "Is there any orange juice left?"

Daphne poured her a glass. "Cereal?" she asked, offering the box.

"No, thanks. Without the prize, what's the point?"

Daphne grinned. "I like the way you think."

Kim grinned back, liking the ease she felt with this girl.

"Good morning," said her mother, bustling into the kitchen. She looked fresh and younger than her age in a Fair Isle sweater, jeans and Ugg boots. In fact, she looked younger than her old self, the upper Manhattan maven in St. John's suits and pearls. Tying on an apron, she said, "Did you sleep all right?"

"Well enough." Kim sipped her coffee. "I was fired. By e-mail."

"Harsh," said Daphne.

"Cowardly," her mother said.

"They're not being cowardly. I'm not important enough to scare them. It's just more convenient."

"I'm so sorry," her mother said.

"Don't be. It was the worst job ever." Not really, but she felt better, saying it.

"And here I thought you enjoyed it," her mother said.

"What do you do?" Daphne asked. "Or—past tense. What did you used to do?"

Kim took a seat across from Daphne and peeled a satsuma for herself. "Sports media relations. It seemed like a good career for me. I was always into sports, all through school and college. After graduation, I went to L.A. to look for a job. On a whim, I tried out to be a Laker girl. I was completely shocked when they chose me as an alternate. It was probably the most grueling three months of my life. And the steepest learning curve. The training I could handle. Even the politics—I watched other girls crumble, but I got along fine. It turned out what I was best at was PR. When I was injured—"

"You were injured?" Daphne asked.

"Tore my rotator cuff." Unconsciously her hand went to her right shoulder. "It put an end to a very short, inauspicious career as a Laker girl. Going into sports PR seemed like the obvious next step for me. Clearly I didn't have the chops to be a top athlete, but I knew what it took to represent them."

She'd been assigned to look after a second-string rookie, Calvin Graham. In the wake of Hurricane Katrina, he was being hounded by the press about the Lower 9th Ward neighborhood of New Orleans, where he'd been born and raised. Seeing him floundering, she'd stepped in. Within a week, Calvin Graham was serving as honorary chairman of a relief effort, raising money to help people rebuild. He'd never had much of a career in the NBA but he'd gone on to create a foundation that, to this day, provided low-interest loans to Katrina victims. Kim had found her role incredibly gratifying.

In time, however, she forgot how much she liked her work. Well, not forgot, exactly. The role of mentor got lost as she was assigned to other players. She found herself saying things like "Get your drunk ass out of bed" and "Learn to verify a girl's age before you sleep with her." She missed guys like Calvin. She missed the good guys.

"Sounds like a cool job," Daphne remarked.

"Sometimes, I have to admit, the work was so satisfying. A lot of people with a God-given athletic talent are brilliant to work with. It was my job to smooth the rough edges."

"How rough?" asked Daphne.

"I worked with guys who were fearless at facing a wall of defensive linebackers out for blood, but who tended to crumble in front of a microphone. I helped them with that part of their career. It went well most of the time. But something happens when you work with people like that. It's hard to describe. You're working with clients on a strangely intimate level, even though it's just a job. I never let things get too personal—until Lloyd." She shook her head, remembering. "The two of us just clicked—at first, anyway." She felt again the bittersweet joy of falling for a guy while doing media training with him. It was like a second-rate romantic movie—if she succeeded in grooming him, then that meant losing him, because once he had mastered the art of handling the press, he would move on.

Except that didn't happen with Lloyd. Her mistake was in letting herself believe it could work out for them. She wouldn't be that stupid again.

Six

Bo woke up early, shivering from the cold as he groped for his comforter. Then he remembered he'd given it to AJ last night, and that thought caused him to sit up instantly, squinting through the morning light.

There, the lump on the sofa confirmed it. His kid was staying with him. His son. Bo waited to feel…what? Paternal? Not happening. The kid was his flesh and blood, and Bo was going to do everything in his power to reunite AJ with Yolanda. But fatherly feelings eluded him.

He yawned and stretched, tried not to make any noise as he got out of bed and headed for the john. He never got up this early unless he was in training. It was funny, how easy it was to get up in the morning when he hadn't sucked down a bunch of beers the night before. Well, not funny ha-ha, but funny as in, he might ought to consider doing it more often.

Call me, read a message scribbled on a Post-it note stuck to the bathroom mirror. *Chardonnay*—and her phone number. The message was punctuated by a lipstick kiss. It was kind of depressing to realize he had actually dated a woman named Chardonnay. That was really all he remembered about her.

Bo snatched the note and stuck it in a drawer. Then he changed his mind and stuck it in his pocket. In the drawer, he spotted a box of rubbers. Whoa. He shoved the box in the cabinet under the sink, back behind the pipes, then gave the place a once-over to make sure there weren't any other sketchy things lying around.

He didn't consider himself the kind of person who kept secrets, but for the time being, there was a kid in his life, and he had to make room for that. The sudden responsibility felt crushing, but what was he going to do? Clean up his act, for one thing.

When Bo himself was a young boy, his mother had shielded him from nothing—not the late-night visitors, not the laughter or the fighting, not the strangers he encountered in the house when he got up in the night to take a leak. Things like that had taken a toll on him, made him a distrustful and cautious child, who had grown into a distrustful and reckless man.

He had enough sense to know there were some things a kid just didn't need to see. At least until someone other than Bo could explain them.

Although Bo and his brother, Stoney, had grown up without a father, they'd had a lot of uncles. Not uncles by blood, of course. "Uncles" was a euphemism for whatever shitkicker or oilfield trash happened to be banging his mother.

So even though he didn't know a damn thing about raising a kid, he understood that you didn't put stuff in their face before they were ready to deal with it. He remembered lying awake too many nights, feeling sick to his stomach as he listened to the low voice of a stranger through the thin walls of the trailer where they lived. One of his earliest memories was hearing his brother say, "I swear, if you piss the bed again, I'll pound your face. Swear to God, I will."

He and Stoney had taken to peeing in empty Coke bottles rather than getting up in the night and risking an encounter with Uncle Terrell or Uncle Dwayne, or whoever else was keeping their mama from getting lonely that night.

That was how she explained the visitors to her boys. "It keeps me from feeling too lonely."

"I can do that," Bo used to tell her, when he was really little and didn't understand. "I can keep you from getting lonely. I'll sing to you, Mama. I'll play the guitar." He wasn't very good, but he knew all the words to "Mr. Bojangles," his namesake song.

His mama had tousled his hair, offered a sad smile. "This is a different kind of lonely, baby boy. It's the kind you can't help me with."

In time, Bo had grown into an understanding of what she meant, but he never forgot the feeling of being a scared kid. He would never subject AJ to that. For the rest of the weekend—or however long the boy was with him—Bo Crutcher would be a monk.

Yeah, right. He could just hear his friends now. People who knew him had never seen him go more than a week or two without a date.

He tried to be as quiet as possible as he moved around the apartment. Until last night, he had considered it a luxury to live in a place that didn't require him to get behind the wheel at the end of the night. Situated above his favorite bar, where he worked most nights, it allowed him the world's shortest commute after work. He simply went upstairs and did a face-plant in the bed.

Unless, of course, he got lucky, which he did with decent frequency. It was always a pleasant feeling, waking up with a woman in his bed. He loved everything about women. He loved their soft skin and all the good-smelling preparations they used to keep it that way. He loved the sound of their sweet voices, laughing at something he'd said or sighing with pleasure in his ear when he held them close. He'd had a lot of girlfriends over the years and he'd loved each and every one of them as thoroughly as he knew how.

And when each one left him, she always walked away with a piece of his heart. He never told them, though. Never complained. He was grateful for whatever time and whatever loving they'd given him.

Most of his girlfriends left believing he'd forget them the moment they were out of sight. They couldn't be more wrong, though. The women he'd loved and lost were etched in his mind like beautiful dreams that never quite vanished with the morning.

Knowing how to love a woman had never been a problem for Bo. Knowing how to keep her, now, that was a different story. A lot of them left as soon as they realized he didn't know shit about sharing his life, planning a future, keeping a bond strong enough for a lifetime. Others took off when they discovered that all professional ballplayers were not created equal. Yes, the Can-Am League was an organization of professionals. But the players were in it because they purely loved the game, not because they were being paid a fortune. To some women, this was a bit of a rude awakening.

In the case of Yolanda Martinez, she'd walked away with more than a piece of his heart.

It was only months later, after Yolanda had forced a goodbye on him, that Bo learned he'd become a father. There was no way to pinpoint the exact moment of conception because the fact was, once he and Yolanda got started, they did it all the time. They were just kids, seventeen and revved up by hormones, and they were in the first flush of tenderness and excitement.

They had met in English class, when they'd both been struggling through the leaden phrases of *Last of the Mohicans,* which felt like a punishment, yet gave them a feeling of kinship in their shared suffering. They took to staying late in the library to study, quizzing each other on vocabulary words no living human would ever have occasion to utter: Vaunted. Cunning. Chaste.

The study sessions were only an excuse to sit close, to eye each other over the pages of the musty tomes, to trade smiles first, then touches that escalated from accidental to deliberate, and finally whispers that bloomed into kisses. She roused in him a sense of protectiveness that made him feel as though he could take on the world. Although she was an only child of strict parents, he persuaded her one hot September day to drive out to a rice well he knew of, where cool water cascaded through a thick pipe, emptying into a vast natural holding tank the size of a baseball diamond. For people who had no money, there was no better swimming pool to offer blissful relief from the heat.

Holding hands, they leaped into the crystalline depths, laughing and paddling, kissing while the water eddied around them in a swirl of sensuality. Later, they lay together on a bed of towels in the back of his rusted-out El Camino.

Bo wondered if Yolanda knew he'd never been laid. While all his friends were getting it on, Bo had foolishly clung to some chivalrous ideal about girls. He didn't want to be that close, that intimate with a girl unless he loved her. There were tons of reasons this made no sense, not the least of which was that he wasn't real sure what love was. How could he, growing up the way he had? His mother drifted from fellow to fellow the way a bee gathered nectar from flower to flower, sucking one dry and then moving on to the next without a backward glance.

Bo had grown up watching this changing array of guys parading through their lives. Sometimes she admitted she liked a guy because he let her drive his nice Volvo whenever she wanted, or because he worked at a music store and gave her free CDs. When Bo was old enough to question his mother, she explained herself with a self-deprecating laugh. "Baby boy, I got to use my looks while I still have them."

As a little boy, he'd wondered where a person's looks went. Did they get left in a heap in the bottom of a closet, discarded like last year's Halloween costume? And why would guys quit liking her, unless the only thing they liked was her looks?

Whenever Bo tried to pinpoint what love was, he thought of his coach, Landry Holmes, and Emmaline, his wife. Emmaline was, to put it in the kindest of terms, a plain woman. Yet Landry had a way of looking at her that made her beautiful, simple as that. He'd get this peculiar expression on his face, and when she looked back at him, she was lit from within, and beautiful didn't even begin to describe how she looked in those moments. Bo's mother worried about losing her looks but Emmaline would always have hers.

That was the kind of feeling Bo was meant to find; he was convinced of this. He hadn't had much luck...until now. His hand shook as he peeled off her swimsuit. He'd been overwhelmed by her beauty, her flickering shy passion. They were each other's first time, with all the attendant awkward tenderness. He was clumsy with the condom, and there was blood and discomfort, but she clung to him and said she wept because she loved him. Over time, their passion and boldness grew and he learned how to please her, nearly weeping himself when she cried out in ecstasy. Afterward, replete with a soaring sense of accomplishment they called love, they lay together and built a future out of words. He would play baseball and go to college. She would work at her sewing, which she loved, making bride gowns and fancy dresses. One day they would marry and have a home of their own, with a porch and a little garden patch where they'd listen to the cicadas singing at twilight.

Bo remembered trying to close that moment into his heart, knowing it was his first time to feel the utter wonder of perfect happiness. As the weeks went by they learned to steal away to secret places, where they would make love, sometimes with frantic, hungry haste and other times with unhurried, delicious passion. He would never know precisely which night the condom had failed. But indeed it had, and Yolanda's blossoming, fertile body had done what it was made to do. The unseen division of cells that would one day be his son happened without his knowledge.

His first inkling that something was amiss occurred when Yolanda stopped coming to school. Worried, he breached her cardinal rule and picked up the phone, even though she told him never to call her. In stern tones her father said Bo must not try to speak to her again. Bo persisted, going to her apartment, only to be turned away by her furious father, Hector Martinez. After that, Bo stole a ladder from a construction site to climb to her window late one night. She was startled awake by his tapping and greeted him, fearful and swollen-eyed, with an urgent whisper. The sight of her gave him an immediate hard-on, which made him vaguely ashamed, since she was clearly the opposite of turned on.

"Go away," she begged him. "If my father catches us, he'll hurt you."

"What's going on?" Bo asked in desperation.

"The end of us, is what."

"But why? I love you, Yolanda. I can't stand being without you."

She'd cried, her cheek to his chest. She felt so small and fragile. "I loved you, too," she whispered, "but we can't be together. I'm pregnant, Bo, and you can't be a part of this."

Pregnant. The word had twisted him into knots. He felt no joy, only abject fear, confusion and disappointment. "I'll help you," he said. "We'll do this together."

That only made her cry harder. "We can't. Everything's changed. I'm not the same person now. I'm not that girl anymore, not that girl who liked making out in the school library and sneaking away to the rice wells. This is real life. This is a baby, and neither of us is ready. But I don't have a choice. You do."

"I choose to stay with you and help you through this."

"You don't get 'through' a baby. I know you mean well. And I know you'd do your best. But the two of us—we have nothing, Bo. Nothing. And that won't work."

"I'll leave school, get a job—"

"What about baseball?" she asked. "What about your dream?"

"It's not as important as you."

She smiled sadly. "I knew you'd say that. I don't want to be with you, though. I don't want to be with someone who sacrificed a dream for me."

"It's not a sacrifice," he protested. As soon as he spoke the words, he knew he was lying. He hoped she couldn't tell.

He never found out. Her parents burst into the room and made him wait in silent misery on the stairs while they called the police.

"Mr. Martinez, I want to take care of her. Swear to God," Bo said to her father.

Just as Yolanda had warned him, her father backhanded him across the face. Blood trickled out the side of his mouth. He didn't make a sound. His mother's boyfriends had trained him the hard way that it was no use.

He was arrested for breaking and entering, and for stealing the ladder. The last he saw of Yolanda was her face in the lighted window, her dark eyes enormous with sadness.

At the substation, they recognized his name thanks to their familiarity with his brother. "I figure it was only a matter of time before we met the other Crutcher boy," said the arresting officer. His partner was more sympathetic. Maybe it was Bo's age or the bloody and swollen lip. The

cop said, "I'm a Stings fan. Played for them myself when
I was in high school. You got a hell of an arm, boy."

"Yes, sir." Bo didn't know what else to say. Then he
found himself telling the whole story to the cop, who
proved to be a good listener.

"Son, I know you're on fire for this girl right now, but
trust me. It'll be best for all concerned if you let her family
deal with this in their own way. Fighting them will only
cause more grief and you won't win anyway. Best to move
on. Trust me on that."

The charges were dropped on condition that Bo stay
away from Yolanda for good. Since he couldn't afford a
lawyer to fight an actual charge, he conceded defeat. Her
family moved away and he could find no friend or neighbor
to say where she had gone. He later heard she'd been sent
to live with her father's sister in Laredo.

Not long after, the chance of a lifetime had appeared before him—an opportunity to train with a farm league team
affiliated with the Houston Astros, and Bo had seized it.
He told himself he'd never stop searching for Yolanda, but
he was out of ideas.

And that, he admitted to the sleeping boy in his living
room, was only the first time he'd turned his back on his
kid. Although Yolanda had forbidden him to see the boy,
Bo now wished he'd fought harder for his rights as a father.

Moving quietly through the small apartment, he opened
the plastic zipper pouch with AJ's ID in it, studying the
copy of the birth certificate. Hell, no wonder the kid went
by AJ instead of his whole name. Place of birth: Laredo,
Webb County, Texas. He stared at the date, unable to re-

member what he'd been doing that day more than twelve years ago.

After Yolanda, Bo dated any girl who said yes to him. He wanted to see if Yolanda was right—if he was in love with her specifically or if he was in love with love. Turned out Yolanda was neither wholly right nor wholly wrong. He loved every girl he was with. Yet the moment Yolanda called, he was prepared to drop everything and rush to see her, but she still didn't want that. "This is just to tell you I had a baby boy last night. AJ. AJ Martinez," she stated.

"Can I come see him?"

"That's not a good idea."

"Hell, Yolanda, then why'd you even bother to call?"

"I thought you'd want to know."

"What I want to know is why you cut me off when I said I wanted to be with you. What I want to know is why I'm not a part of this."

"Because we're living in Laredo now. My aunt has a bridal shop...."

He told her about the bank account then, the one he'd opened for the baby. Coach Holmes had helped him set it up and explained how it would work. A bank official had opened an escrow account that could be accessed by the child's legal guardian. It wasn't much because he didn't earn much, doing odd jobs wherever he could. But he promised he would always add to the fund.

"Why would you do that?" Yolanda asked after a long silence.

"Because you won't let me do anything else," he said.

Bo tried not to resent Yolanda for keeping AJ from him, only bringing them together when disaster occurred and she had nowhere else to turn. Fact was, even if she'd invited him to be part of AJ's life, Bo probably would have kept his distance. The child-support payments he voluntarily sent were, for him, a kind of penance. He'd caused a child to come into the world, after all.

He went to the sofa and checked on AJ. Still asleep. The boy's face was erased of all the tension and anxiety and anger of last night. He was a good-looking kid, despite being puny. He probably took after his mother. Bo remembered her pretty smile and thick eyelashes, large doe eyes that seemed to sparkle just for him. Bo didn't know what AJ's smile looked like. The boy looked as if he'd never smile again, and Bo really couldn't blame him.

That sleeping face held secrets Bo knew nothing about. There was a tiny whitish scar by his mouth. A Band-Aid around his right thumb. Was AJ right-handed? Or left, like Bo?

AJ was only here temporarily but if he did nothing else for the boy, Bo would make sure they got to know one another. That was the least he could do.

He took a quick shower and dressed for the weather, with thermal layers and thick socks under his jeans. When he popped his head through the neckline of his undershirt, he felt someone watching him. "Hey, AJ," he said.

The boy was sitting up on the sofa, surrounded by the rumpled covers and slowly blinking in the half light. He reminded Bo of a just-hatched chick, disoriented and looking for something to lead him in the right direction. His dark hair was tousled, his face a little puffy. He looked chastened, as though someone had yelled at him. Hell, maybe he did get yelled at. Maybe worse. The thought of anyone hitting this kid made Bo fierce. Yet he acknowledged that the feeling of protectiveness came about twelve years too late.

"Can we call my mom?" asked AJ.

"Sure." Bo dialed the number in Houston, same as he'd done the day before, several times. He doubted anything had changed, but went through the motions anyway. "No answer," he reported when it went to voice mail.

"Let me try."

Bo handed him the phone, watching the boy's solemn face as he listened to his mother's cheery bilingual greeting. The large brown eyes flooded with an expression so sad it made Bo want to put his fist through the wall. He knew nothing had changed since they'd called from the airport, but hell. The kid needed to see him doing *something*. "Let's try the detention center." He used the number Mrs. Alvarez had given him. It kicked immediately over to a frustrating bilingual menu, requiring him to press numbers until he was ready to pound the phone into the floor. After several minutes of button pressing, he made his way to a recorded message. With exaggerated care, he shut off the phone. "The center's closed on weekends and after hours, except in case of emergency."

"This is an emergency."

"I know it feels that way. Hang in there, okay? Is there anybody else you can call? A relative or neighbor?"

"Mrs. Alvarez, maybe. Or my teacher, Mrs. Jackson."

"I've got them both in my cell." Bo navigated to one of the numbers and hit Send. Both numbers went straight to voice mail. "We'll try them later," he said gently. "So, how about your...stepdad?" Yeah, how about him? Yolanda had married Bruno, and they'd moved to Houston. The guy had played the role of AJ's father for several years. He might not be able to help with the current situation, but it could be reassuring for the kid to hear a familiar voice.

"I can't call him," AJ said.

"Why not?"

"I don't know his number."

Son of a bitch. Bo bit his tongue. What kind of loser just fell out of touch like that? He flinched, feeling a sting of guilt. He liked to think he'd have stuck around, but would he?

He grabbed a thick Irish fisherman's sweater and put it on. His best friend's wife, Sophie, had given him the sweater for Christmas. Bo wasn't Irish and he wasn't a fisherman, but she had told him there was some quality of the wool, from blue-face sheep, that kept a man warm and dry. The pattern of cables and other fancy stitches used to be the knitter's signature, surrounding the wearer with her spirit, protecting him from harm and bringing him luck.

He hoped like hell the sweater would bring him luck today. He and AJ were going to need it.

"Damn, this thing itches," Bo said, running his index finger around the neckline of the sweater.

"Then why are you wearing it?"

"Because Sophie gave it to me. And we're going to see her about your mama today and it's always a good idea to wear something a woman gave you when you're going to see her. Women like that. Yeah, that's a good rule. One thing I know for sure is that when a woman gives you a sweater, you'd better by-God wear it."

"Even though it itches."

"I've suffered worse than that to please a woman," Bo

said, with a flash of memory he'd thought long gone. "Do you know, I used to eat hominy grits for breakfast every time my mama fixed them. You like grits?"

AJ clutched at his throat and made a gagging sound.

"My thoughts exactly. Speaking of food, let me get you something to eat." He went to the kitchen and opened the fridge. "We got that pie we brought home from Friendly's, and… You like pepperoni pizza?"

A nod.

"Then get over here and eat. You sleep okay?" he asked the boy.

A shrug. "It's kind of noisy around here, so—" A loud beeping from outside drowned out the rest of his words. The racket came from a garbage truck backing up, and the beeping was followed by the hiss of hydraulic lifts and the crash and bright clatter of the Dumpster being emptied.

When the racket subsided, Bo said, "At night, the bar downstairs can get pretty rowdy, especially on the weekend." Living over the bar used to feel like the best of all worlds. Now it made him feel…inadequate, somehow.

"Tell you what," Bo said to AJ, trying to sound cheerful, "how about you get dressed and we'll head over to Sophie's, and she'll get to work figuring this out."

AJ grabbed some things out of his suitcase and headed into the bathroom. The shower hissed to life.

Then, a few minutes later, he emerged from the bathroom, backlit by a cloud of steam from the shower. He was dressed in jeans and a T-shirt, the garments wrinkled but clean-looking. His hair was slicked into place, parted on the side with knife-blade sharpness. His olive-toned skin glowed from a vigorous scrubbing. In the diffuse light, he looked like an angel, so beautiful Bo was momentarily speechless.

Their bellies full of cold pizza, apple pie and Orange Crush, which was the closest thing to juice Bo had, they headed downstairs. It had snowed all night, and the car's windshield was crusted with ice and dusted with snow.

Bo swore, then caught himself in mid-cuss, inventing a new word on the spot. "Fuuu—dge-a-mania," he improvised, retrieving a scraper brush from the trunk of the Z4. "Hard to believe people choose to live in this sh—stuff." He shut up, realizing AJ wasn't listening at all.

The boy was scuffing his feet across the crusty surface of the parking lot. His eyes shone with fascination. Steam rose from his still-damp hair and puffed from his mouth. There were tall heaps of snow from the plows, blanketed by a fresh coat. The snow had nearly buried a couple of cars, which had been left by regulars who knew better than to drive themselves home after they'd had a few too many. From the hilltop vantage point, there was a long view of the town below and the lake in the distance, the rooftops dusted with more snow.

He tried to imagine what this world was like for AJ. No one had asked his permission to pluck him from the southern metropolis of Houston and plunk him down in the small snowed-in town of Avalon. He was a stranger in a strange land.

"Crazy, huh?" Bo said. "All this snow."

"It's so cold," AJ said. He all but disappeared inside Bo's olive-drab parka, size Large–Extra Tall. The parka reached AJ's knees, the sleeves hanging well below his hands.

"Damn cold. Especially for a Houston boy." Bo wondered if saying "damn" was okay in front of a kid. "Be careful on the ice," he added.

AJ slid his feet across the crusty surface of the parking lot. His low-top Chuck Taylors had no traction at all, and he held his arms out to steady himself. "I've never seen snow before," he said.

"Yeah, well, you'll see plenty of it in this town," Bo assured him. "Can't stand the stuff, myself."

AJ scooped some off the hood of a parked car, flinching at the cold as he watched it melt from the palm of his hand.

"We'll get you some warm clothes and boots right away," Bo promised. "And I need a cup of coffee, bad. Then we'll go see Sophie and figure out the best way to help your mom." He finished brushing the snow off the roadster and they got in. He showed AJ the button to push to heat the seat. The boy's startled expression when he felt the heat come through made Bo smile.

"Can we have the top down?" asked AJ.

"It's freezing out."

"I'm plenty warm in this coat."

Bo hesitated. It was the boy's first snow, he reminded himself. Bo had never had a "first snow" as a boy. He'd had hurricanes and hail storms, floods and plagues of fire ants, but he'd never seen the snow until he was an adult. "Just remember," he warned, blasting the car's heater, "you asked for it." He pushed a button on the console, and the canvas top of the convertible retracted, neatly folding itself away. He steered out onto the street and headed toward the center of town. "People are going to think I'm outta my gourd," he muttered.

It was worth it, though, to see the way AJ's eyes sparkled. It was one of those rare winter days that was as clear as the air was cold. The sky shone with a depth and clarity that seemed sharp enough to shatter. The sun laid golden fronds over the brilliant white landscape. Too bad it was so freaking cold. The heated seats and warm air blowing from the vents kept them from freezing to death as they rode with the top down on and the radio turned up loud, playing Stevie Ray Vaughan.

They garnered a few looks from shoppers in the town square as Bo trolled for a parking spot. For a few minutes, he felt…kind of glad. He hadn't been expecting that. The happiness. The feeling of connection. It was a terrible thing, what was happening to AJ, and Bo was going to do everything in his power to fix it, but for these few moments, driving along in the sunshine with his boy, he felt happy.

"It sucks that we're meeting because of what happened with your mom," Bo said, "but I always wanted to meet you."

"Then why didn't you?" AJ asked. The question was simple, direct and devastating. "It's not hard."

"Your mom didn't think it was a good idea, and I had to respect that." There was a lot more to it than that, but he didn't think AJ needed to hear all of it, not now.

He turned up the car's stereo. As he came around the corner, his gaze was drawn to a long-legged redhead in the distance, coming out of women's shop called Zuzu's Petals, carrying a big shopping bag. He felt a flicker of interest. Could it be…? Nah, he realized. Just wishful thinking.

Seven

The thump of a car stereo caught Kim's attention as she exited the clothing boutique. She'd armed herself with the basics—thermal underwear, wool pants and a couple of sweaters. She was already wearing new jeans and boots and a new jacket, and was ready to embrace winter. This was something she'd missed, living in southern California. Crisp white winters, ice-skating and snowboarding.

She had never worked with winter-sports athletes. Well, there was one, almost. She'd been assigned to work with a hockey player named Newton Granger, and he'd been missing so many teeth, he sounded like he had a speech impediment. Despite facing the myriad perils of the hockey rink, he had a pathological fear of dentists. Kim had tried to create an image of the strong, silent type, but the guy had a goofy, spontaneous and gap-toothed grin that spoiled the effect every time.

Athletes, she thought. Never again. She was forging ahead to bigger and better things. She wasn't sure what things, but they would definitely be bigger and better.

Parcels in hand, she spotted the source of the thumping stereo. It was a low-slung sports car—with the top down— just rounding the corner into the main square of town. Sunlight flashed over the convertible, which looked as if it would be more at home in Malibu than upstate New York in the dead of winter.

The car swung into a parking space in front of the Sport Haus, a shop that specialized in winter garments and gear. Its black canvas top arched up and over, obscuring the driver and passenger. A moment later a tall man got out. For a second, recognition flared, but she couldn't quite place him. A moment later, a half-grown boy exited the passenger side. The kid looked as cold as Kim felt, huddled into an oversized jacket, no hat, hands shoved into his pockets. He kept looking around with an expression of wonder, like the groundhog poking his head out. The guy looked—all right, she was not completely numb—like the type proper girls weren't supposed to like. He had an easy way of moving that hinted at a bit of an attitude. Kim had made a study of these things. It was her job to observe the image a person projected, and—in the case of her clients— to hone that image into a public persona.

While she was shopping, Kim's appetite had kicked in. It occurred to her that she hadn't felt hungry since the black-tie affair in L.A. The fare that night had consisted of tiny samplings of baby vegetable timbale and field greens dressed in champagne vinaigrette and truffle oil.

Screw the diet, she thought, and went into the Sky River Bakery, one of the oldest and indisputably the most popular establishment on the square. Kim always visited the land- mark bakery when she was in Avalon.

The moment she stepped into the glowing warmth of the crowded bakery, it felt like the only good decision she had made in a long time. Sweetness literally hung in the air here, the scents of sugar and yeast and butter filling her until there was room for nothing else. The warmth and smells were nearly unbearable—cinnamon, chocolate, brewing coffee, baking bread. The hiss and gurgle of a cappuccino maker punctuated the sound of laughter and conversation. The place looked wonderful, too, with its checkerboard tile floor and funky, eclectic decor.

Kim perused the gleaming glass cases, abundant with a dizzying array of baked goods—kolaches and butterhorns, croissants stuffed with marzipan, raspberry or chocolate, gorgeous cakes with hand-crafted sugar-dough decorations, rustic loaves of bread. She ordered a cup of tea and an iced maple bar. As long as she was going to go off her diet, she might as well go big, as her mother might phrase it. In her old neighborhood in L.A., consuming a pastry like this would be considered a felony.

She browsed the bakeshop while waiting for a seat to open up. Maybe she was just hyperaware of happy couples, but they seemed to be everywhere—smiling at each other across the café tables, holding hands as they waited in line for their orders, sharing intimate glances. So soon after the demise of her relationship with Lloyd, she should not feel a twinge, but Kim couldn't help herself. She didn't like the feeling of being alone in a crowd. Didn't like the feeling of being alone, period.

Good thing I've got a house full of people to keep me company, she reminded herself.

The weekenders and day-trippers from the city looked

delighted to be heading to the great outdoors of Catskill Park, a natural preserve designated as "forever wild." Winter sports abounded in the area, where the pristine snowfall could always be counted on to cover the landscape in a picture-postcard blanket of white. Bundled in their colorful parkas and hats, people talked in animated fashion about the perfect weather—new snow, clear skies. She imagined some were headed to Deep Notch for ice climbing, others to Saddle Mountain for a day of skiing. There was also skating on Willow Lake, snowshoeing or snowmobiling in the backcountry. Everyone seemed excited about spending the day out in the bracing cold, away from cell phones and e-mail, firmly in the raw grip of Mother Nature. They all seemed so…content. It was a feeling that had eluded Kim in every relationship she'd ever had. She'd stopped even believing it was possible.

I used to love the winter, she thought. Perhaps she still did. Lately, she hadn't paid much attention to her own likes and dislikes.

A seat opened up at the counter, facing out the shop window. She settled down at the window bar with the newspaper, her pastry and mug of tea. The moment she sank her teeth into the soft, rich pastry, she saw stars. It tasted like pure ecstasy. It was all she could do not to moan. In those few moments, she forgot about Lloyd, and her exploding life, her crazy mother and uncertain future. If everyone would start the day with an iced maple bar, she thought, we would have world peace.

She noticed a display of art photographs, beautifully matted and framed, showing off Avalon, Willow Lake and

Catskill Park at their best—bathed in golden light, the colors soft and muted, as though painted by a master.

Near the cash register, there was also a stack of books on display marked, "Just published! Signed by the author." The title of the oversized book was *Food for Thought: Kitchen Wisdom from a Family Bakery* by Jennifer Majesky McKnight. The book's cover image depicted an older woman's flour-dusted hands, working a pale globe of bread dough.

An array of daily papers lay on a side counter. While waiting for her tea to cool, she paged through the *Avalon Troubadour*. In addition to the bakery book, Jennifer Majesky McKnight had a regular column; today's topic was a deep meditation on the attributes of black cocoa.

Kim sipped her tea and skimmed the pages, wondering idly at the juxtaposition of births, deaths and marriages, all on the same page. Beginning, middle, end. With a whole lot left out. There was a column headed Milestones—graduations and job promotions. And Engagements, featuring smiling people, supremely confident of their future. Why didn't people announce breakups? Kim wondered. Surely the end of love was a significant life event. People trumpeted it to the world when they got engaged. Why not when they got dumped? Why was it treated like a secret, or like something shameful? Why not announce it as a major milestone, certainly far more significant than a graduation or a promotion at work. Or a demotion, for that matter. Or getting fired.

Kim was a spin doctor. She'd been in sports PR and media training since graduating from USC, and she was good at it. She couldn't believe breakups and divorces had not been spun into an industry by greeting card and chocolate companies. She imagined her own announcement for the press. "Kimberly van Dorn proudly announces her breakup with Lloyd Johnson, NBA star and point guard for the L.A. Lakers…"

The "Pride of the Lakers," as Johnson had been dubbed, was her star client. When he had fired her, loudly and publicly, in a room full of everyone who was anyone, she'd committed the ultimate faux pas of dropping her champagne glass. The tinkling, shattering sound had drawn the attention of everyone in the room. And it wasn't just the sound of shattering glass. It was the sound of her career imploding. The ensuing scene in the parking lot—well, thank God no one else had witnessed *that*.

The tea boiled in her stomach, and the smells of the bakery nearly overwhelmed her. How would she ever eat anything again? How would she ever face the world without panic clawing at her throat?

To distract herself, she checked out the funny pages in the local paper, pleased to find her favorite syndicated comic strip. *Just Breathe* was about a young woman who'd moved in with her mother after her life fell apart. *Ouch.* This morning, that hit too close to home. Kim doubted she'd ever find any humor in the situation.

Setting the paper aside, she studied the scene outside the window. Back in California, she used to wake up to a landscape misted in smog and filled with the roar of L.A. traffic. The current view of the quaint, beautiful mountain town made her feel as though she had entered a different dimension. The old-fashioned brick buildings of Avalon's main square stood shoulder to shoulder, and shops and establishments were rolling out their awnings and salting their sidewalks as the day got started.

Kim felt like a virtual stranger here in this obscure, storybook-pretty town, especially in winter, when everything was draped in a pristine veil of new snow. While she sat, gazing out the window, the tall man and the boy she'd spotted earlier walked diagonally across the square toward the bakery. The man moved purposefully, the boy following a few paces behind. He was bundled into a navy blue ski parka and gloves. He flexed and unflexed his hands as though unaccustomed to the feel of the gloves.

A few minutes later, they entered the bakery, the bell over the door jangling brightly. Kim didn't want to be obvious about checking them out, so she studied their reflection in the glass. The man still looked familiar to her, but she couldn't place him. Then he brushed back the hood of his jacket, freeing his long hair.

Oh, God. Now she realized why he'd caught her eye—that lion's mane of hair. Kim stiffened, hunching up her shoulders as the guy helped himself to coffee at the side counter. The boy stood next to him, eating a kolache. A few minutes later, the guy paid at the register, chatting quietly with the counter girl. Kim saw him pick up a bakery box tied with string.

"Come on, AJ," the guy said. "We'd better get going."

Kim kept her eyes down. As he passed behind her, she heard him murmur a quick greeting: "Ma'am."

The two of them left the bakery.

Ma'am.

Alarmed, Kim swiveled around on the bar stool and craned her neck to get another look at him. No way. There was no possible way it could be…

They got into the little sports car and were gone before she could make up her mind about whether or not she recognized the stranger.

She did know, of course. A part of her had known who he was the instant she'd spotted him clear across the town square. He was the jerk from the airport. Of all the little backwater towns in upstate New York, he had to pick *her* backwater town.

Eight

"You're going to like Sophie and Noah's place," Bo said. With a new jacket, boots and gloves for AJ, and a box of warm kolaches as an offering, they were headed to their meeting with Sophie. She had an office in town, but was adamant about staying home with her family on the weekends. "I guarantee it. They live on a farm, and he's a veterinarian. You like dogs?"

"I got bit last year when I tried to pet one." AJ touched the side of his mouth, where a subtle white line formed a scar.

So that was where the scar had come from. "No dog's going to bite you," Bo assured him. Privately, he thought, *strike one.* "How about cats?" he ventured. "You like cats?"

AJ shrugged.

Strike two. "Horses, then. Everybody likes horses, right?"

"They make me sneeze."

Strike three. He's outta there.

"I have a confession to make," Bo said. "I'm not all that keen on horses myself. When I first moved up here from Texas, everybody thought I was a cowboy."

AJ didn't say anything.

"Geez, AJ. How about pygmy hamsters? You got anything against pygmy hamsters?"

"Never saw one. So they got pygmy hamsters at this place?"

"Dunno," Bo admitted, navigating the road that curved along the lakeshore. "Look, I know it's weird for you, being here. And I know you're worried about your mom. We're going to do everything we can to help her. Okay?" He glanced over at the boy.

AJ sank his chin into the downy pile of the jacket, nodding his head.

"Sophie will know what to do," Bo assured him, "and I'm not just saying that. She used to work at an international court in The Hague. That's somewhere over in Europe."

"In Holland," AJ said. "Seat of the Dutch government."

"You're pretty smart," Bo said, impressed. "Most people have never heard of The Hague. I don't know much about it myself, just that you have to be a hell of a lawyer in order to work there."

He had total confidence in Sophie, who had married his best friend, Noah Shepherd, the previous spring. She'd been involved in some kind of violent incident over in The Hague, and the experience had brought her back home to Avalon. She had two kids from her previous marriage, and she and Noah had recently adopted two young children, a brother and sister from a small country in southern Africa. Bo was a little in awe of Noah and Sophie for taking a leap of faith like that, getting married and having kids all at once. He couldn't imagine it, couldn't imagine being so sure of himself, so sure of loving a woman and so confident about being a father, to do such a thing.

He could barely make his own life work. Marriage, a family—all that stuff felt far from his grasp, as distant as the moon.

AJ's unexpected arrival was a fly ball out of left field. Through the years, Bo had given this boy plenty of thought, as well as a monthly check. Yet this was the first time he'd considered AJ as a flesh-and-blood person with needs and feelings and eyes so full of pain and fear that Bo felt it like a knife wound. He hurt for this kid; having his mother ripped away from him and being shipped to a strange, cold place was the stuff of nightmares or dark fairy tales. Having a loser stepfather, who wouldn't give him the time of day, much less his phone number, only made matters worse. And now the boy had Bo Crutcher for a father. He must be wondering what he'd done to deserve this.

Once a dairy farm, Noah's place sprawled out on a slope overlooking Willow Lake. There was a big, old-fashioned farmhouse and numerous outbuildings, including a storage silo, a barn and paddock, and the animal hospital. A sign reading Shepherd Animal Hospital marked the driveway. The dairy had been founded by Noah's grandparents, and he'd grown up here, never living anywhere else except when he went to college and then to Cornell for vet school. It was hard for Bo to imagine what it was like to belong to a family that had roots, that stayed in one place for so long, that stayed together. Noah was the most well-adjusted, happy person Bo knew, and he suspected that came from a deep, lifelong sense of security. He wished someone had provided that for AJ. It might already be too late, though.

He parked the car at the side of the house, and the minute they got out, a pair of big, furry shapes came barreling down the snowy slope behind the house. AJ moved like lightning, jumping back into the car and slamming the door. Bo was used to the two friendly mutts called Rudy and Opal, but they probably appeared as scary as hell to a boy who had been attacked in the face by a dog.

"Settle down, now," he said as the dogs bounded around him. "Go on now, *git*." Fortunately, they had been trained to mind. They fell back, keeping their distance as he motioned to AJ. "It's all right, they'll stay away. That's a promise."

AJ hesitated.

"It's all right," Bo repeated. "I swear, it's fine. I won't let them near you."

AJ slowly got out of the car and walked up to the porch. Bo didn't take any credit for helping the boy overcome his fear. He knew AJ was simply trying to save face.

Sophie was waiting at the door, greeting them with a smile. She was blond and as soft as a sunrise, attractive despite the well-worn jeans and a sweater with what looked like a grape-jelly stain on it.

"Hey, Bo," she said, and then smiled warmly at AJ. "I'm Sophie," she said. "You must be AJ."

"Yes, ma'am."

He stepped into the foyer and looked around uncertainly.

"Let me take your coats," she said, motioning them into the house. When she had married Noah, she'd changed every aspect of his life, including this house. In Noah's bachelor days, it had been perfect for a guy on his own. Gone were the lighted beer clocks, the foosball table, the drum set in a corner of the living room, where the garage band used to practice. All of that had been relegated to the actual garage, which wasn't such a bad thing, since it was heated and had a refrigerated beer keg.

Noah hadn't made a peep about the changes. He been so damn happy and punch-drunk with love that she could have draped the house in pink chintz, for all he cared. Photos of their brand-new, blended family had replaced the guy stuff.

"Noah's up at the clinic," she said, gesturing vaguely at the building across the way. "The kids are finishing breakfast." She led them down a hall to the big country kitchen, its yellow walls hung with nursery-school artwork—mostly finger paintings that resembled petroglyphs in prehistoric caves.

"Uncle Bo!" His honorary niece, Aissa, waved a piece of toast smeared with grape jelly. She was about four years old, and so cute it kind of made his eyes smart to look at her.

"Hey, shortstop," he said. "You, too, Buddy," he greeted her brother, who was around seven. The little boy's name was Uba, but the Americanized version had quickly replaced it.

Aissa held out a pair of tiny pink snow boots. "I wanna go play outside," she said.

"You're nuts, you know that?" Bo said to the four-year-old. "It's freezing out there."

The little ones were being supervised by their older brother, Max, who was Sophie's son from her first marriage. Max was in the eighth grade, and seemed to be pretty good with the youngsters. Through the introductions, AJ acted bashful and quickly declined the offer of grape-jelly toast and apple juice. He and Max regarded each other with wary awkwardness.

"Kolaches," Bo said, handing the bakery box to Max. "Knock yourselves out."

"Yes." Max and the other two dove right in. He paused before sinking his teeth into one of the pastries. "Uh, would you like one?" He offered the box to AJ.

"No, thanks."

"We've got some work to do in the study," Sophie said, defusing the tension. "Are you okay with these two, Max?"

"Sure, no problem."

They went into Sophie's study, a small, well-organized room with a computer and some filing cabinets, a bulletin board papered with international news articles and maps. The shelves were crammed with a mixture of law books and family photos that looked to Bo like a sea of smiling faces. He knew Sophie had endured her share of tough times and heartache, but the pictures were proof in living color that even the worst troubles could get better.

Sophie put a reassuring hand on AJ's shoulder. The simple touch had a tangible effect on the boy. He relaxed visibly, the tight lines of worry easing from his face. Just like that, a touch could comfort. Other than awkwardly carrying him upstairs while asleep, Bo had not touched the boy. Now, seeing the reassurance imparted by that simple, brief connection, he realized it didn't have to be weird. There was a lot to learn about being a parent. And given the way Bo had grown up, most of it was going to be guesswork on his part.

"I started making calls yesterday, as soon as Bo called me about your mother," Sophie said to AJ. "I know it's a scary time for you and your mom both, so we're going to figure this out just as fast as we can."

"How fast?" asked AJ. "When can I see my mom again? When can I go home?"

"I can't answer that. Immigration cases tend to be complicated. But this is also something that will help us. Anything can happen in an immigration case. I'm working with a colleague, whose firm specializes in immigration." She touched him again, lightly on the arm. "See that document on my computer screen? It's an emergency writ of appeal. We're going to file it in federal court first thing Monday morning. It's telling the court that a minor citizen of the United States has been left without legal guardianship. We're hoping to get emergency temporary status for your mom."

The lines of worry reappeared in his brow. He regarded the computer screen, his expression drawn and miserable. "I just need to see my mom. I can't wait any longer."

Bo wanted to hug him or something, he felt so sorry for the kid. He didn't want to cross a boundary with AJ, though. Damn, he hated this. Remembering the way Sophie had touched AJ earlier, Bo reached out and patted the boy on the shoulder. "It's not going to be forever, but all this legal stuff is going to take some time."

AJ pulled away. "How much time?"

Bo traded a look with Sophie. "No one can say for sure," he said.

AJ glared at him with suspicion. "Why can't I just go to wherever they sent my mom? To the detention center and then to Mexico or whatever?"

"You're an American citizen, and sending you there is just as complicated as bringing her back," Bo said, receiving a nod of encouragement from Sophie. "Besides, that's not what your mom wants for you." Yolanda had been adamant during her urgent phone call. There was nothing but danger and uncertainty for him there, she'd said.

"I'm a kid," AJ reminded him needlessly. "Doesn't that matter? That I'm a kid, and I'm supposed to be with my mother?"

"Actually, that was the law until recently," Sophie said. "The Immigration Reform Act wiped out that option. Used to be, if undocumented parents could prove their deportation would put a U.S. citizen—in this case, you, AJ—at risk, the judge could let them stay. But the act made deportation automatic." She showed them a document she'd printed out. "In the mid-'90s, there were around forty thousand deportations a year. Nowadays, there are around three hundred thousand a year. The INS and ICE will tell you they're getting rid of a criminal element, but that's not always the case. Plenty of working people—even war veterans—get swept up in raids."

"Not helping," Bo said, watching AJ.

"No, I want to know how things stand," the boy said. "Even if it's bad news."

"It's not necessarily bad," she said. "It simply means we have to find another strategy. In the meantime, your home will be here in Avalon, with Bo."

Bo tried not to feel insulted by the expression on the boy's face. "All right, so I'm not father of the year," he conceded. "But I'm ready to step up to the plate." When he was pitching, he could read the batter. He could guess what a guy at the plate was thinking—expecting—based on his stance and posture, where his eyes went and what he did with his jaw. Bo wondered if the technique would work on this boy. If so, the kid's demeanor was telegraphing fear and rage, not a good combination. A batter who faced a pitcher in this state was fully expecting to be capped by a wild fastball.

Bo reached for AJ's shoulder again, trying for another reassuring squeeze, but this time, the boy was prepared, and he jerked out of range. "I'm going to go see if there are any of those pastries left," he said, and headed for the kitchen.

Bo turned to Sophie. "What can I say? The kid loves me."

She smiled, but the suspicious sheen in her eyes told the story. "He's terrified, and who can blame him? You'll both get through this, I know you will."

"So be realistic, Soph. What are Yolanda's chances?"

"It's like I told AJ. Anything can happen. The most important thing now is to research every aspect of the case. We need to learn everything we can about Yolanda, even things she might not want us to know."

"What're you asking?" He felt a twinge of discomfiture.

"I'm not certain. I suspect this is going to take longer than you or AJ want it to." She searched his face. "I'm just trying to be realistic, Bo. Sometimes things don't happen at the most convenient time."

"I can't do this, Soph. I'm completely unprepared. I live over a *bar,* for chrissake."

"Is he safe there?"

"Sure, but the place is tiny. Noisy, too, and probably not the ideal place for a kid to be living. If this is going to go on for any length of time, I'll have to find a new place."

"Then I suggest you do that."

He nodded and dug out his mobile phone. "I need to make a phone call."

"I need a kolache before they're all gone," Sophie said, heading for the kitchen.

Dino Carminucci answered on the first ring. "Yeah, what's up?"

Bo had made Dino aware of the situation the day before. Dino had been incredulous, but then he'd offered the usual innocuous, "If there's anything I can do…"

There might be. Bo brought him up to date on the situation. "Sophie—she's a lawyer—says this is going to take a while," Bo said.

"He all right?"

"No," Bo said. "How can a kid be all right with his mother getting caught in a dragnet while he's at recess? I mean, I've had bad weekends before, but this—" He stopped, took a deep breath. "We're going to have to find another place to live for a while. Above the Hilltop's fine for me, but it's no place for a kid."

"Good thing you called me, then," Dino said. "I got the perfect place. You come see me after the lawyer. We'll work this out."

"This is the 'better arrangement' you were talking about?" AJ stared at the candy-colored mansion, his eyes narrowed with skepticism.

"Dino swears it's a great place to stay. But you know what I heard? I heard it belongs to some crazy widow woman."

AJ's eyes brightened. "Really?"

"Uh-huh. A bunch of my teammates helped her fix the place up." Bo looked around the neighborhood, with its swath of tall, straight trees down the center strip. On either side of the street were stately homes a hundred years old, some even older, centered on broad lawns. Built by wealthy families seeking refuge from the summer heat of the city, most of the houses had been lovingly kept and restored by the new elite of Avalon—prosperous young professionals, who'd made their fortunes in the tech sector or in law or finance. Others had been converted into office and studio space for doctors, contractors and local businesses, but the look of the homes had been carefully preserved.

He glanced over at AJ to see the boy's reaction to the storybook-pretty scenery. The snow gave the whole area a quiet, horse-and-buggy atmosphere, despite the absence of horses or buggies. AJ kept his face turned away, his arms folded protectively in front of him. Already Bo recognized the stance—full emotional body armor.

Fairfield House stuck out like a whore in church, sporting a garish paint job. All its fine architectural details had been painted in varying shades of pink. There was a sign on the wrought iron fence in the front. Fairfield House, Circa 1886. Rooms to Let.

"The landlady has a two-room suite available on the top floor," Bo told AJ. "She provides a serve-yourself breakfast each morning and dinner each night, which is more than I get, living over the bar." Even so, the pink-wedding-cake style of this place gave him the willies. Playing it cool, he got out of the car and motioned for AJ to do the same. He opened the gate, cringing at the rusty jangle of the hinges. Their footsteps crunched on the salted walkway that led to the painted steps of the porch. The porch furniture was fussy-looking white wicker, currently clad in zipped-on plastic covers. Several skeletal plants hung sadly from the eaves, forgotten remnants from warmer weather.

Bo squared his shoulders and rang the bell. At the last second, he snatched off his hat, recalling that Dino had described the owner as proper. AJ stood back, hovering in Bo's shadow. The kid was probably mentally calculating the time it would take to sprint back to the car. Impatient, Bo pushed the button again.

The bell was more like a gong. The wavy leaded glass in the front door was dressed in a froth of lace curtains. Through it, he could see someone approaching. Already Bo felt completely out of his element. Mrs... He dug the card Dino had given him out of his pants pocket to check the landlady's name. Mrs. Penelope van Dorn.

Van Dorn. Now, there was a classy-sounding name. A very prim and proper name. She was probably some kind of schoolmarm.

The door opened abruptly. "Can I help you?"

For a moment, Bo couldn't speak. Or move, or think, for that matter.

This was no marm.

She was approximately five feet nine inches of glorious sex. Her long, glossy hair fell in waves to the middle of her back; despite her height, she was curvy enough to create a halo of cartoon birds and bees swirling around his head. Jimi Hendrix's "Foxy Lady" twanged in his ears. As he gaped at the impossibly gorgeous redhead in the doorway, his mouth went dry, and his tongue turned to acrid dust. And when he forced his brain back into gear, only one thought pounded at him.

He was so screwed.

Nine

Oh, this could not be happening, thought Kim, stepping aside to let her visitors in. Her mother couldn't have known what a curveball this was. Mom had told her to expect two new guests at Fairfield House. Kim had never dreamed it would be this character. What were the chances? she wondered. Maybe she *had* angered the universe.

One of the most cursed things about being a fair-skinned redhead was the blushing factor. It was impossible to hide a blush, and she tended to blush whenever she was flustered, upset, embarrassed, intrigued or all of the above.

At the moment, she was all of the above, and her face flared a heated shade of pink to prove it. Maybe he wouldn't remember. Of course he wouldn't, she reassured herself. Their paths had crossed at the airport, he'd been a jerk to her and that was that. Guys tended not to remember being jerks, so she was probably safe.

"Ma'am," he said. "I remember you from the airport. Reckon it's time we were properly introduced."

An awkward beat of silence stumbled past. So he did remember after all. Which meant either he didn't think he'd been a jerk, or he didn't *care* that he'd been one. She narrowed her eyes at him, not about to be taken in by that faux aw-shucks charm. "I remember you, too, Mr...." She checked the appointment card her mother had handed her, asking her to greet the new arrivals. "Crutcher," she read. "And son."

The boy looked from the tall guy to Kimberly. He carried a backpack slung on his shoulder. He had beautiful thickly lashed eyes and an unsmiling mouth that gave him a very solemn, very unkidlike air.

She wondered exactly how old he was, who his mother was. *Where* his mother was.

"I'm AJ," he said in a gravelly, curiously endearing voice. "AJ Martinez."

"Hello, AJ," she said, smiling. It wasn't the boy's fault his father was a tool. "I'm Kimberly van Dorn. Call me Kim."

He looked around, wide-eyed. He was small and uncertain, quite unlike his father.

"Feel free to check things out," Kim said, taking his jacket. "The kitchen's in there, and there's a library and TV room. The big round room with all the windows is called the rotunda."

He followed Bo's lead, parking his boots in the boot tray by the door. Then, with his hands in his pockets, AJ wandered through the downstairs, as silent and careful as a museum visitor. That, at least, was a good sign. Her mother had been concerned that a child in the house might be too noisy and rambunctious for the other guests. "So, Mr. Crutcher," Kim said, "is he always this quiet?"

"Yeah, so far, he's been real quiet."

So far, she thought. So far as what?

"My name's Bo," the guy said.

She took a moment to study him. He was handsome in such an unconventional way—lanky and long-haired, with soulful eyes and a gentle smile. At the same time, there was something hurting and mysterious about this guy.

"Bo," she said, trying out the name. "Like Beau Bridges? Or Beau as in Beauford, or Beauregard?"

"Ma'am, I can barely pronounce Beauregard."

"Then how about Bo, as in...Peep?"

His grin widened. Yet at the same time, it was guarded, revealing little. "That's a good one. My mama wadn't a real good speller."

"And what about you? Are you a good speller?"

"I'm good at a lot of things."

"Like being polite in the airport?"

"That's not one of the things. Now, making friends with a pretty woman—I'm usually good at that."

"Wonderful. My own personal airport Lothario is moving in."

"Who?"

"Lothario. A literary reference."

"I'll take it as a compliment." He grinned.

She liked his smile, and she hated that she liked his smile. "You seem easily amused."

"Just trying to figure out how to explain to a girl like you—"

"A girl like me. And what kind of girl would that be?"

He shrugged. "Dunno. The kind who doesn't know many guys named after country songs."

"You're named after a country song?"

"'Mr. Bojangles.' My full name's Bojangles T.

Crutcher." He looked apologetic. "Used to embarrass the heck out of me when I was a kid. It's an okay song, but carrying that name around has been a burden all my life. Mama had a thing for Jerry Jeff Walker. She loved his songs so much that she had his initials, JJW, tattooed in the small of her back."

Kim kept her face composed. "She must be quite a fan."

"She changed her own name, Gertrude, to 'Trudy,' which is also a song of his. I got a brother named Stoney, too."

"Another Jerry Jeff Walker number," she guessed.

"That's right. It's from a song about a wine-drinking mystic. I'll play it for you sometime."

"So are you a musician?"

"I play bass, and sometimes pedal slide guitar. Strictly an amateur, though," he said. "And don't worry, I'll practice with the headphones on, I swear."

"And where do you work?" she asked. A fair question. She was new at this boardinghouse business, but surely she should ask it.

"I've been pitching for the Hornets here in Avalon. Tending bar at the Hilltop Tavern in the off-season when I can't afford to go south for the winter. Come spring, I'll be training with the Yankees, trying to get a spot on their top-forty roster."

"The Yankees," she repeated, feeling a sinking sensation in her stomach. "As in the New York Yankees?"

"Yes, ma'am. It's been a long time coming. I was at November tryouts down in Florida, same as I am every year. And I figure every year, I'm going to get the same song and dance—no room on the roster. This year, there was an opening on their pitching staff."

Kim felt queasy. A bass player she could handle. A tall

guy with long hair and blue eyes—she could deal with that, too. But an athlete? A major leaguer? It was a nightmare. After the Lloyd fiasco, she didn't want a thing to do with athletes in any way, shape or form, ever again. And here was one expecting to move into the house where she lived. She must be cursed. What god had she angered? What karmic boundary had she crossed?

His smile faded as he stared at her. "You all right?"

"Um, yes. Why do you ask?"

"You look a little green around the gills. I usually get a different reaction when I tell people I'm going to pitch for the Yankees. Or at least, accused of being delusional."

She swallowed hard. "No, I believe you. It must be very exciting."

"No sh—er, yeah, it is." As though he couldn't help himself, he smiled again.

Under different circumstances, this would be an auspicious meeting—a media relations expert and a newly minted major-league player. And—she couldn't help herself—it was in her nature to assess a guy like this. The first thing that struck her was that, for a rookie, he was long in the tooth. Judging by his looks and the age of his son, Bo Crutcher was in his late twenties or early thirties. Already, she caught herself speculating about him—what was his story? In spite of herself, she thought about his image. If this was true and not some fantasy, then this guy needed some serious work.

She had a sixth sense about what it took to make it in sports. Talent was only the beginning. Pro athletes today were packaged, and everything had to be in that package. Talent—of course. But there were other elements crucial to an athlete's success. His determination and heart. His looks and personality, the way he presented himself. Especially when it came to the Yankees. During the season, at any given time there might be fifty members of the press in the clubhouse, and only a couple of areas were off-limits. A guy's public persona was extremely crucial. This guy—Bo Crutcher—there was something about that lion's mane of hair, that face...she had a hard time looking away from him. Then she caught herself noticing the icy clarity of his blue eyes, and the shape of his mouth and—

Kim made herself quit speculating. This guy wasn't even close to ready. She wondered if he knew that. She wondered why she cared. She felt a flare of irrational anger at her mother, who had gone to the market, leaving Kim in charge. Penelope had told her the newcomer would be a "nice young man and his son" who had come on Dino's recommendation. But never in her most lunatic moments had Kim imagined it could be a a professional athlete. She tended not to connect "nice" with "professional athlete." Sure, there were probably plenty of nice ones out there, but she always seemed to encounter the other kind.

"This feels like my lucky day," he said. "I wanted to explain about the airport—"

"That's best forgotten," she interrupted. "Mr. Crutcher—" She caught his look. "I won't lie to you. If it were up to me, I'd ask you to find someplace else to live. But this is my mother's establishment, and, based on Mr. Carminucci's reference, she wants to accommodate you."

He offered her the warmest of smiles, as if she'd just welcomed him with open arms. "We're going to get along just fine," he said. "I got a feeling a house like this is just what AJ needs."

Through the doorway, they could see the boy in the rotunda. Pale winter light flooded through the mullioned windows. He was checking out the shelves of well-thumbed books, a collection of Meerschaum pipes, her grandfather's chess board, the pieces lined up in readiness like an army geared for battle. The ship-in-a-bottle never failed to fascinate. AJ treated the objects in the room with respect and reverence. This might be because he knew he was being watched. Then again, unlike his father, he might just be a well-behaved kid.

Who needed a place to live.

Suddenly Kim felt petty. "Why don't you hang up your coat?" she said to Bo. "I'll show you around." On autopilot, she led the way into the kitchen, which adjoined the dining room through a set of double doors covered in green baize. "Breakfast and dinner are served buffet-style every day. Guests help themselves in the kitchen, and everyone eats in the dining room. Er, if you decide this is going to work for you, that is." *Please say no,* she thought. *Please say you need to keep looking.*

"It's just right," Bo said.

AJ was checking out the kitchen. Like everything else, it had been painted in startling colors—walls the color of a lime Lifesaver, tangerine trim. Yet it still retained its old-fashioned character, with bead-board wainscoting and high ceilings, tall cupboards with wavy glass cabinet doors and a deep farm sink. There was a butcher-block island and a long wooden table, lace curtains in the windows.

"This used to be my grandparents' house," she told AJ,

suddenly flooded by a rush of memories, the smells and sounds of cooking and conversation. "We spent every Thanksgiving here." She could still see her grandmother in a flowered apron and huge oven mitts, bringing the feast to the table. Her grandfather, who had turned Kim's own childhood to days of magic, used to ad lib prayers of thanks that were as natural as conversation.

"This is a really nice house," AJ commented.

Kim showed them to the sitting room, which was equipped with TV, stereo and shelves of books. "I'm glad you like it. I spent a lot of happy hours here when I was a kid." Long ago, she'd been filled with hopes and dreams, but those had been the dreams of a girl who didn't know who she was. Now here she was, years later, and she still didn't know. Not anymore. It was a bit depressing that she'd built a fine career for herself in California, then lost it all in a single moment. Thanks to a strict employment contract, her other clients would stay with the firm, not with her.

"Your lodgings are on the third floor," she said, heading for the stairs.

Many questions occurred to her, but she didn't ask them. It was a tricky thing, this concept of a boardinghouse. Her mother called the residents guests, yet they weren't, not really. They hadn't been invited, and their stay lasted much longer than a few days. In reality, this was a house filled with paying strangers. Her mother swore they came by referral only, and provided impeccable references. Bo had been referred by Dino, whom Penelope seemed to trust implicitly.

Still, Kim didn't think she'd ever get used to the boardinghouse arrangement, nor could she imagine getting accustomed to the invisible fine line between intimacy and privacy. Not that it was up to her. So long as she was a member of this household, she went by her mother's rules.

She imagined how Bo's references would read: *A natural at baseball and flirting.*

A man with a child and, apparently, no wife.

She opened the door to the top floor and stood to the side, feeling a bit like a hotel bellman as she invited them in. A glow of soft light, reflected by the snow off the sloping roof, filled the room. The stream of light through the gabled windows reminded her of moments long past, when she used to gaze outside on white winter days, imagining herself a snowflake from *The Nutcracker,* an inhabitant of an enchanted kingdom. She wondered if AJ would do the same, or if he was too old for childhood fantasies.

The room was L-shaped, with a twin bed in an alcove and another around the corner, a sitting area with a desk and small television, and an adjoining bath.

"Is this where we're staying, ma'am?" AJ asked.

She smiled at the boy, turning her back on Bo. "You can call me Kim," she said.

"Yes, ma'am. Kim."

"Ah, I'm guessing you're from Texas, then. Boys from Texas say 'ma'am' a lot."

"Yes, ma'am." He flashed his first smile since stepping through the door, and that smile took her breath away. It was like seeing a glimpse of the sun in the midst of the darkest days of winter—rare and bright, fired by an invincible spirit. When he saw her watching him, he quickly turned solemn again.

"This looks fine here," Bo declared. "It's just fine."

So his mind was made up, she thought with a shudder of nerves.

"How about you put your things away," Bo suggested. "I'll go down and get the rest of the stuff."

AJ nodded without looking at him, and set his backpack on a chair. "Okay."

"See this bookcase?" Kim asked, feeling a thrum of tension emanating from both of them. "It's got all my favorite books from when I was young—*Superfudge, Maniac Magee,* the whole series of Matt Christopher books. My friends used to think I was weird because I liked Matt Christopher books so much."

"Why is that weird?"

"They're sports books, and I guess some people didn't think a girl could be interested in sports stories. I was, though. I still am. What about you?"

He shrugged. "I don't really like sports."

At that moment, Bo Crutcher stepped into the room, laden with bags. His color was high from the cold, his eyes bluer even than they'd looked a few minutes ago. "Hey," he said, "I thought it was just baseball you didn't like."

AJ stiffened, tossed his glossy straight hair out of his eyes. "I'm not a big fan of any sports," he said. "It's not like that's a crime or anything."

Bo regarded him warmly, ignoring the attitude. "It's not a crime. Just a surprise. I don't mind a surprise every now and then."

AJ nodded. "Okay."

Interesting, Kim thought, watching them. They acted like strangers. Yet when each didn't think the other was watching, they took turns studying each other with hungry eyes. She showed AJ a recreation guide to the area. "There's lots to do around here," she said, spreading out a colorful map. "That's the golf course, Avalon Meadows. In the winter, it's used for cross-country skiing and sledding on the hills." She indicated Saddle Mountain at the western edge of town, scored with cleared ski runs and webbed by the black threads of the ski lifts. "Up there, that's a ski resort. A lot of the kids are into snowboarding, too."

AJ shaded his eyes to look, but made no comment.

"My favorite winter sport is sitting by the fire, watching a football game on TV," Bo chimed in. "What about football, AJ? Think you'd like watching football?"

"Not really," the boy said.

"Winter sports are my favorites," Kim told AJ. "I love snowboarding, sledding, ice-skating—anything in the great outdoors. Willow Lake freezes hard enough to skate on. Ever tried ice-skating?"

"I've never tried any snow sports," AJ confessed.

"Maybe you'll give them a shot this winter."

"To me, being out in the snow is about as much fun as a trip to the dentist," Bo said. "Never tried skiing or snowboarding. Never had the urge. I think it's purely nuts to strap a board on your feet and head down a mountain at sixty miles an hour. You won't see me doing it, not in a million years." He turned on the television, handing the remote to AJ. "You get settled in, okay? I'm going to go downstairs and have a word with Miss van Dorn."

She sensed he was leaving a pause so she could say, "Call me Kim." She didn't. "AJ, we'll be down in the front room." She was dying to hear what was going on between this man and the boy he seemed to barely know. She led the way down to the main floor, keenly aware of Bo's eyes on her. What did he see? she wondered. The person he'd accosted in the airport? A woman who'd been defeated by her own career? Or a throwback to a simpler time—a landlady?

When she reached the bottom of the steps, she turned to look at him, and saw him checking her out. Great. Just what she needed. "Do you mind?"

"Sorry," he said, "I don't— I mean, just...give me a minute."

"A minute for what?" She reached up and touched her hair.

"You know, when I saw you at the airport, I thought you were the prettiest thing in the world."

His words disarmed her. Despite all her experience in the PR business, she could still be disarmed by certain things, like a tall, blue-eyed baseball player looking her in the eye and telling her she was the prettiest thing in the world.

"I was wrong, though," he went on.

Oh.

"Now I'm thinking you're the prettiest thing *anywhere.* Seriously."

Oh.

"Mr. Crutcher—"

"I know, I shouldn't have said anything, but everybody who knows me says I got a mouth like a bullfrog in springtime. I go on and on. My agent—I just started working with him—says I need to quit talking so much."

She fought to master the creeping blush, lost the battle and said, "Would you like something to drink?" Immediately, she regretted the offer. It sounded too social.

"Maybe in a while," he said easily.

They went to the living room, the largest of the down-stairs spaces. It was filled with her grandmother's furniture and keepsakes, her old-fashioned lamps and art on the walls. It had been painted a startling shade of robin's egg blue, another discontinued color. Her mother called this a house of discontinued colors.

Bo took a seat on a spindly legged chair, his lanky frame dwarfing the piece. He leaned back, settled his ankle on the opposite knee and watched her expectantly.

She grew unsettled by his scrutiny. "Tell me about you and AJ. He seems like a good kid."

"I hope so, but to tell you the truth, I wouldn't know."

What an odd thing to say about one's child, she thought.

"AJ's twelve years old," Bo continued. "He was born in Texas and lived there all his life. I never met him until yesterday morning. That was what I was doing at the airport, when we—when I was there to meet him."

"You hadn't met him before then?"

"His mother's choice, not mine. After AJ was born, she married some other guy, and he was the only father AJ knew. Yolanda—his mom—didn't want me coming around, confusing the kid." Bo's voice was low, filled with regrets. "I never had a dad, growing up, so it bugged the sh—heck out of me, knowing AJ was in the world but never seeing him. I respected his mama's wishes, though. Never tried to see him, until she called me Friday and said she needed me to look after him for a while."

Kim tried to imagine what would compel a woman to send her own child to a person he'd never met. "Is she…all right? What made her change her mind about getting you and AJ together?"

"It's a long story. Her husband left her, and she got in trouble with the INS."

"You mean, the Immigration and Naturalization Service."

He nodded, pressed the tips of his fingers together. "She was sent immediately to a temporary holding center in Houston. No advance warning whatsoever, and there was no one to take care of AJ. They've got no other family in this country, no friends or neighbors who could help. See, she's an only child. After her father passed away, her mother moved back to Nuevo Laredo. That's in the Rio Grande valley, on the Mexican side."

Kim's heart lurched. "You mean, his mom just went to work one day, and wasn't allowed to come home?" She could scarcely imagine what that had been like for the boy.

"That's right," said Bo. "So I wasn't about to let him be sent to foster care. But I've been living in an apartment above the Hilltop Tavern. It's too noisy there for a kid. We came here because I wanted him to be in a place that felt more like home. And here we are."

"In a place that feels like home," she said quietly. And for the first time, she understood her mother's enthusiasm for this new enterprise.

"That's right. If I hadn't been around, AJ would've had to go into foster care. And believe me, foster care is a total crapshoot. It can be the best thing that ever happened to a kid, or it can be a nightmare."

Her expression must have been easy to read, because he said, "Yeah, I know the system from direct experience."

She flashed on her own childhood, secure and predictable. Despite her father's financial missteps, she had never for a moment had to worry about being abandoned. "You were in foster care?"

"A couple of times. The first time it was straight out of a Stephen King novel. After that, another couple took me in, and it was the best thing that ever happened to me. Sometimes, when my mama hit a rough patch, I'd go stay with my coach, a guy named Landry Holmes. We didn't have much when I was a kid, but Coach Landry taught me to focus on what was important."

Kim couldn't help being intrigued, and she caught herself thinking like his publicist. He had a strong personal story. It was a little messy, but that was all just part of the challenge. His matter-of-fact honesty reminded her of the kind of clients she'd started with before she was saddled with guys like Lloyd. She much preferred the ones who deserved a shot, as opposed to the ones who believed they were entitled to one.

The jerk from the airport was fading fast, obliterated by a flesh-and-blood person. AJ's situation made Kim's troubles pale in comparison. "He's just a child. I can't believe they can separate a mother from her child."

"Happens a lot apparently. More than you or I know."

"So what are you going to do?"

"I've got a lawyer on it. Sophie Bellamy-Shepherd. You know her?"

"I know the name Bellamy, but no. Not Sophie."

"Married to a friend of mine, Noah Shepherd. She's already found an immigration specialist, and they're filing paperwork with the Board of Immigration Appeals. Someone's doing a records search on Yolanda's family, but Sophie warned me that this could take some time."

"Meanwhile, AJ is with you."

"That's right."

"He must be so worried about his mom," she said. She also assumed this turn of events was wreaking havoc with Bo's plans to devote the off-season to preparing for the Yankees. Either the guy was in denial about that, or he was hiding his agitation for the sake of the boy.

"He's worried, all right," Bo assured her. "How can he not be? He's keeping it all inside, though. At least, that's what I think he's doing. Wish I knew him better."

The situation of this man and his son didn't just intrigue Kim; it moved her. She hadn't expected that. But sometimes people clicked on a deep level right away, and it wasn't a matter of how long they'd known one another. It was a matter of interest. She wondered if he was sensing that from her.

"So in the meantime," she said, "you plan to stay here."

"Yes, ma'am. He's going to have to enroll in school, right here in Avalon. Starting Monday."

"Maybe he'll be glad about that. Some kids like school."

Bo sent her a dour look. "It's midyear, he's from a different state and he doesn't know a soul."

"All right, perhaps that was a little optimistic."

"I reckon I'll tell him tonight. Maybe after dinner." He looked around the room, seeming shell-shocked. "Anyway, thanks, Kim."

Well. She'd been upgraded from ma'am to Kim. "For what?"

"For not freaking out when you saw me."

"Why would I freak out?"

"When you answered the door, I thought I was totally screwed."

She was not exactly flattered by this. "About that...the way I behaved at the airport that morning. That's not me."

"I figured you were probably having one of those days," he said.

"One of those *lives*," she replied, then shook her head. AJ Martinez was proof positive that there were worse things in the world than Lloyd Johnson. In the wake of her sudden departure, there had been a flurry of calls from her former colleagues, but the calls had already tapered off. Soon— probably before the end of the day—they would cease altogether. That was the nature of this business. It chewed people up and spat them out, all used up and worse for the wear. She used to have the stomach for it, but not anymore.

"That doesn't sound good," Bo Crutcher observed. "So what were you doing at the airport, all dolled up like that?" he asked.

"I had to leave L.A. in a hurry. There wasn't time to change."

"You on the lam from something?" He was checking her out closely.

She offered a brief, humorless laugh. *From my own life,* she thought. "You ask a lot of questions."

That smile again. She could almost swear he was flirting with her. "But you don't answer many," he said. "Everything okay?"

She thought about AJ again, and the uncertainty he faced. And Bo himself, picking up a suddenly motherless son he'd never met. "I'm all right," she said.

"Maybe one of these days, you could tell me about yourself. We'll have to get to know each other."

No, we won't, she thought, dangerously attracted to the

smile that seemed to hover on his lips, even when he spoke of troubling matters.

Daisy Bellamy was late again. Even though Charlie was a year and a half old, she still hadn't mastered the art of coordinating everything she needed and getting out the door on time, even for a simple trip up to Camp Kioga for a family gathering. No matter how far in advance she started getting ready, something always delayed her. This evening, she had everything all planned out—Charlie's outfit, his bag of gear, her camera bag—but just as she was heading out the door, Charlie found an old Oreo cookie somewhere. By the time she caught him, he was wearing a dark-chocolate grin and a massive smear of damp cookie all over the front of his sweater.

"Oh, Charlie," she said. "That's the sweater your grandma O'Donnell made for you, and she's going to be there tonight." His paternal grandparents had made a special trip up from Long Island just to see him. Daisy grabbed a sponge and tried to clean the sweater, but her efforts only made it worse. Charlie babbled good-naturedly at her and grabbed the front of her shirt with a grubby hand, managing to soil her, as well.

"That's right," she said through gritted teeth. "All dirty." She took off the sweater over his head, managing to smear more wet cookie on his face and hair. Barely holding on to her patience, she wiped him off as best she could, washed her hands and found clean shirts for both of them. So much for dressing up for the party. Or for being on time.

"This is not what my life was supposed to be," she said, hurrying out to the car before anything else happened.

"No," he agreed, using his favorite word.

"At least we agree on something. I swear, Charlie, sometimes…" She didn't let herself finish. Even though he was too little to understand, she didn't want him to hear her complain. She buckled him into his car seat and headed north along the lake road, toward Camp Kioga. At times like this, the reality of her life felt like too much. She had her photography work. And Charlie. And school. And Charlie. Always Charlie. He was everything to her, and her love for him was almost frightening in its intensity, but the responsibilities were relentless and never-ending. Charlie got up at the crack of dawn, without fail, and once her day got started, there was no downtime. Never, not once, had she deluded herself that being a single mother was going to be easy. Sometimes she wished she could curl up in a ball and escape, just for a while. With an active toddler, that wasn't an option.

She shook off her sour mood by focusing on the stark beauty of the twilight. Trees bowed with the weight of fresh snow over the road, creating a tunnel effect. As she rounded a curve, her headlamps illuminated the vast, snow-covered surface of the lake. The dashboard clock indicated that she was only twenty minutes late. Not too bad.

Her cousin Olivia, and Olivia's husband, Connor, had transformed Camp Kioga, a rustic retreat that had been in her family for generations, into a year-round resort. Olivia and Connor were hosting a farewell celebration for Connor's brother, Julian Gastineaux. Julian was headed to South Carolina for special ROTC training. He told people he'd signed up for Reserve Officer Training in order to finance his education. Daisy knew there was another reason.

Julian also loved the rush of doing dangerous things—parachute training, marksmanship, field maneuvers. He was actually entertained by the notion of staying up all night in the wilderness, training for sniper combat.

Everything about Julian Gastineaux fascinated Daisy, and had for a long time. She'd been half in love with him since the first summer they'd met a few years back. But only half. The other half had done crazy things, like sleeping with another boy, getting pregnant, having a baby out of wedlock. Sometimes she thought Julian wanted to love her back, but she wouldn't let him. He was on the verge of living his own dream, and she wasn't a part of that. There wasn't much point in dreaming. Julian was on a path that included college and a military career, a path that led far away from her.

The road leading in was newly plowed and well lit. She parked, shouldered all her gear and got Charlie out of his seat. He insisted on waddling in his tiny boots to the main lodge, so it took a good five minutes to get inside. With a toddler, everything took ten times longer than normal. She considered herself a patient person, but sometimes she couldn't help murmuring, "Come on, already…" under her breath.

She arrived to find the party already in full swing, the air alive with music and conversation. Tables were laden with a buffet. The roaring hearth crackled with burning logs, gilding everything with an amber glow. Daisy set down her things and left their coats on a rack by the door. She saw her cousin Jenny and Jenny's husband, Rourke, but they didn't see her. They were holding hands and talking. Jenny's very pregnant form was outlined in the firelight. Daisy felt a twinge of envy. The two of them were having a baby the right way—together. Partners, who would support each other through the scary, exciting birth, the night feedings and unending laundry. They'd share the moments Daisy had experienced alone—their child's first smile, his first tooth, his first wobbly steps. And she didn't begrudge them these things. But sometimes she wanted that so much that it felt like a physical ache.

Hearty laughter erupted over at the bar, and glasses clinked. Suddenly bashful because of the noisy crowd, Charlie whimpered and clung to her leg. She scooped him up and settled him on her hip, the movement by now as natural as breathing. "It's all right, kiddo," she said. "These are our friends and family, and everyone in this room is ga-ga over you."

"Ga-ga," he echoed.

Scanning the group at the bar, she easily spotted Julian. She hung back for a minute, studying him. Her reaction to him was always the same—the pounding heart, the fluttering stomach. The shaved head was a shock. All those glorious, riotous dreadlocks, shorn. Yet somehow, the eight-ball look only accentuated his amazing cheekbones and sensual mouth, the dark eyes and warm café-au-lait skin.

As though he sensed her scrutiny, Julian spotted her. A smile of pure happiness lit his face, and he wended his way across the room to her. For a few seconds, Daisy allowed herself a fantasy. He would cross the room, scoop her into his arms, swing her around and declare that he loved her.

Instead, he gave her a brief hug. "Hey, Daze," he said, then lightly ruffled Charlie's downy red hair. "Hey, short stuff. How you doing?"

Charlie tucked his face into the curve of Daisy's neck.

"Must be the haircut," Julian said. "Come on. I'll get you something to drink. You want a beer?"

"Sure." They had both just turned twenty-one. Having a beer in a room that included her father, various aunts and uncles, and her grandparents, felt a little strange, but she accepted a chilled bottle of Utica Club. She clinked her bottle with his. "Cheers," she said. "You must be excited about your trip."

"Completely. But, Daisy…" He grew serious, the merriment leaving his eyes. "I'm going to miss—"

"Da!" Charlie started bucking in Daisy's arms, causing her beer to erupt, sprinkling both her and the baby. "Da!" he said again, scrambling to get down.

Daisy knew even before she turned who had arrived. Charlie had this reaction to only one person. "Hi, Logan," she said, greeting the father of her child.

Charlie practically launched himself at Logan. They both shared bright red hair and a sunny outlook on life. Logan was Julian's opposite in nearly every way. Perhaps that was why she'd slept with him, long ago, back when she was angry and stupid. Logan grabbed the boy and swung him up in the air. "Hey, big guy," he said, flashing a grin. Then he greeted Daisy and Julian. There was an awkward moment when he focused on the beer bottle in her hand. He was in recovery, but staying clean and sober was an everyday struggle for him.

"Why don't you take him to see your folks?" she said, holding the bottle low against her leg. Silly. He'd told her many times that he didn't expect her to avoid drinking around him. Staying sober was his job. Still, she couldn't help feeling bad.

"Okay, they've been asking where he is. Let's go, big guy."

She watched him walk away with their son, confused by her own emotions. Despite their rocky, unplanned beginnings, Logan had turned out to be a loving father. Sometimes, when the three of them were together, she could so easily picture them *staying* together. She glanced again at Jenny and Rourke, awaiting their baby together, ready to be a family.

"Remind me again," Julian teased, "what are the O'Donnells doing at my farewell party?"

She gently slugged his arm. "It's a family thing, and you know it. Thanks to Charlie, they're family."

"It's cool. I never had much in the way of family."

"You do now," she pointed out, gesturing around the room. He and his brother, Connor, had reconnected a few years ago, opening a world to him. He'd told her so, and he'd talked a little about his childhood, being raised by a single mom. He'd admitted it was lonely.

She set down her beer, no longer thirsty.

"You all right?" he asked.

"Sure. I'm jealous of you, though, heading for another adventure. And Sonnet, studying abroad." She thought about her best friend, spending the semester in Frankfurt. "When she and I were little, we always said we'd travel the world together. I'm jealous because it's not an option for me." She smiled up at him. "Then I look at my little boy, and I get over it, so don't feel too sorry for me."

"I don't feel sorry for you."

What *do* you feel? She wished she had the courage to ask. She thought about the things unsaid between them. She thought about the one time he'd kissed her. It had happened a year ago, but it was the kind of kiss you thought about forever. She wished he'd do it again. But there never seemed to be a good time for them.

"Go mingle," she said, shooing him away. "All these people are here for you."

"What about you?" he asked. "Are you here for me?"

She teetered on the verge of giving him an honest answer. "I'll meet you at the station when you leave next Monday," she said.

He offered a half smile, and a look that said so much more than words. "Seems like I'm always telling you goodbye."

Ten

In the fussy candy-colored mansion, Bo felt like a bull in a china shop. He was surrounded by fragile knicknacks, precariously displayed in rooms that had names that made him think of that old board game—the parlor, the library, the rotunda. The butler did it in the pantry with the meat mallet. The maid did it with the feather duster in the linen closet. The baseball player did it with Kimberly van Dorn in the bedroom....

Yet despite the ornate furnishings, waking up at Fairfield House was unexpectedly pleasant. In his little alcove bed, AJ slept like the dead, and Bo was careful not to awaken him. Sleep was the only escape the poor kid had from worrying about his mother.

On the nightstand beside the bed was a small photograph in a plastic sleeve. It was the only photo AJ had of his mother. The shot depicted the two of them with their arms around each other, grinning straight at the camera. In the background was some kind of fair or carnival. In the smiling, dark-haired woman, Bo tried to see the girl he'd once loved, but too much time had passed. She looked like a stranger to him. Yet in the photo, the bond between her and AJ was tangible. The kid clearly adored his mother, and having her ripped away from him was probably the emotional equivalent of an amputation. Bo just hoped they could resolve this soon and end the boy's hurt.

Bo went down to the kitchen for coffee, where he encountered Kimberly van Dorn. The moment he spotted her, he'd felt an instant surge of attraction, a reflex as automatic as breathing, because she was *that* beautiful. Never mind that she had been sending out not-interested signals since the moment he'd shown up on her doorstep.

"Hey," he said.

"Good morning." In plain jeans and a sweater, her hair still damp from the shower, she looked kind of vulnerable, maybe fragile in a way. "Help yourself to breakfast."

"Thanks." He grabbed an orange from a fruit bowl and stood over the sink, peeling it.

"Is AJ all right?"

"As all right as he can be, given the situation. Thanks for asking."

She nodded and took her coffee into the dining room. Bo felt a little easier after the exchange. She seemed cautiously willing to give him the benefit of the doubt. Maybe he shouldn't have said anything about how pretty she was, but damn. That would be like walking past a *Playboy* centerfold and not stopping to admire it. For the time being, *Playboy* was going to be as close as he could get to an actual relationship with a woman, because having a kid didn't leave him any time for dating.

On the AJ front, things were not going so hot. He'd

come downstairs and refused breakfast. A few minutes later, he sat slumped in the passenger seat of the Z4, staring out the window and staying conspicuously silent as they drove into town, on their way to register him for school.

"I never saw the snow except in pictures," Bo said, "until I moved up here in '04 to play baseball. Why anybody would want to move here if he didn't have to is beyond me."

En route, they passed the offices of Peyton Byrne, Esq., a local lawyer, the establishment marked with a discreet hand-lettered sign. Bo never looked at that sign without feeling an unpleasant twinge of memory. Last year, Byrne had repped some crazy-ass woman in bringing a paternity suit against him, and he'd had to hire Sophie Bellamy just to get the test results—negative—admitted before the court. After AJ, Bo had been scrupulous about birth control.

Bo decided not to share that particular Maury-Povich moment with his son. He did want to get more friendly with the boy, though. Win him over a little. Ordinarily, this was not a chore for Bo. Growing up as he had, he had learned at an early age to turn on the charm in order to get what he wanted. Sometimes, personal charm was the only thing in his arsenal.

"There's a winter carnival every year," he continued, gesturing at Blanchard Park as they passed it. "They'll build an ice sculpture as big as a house. They cut huge chunks of ice from the lake."

"Uh-huh," AJ said, his breath misting the car window as he kept his gaze trained away from Bo.

"You ever read a book called *The Last of the Mohicans?*" Bo asked. AJ liked books. Maybe they could find something in common.

"Nope," AJ said.

"It's by James Fenimore Cooper. I had to read it for English class when I was in high school. And I'm sorry to tell you, it was the most god-awful, boring thing I've ever read. It's about the Indians who lived here when the French and English guys first came over. They had a word for the big water between the forested mountains—*Glimmerglass.* I didn't much care for the book, but I still remember that word. When I look at the lake, I can kind of see how the guy came up with a word like that. I swear, in the summer that's just how it looks. The rest of the story, I can do without. I usually like fighting in books, but in this one, even the fighting was boring. The whole thing is about a white guy named Natty Bumppo, living with the Indians. Who the hell could take him seriously with a name like that? Natty Bumppo, for chrissakes."

"How is that any less weird than Bo?" asked AJ.

"You got me. Hey, listen, I thought after we finish with the school stuff today, we could go to the gym. I have to stay in training. Sixty throws a day, minimum. You might like the gym. Good pickup games of basketball, a pool. Great snack bar, too. What do you say?"

"Sounds okay."

So much for trying to sweet-talk the kid. And honestly, Bo didn't blame him for being unhappy and suspicious. Given the way Yolanda had misrepresented Bo to AJ, it was no wonder the boy didn't trust him. To salve her own conscience, or perhaps to mollify her now-ex-husband, she'd led AJ to believe his biological father had never cared enough to want to see him, and that the presents and monthly checks were sent out of guilt. She'd characterized him as a ballplayer living the high life. That part, at least, had a grain of truth. He was a baseball player. If drinking and getting laid regularly constituted the high life, then yeah, he'd cop to that. What was omitted was the fact that, up until a couple of months ago, he'd earned next to nothing from baseball. The checks often represented his food budget for the week. Yet he'd never once considered stiffing AJ. Bo remembered what poverty was like, and he wouldn't wish it on any kid.

No doubt the idea of a new school was contributing to AJ's sullen mood.

Bo didn't say anything, though, and he didn't let AJ's silence bother him. The boy was doing okay, considering everything he'd been through.

They turned down a freshly plowed street toward the town square, a bustling area of shops and restaurants and old-fashioned brick buildings. A few blocks later they arrived at their destination—Avalon Middle School. The moment the Z4 nosed into a visitor's spot in the parking lot, Bo had the sensation that all the air had been sucked out of the car's interior. The tension was that strong and palpable.

"It's going to be—" He broke off, regrouped. No point in filling the kid's head with platitudes. "Listen, we got no choice about this. The best thing you can do for your mother is toe the line, and that means going to school—"

AJ took a deep breath like a swimmer about to dive into frigid water, and pushed his way out of the car. At the main entrance, Bo identified them through the intercom and they were buzzed inside. A sign indicated that the main office was about halfway down the hall. It was a long, deserted hallway lined with lockers on one side and banners and announcements on the other. There was a flyer announcing a broomball tournament, a sport that was probably as foreign to AJ as kabuki theater. The classroom doors were shut, though he could see AJ's nervous glance darting to the narrow glass windows as he sought a glimpse inside at the other students.

AJ's pace quickened, as though he didn't want to linger in the hall. His instincts proved correct, because a few seconds later, a bell shrilled through the hallway. Damn. Bo had forgotten that singular shriek of the school bell, but AJ clearly had not; he shoved his hands in his pockets and tried to hunker down into his parka like a turtle into its shell. The floodgates burst open and students flowed in a churning mass from the classrooms.

Another thing Bo had forgotten—how god-awful loud kids tended to be. There was shouting, laughter, the stamping of feet. A few kids spotted Bo and gave him a wide berth; he was an adult. An interloper. Fewer still noticed AJ, but those who did stared holes through him. Watching them, Bo realized diversity was not a strong suit at this school. Amid the mostly-Anglo kids, AJ already looked like a misfit.

Battling the current of students flowing through the hallway, they made their way to the office. Though quieter than the corridor, the office was a hive of activity, with clerical workers at computer terminals, teachers checking their in-boxes, the school nurse dealing with two peaked-looking students. At the front counter, Bo waited for a few minutes. No one noticed them.

"Pardon me, ma'am," he said to one of the women working at a computer.

Glancing up at him, she seemed harried and over-worked, with wispy pale hair and an air of distraction. The sign on her desk identified her as Ms. Jensen, the attendance clerk. "Can I help you?"

He offered his best smile, the one that usually worked even on the crankiest of females. "Bo Crutcher," he said, "and this is my son, AJ Martinez. I called earlier. I'm here to enroll him."

The smile failed him. She pulled her mouth into a prune shape. Then she took out a clipboard and handed it to him. "You'll need to fill out this release for his records. Date and sign it at the bottom."

Her brusque manner irritated Bo. AJ didn't seem surprised. Just subdued.

Bo had come prepared—Sophie had told him to bring all the documentation he had. He handed Mrs. Jensen a thick manila envelope. "Here's his birth certificate, immunization record and latest progress report and contact information for his school. And an emergency guardianship form. He just moved here from Houston."

She paged through the documents. "What's the emergency?"

"His mother had to go away...temporarily."

"How is that an emergency?"

"How is that your business?" Bo asked the question with a smile, but the question made his point.

She sniffed. "Proof of residency?"

"Right here." He indicated the lease agreement he'd just signed with Mrs. van Dorn.

"Social security card?"

Bo turned to AJ. "You got one?"

AJ shook his head.

"Will mine do?" Bo asked, taking his from his wallet.

She narrowed her eyes at him. "He has thirty days. In this country, it's standard."

Now he got it—the attitude, the suspicion. This woman had made up her mind about AJ, tried and convicted him, knowing nothing more than the kid's name. "In this country, it's mandatory for a kid to go to school," he said.

"Does he speak English?" she asked. "Because the ESL classes meet on a different campus—"

"Lemme check on that," said Bo. "Yo, AJ, *¿habla inglés?*"

"Dunno. Is that what they speak in this country?" AJ asked quietly but pointedly.

Mrs. Jensen pruned her mouth at him, then studied the paperwork they'd brought. "This isn't certified," she said, handling the birth certificate as though it smelled bad.

"It's a certificate," Bo said. "Doesn't that mean it's certified?"

"I need a certified certificate. Not a hospital certificate. Not a mother or souvenir copy. A *certified* certificate. He cannot be enrolled until I have that, along with the records from his previous school. And I can't send for the records until you complete this form." She indicated the pages on the clipboard.

"I'll be quick, ma'am," Bo said, filling out the form. He bit his tongue. He knew if he let go of it, he'd be in big trouble. But he couldn't help himself. As he handed over the clipboard, he said, "I know you must be in a hurry to get to your doctor appointment."

The woman scowled. "I don't have a doctor's appointment."

"Really? You might need one, ma'am."

"I beg your pardon?"

"You know, to do something about that stick."

"I'm sure I don't know what you're talking about."

"Sure you do. That stick. You know, the one you got stuck up your ass. You'll be a lot happier once that's removed. Come on, AJ. Let's go."

The hallway had cleared out by then. "You shouldn't have said that," AJ whispered.

"It was totally worth it," Bo said, feeling the first flicker of camaraderie with him. "Did you see her face?"

At the end of the hall, by the exit, a janitor was swabbing snow and slush with a mop. It didn't escape Bo that this was the only Hispanic person they'd seen all morning. Glancing at AJ, he guessed that the boy had noticed this, too.

He said nothing, but checked the new-student brochure. "Looks like we've got to pick up some school supplies for you," he said, adding it to his list of errands. As he planned out the things they had to do before AJ started school, Bo finally had to acknowledge that his life had just gotten immeasurably more complicated. Suddenly finding himself in charge of a boy was not quite the same as rescuing a kitten or getting a goldfish. Here was somebody depending on him, twenty-four/seven. His life was not All About Bo Crutcher anymore.

People juggled work and family all the time, he reminded himself. He'd never thought about just how they did, though.

Before the phone call from Yolanda, he was happily immersed in his career. The pre-season agreement with the Yankees was the answer to every dream he'd ever had, yet he hesitated to explain to AJ exactly what it was going to mean in practical terms. A major-league career was all-consuming, and the three-ring circus was about to begin. Bo was supposed to hit the road soon, heading down to Virginia for the annual rookie development program, known as Fame School.

He didn't relish telling AJ. The boy had already been ripped from his mother. And although Bo wasn't any kind of father, he was all the kid had, for the moment, anyway. He suspected AJ might not warm up to the idea that Bo, too, had to go away, regardless of the reason. He kept rehearsing ways to explain the situation, but there was really no good way to say it—except to say it.

Tonight, then. At dinner, Bo would explain about the Yankees contract, and how he had to go away for the rookie development program.

Which would probably go over like a fart in church.

"Now what?" AJ asked peevishly, buckling his seat belt. He felt totally freaked out. Enrolling in school was huge. It seemed to take him even further away from his mom.

"How about we have a little fun this afternoon? Let's head to the gym."

"That's your idea of fun?"

"We could always go back to the school, bug the attendance clerk some more."

AJ knew what Bo was up to. He was trying to keep him from being homesick for his mom. It kind of worked. A little bit, sometimes.

"I know what you're doing," AJ said.

"I'm glad you do," Bo said with laughter in his voice. "Because most days, I haven't got a clue."

"I mean, I know what you're doing with me. You're try-ing to make me like it here by doing all this fun stuff with me."

"Oh, busted," Bo said. "So is it working?"

"Maybe a little bit. Sometimes."

"Nothing's going to keep you from missing your mom, AJ. That doesn't mean you have to suffer every second she's away. It doesn't help her, and she wouldn't want you to be miserable. Agreed?"

He shrugged, looked out the window. It was weird how he was already getting used to the small town. Probably because there was so little to it—Main Street and the town square, the city park at the lakeshore, the train station.

Bo turned into the parking lot of the big barnlike build-ing that housed the sports complex. School was out for the day, and kids were hanging around. It made AJ miss his *cholos* back home. They never went to a gym or anything. There was no money for that. AJ thought about all the flyers given out at school—*Sign up for Youth Soccer! Little League tryouts next week! Swim Team starts soon!*—that had never made it home. His mom's reaction was always the same: "It's a lot of money, *chico tierno...*" By second grade, he'd learned to leave the flyers in the trash.

"Here we are," Bo announced. "The Arthur Rey Gym-nasium and Aquatic Center. Sophie loaned me some of Max's gym shorts for you. We might be able to find some swim trunks in the lost and found."

"I'm not swimming," AJ said, folding his arms across his middle.

"Not right away, you aren't," Bo said. "We're going to have a game of one-on-one first."

"Forget it."

"Fine. You can sit on the bench while I find a pick-up game."

AJ hesitated. "See? This is what I hate. I only get two choices and they both suck."

Just for a second, hurt flashed across Bo's face. AJ wished he hadn't seen it. He wished he hadn't caused it. He wished he wasn't starting to care whether or not Bo's feelings were hurt. "Why do you keep trying to turn me into someone I'm not?" he lashed out.

"What the hell is that supposed to mean?"

AJ scowled. "You want me to be athletic like you. I'm not like that. I'm not cool and I'm not athletic."

"Let me tell you something," Bo said. "The only thing wrong with you is your attitude. You know I'm right." He killed the engine and turned to face AJ. "When I was in junior high, I was like every other kid in Texas. I wanted to go out for football. I would've made it, too. But at try-outs, the coach sent me home."

"Why? Weren't you any good?"

"I was okay. And sure, I could have played football. But the coach took me aside and said I even had a decent shot at a football scholarship at one of the smaller schools."

"So why did he reject you?"

"Because he wanted more for me. And he didn't want me getting hurt. See, playing football, I'd end up with injuries, maybe one that would end up doing permanent damage. Or keeping me from playing a sport I'm a lot better at."

"Like baseball."

"Uh-huh. But, man, I was humiliated. Back then, I didn't understand what a huge favor they were doing me."

"I still don't want to put on gym clothes. And I really don't want to put on swim trunks. People will think I'm a freak."

"I'm not going to force you to put on anything." Bo got out of the car and grabbed a gym bag from the trunk. He leaned way down into the car. "You can either follow me...or freeze. Your choice."

AJ got out and slammed the door.

"And something else," Bo said as they headed inside. "You wouldn't worry so much about what people think of you if you knew how little they did."

In the locker room, they changed into gym clothes. AJ wore a large gray T-shirt and some long shorts that were too big. He felt like a total dweeb, but nobody paid him much attention. The basketball court was busy with people who were totally focused on playing. The court was filled with the sounds of thumping basketballs and shoes squeaking on polished wood. Bo grabbed a ball and effortlessly dribbled it in a circle around himself, then passed it to AJ.

He put up his hands to protect himself, stopping the ball. "I suck at this," he said.

"Naw, you just need some practice." Bo got out another ball and demonstrated some dribbling techniques. "Loose," he said. "Loose and easy. Treat the ball like it's a dinner roll, hot out of the oven. You barely need to touch it."

The advice worked pretty well. They practiced dribbling and passing. Bo didn't seem too concerned about shooting hoops, which was fine with AJ since he'd probably end up missing anyway.

"Quit thinking so much," Bo said.

"How can you tell I'm thinking?"

"It makes you slow and stiff."

"So how do I stop?"

The ball flew straight at his face, fast and hard. He plucked it out of the air and bounce-passed it back to Bo.

"Like that," Bo said with a grin. "You let your reflexes take over. Give your brain a rest."

AJ didn't understand why the technique worked, but it did. Pretty soon, he was dribbling and feinting like a real player. Weird. No one had ever bothered to show him how to play a sport before. His stepdad always used to be busy, and his mother didn't really know any sports. Bo kind of led him into practicing shots. AJ missed more than he made, but he sank a few.

"You're quick study," Bo said.

AJ glanced at the clock. To his amazement, an hour had gone by. He was drenched in sweat, and so was Bo.

"One game of twenty-one," Bo said, and explained a few simple rules. "Winner gets to pick what we do next."

"No fair," AJ protested.

"Life's not fair. Deal with it."

AJ was determined to win, but he was hopeless against Bo. That didn't stop him from trying. He feinted and spun around, tried shot after shot and made some headway, but in the end, Bo reached a winning twenty-one long before AJ.

"Don't take it too hard," Bo said, tossing him the ball to put away. "Nobody beats me at games. Ever."

"Good to know."

Two kids had come in and were watching him. He figured they'd start snickering or whispering about him but instead, they came over when Bo waved at them.

"Hey," one of them called. "How about a game?"

AJ checked with Bo, who nodded. "Go ahead. I'm going to get some water."

The game with the other kids went okay. He didn't win but he held his own. After a short while, they were all as hot and sweaty as AJ. The boys told him their names were Shane and Lehigh. They went to the middle school. And both of them knew who Bo Crutcher was. AJ wondered if that meant Bo was famous.

"Let's go jump in the pool," Shane suggested.

"Yeah," said Lehigh. "Come on, AJ."

"I don't have my trunks."

"Just wear those," Bo said, indicating his long nylon shorts. He'd been watching from the sidelines, guzzling water from a plastic bottle.

"I don't have a towel."

"There's a clean one in my gym bag."

Great. AJ followed the others to the pool. Best just to bite the bullet, he decided.

He left his shoes and socks under a bench, then peeled off his shirt one-handed. As fast as he could, he streaked through the shower and ran and dove into the deep end. He wasn't a good swimmer, but he was fearless. Growing up in Houston, every kid had to learn to swim, or risk drowning in an apartment complex pool.

Bo joined in, doing giant cannonballs off the diving board. He made huge splashes and swam like he'd never left Texas, with long, easy strokes.

"Your dad's cool," said Lehigh, treading water next to AJ.

"I guess."

"You guess? What? It's not cool enough to have a dad on the New York Yankees? Does he beat you or something?"

"Only at basketball," AJ said quickly. "He's okay. He's just… We're new to each other," he said, not wanting to elaborate. "I've never spent any time with him before."

"Where's your mom?" Lehigh asked.

"She's…away. Kind of going through a bad time. So I'm staying with my—with Bo for a while." AJ couldn't believe he was able to talk about her without bawling like a baby.

"Heads-up," somebody called, lobbing a water-polo ball at them.

AJ didn't think, just snatched the ball out of the air. Bo was right about that, at least. Things were easier when you didn't think so much.

Eleven

AJ quit asking about his mom, because every time he asked, there was more bad news. Another delay. A report that additional documentation was needed. Another that the documentation was insufficient. A few days ago, she'd been transferred with a large group from temporary holding to something called a contract detention center. From there, she wasn't allowed to call out, but he could leave a recorded message for her each day. Big whoop. Like that was supposed to make them both feel better. He sounded so phony, saying the same thing every time—*I'm fine, don't worry about me, we're getting you help. The lawyers are really good.* AJ worked hard to sound confident. Bo had not had to warn him that it did no good to complain.

Although he knew it was no use, he dialed their home phone number. He just wanted to hear her voice, even though he knew how much it would hurt. "It's Yolanda. Leave me a message, and I'll call you back." It wasn't the words, but the sound of her voice, followed by the open invitation signaled by the beep. "Mom," he said, "Mami, where are you? I'm really scared and I want to be with you again." He knew she wasn't home to hear the message, but he added, "I love you, Mom. *Te quiero.* Okay, bye."

Every time he turned off the phone, he would study the only photo he had of her, the shot taken at last year's Houston Livestock Show and Rodeo. It was just by luck that he had the picture in a pocket of his backpack. Otherwise, he'd have nothing at all.

After studying the photo, he would close his eyes and conjure memories of her, trying to bring her closer to him. Her smell and the way her hand felt, brushing the hair off his forehead. The sound of her voice when she sang along with the radio. The frown of worry that creased her brow when she didn't think he was watching, and the way she twisted the phone cord around her finger and talked in a low voice so he couldn't hear. He remembered the good times, too. Like in the summer, when it was so hot you almost couldn't see straight, she'd take him to a secret place for swimming—a big holding tank called a rice well, fed by cool, clear water pumped from the ground.

"This place is special to me, *niño,*" she'd once told him.

"Why?"

A faraway look had softened her eyes. "It reminds me of a special time in my life."

"What special time?" he persisted, but instead of answering, she'd laughed and ducked him under water. Afterward, they'd stop at the Sonic for soft ice cream cones, and AJ would find himself wishing his mother had more time off work.

Each Fourth of July, she used to take him to the bayou spillway west of town, and they would sit at the top of a steep bank, watching the fireworks, soaring in patriotic colors. He could still picture the glow on her face and the way her eyes sparkled as she lifted them to the sky and watched in wonder. "Do you see, *hijo?* Flowers blooming in the sky. Anything is possible. When I was your age, my parents used to take me to a place by the Rio Grande, to see the flowers."

"Tell me about when you were little."

Her face had grown sad, her eyes soft with a faraway gaze. "We lived in Laredo, down in the valley, and there was music every night, and wonderful food... My papa was hardworking and stern, but he loved me, and my mother was a wonderful cook. It was not such a big problem to cross the border in those days, and sometimes we visited my mother's family in Nuevo Laredo, on the other side of the river. The Mexican side."

According to his birth certificate, he'd been born in Laredo, though AJ barely remembered his *abuelos.* He hadn't seen them since before he started kindergarten. He remembered his mother's sadness when she told him his *abuelito* had died, and his grandmother was moving back to the valley, to live in Mexico. By then, his mom had married Bruno and they moved to Houston for work.

When AJ would ask if they could go visit his grandmother, the sadness returned to his mother's eyes. "It's not safe," she said, and now he understood what "not safe" really meant. It wasn't safe to be Latino, and poor. Sometimes you had to show proof of who you were, and he was fast finding out how hard that could be for people like his mother.

People seized in the raid were told they could agree to immediate voluntary deportation, or choose a hearing. Mrs.

Bellamy-Shepherd, the blond lawyer, had explained that a hearing was when you went to a federal judge and explained why you should have the right to stay in the country instead of being forced to leave.

The bad news about that was, waiting for a hearing could take a long time because of something called a backlog. Even though the lawyers had filed emergency papers, the delay might last for weeks or months. Plus—and AJ had figured this out by looking at the Internet on Bo's MacBook—the detention center was pretty much a jail.

A jail. He couldn't picture his mom in jail. He could picture her listening to him read a poem aloud. He could picture her sitting in her bathrobe on a Sunday morning, sipping coffee from a mug and listening to the radio. He could picture her waiting in the school hallway for a parent-teacher conference. She always wore her nicest blouse, the sleeves pressed with a crisp crease, her hair pulled back in a clip, her mouth shiny with lipstick. He could picture his mom coming home late from the plant, so exhausted she had to fight to find a smile for him. And he could picture her brushing the hair from his forehead and saying, "You need a haircut, *mi hijo,* so I can see those beautiful long eyelashes."

He could picture his mom a hundred ways. But he couldn't picture her in jail.

Even worse, Mrs. Bellamy-Shepherd had explained that challenging detention was risky because they would almost certainly accuse his mom of doing something illegal.

"She hasn't done anything illegal," he said.

"I believe you're right," she said. "But something might come up—a parking violation or an expired tag, littering or filling out a form wrong. There are cases on the books of people who were deported for voting. Or taking a class in English without proper documentation. Sometimes, people get in trouble just by being in the wrong place at the wrong time."

"She was at work," he said. "Same as every day." He knew what the real problem was—his mom had brown skin and spoke English with an accent.

"I'm sorry, AJ. The system is extremely flawed, and sometimes people like your mother pay the price."

So here he was, a few thousand miles from the only home he'd ever known, living in this crazy house with a group of strangers.

And here was the weird thing—it was sometimes like having a great big family.

Of course, he would consider it way cooler if he wasn't so worried about his mom. If he was back together with his mom, maybe if he could live at a place like this with her, then that would be awesome. He'd always wanted a bigger family, even though he knew brothers and sisters fought with you and took your stuff. He just liked the noise and the feeling of being surrounded by a big group of people in a place where he belonged. After Bruno left, it was just AJ and his mom, which meant it was really just AJ most of the time, because he was home alone so much while Mom worked.

Being in this snow-white small town, in this big crazy house, meant that at least while he waited for her to come home, he wouldn't be bored. So that was something. The house itself was like a mansion out of an old-fashioned novel, both elaborate and slightly creepy. The place had a turret—a round tower three stories high, and old-fashioned rooms with tall ceilings and carved woodwork. The furniture was old, too, but well cared for, and the yard was crisscrossed by fresh tracks from some small animal or other. And the whole thing was presided over by Mrs. van Dorn. She had an open face and kind eyes, and she was a pretty good cook, judging by the nightly dinners around here.

All in all, it wouldn't be too bad, except for the thing with his mom.

At dinnertime, AJ helped himself to a plate full of spaghetti and meatballs, and a side of salad with big toasted croutons. He took his seat next to Bo in the brightly painted dining room. Music drifted from a speaker behind a plant, mingling with the murmured conversation of people greeting each other, complimenting Mrs. van Dorn on the food. It was weird, in a good way, to be living with this group of people. One big not-happy-but-at-least-not-bored family.

Mrs. van Dorn sat at the head of the table, with her back to the swinging kitchen door. To her left was a guy called Dino Carminucci, the manager of Bo's baseball team, some outfit called the Hornets. To Mrs. V's right was the Hornets' catcher, Bagwell, who went by the nickname Early. Bagwell usually played winter baseball in the Dominican Republic, but he had a wrist injury and was sitting the season out.

Across from AJ sat Daphne McDaniel. He silently called her "Daffy" on account of the pink hair, tattoos and facial piercings. She worked at Mrs. Bellamy-Shepherd's law office, even though she didn't look like the type to be doing office work. What she really liked was anime. She was obsessed with drawing, and even had a series going called "Steel Angel."

At the opposite end of the table sat Kim, who was Mrs. V's daughter. With her long red hair and that face, she was like a movie star or something. She was even prettier than the Miss Texas he'd seen at the Houston Livestock Show and Rodeo. It was hard not to stare at her, but AJ was pretty good at being cool. And Kim just acted like a regular person, although Bo seemed to make her nervous. AJ wondered what was up with that.

"More milk?" Bo offered, startling him.

"Uh, no thanks." To tell the truth, AJ pretty much hated it here. He didn't quite know what to make of Bo. What kind of guy had a kid and then blew him off for twelve years? Sure, he was trying to figure out a way to help AJ's mom, but that was just so he wouldn't have to deal with AJ anymore.

AJ figured the feeling was mutual, although Bo acted all buddy-buddy with him, even razzing the attendance clerk at the school AJ had no intention of going to. A school full of strangers. He might have to give in and go, though. More than anything, he wanted to keep the focus on getting his mom out of detention. The quicker that happened, the better for everyone.

The people at Fairfield House didn't ask him a bunch of nosy questions, so that was something. There was no reason for them to be interested in where he came from and how he'd ended up here. He just wanted to get back together with his mom. Every time he thought of her, he got a lump in his throat, big enough to hurt really bad. He tried not to think about his mom and concentrated on the meal and the people around the long table.

At a pause in the conversation, Mrs. van Dorn turned to smile at AJ and then Bo. "Now that you've had a chance to settle in, is everything all right?"

"Absolutely, ma'am," Bo said immediately. "Isn't it, AJ?"

"Yeah, sure. Um, yes, ma'am." AJ figured a show of good manners would get him further than copping an attitude.

"Well, we're very glad to have you, aren't we, Kimberly?"

"Absolutely."

"We're much obliged to you," Bo said. "Dino and Early told me you're the best cook in Avalon, and they weren't pulling my leg."

Mrs. van Dorn's eyes lit even brighter. "When my daughter said you were a charmer, she wasn't pulling *my* leg."

Bo grinned at Kim. "A charmer? Did you really call me a charmer?"

"Indeed, I did." She was trying to act all cool, but AJ saw her face turn red. "But why would you assume it's a compliment?"

"Maybe she means you're like a snake charmer," Bagwell said.

"Dino told me he's known you for years," said Mrs. van Dorn. "He knows I'm very particular about my guests."

Bo grinned again and caught AJ's eye. "We're going to be on our best behavior."

"So, AJ, how about your old man?" asked Dino Carminucci, beaming at Bo. "That's some news, eh?"

It was weird the way everybody liked Bo so much.

Bo's grin disappeared. "Yo, Dino—"

"What news?" asked Mrs. van Dorn.

Good question, thought AJ. "What news?" he asked.

Bo set down his fork, used his napkin. "Well now, I

meant to talk to you about this today, AJ, but Dino let the cat out of the bag."

What cat? AJ wanted to know. What bag?

"I'm going to be in a special training program for rookies."

"Where?" AJ asked suspiciously.

"Virginia. It's not for long."

AJ turned himself to stone. This was the only way to keep from cracking into a million pieces.

Daphne seemed to pick up on AJ's quiet mood. "So are you a baseball fan?"

He was pretty freaking tired of that question. Everyone he'd met so far just assumed that because Bo played ball, AJ not only was a big fan, but he played, too, and played it well. Which was all a bunch of bull. He couldn't care less about baseball. "I don't really like any sports," he said bluntly.

"What do you like to do for fun?" Bagwell asked.

The question cut deep. Nothing was fun. How could anything be fun when your mother was being held at some detention center like she was an international criminal? AJ was tempted to say, "Well, I like pulling the legs off insects. That's pretty fun." But he kept his mouth shut.

Here was the problem. He couldn't blame this situation on anyone. No, wait. He could, too. He could blame Bo. If Bo Crutcher had done the right thing when he learned he'd gotten AJ's mom pregnant, and married her, then his mom would be totally legal and none of this would be happening. So this was really Bo's fault.

"I see you're a southpaw like your dad," Dino observed, beaming at him.

AJ set down his fork. "Yes, sir."

"How about another roll?" Kim offered, holding out a

basket. She alone seemed to sense how much he was hating the conversation.

"Thank you," he said, and ate the roll in record time. Then he asked, "May I be excused?" Before anyone could say no, he set aside his napkin and left the table. He was blinking fast as he moved, heading for the room Mrs. V called the rotunda. It seemed like a refuge to AJ, a big round room filled with books. There was a sitting area, and lots of windows hung with lace curtains. AJ flung himself into a big armchair and ground his fists into his eyes.

Don't do it, he warned himself. *Don't cry, whatever you do.* By pressing hard and clenching his jaw, he managed to stave off the tears. If he let himself get mad enough, the heat of anger would cause the tears to boil away like drops of water on a hot skillet.

Nobody came after him, not right away. AJ couldn't tell if this meant Bo was being decent, knowing AJ didn't want anyone to see him, or if Bo was just blowing him off because he didn't care. Probably that, yeah. He didn't care. He hadn't cared for twelve years and he sure as heck wasn't going to start now.

AJ went over to Bo's laptop, which Bo said he could use whenever he wanted. Back home, AJ hardly ever got to use a computer. The ones at his school were always swarmed, and he always felt out of place at the public library. Having a Mac all to himself was pretty amazing. He looked up stuff about immigration, finding a ton of agencies claiming they could help. And most of those agencies had an address in New York City, which was just a train ride away. He went looking for a train schedule, but then he heard Bo coming and quickly shut the browser. Snatching up a heavy illustrated book about Greek mythology, he acted as though he'd been reading the whole time.

"Hey," said Bo.

"Hey." AJ didn't look up. He focused on a story about a guy named Kronos, who envied the power of his father so much he castrated him with a sickle, which totally skeezed AJ out, but that was a Greek myth for you.

AJ didn't really know what it was like to have an actual dad. Bruno had never paid much attention to him. Bo was a stranger.

"You okay?" asked Bo.

AJ gave a shrug, still not looking up. The sickle thing backfired on Kronos, though, because when his father bled into the sea, the Titans were born, and everybody knew you don't want to piss off a Titan.

Maybe he'd better not piss off Bo, either, because stranger or not, Bo was the only thing standing between AJ and a foster home, the only one paying the lawyer and the only one who seemed to give a hoot about getting AJ's mom back.

"I didn't mean for you to hear about the rookie trip that way," Bo said. "I wanted to tell you myself, without a bunch of other people around."

"Doesn't matter to me. I mean, congratulations and all, but it doesn't matter if I found out when everybody else did," AJ said. He did not want Bo to give him any kind of special status. As far as he was concerned, they were room-mates. He studied a drawing of Kronos facing down a bad-ass Titan called the Cyclops.

Bo didn't say anything for a few minutes. AJ pretended to read, but the words blurred before his eyes.

The chair across from him exhaled as Bo sat down on the leather cushion. "I know it's a lousy break, this thing that happened to your mother," Bo said.

Duh. *Tell me something I don't know,* thought AJ.

"And what probably really sucks is hearing people talk about my news."

"Why would that suck?" AJ asked.

"I figure the last thing you want to hear about is somebody else's good news."

AJ glanced up from the book at last. He hadn't expected this—hadn't expected Bo to understand. "It's cool," he said tonelessly. "The Yankees thing."

"That's nice of you to say, but we need to talk about you."

AJ quit trying to pretend he was interested in the book of myths. "Talk about me."

"Looks like you might be stuck with me for a little longer than we thought. According to Sophie, the soonest your mother can get a hearing is in six weeks."

AJ stomach knotted. He wished he hadn't eaten so much spaghetti at dinner. Six weeks. A month and a half. And that was just for a *hearing.* Who knew what would happen after that?

"Anyway, Mrs. V. is fine with us staying for as long as we need to, so that's something," Bo said. "But there's one thing…."

The knot in AJ's stomach tightened. "What? Just tell me."

"I need to explain about the thing Dino mentioned earlier. He didn't realize I hadn't told you yet about the rookie program. They coach new players on how to handle reps, sportswear executives, the press, fans, that sort of thing. See, in the major leagues, baseball isn't just baseball. It's like learning a whole business. The trouble is, I'm supposed to go the week after next."

AJ sat there, smoldering mad, trapped. "Yeah? So?"

"So I got a dilemma now. I'm responsible for you. I can't just go taking off."

AJ couldn't resist. "Why not? That's what you've done my whole life."

"Hey—"

"You can just go," AJ stated, getting up and putting the book back on the shelf with a decisive shove. "I'll be fine." To his relief, Bo didn't try to stop him as he stalked out of the room.

He kept his head down and took the stairs two at a time, nearly colliding with Kim on the stair landing. "Sorry," he mumbled.

"No harm done. AJ, you look upset."

He was amazed to see what he saw in her eyes. They were soft with kindness and understanding. What was up with that? He was even more amazed to hear himself say, "It's cool and all that Bo's going to be a Yankee, but *I* have to go to school starting Monday, and that is not cool." There was still no certified birth certificate, but Bo had gone over the attendance clerk's head and sweet-talked somebody at the school into giving AJ provisional enrollment.

"I'm sorry."

Most grown-ups would probably tell him all the good things about school. Not Kim. She said, "I used to hate school, myself. How about you?"

He shrugged. "It's okay, I guess." He thought about Mrs. Jackson, and how he always felt all proud to be in the top reading group, even though it meant reading harder books. And he liked Mrs. Alvarez, the teacher's aide, who spoke Spanish most of the time, because most of the kids in class were Latino. His school in Texas, with its open-air walkways and sunbaked playgrounds, was completely different from the snowbound brick building in Avalon, filled with suspicious-looking Anglo kids.

"But you feel funny about being new," Kim said, guessing correctly.

He nodded.

"What can I do to help? Don't look at me like that, AJ."

"Like what?" But he knew. He'd squinted his eyes, wondering why she cared.

"Like you think I'm being phony. I'm not. I really want to know if there's any way to help you. I'm new to this, you see—"

"To what?"

"To you. To having a friend your age. I like you, and I don't want to see you hurting. So tell me what I can do."

Her words startled him. And she was getting really emotional. He didn't quite know how to handle that. There was only one person in the whole world he could count on, and that was his mother, and she was gone. Yet here was this stranger who didn't seem to want anything except to be nice to him. Part of him wanted to break down and wail, but he wasn't about to do that in front of her. Or anybody.

"AJ?" she prompted softly.

He took a deep breath, hardening himself. "Nothing. It's just going to suck. Everything sucks."

Again, she didn't try to act all cheerful about it. She touched him on the shoulder and gave it the lightest of squeezes. "I know the feeling."

Twelve

"I'm not going." AJ glared at Bo across the darkened kitchen of Fairfield House.

Bo clenched his jaw, silently vowing not to let this turn into a fight. They were the first ones up on a freezing Monday morning. Snow had come down all night, but according to the local radio reports, there was no hope of a snow day. This town was well-prepared, and snowplows were already out, clearing the streets.

"Yeah, you are." Bo braced his hands on the countertop and glowered at the coffeemaker, willing it to hurry up and brew. He hadn't had to get up for school in years, and he'd forgotten how brutal these early-morning wakeup calls could be.

"I'm not, and you can't make me."

Drip, drip, drip. Outright defiance was something Bo hadn't expected and wasn't prepared for. The words sounded strangely intimidating, especially coming from a kid. *You can't make me.* Bo had endured every sort of taunt and chatter on the baseball field, yet none of that rattled him the way AJ did. It was, he realized, because when all was said and done, baseball was a game. This, on the other hand, was not.

He glanced at AJ over his shoulder, sizing him up swiftly, the way he would a power hitter fresh from the dugout. The boy's face was stiff, his eyes hard with belligerence.

"Hate to point this out, buddy," he said, keeping his tone easy and reasonable. "But I *can* make you. So you might as well get used to the idea." At last, the coffeemaker finished, and Bo filled his mug. Two sips later, he felt almost human. "Look, we talked about this. It can't be avoided. You have to go to school, same as any other kid."

"I'm not the same as any other kid," AJ stated, his voice quiet but still obstinate. "Who cares if I go to school or not?"

"I care." Bo's words came out sounding testy. Well, hell. He *was* testy. Working on autopilot, he fixed AJ a glass of juice, handing it to him. "And you're going. You don't have to like it—you probably won't. But it won't be the end of the world, either."

"Not for you, it won't be. And you don't care if I go to school. You only care if I stay out of your hair so you can go away to Virginia."

"That's bullsh—baloney, AJ, and you know it." Bo held up two different boxes of cereal. AJ picked the one in his left hand, and Bo filled two bowls. He peeled a banana and started slicing it, then noticed AJ had fallen silent. "What?" he asked.

"Nothing." AJ took a seat and waited.

Bo set down the cereal bowls, then sat on a counter stool next to AJ. "Eat something. You need breakfast."

"I'm not hungry. I feel sick."

He probably did. He sure looked a little green around the gills.

"I get butterflies real bad when I'm up against something new," Bo said, digging in. "I've even thrown up, a time or two. That's what happened before I had my first game in a farm-league team when I was just out of high school. I got cut right away that season, and I always blamed it on nerves. Looking back, I think I was distracted, too."

AJ took a bite of his cereal. "Distracted by what?"

"Honestly, by your mother. By that time, she'd moved from Texas City down to Laredo with her folks, and I couldn't stop thinking about you, even though there wasn't technically a 'you' yet, since you hadn't been born."

The boy took another bite. "But you still managed to blame me for messing up your career."

"C'mon, AJ." Bo reminded himself not to get defensive. The kid was clearly looking for buttons to push. At least he was eating his breakfast. "You want the honest truth? I was a dumb-ass kid pretty much on my own, and I was scared I'd mess you up. But that didn't stop me from thinking about you all the time."

The boy shoveled the cereal steadily now. "Don't you have a family?"

"My mother—her name was Trudy—passed away five years ago. And my big brother, Stoney. He works offshore, on an oil rig. I bet he'd like to meet you one day." He refilled AJ's juice glass. "I wish I didn't have to go," Bo reiterated.

"Yeah, right," AJ said. "I'm sure you're just dying to stay here in the snow and babysit me."

He hated that the boy's accusation did have a ring of

truth to it. And that look would haunt Bo—an angry expression, underscored by the deep hurt of betrayal. It was an expression Bo hadn't seen in a very long time, but he remembered it well. He used to see that same face every time he looked in the mirror. And it bugged the heck out of him, because he knew just what AJ was feeling.

"I didn't say that, either. I'm supposed to go to Virginia for this special program. It's business, AJ." *It's my life.* "While I'm away, you've got Dino and everybody else here to keep you company. I'll be back before you know it." Even as he spoke, Bo could imagine how that sounded. AJ's mother had gone to work one day, too. And she'd never come back.

On one level, they both knew this was different. The INS or Homeland Security was not going to catch Bo in their dragnet. But on a deeper level, this was one more person abandoning AJ. In his short lifetime, the boy had lost his grandfather, and his grandmother had moved south of the border. He'd lost a stepfather and, most devastating of all, his mother. Now Bo was planning to take off. He didn't fool himself that he meant all that much to AJ, but this was probably the last straw.

"Everybody goes to school," he said. "No exceptions. You'll get through the day. Hell, you might even like it. Be who you are, because you're a hell of a kid. Make some friends—"

"I'm not going."

To Bo, AJ's defiance felt like being confronted by a weasel or a wolverine—startling and threatening. You didn't know how to handle it. He felt like a fool, being intimidated by a kid, but he couldn't quite get past the discomfort. How the hell did people do this?

"I don't want to fight with you about this," he said, keeping his voice even. Reasonable. "You need to get your stuff together. You don't want to miss the bus on your first day. Unless you changed your mind and want me to give you a ride." Bo had offered him a lift earlier, but AJ had declined, horrified by the suggestion.

"I didn't change my mind. I'm not riding with you," AJ muttered. Then, to Bo's relief, he shrugged sullenly into his parka, stuffed his feet into the warm snowmobile boots Bo had bought for him and tugged on his gloves.

Encouraged by the air of cooperation, Bo asked, "Got everything you need?"

"Yeah, sure," AJ said. "No—wait." He ran back to their room, feet thudding on the stairs, and came back down, zipping his photo of Yolanda into a pocket of his backpack.

The gesture made Bo wish he could give the kid a hug, tell him everything was going to be all right. But the kid didn't want hugs from Bo, and nothing was right, so Bo kept his mouth shut. Starting at a new school was hard for any kid. Bo of all people should know. He'd lost count of the times in his own boyhood when he and Stoney had been in charge of getting themselves up and off to school. If a kid showed up wearing the wrong thing, or smelling weird, or looking somehow different from the other kids, he was toast.

"Wait! Lunch money. You need lunch money." Bo fished a wad of bills from his pocket and handed AJ a twenty. "I don't have anything smaller, but that ought to cover it," he said. "Don't you think?"

AJ hesitated. Then he said, "I think I'm supposed to buy a punchcard."

Oh, yeah. Sophie had mentioned the card situation, but Bo hadn't paid close enough attention to the details. When she'd first spoken of school and other long-term plans, Bo had still been in denial. He'd felt sure the whole AJ situation would be resolved quickly, or that somehow, things would magically take care of themselves. It had taken a few days, and lots of meetings with Sophie about the legal situation, for reality to sink in. AJ wasn't going anywhere soon.

Bo fished out another twenty and handed it over. "I don't know what one of those cards costs. Better safe than sorry." If it turned out the punchcard cost a hundred bucks, he'd gladly pay it. He'd pay any price if it meant AJ would cooperate. "What else? Did we get everything at the store the other day? Paper and pencils? A…what do you call those curvy things? A protractor?"

"A French curve," said Kim, breezing into the kitchen. "Morning, AJ. Morning, Bo."

The moment she entered, the air shifted. Even the light seemed to change, as though more of the sun's rays were allowed to leak through the brooding clouds. She looked like a model in a mattress commercial, well rested and effortlessly beautiful.

"Coffee?" Bo offered.

"In a minute." She turned to smile at AJ. "I caught you just in time."

As usual, Bo couldn't take his eyes off her. She wore a black turtleneck dress, black stockings and high-heeled ankle boots, hoop earrings and pink lipstick. There was no better-looking outfit for a redhead than all black.

She handed AJ a sack. "Just a few things for school," she said. "Some folders, a binder and spiral notebooks. A calculator and a ruler. A French curve and a protractor. I hate to say it, but you're probably going to need a protractor. Math teachers love giving problems with angles, don't they?" As she spoke, she fixed herself a cup of coffee. Skim milk, no sugar.

"Thanks," AJ said. He peeled off one glove, reopened the backpack and stuffed in the extra supplies.

Bo was amazed. She'd managed to come up with most of the things he'd neglected to get at the store. He caught her eye, adding a nod of thanks. "Well," he said, "better get to the bus stop." He walked to the front door with AJ. "You take care, now," he said. "I'll see you after school."

"'Bye." AJ went out the door, into the cold semidark of the winter morning. He headed down the long walk that bisected the snow-covered yard and turned onto the lane leading to the street. In the bluish light, his shoulders hunched against the cold, he resembled a condemned man walking the Green Mile. He shuffled along at an old man's gait, with his eyes on the ground and his shoulders hunched up. Halfway down the block was the bus shelter, where a few kids had already gathered.

Bo shut the door against the cold, though he stood in place, looking out until AJ disappeared into the shadows. "Dammit," Bo muttered, taken aback by the pain he felt. Hurting for a child was unexpectedly intense. "Dammit all to hell."

"That went well," said a soft voice behind him.

"You think?" He turned to Kim. "I wanted to give him a ride, at least on his first day. He said he didn't want me to."

"Then you're smart to respect his wishes."

"I had no idea it would be this hard."

"I don't think this is supposed to be easy." She glared

at him, a challenge. "I'm no expert on parenting, but I do know that much."

"Just because there's nobody to be pissed at doesn't mean I'm not pissed. I'm no expert, either. Most people get a chance to adjust to being a parent. I'm still adjusting. My being a father was just an act of biology." He turned to her, not bothering to hide the genuine pain in his eyes. "I thought I'd spend the winter getting a crash course in major-league baseball, but what I need is a crash course in being a father. I don't have the first idea how to do that."

"Well, guess what? You don't have time for a crash course. AJ needs you to be a father now. He needs you to be present now. Don't worry about getting it perfect. Sometimes you just have to be there. Just be what he needs."

Bo kind of liked it when she got all bossy like this. "I hear you, coach. How'd you get so smart?"

"I'm not smart."

He studied her face, pretty even when she was being serious. She wore makeup every day, expertly applied, but still, he could see a fading, nearly undetectable bruise under her left eye. The makeup camouflaged it—almost. But growing up the way he had, Bo knew how a woman looked when she was trying to hide the fact that somebody had hit her. He knew she'd get mad if he said anything, so he just kept quiet.

She headed back toward the kitchen. "Come on. I'll buy you a cup of coffee."

"Why are you being so nice to me?"

"Because I feel bad for you and AJ."

"Does this mean you're starting to like me? Maybe just a little?"

"It means I feel bad for you."

Okay, he thought. From a woman like this, he'd take what he could get. "I just wish I could wave my hand and make all his troubles go away," he said.

"If you did that, you wouldn't be a father. You'd be a comic-strip character or a, I don't know, a superhero. Listen, AJ has to go to school, no matter what. Once he gets past the initial awkwardness, he'll be all right."

"Yeah, but—"

She put her hand on his arm. It was the first time she'd touched him on purpose, and it had an amazing effect on him. A warm, alive connection that made him feel, right or wrong, that he wasn't so completely alone with his troubles. He hoped she didn't notice, though. She'd probably think it was weird.

"Quit worrying," she said. "He'll be just fine."

Heading down the lane for the bus stop, AJ sneaked a look back over his shoulder at the big, colorful house behind him. Bo had moved away from the door, probably with a huge sigh of relief. AJ knew Bo couldn't wait to get rid of him.

A few kids were gathered at the bus stop, which was basically a bench with a roof overhead. He could hear them talking, two guys and a girl, their chatter punctuated by the occasional laugh. Their breath frosted the air like speech bubbles out of the mouths of cartoon characters.

They hadn't spotted him yet. In the early morning gloom, he was all but invisible. He felt like a foreign spy, slipping in and out of shadows, camouflaged by the trunks of trees lining the sidewalks.

The deep thunder of a diesel motor sounded as the bus turned onto King Street. It was coming for him. Its owlish headlamps swept the area like a searchlight. Without even thinking, AJ plastered himself against a tree trunk twice as big around as he was. He held himself perfectly still, not even breathing lest the frozen vapors give him away. If he was going to catch the school bus, he'd need to hurry.

Still, he didn't move, not even when he heard the shush of the bus's air brakes and the cranking of the door. Then, a few minutes later, the door clanked shut and the bus drove off in a noxious cloud. Snowy silence descended again, and AJ slowly let out the breath he forgot he'd been holding. Oh, man. What had he done? Was he skipping school? When had he decided that? He'd never skipped school in his life—ever. Not that he loved school all that much, but he hated trouble more. And skipping school was trouble.

That was how he used to see it, anyway. Now, however, he tended to see things in a different light. Once your mom got detained by the authorities, stuff like skipping school didn't seem like such a big deal.

A cold wind was blowing, and the snow flurries flew at him, stinging his face with tiny needles. AJ had no plan. He had acted totally on impulse. One thing he knew for sure—he couldn't just stay here until he turned into a human Popsicle, waiting for the sun to come out.

He couldn't go back home, either. Not that Fairfield House was any kind of home. If he headed back there, Bo would put him in the car and drive him to school. Being driven to school like a kindergartner, and arriving late, would make a bad situation even worse.

His hand stole to a pocket of his backpack. Last night,

he'd printed off some maps and information from the Internet and stashed them away. So maybe the plan had been forming even then.

Lowering his head into the wind, AJ started walking. The journey of a thousand miles begins with a single step, so people said, anyway.

The whole town was strange to him, but he knew in a vague sense that if he headed down the hill toward the lake, eventually he would find the main part of Avalon. There was an area of shops and restaurants, the city hall and the public library.

And the train station.

According to Bo, there were daily trains to New York City.

AJ's heart sped up, and so did his footsteps. He still had no plan. He knew this was crazy, that he was totally unprepared. All he had was his backpack full of school supplies, the maps and directions and forty dollars in his pocket.

Which was probably more than his mom had when they deported her.

It wasn't hard to find his way around the small town, what with the big, flat, white lake in the distance, its surface tinged pink with the rising sun. If Bo hadn't pointed it out to him, AJ wasn't sure he'd even recognize it as a lake, since it was completely frozen over, the snow forming a perfect covering, so cold and beautiful it made his eyes hurt. On closer inspection, he saw hints of the Willow Lake of summer. There were houses with docks projecting out into the flat whiteness. Passing a deserted park, he could see a chair on a scaffold with a sign: No Life Guard on Duty.

He made his way to the main part of town. The streetlights were just winking out, yielding to the day. A couple of restaurants were open, and the Sky River Bakery was jammed with people, its glowing windows misted with fog. Despite the delicious aromas emanating from the bakery, AJ kept walking. He spotted a railroad crossing and followed the tracks a short way to the train station.

Okay, he thought, joining the stream of commuters heading into the old-fashioned terminal building. Here we go.

He immediately lost confidence, however, when he looked up at the schedule board with its flashing lights and bewildering array of place names. How was he going to figure out which train would take him to the city? And once he got to New York, then what?

He stood in the terminal building, grateful for the big blowers on the ceiling generating heat. Behind him was a row of posters advertising Avalon and Willow Lake, showing happy families paddling canoes, watching fireworks, skiing and looking at autumn leaves. Studying the pictures, AJ could only shake his head. When he was younger, he used to believe families like this were real, but now he knew better. The people in the pictures were hired models. They probably didn't even know each other.

AJ took his mind away from the random thoughts and focused on figuring out what to do next. There were four platforms, and a ticket kiosk and some vending machines dispensing tickets. He observed a few passengers. They would buy a ticket, insert it into a slot on a turnstile and then pass through, collecting the ticket on the other side. Once, he spotted a teenager who looked both ways, then oh-so-casually braced his hands on the sides of the turnstile and jumped over, quick as the blink of an eye.

You really had to know what you were doing if you were

going to sneak on without a ticket. AJ decided against trying it. He'd get caught for sure. Better to blend in and stay
under the radar. He checked out the other commuters—
people talking on cell phones or checking e-mail, some
making small talk with each other.

"...call me when you get to New York, okay?" someone
asked. A soft, female voice.

"You know I will," a deep voice replied.

AJ edged closer to the couple. Now he was getting
somewhere. The guy was going to New York. All AJ had
to do was copy everything he did and get on the same train.

The guy was a really tall black man with a shaved head,
and his girlfriend was blond and pretty, pushing a baby
stroller. The baby was bundled up in a fleecy blue thing,
with a hood that had small animal ears attached. With pale
skin and a fringe of carrot-colored hair sticking out of the
hood, the baby reminded AJ of one of those staring-eyed
dolls you won at a carnival.

"Take care, Julian," the young woman said. She indicated
the stroller. "Charlie and I are going to miss you so much."

The tall guy hunkered down in front of the baby. "You
take care of your mama now, okay?" he asked.

The baby made a noise and squirmed. The guy stood up.
"See you around, Daisy."

Her face turned tragic and she hugged the guy, hard and
fiercely. "You will see me," she said. "Promise me you'll
call. And write."

"Every day," he said, bending down and inhaling, as if
he was trying to smell her hair. "I will, swear to God."

AJ felt kind of squirmy, watching them, like he was spy-
ing on them or something. He wasn't. He just needed to

see how to get the train to New York. At least the tall guy didn't kiss her or anything, even though he acted like he wanted to. He gave her one last squeeze and then went to a short line of people at the ticket machine. The blond girl named Daisy watched him with tears in her eyes.

Maybe, like AJ, the guy was going a lot farther than New York City.

AJ slipped into line behind the guy. His duffel bag had a label with his name: J GASTINEAUX—and a school name—Cornell University. He slid a twenty-dollar bill into the machine and punched some buttons. AJ observed his selections carefully.

The machine regurgitated some change and a printed ticket.

When it was AJ's turn, he fed his lunch money from Bo into the machine, pushed the same buttons as the guy before him, held his breath and waited. The seconds seemed endless, but at last, the machine coughed up some change and out came the ticket with its magnetic strip. He hurried to the same turnstile the guy had used, and the ticket worked like a magic key. He half ran to catch up with the guy, who went up some stairs, across a wire-caged pedestrian bridge and down to platform number four.

There was a glassed-in waiting room, crowded with passengers. AJ wedged himself just inside the door.

Now he was forced to think about what was next. When he got to New York, then what? Did he try to make his way back to Houston? His mom wasn't there anymore. He had a few friends, but they wouldn't take him in, because they'd probably get in trouble. Their parents would probably worry about breaking the law or something. The reality was, he had no good option, none at all.

The train came into the station, big and boxy, in a swirl of steam. Passengers poured onto the platform and climbed aboard. AJ stuck close to Julian. He didn't know why. Maybe because the guy had been nice to the little baby. Whatever. All that mattered to AJ was that now he was on his way.

Thirteen

Julian Gastineaux scooted over to make room for the dark-haired kid. "Go ahead," he said. "It's not taken."

The kid sat down, holding his backpack in his lap.

Julian turned to stare out the train window. There was nothing to see. Daisy was long gone. Still, he could picture her perfectly in his mind, could even smell her hair.

He should have kissed her goodbye. He wished he had.

And this, of course, was the essence of his relationship with Daisy Bellamy, and had been ever since he'd first laid eyes on her one summer. Their relationship seemed, sometimes, to be made up of a series of goodbyes. Awkward ones. He spent a lot of time looking back over his shoulder, wishing he'd done something, or said something, instead of just letting her go.

When it came to Daisy, he had no sense. He was all heart and no head. So many times over the past few years, he wished his damn heart would just tell him to walk away…and stay away. His life would be a whole lot simpler if he'd surrender to circumstances. But of course, where Daisy and Julian were concerned, nothing was simple.

Stretching his long legs until his feet slid under the seat in front of him, he took out a battered paperback novel and folded it back on itself, grateful in a way for the long ride into the city. Enforced downtime. It was a rare thing in Julian's life. Making the grade at Cornell, especially in his chosen major—Engineering and Applied Physics—took everything he had. And on top of that, he was in the ROTC for the Air Force, so he could afford the degree that was sucking his life dry. The reserve officer training for the Air Force was a huge commitment, but not as huge as the tuition bills for an Ivy League college. Some people thought he was out of his gourd, signing up for the military. But the the military had a concrete plan, something he'd lacked all his life. There was a certain satisfaction in knowing exactly what was expected of him.

Besides, when he considered the alternatives, there was no question that he was doing the right thing. If he hadn't worked his butt off to get into college, he'd be in some greasy spoon in a no-name suburb in Southern California, wearing a disposable paper hat at work instead of a parachute pack.

Daisy was scared for him on this J-term training mission. She knew he was going to practice, among other things, how to jump out of an airplane at 20,000 feet, and survive.

And of all the things the ROTC demanded of him, all the mental and physical challenges—the early-morning wakeup calls, punishing endurance training and numbing drills—this was surely the coolest.

The kid next to Julian shifted restlessly in his seat. Julian could tell he was anxious about something. No, scared. That was what Julian sensed, and he grew mildly curious. The boy exuded a kind of toughness most people would find off-putting. Not Julian. He had no idea who the kid was, but he recognized him, because not so long ago, he'd been there. He'd been alone in a crowd and scared shitless, and he covered his fear with that same tough, slit-eyed reserve.

"How you doing?" he asked. Not in a phony-interested way. He was just cracking the door open a little in case the kid felt like talking.

The boy turned and eyed him briefly. Julian knew he intimidated some people. He was biracial, but he looked a hundred percent black. He was naturally big, and had grown broader and more muscular from the Air Force's relentless physical training. His head was shaved like an eight ball. He used to have dreadlocks but, of course, they were anathema to military training, so he'd left them on the floor of a barbershop the day of his induction into the program.

The Latino kid merely shrugged. "I been better," he said.

Julian didn't want to push, but his curiosity was piqued. "Yeah? How's that?"

"I'm okay," the boy muttered, obviously thinking better of trusting a stranger.

"You headed to the city for a visit?" Julian inquired, still casual, not pushing at all.

"Yeah."

Julian wasn't sure how he knew, but the kid was lying. Or hiding something. Or both. "Me, I'm headed down to Montgomery, Alabama," he said, then stuck out his hand. "Julian Gastineaux."

"AJ," the boy replied. He shook hands, though he leaned away from Julian.

All right, I can take a hint, thought Julian. He tried one more time. "You from around here?"

"Nope." The kid's hands tightened on his backpack.

Okay, then. Julian decided to make one final attempt to draw the boy out. "I grew up in New Orleans."

No response from Mr. Happy, so Julian sat back, shut his eyes for a few minutes, thinking about New Orleans. It was just Julian and his dad, back then. The two of them against the world. A physicist at Tulane, Maurice Gastineaux had raised Julian in a loving but haphazard fashion, pretty much what you'd expect from an absentminded professor. Maurice had been a rocket scientist, same as Julian aspired to be. Except unlike his late father, who was all cerebral, Julian hungered for action. He didn't simply want to be a rocket scientist. He wanted to be the *rocket.*

He dozed a little, then was awakened by the vibration of his mobile phone, indicating a text message. He flipped it open. Miss you already, Daisy had written.

There was nothing to say to that. She already knew the way he missed her. It was the kind of missing that felt like a limb blown off, a huge void of hurt beyond imagining. His roommates at Cornell told him repeatedly that he was nuts. What guy in his right mind fell for a girl who lived a three-hour drive away, and who had another guy's baby, for Christ's sake?

Then Julian would show them a photograph of Daisy and they'd be like, oh. Now we get it.

She had the kind of looks that made people stop and stare, dropping whatever they were doing for a few seconds. She had that yellow-haired goddess thing going on; you could picture her in a Renaissance painting, surfing on a half shell, her long blond hair twisting in the wind. But the thing Julian's roommates didn't get was that, even if she looked like one of the gorgons, Julian would still probably be into her.

But her life was complicated. She had a baby. And not just any baby. Charlie had the red hair and blue blood of his father, Logan O'Donnell. Logan was the opposite of Julian in every way. Lily-white, he'd grown up surrounded by wealth and privilege. The only thing Julian and Logan had in common was that they were both in love with Daisy Bellamy.

Agitated, he opened his eyes again. The kid next to him was watching intently out the window. Julian studied him for a moment, remembering the seminar in military intel he'd taken as part of his training. The boy was exhibiting signs of stress—jiggling his foot, chewing his lip. Something about this boy reminded Julian of himself when he was younger. He'd been about the same age as this kid when his dad had wrecked his car, eventually dying of his injuries. Julian used to deal with his own stress and uncertainty by taking physical risks, anything from jumping off a high dive to skateboarding a dry concrete spillway, knowing it could flood without warning at any moment.

"So you're headed to the city to do what, if you don't mind my asking?" Julian said.

"I mind."

"Just trying to make conversation. It's a long way to the city." Julian shrugged and turned his attention to his phone. He felt a little strange doing it, but he sent a message to his brother, Connor Davis. Connor's brother-in-law was Rourke McKnight, Avalon's chief of police. This kid was no criminal, but it probably wasn't a terrible idea to let someone know.

Fourteen

Kim took a break from going over her mother's books. She pushed the papers away from her on the library table and stretched her neck one way, then the other, frowning as she kneaded her tense muscles.

Bo was across the room at his laptop, where he'd been alternately muttering under his breath and shifting in his seat for the past hour. The downstairs rotunda was the designated place for work, and at any given time, one of the guests could be found here, checking e-mail or surfing the Web. Kim suspected it was no coincidence that Bo had decided to work at his computer the same time she did.

Her stomach knotted as she sat back down and stared at the screen of her laptop, which displayed a spreadsheet.

"Everything okay?" Bo asked. "You're looking stressed out there."

She nodded, the figures blurring before her eyes. "Money troubles," she admitted, then paused. *A person's finances are a strictly private affair.* She could still hear her father's imperative voice, echoing across time. She used to regard this as an admirable notion, but now she knew why he had refused to talk about money.

Guess what, Dad, she thought. *I'm breaking the cycle.* "I've been trying to get a handle on something here," she told Bo. "My mother was widowed a few years back, and that's when she discovered that my father had incurred a massive debt. Neither she nor I had any idea he was in trouble. She kept it from me until recently, taking a crazy loan against the value of this place. She also bought some kind of annuity and an insurance policy, both of which appear to presume she'll live to be a hundred and fifty." Kim found herself revealing a list of disturbing discoveries she'd made as she parsed through the records. Her mother had been paid a visit by a smooth-talking salesman. He'd managed to disguise the liability aspects of each transaction until the deal was closed and he was long gone. The next month, Penelope had been hit by exorbitant origination fees and crushing monthly payments.

"She didn't even tell me," Kim said. "She just started falling behind every month, and then taking in boarders. I can't believe she didn't tell me."

"Probably didn't want to worry you," he said. "Or embarrass herself. People will pay almost any price to save their pride."

She thought about the explosive night in L.A., and nodded glumly. "True."

He leaned back in his chair, folding his arms behind his head. "Well, I'm not saying I know much about this stuff, but I bet there's help available. See, this state has laws to protect people from predatory and pressure sales of financial products."

She lifted her eyebrows in surprise. "How would you know?"

He indicated a fat three-ring binder on the table next to him. "Part of my rookie training," he said. "Most rookies are a lot younger than me, and even more ignorant."

She thought of the cars, jewelry, boats and even airplanes some newly fledged professional athletes often flaunted. So-called financial advisers circled like buzzards, enticing naive players with too many bewildering and expensive choices.

"Something tells me you're not ignorant at all. Do you have some kind of hidden talent for finance?"

"Not particularly, but I've been broke before. You learn a lot about yourself, being broke. And if you're smart, you learn how to avoid it in the future." He flipped through the pages of his binder. "If you think your mother's been victimized, you should call the state attorney general." He handed her a page from his reading, and she copied down the number and e-mail address.

"I feel so bad for my mom," Kim said. "She's supposed to relax and enjoy her retirement. Instead, thanks to my late father, she's in a world of trouble. And it looks like she unknowingly compounded the problem with this horrific loan."

Kim caught the look on Bo's face. "My father wasn't a bad man," she said. "He wasn't even a bad father. But it turns out he was a lousy businessman, who happened to be good at covering his tracks."

"Was he doing something illegal?" Bo asked.

"No. Just lived beyond his means. Far, far beyond."

"It's the American way," he said with an ironic smile.

"In my father's case, it was his pride run amok. I wish

I'd known that, but I never really saw his heart. God, there was a time when I would've done anything to please him." She'd lived her life to fulfill some vision he'd had. She thought if she could just be the daughter he wanted her to be, her life would be perfect. Her father had taken up so much room in her life, and all along, the things he'd valued were built on a false and shaky foundation. She wondered how much her father had to do with the choices she'd made. He'd been so proud of her career; he'd loved knowing she had an exciting, dynamic job that seemed both glamorous and prestigious. The fact that her father was so impressed by her career probably kept her on the job long after the fun had gone out of it.

"He always expected so much from me," she confessed to Bo. "He wanted my B-pluses to be A's. My performances in music and sports always had to be first-place finishes. And my father was all about social connections, too. The older I got, the more he would urge me to cultivate the 'right' friends." She'd attended the best private school in Manhattan, not only for the education but for the boost it would give her in her climb to the heights of society.

"Maybe it would have been sort of all right," she said, "if he'd really had the money he wanted everyone to think he had. Instead, it was all a pretense. He wanted the world to think he could afford our lifestyle—and for what? I wonder if he even thought about what would happen after he was gone." She flipped through an old file, the pages marked with the slash of his signature. "Now I'm finding out things I never knew about him. Things I was happier not knowing."

"Be glad you knew him, even a little," Bo said. "Mine

was almost never around. My brother, Stoney, and I grew up half wild. Our mom wasn't big on supervision."

She tried to envision him and his brother—*Stoney*—as wild kids, making a mental picture of long hair, skateboards, black T-shirts, ripped jeans. As a girl, she would have been fascinated. But in high school and college, she'd dated only the most conventional of boys. She knew instinctively that Bo had not been the sort you introduced to your parents. Her father always wanted to know the most random things about a guy—who his parents were and where they'd gone to college and what business they were in, what clubs they belonged to and what their politics were.

Once, she'd asked her father to explain his obsession with connections. She had expected him to dismiss her. Instead, he'd actually given the question some thought. "Safety and security," he said. "That's why connections are important. When someone is well connected, it means he is offering so much more than himself."

Now she stared down at the quagmire of paperwork he'd left behind, and the remembered words echoed with cruel irony. "I was *over*supervised," she told Bo. "That's got its downside, too."

"Do yourself a favor," he said. "Don't be too hard on the guy. It's tough, arguing with a ghost."

"I take it that's something you've tried."

"My mother's been gone five years, and sometimes I still catch myself."

"I'm sorry." She watched the play of firelight on his face, feeling an unexpected bond with him.

"It's okay," he said. "Makes me want to do a good job with AJ."

"You will," she told him. "You are. And thank you for this." She indicated the information he'd given her. Kim felt her stomach unknot a little more. "It's funny, how things work out. I had no idea she was in such trouble, and if I'd stayed in L.A., I still wouldn't have known. So even though it wasn't part of my plan, coming back here turned out to be a good thing. For my mom, anyway." She watched the flames dancing in the fireplace. "Maybe for me, too. I tried to plan out every detail of my life and ended up walking away from it all. I should feel bad about that, but I don't."

He provided a surprisingly sympathetic ear and it was a relief just to share the burden. To look into his sapphire-blue eyes and see real interest there. *Don't be attracted to him,* she admonished herself. *That's the last thing you need in your life.* Yet it felt so good to simply talk to someone. It had been literally years since she'd had genuine people in her life, yet she'd been so busy in L.A., she hadn't even noticed.

"Yeah, I gave up trying to plan stuff out," he said. "That way, everything that happens to me is a surprise." When he smiled, his blue eyes conveyed a message of utter sincerity. So much for not being attracted to him.

"I take it you like surprises," she said.

"They're a mixed bag. Getting tapped for Yankees spring training, with a shot at the roster—I'd call that a good one. Being asked to take care of AJ—now, that's a mixed bag. Don't get me wrong, it's a dream come true, getting to meet him at last, but I wish the circumstances were different."

As she often had since meeting AJ, she wondered about his mother. Yolanda Martinez. Judging by AJ's looks— creamy skin, deeply expressive brown eyes, a thoughtful

mouth and rare, heart-melting smile—Yolanda was probably beautiful. And judging by AJ's devotion to her, she
was a good mother. Yet she'd never let Bo see his son. Bo
was her last resort.

"You look as if you're about to ask me a hard question,"
he commented, correctly reading her expression.

"I don't know if it's a question or not," she said. "Just
wondering about AJ's mom."

"Wondering why she didn't want me involved in AJ's
life, you mean. She married somebody else when AJ was
a baby, didn't want him to get confused." Bo didn't seem
self-conscious about letting Kim see the world of hurt in
his face. "Guess she didn't realize, a kid is *never* confused
about stuff like this." He glanced at his watch. "This is the
longest damn school day in the history of the world. Whose
idea was that to make the school day so damn long?"

"I just hope he's having a good time," she said.

"It's school," he replied. "How good can it be?"

"You could call the main office and ask," she suggested.

"I thought about doing that," Bo said, "but he's so touchy
about me right now, I don't want to push it. Maybe later."

"The first day of school is scary no matter what," she
said. "I don't know if there's any way to make it easier."

"And here I am making it harder on the kid," he said.

"Because you're going away to fame school." She could
tell it was weighing on him.

"I'm contractually obligated to go. Now, I could blow it
off, stay here with AJ and hope for the best, but according
to my agent, that's a huge risk. If I go, if I make it in this
career, it could make a huge difference not just in my life,
but in AJ's. His mother wouldn't have to work all the time.

He could live in a house, go to college. Anyway, it's only temporary. Dino's going to take care of AJ while I'm gone. He says he wants to do it."

Kim hesitated. She could tell Bo was trying hard to sell himself on the idea. She could only imagine what it had been like for him, to discover in the middle of his big career break that he was responsible for a child. "In this house, he'll get plenty of backup support," she said, trying to sound reassuring.

"That's real nice of you to say. Funny thing about AJ. He tends to bring out the 'nice' in everybody."

"I've noticed. He's a special boy."

"Yeah, I'm proud of him, though I can't take any credit."

Kim's computer signaled an incoming e-mail. She glanced at the screen and saw that it was from Lloyd Johnson. She quickly hit the delete button. "Are you sure you want to delete this message?" asked a pop-up window. She stabbed the Enter button. *Yes.* Then she slapped the laptop closed. The tension in her neck and shoulders returned full force.

"You look like you could use a neck rub," Bo suggested.

She flushed at the knowing expression on his face. For a fraction of a second, she was tempted by the offer. There was nothing quite like the sensation of a pair of large male hands gently massaging away the tension. Unfortunately, the large, male hands always came attached to a large male.

"No, thank you," she said.

"I wouldn't hurt you," Bo said in a quiet voice.

Kim's stomach dropped. She realized then that he knew. Either he could see past the makeup, or he'd figured out why she'd flown across the country without so much as a change of clothes. Her throat felt dry and prickly, hurting as she asked, "Is it that obvious?"

"Probably just to me. The way I was raised... Let's just say I know what a woman is like after some son of a bitch hits her. My mother couldn't seem to stay away from guys like that."

"I'm sorry," Kim said. "It must have been terrible for you."

"Are you safe now?" he asked, his voice still quiet.

"Yes, yes, I am. Let's just say I'm a fast learner." Lloyd was too busy and self-absorbed to come looking for her— that was what she believed, anyway. Now here was this man, asking her if she was safe, offering to comfort her, and the concern in his eyes made her want to cry.

"You want to talk about it?"

Yes. "No," she said quickly. "I'm fine, really. I don't need rescuing, if that's what you mean."

"Maybe not," Bo said quietly. "I don't pretend to know all that much about women, but you're not that hard to read."

He was amazingly easy to talk to; he'd already proven to be a good listener. She didn't feel the need to protect him from the ugly details as she did her mother. "His name is Lloyd Johnson," she said. She could tell by Bo's expression that he knew exactly who Lloyd was. "He started out as a client with my PR firm. We dated for a while, and for the past few months, it had been serious. We were going to get a place together."

The thought now caused a chill to slide across her skin. "The night I left, there was a reception at a private club," she said. "A very big night for Lloyd. And for me, too. He had just agreed to sign with Fandango, an athletic wear company. I'd worked for weeks to make it happen." It had been so much more than a publicity project for her. She'd helped broker a major deal, one that paved the way to her future. She could still remember the high ripples of anticipation that had buoyed her along that evening. Everything had fallen into place for Lloyd…and for her. The one thing she forgot to consider was the one thing that never varied for athletes of his caliber—his ego. "The sponsor's daughter came with a date—Marshall Walters—who just happened to be Lloyd's biggest rival, both on and off the court." The two had been in a brawl on the court earlier that season. The altercation had resulted in Lloyd being suspended for a dozen games. It had cost him millions, and was a constant sore spot.

"I saw their latest fight on the news," Bo said. "Too bad they're not boxers."

"Mute boxers," she added. "I've always thought the world would be a better place if we didn't have NBA players asking each other 'How does my ass taste?' in public. And don't you dare laugh."

"Not laughing," he said.

"I won't defend Lloyd, but Marshall Walters was pushing his buttons that night. For a while, I managed to keep them on opposite sides of the room. Lloyd was mad at me, but I figured that was less dangerous than letting him get mad at Walters. After he got a few drinks in him, Lloyd decided Marshall's presence was all my fault," she continued. "I was in charge of the guest list. The daughter was listed as bringing a plus-one, but I stupidly didn't bother to research who that might be. It was a setup, an ambush—Walters knew his presence would drive Lloyd crazy, and as for the daughter—I don't know what she was thinking.

And Lloyd took the bait. He was going to confront Walters, so that's when I stepped in. That's what was caught by the stupid cell-phone video somebody shot—me, throwing myself under the bus."

"You picked a fight with him so he wouldn't fight with Marshall Walters."

She remembered clearly Lloyd's words. He'd called her a name that made her flinch even now. He loudly declared he was firing her, and claimed she'd never work in the business again. "Not exactly a high point in my career," she said, "but it gave me an unexpected moment of clarity. And I realized nothing—no career, deal, boyfriend and no amount of money could keep me there, doing what I was doing. That's when I walked out. I thought that was the end of everything. What I didn't count on was him following me to the parking lot."

She could still hear the echo of his furious voice: "You're walking out on me? You're walking out on me." He'd answered his own question.

"You fired me. Good night, Lloyd."

"Not so fast. You don't walk out on me."

"Watch me." She'd turned on her heel. She shouldn't have shown that flash of defiance. That was all it took to spark his temper. Yet, even then, she hadn't anticipated his violence. It was like an accident she played over and over in her mind. What could she have done differently?

She got up and wandered over to the fireplace, staring into the flames. "That's why I showed up here with nothing," she whispered.

Bo Crutcher didn't say anything. She didn't need for him to say anything. It was enough that he'd listened. Nothing had changed, yet at the same time, she felt something shift between them.

"I don't regret what I did," she said, "but I definitely picked the wrong time to show up penniless on my mother's doorstep."

The ensuing silence felt...safe. Comfortable. They were easing into a friendship, Kim realized. She felt him watching her. "What?" she asked.

"So do you still want that neck rub, or am I a jerk for asking?"

She couldn't take her eyes off him. "You're not a jerk."

"Not today, anyway," he said, slowly getting up from the table.

She forgot to say no. She didn't want to say no. The look in his eyes hypnotized all the words out of her. She was already imagining how his hands would feel when the phone rang, shattering the moment.

The sound kicked her back to reality as she snatched up the receiver.

"This is Kimberly van Dorn."

"Miss van Dorn, it's Rourke McKnight of the Avalon Police Department."

She frowned, hoping her mother wasn't in even more trouble. She glanced at Bo, finding an unexpected sense of balance as she gazed into his eyes. "Yes?" she prompted.

"I'm just calling to check on something," said Chief McKnight. "It's about one of your guests."

Fifteen

Grand Central Station was one of those places people mentioned when they wanted to describe something really busy.

"It's Grand Central Station in here," a teacher might say
about a classroom.

The real Grand Central Station lived up to the description. It reminded AJ of a human anthill inside a marble
cube, with everyone scurrying in different directions.

AJ had no idea which direction to scurry. Still, he knew
better than to stand around looking lost, so he joined a
stream of people heading for the exit. Along one wall he
spied a bank of pay phones. Almost no one used pay
phones anymore, except people who couldn't afford a
mobile phone. Like AJ.

There were stickers on the wall around the phones, advertising bail bonds, help for suicide prevention, addicts,
runaways. AJ wondered if that was what he'd become—a
runaway. A knot of fear formed in his stomach, compound-
ing the lump of sadness in his throat and the keen sense of
yearning that burned in his chest. All these emotions to-

gether made him want to throw up, so he followed some signs to the men's room.

A couple of guys there halted their conversation and glared at him, making AJ change his mind and back out the door. He cast about for somebody to ask for help, but suddenly everyone looked sketchy to him. A group of teenagers poured in through one of the entrances, and a couple of them checked him out. He could feel their stares from twenty yards, and something told him they weren't like the guy he'd sat next to on the train. He tried to act all cool, putting on the dangerous slit-eyed expression and unhurried saunter of the gangbangers at his old school. He headed for daylight and found himself on a busy street jammed with traffic, mostly yellow taxis and delivery trucks. Honking horns, whistles and shouts clouded the air, along with the cindery smell of exhaust.

Although there was no snow here, the city felt cold. He should never have come here. Bad things happened to kids who ran away to the big city.

On the other hand, what could be worse than losing your mother?

At least he fit in a little better here. There were plenty of brown-skinned people everywhere, workmen in blue jumpsuits doing street repairs, guys in hard hats on a scaffold, people stopping for a chat at the coffee carts on every street corner. As he wandered along the street, he occasionally caught Spanish being spoken, just a whiff, like the scent of hot dogs in the air.

He dug the slip of paper out of his pocket, something he'd printed off Bo's computer last night. It was a place with a New York City address: *Casa de Esperanza*. The

House of Hope. Although he hadn't planned this trip out, he'd hung on to the printout, somehow knowing it would be important. He studied the address and prayed it wasn't far, shivering as a gust of wind howled through the street. He didn't understand how people could live in this cold weather. In Houston, people complained about the heat, but here in the cold, you had to curl up against the wind and hope you wouldn't freeze to death.

He scanned the throng of people, trying to figure out who to ask for directions—the guy with the coffee cart on the corner? The grim businessman with the briefcase? The skinny girl with a long scarf wound around and around her neck? He approached a lady with graying hair, wearing a plain cloth coat and worn leather gloves. There was something about her that seemed to be friendly enough. Unlike most people in the crowd, she didn't act like she was in a hurry.

"Ma'am," he said, "I'm looking for One Hundred and Sixteenth Street East. Do you know how to get there?"

"Sure. Go a block over to Third Avenue. Almost all the buses there go uptown. You all right?" she asked, checking him out.

"Fine, thank you." AJ thought it was nice of her to ask. It usually sucked, being puny, because people often thought he was younger than he actually was. Sometimes, though, it made a certain type of person act nicer to him. As he headed in the direction the woman had indicated, he tried to remind himself that there were kind people in the world, and that things had a way of working out. Yet as he progressed, he felt more and more lost and out of place. He was as homeless as the guys he passed in church doorways, huddled against the cold. And AJ was hungry on top of everything else. Food vendors were everywhere, scenting the air with the aroma of roasting hot dogs, peanuts and pretzels. There was more exotic stuff, too, sold by people with heavy accents and big iron pans of chicken and lamb skewers. AJ resisted temptation, though. He kept his shoulders hunched against the wind and put one foot in front of the other.

He reached Third Avenue but didn't spot a bus stop right away, so he walked in the direction of the traffic. The street numbers got higher as he went along, so that was something. He hoped the Latino place wasn't much farther. Finally, when his toes went numb, he asked directions again and hopped on what he thought was the right bus. He paid the fare, found a seat and began counting off the streets as it crawled through the lurching traffic.

The neighborhood changed every few blocks, from grimy shopfronts to fancy apartment buildings to official-looking government and school buildings. Then the bus nosed its way into a neighborhood with shrines of flowers on some of the street corners, familiar-looking *tiendas,* rows of brick buildings, walls exploding with graffiti and a big covered mercado with colorful displays of pepper wreaths, lacy *quinceañera* dresses, piñatas hanging from the awnings and bottled imported drinks lined up on open counters.

He stepped off the bus, thinking, *now I'm getting somewhere.* Yet he didn't fit in around here, either. Down one block, he spied a school. At least he thought it was a school, although it looked a lot different from his school in Texas. This one was an old brick building, with ball courts surrounded by a chain-link fence, mounds of dirty snow in the corners. He hurried in the opposite direction, sticking to the street with all the shops. Everyone seemed to have somewhere to go or a job to do.

Just as AJ started to feel completely invisible, someone noticed him. "Hey, kid," a voice said, "whatchoo doing? Skipping school?"

AJ saw a boy who looked just a little older than him, gesturing him over. Although the kid seemed friendly enough, there was something about him that made AJ nervous. He tried not to let it show as he said, "Just looking for an address."

"Yeah? What's that?"

AJ showed him the address on the printout.

"I know where that is," the kid said. "Come on. I'll take you." He fell in step with AJ. "I'm Denny."

"AJ." He stuffed his hands in his pockets. Looked around the street. Buses, taxis, delivery vans. They passed a worn-out city park, where the trampled grass was dead and pigeons littered the sidewalks.

"Where you from, AJ?"

"Texas."

Denny took out a phone and swiftly texted something. He barely had to look at the keypad as his thumbs pressed the buttons. AJ frowned. "What are you doing?"

"Texting my *cholos*. We can all hang out."

"Maybe later," AJ said. "I better check in at this place."

"Yeah, okay, but I gotta make a stop along the way. It's not much farther."

AJ didn't like Denny. It was something he knew in his gut before he admitted it to himself. Denny looked normal, except maybe he was wearing eye makeup. That was definitely weird. And he smelled of something AJ couldn't quite identify. Pine-Sol cleaner, maybe.

Before long, the *cholos* joined them, and that was when AJ knew without a doubt that he'd made a bad decision. They were some tough-looking customers for sure, two boys in baggies and big parkas, and a girl wearing lots of fake-looking jewelry. She had on lots of makeup and a scare-do—hair teased up high.

"You said it was nearby," he reminded Denny. "That was like twenty minutes ago. I bet you don't really know where this place is."

Denny laughed, but it wasn't a happy sound. "What's your hurry, eh? They're all churchy and boring at that place, and they'll get you in trouble."

"C'mon inside where it's warm," the girl invited, pushing open a heavy door. AJ felt a momentary relief from the cold, but that was quickly eclipsed by an itchy, restless anxiety. They went up the stairs of a building that smelled of frying onions and urinal cakes.

Graffiti covered the walls. On the third floor the girl unlocked a battered door that looked as if it had been kicked in a few times and repaired. A tinny-sounding radio played somewhere. Two teenagers lounged in front of a TV with the sound turned up to compete with the radio.

"I'm gonna go now," AJ said, lingering by the door.

"Man, don't be such a *chonger.* Hang with us for a while. You don't need the *Casa.*"

"I'll check it out and see for myself," he said.

"Just stick around," Denny insisted. "It's better that way."

"What way?"

"Our way."

"No, thanks." AJ made a snap decision. Instead of trying to act all cool for a bunch of strangers, he forgot about pride.

He remembered something Bo had told him—*There's no shame in looking out for yourself. Be who you are.*

He acted like the scared kid he was, and ran.

In all his years on this earth, Bo figured he knew what it was like to be afraid. He knew what love and hate were, and what it felt like to be abandoned. He thought he knew fear—the way it tasted and smelled, the way it trickled across your scalp and down your neck.

He was wrong. He'd never, ever in his whole life felt a fear like this, like knowing someone small and defenseless was at risk. It was a painful physical affliction, like freezing to death or suffocating. The moment he'd been informed that AJ never showed up at school, this new horror superseded all other fears he'd ever felt. Until AJ, he'd never known this kind of terror existed. Picturing his boy alone in the world, and lost, Bo could think of many dangers, so many he felt as if his head might explode.

And it was a kind of madness, too, so intense that Kim insisted on going with him to the police station. The second Bo had hung up the phone after speaking to Chief McKnight, she had said, "We'd better get going. I'll drive."

He'd been too freaked out to argue. Kim gathered up the things the chief had told them to bring—laptop, ID, photograph—and took him straight to the station.

Lt. Brenda Flynn immediately took charge of the case. When a child went missing, there was no delay or lag time. No designated waiting period. The assumption was that the kid was in trouble *now.*

Bo had a few pictures of AJ on his cell phone. His hand spasmed and trembled as he gave it to an assistant. These were uploaded to a database to go out with the alert. The lieutenant questioned Bo and Kim about what they knew. He told her about Yolanda, as much as he knew.

Had she been in touch with AJ?

No.

Did AJ have a cell phone?

No.

Did he have friends or relatives in New York City?

Not that Bo knew of.

Was he ill? On medication? Mentally altered?

No, no and no.

Each question was another turn of the screw.

"I'm an idiot," Bo muttered. "I believed him when he said he'd go to school on his own, that he didn't want to be treated like a kindergartner."

"Sign here," Lt. Flynn said. "This gives us permission to access the browsing history of your laptop."

"You got it." Bo understood he was giving up all kinds of privacy, but he didn't care. At the same time, he tried to remember whether or not he'd been looking at porn lately. Nope. He had nothing against porn, but it was completely useless as a substitute for the real thing, so he didn't really spend much time looking at it online.

The lieutenant's assistant, who was also an expert in digital forensics, went through the browsing history and found an online trail through a maze of Web sites.

"Here are a few possibilities," the assistant said. "Your son's been busy." He gave Bo a quick overview of AJ's browsing. No gaming sites or networking with friends. The boy was desperately seeking a swift resolution to his mother's troubles. He'd perused an impressive array of sites devoted to immigration and naturalization, churches and agencies dedicated to helping immigrants regardless of their legal status.

Bo's heart sank as he thought of AJ, sitting for hours at the computer. He'd thought the boy was playing games. Hell, he *should* be playing games. He was only a kid. His head should be full of fun and games and stupid stuff like fart jokes and wacky inventions. Not immigration law.

"He hit print from this page." The assistant paused. "He printed quite a few pages."

The icy fist in Bo's gut twisted a little. "It'll be like finding a needle in a haystack."

"Not quite." Lt. Flynn handed him a MapQuest printout. "I've already uploaded the pictures to a special dispatch. Every substation in New York will see it."

Bo felt ready to jump out of his skin. He got up and paced, feeling Kim's eyes on him. "It's going to be all right," she said.

"Thank you, Pollyanna," Bo snapped.

"I'm not being a Pollyanna," she said. "Just realistic."

"Yeah, what's the view like from behind those rosy lenses?" He was being a prick and he knew it. He shut his mouth before he did any further damage. But shit. She understood nothing, he thought. She'd been raised like a hothouse flower, insulated from things that were harmful or ugly. Hell, she'd probably been to finishing school, for all he knew. Whatever the hell "finishing school" was. People used the term all the time, but he doubted they had any idea what it was. She'd gone from her sheltered childhood to USC to a career in some tony L.A. firm. She didn't know squat about the real world.

Then he remembered the bruise on her face, so artfully concealed with makeup. He was wrong about her. "Sorry," he said.

She waved away the apology. "Look at the guy who phoned about him. Julian Gastineaux. He was just a stranger on a train. He didn't have to send that text message about AJ. He did it because he was concerned."

When she was right, she was right. The pounding in his gut abated. "What am I supposed to do?" he asked the lieutenant. "I can't just wait around for something to happen. Shouldn't I at least go to the city?"

"You should let us do our job," said Flynn. "I know that's hard, but the best thing you can do for your boy is to give us a chance to get all the info into the system. NYPD already has the pictures, train time, description. We'll add the likely destinations next, and—"

Bo's cell phone rang, and he snatched it up. "Crutcher."

Every head in the room turned his way. There was a beat of silence. His heart stumbled.

"It's me," said a small voice. "It's AJ."

Bo slumped against the closed door, giving everyone a thumbs-up sign.

All during the drive to the city, Bo rehearsed what he was going to say. He pictured himself giving a stern but concerned fatherly lecture on decision-making and responsibility. He would explain the need for supervision. He would be the very model of the responsible adult.

Instead, what he ended up doing the minute he saw AJ was driven by nothing but instinct.

AJ stood out in the busy, brightly lit community center.

He was perfectly still, hugging his backpack to his chest. When he spied Bo, his face softened with relief and despair. And whatever Bo had planned to do and say, it all flew out of his head. He opened his arms, grabbed the boy and held him close. AJ seemed to fit perfectly against his chest, warm and alive, smelling of shampoo and the city and peculiar smell that had no name. *My son,* Bo thought. *I'm finally holding my son.* Bo's entire body shuddered with relief, intense and so sweet that it hurt.

"Don't you ever do that again," he said in a rough whisper. "Do you hear me? Don't you run away again."

AJ was trembling, but Bo felt him nod his head.

"Come on," Bo said, his throat hurting with emotion. "It's been a hell of a day. Let's go."

Out on the street, teenagers were circling around the car, tough-looking kids in sagging black clothes slashed with color. The roadster wasn't the kind of car you saw in a neighborhood like this. Bo felt AJ stiffen beside him, and as soon as Bo hit the unlock button, the boy ducked into the passenger side and quickly slammed the door. Amid the murmured Spanish commentary, Bo caught *gabacho*—a term he knew well—but decided to ignore the derogatory comment. He nodded politely to the onlookers, then took his time getting in and heading for the expressway.

"You're okay?" Bo asked.

"Yes."

"Nobody messed with you?"

He noticed AJ twisting around in his seat, looking back through the window.

"Did those kids mess with you?" Bo persisted.

AJ turned back around and adjusted his seat belt. "No."

"Some of them looked pretty tough," Bo said, trying to get the boy to talk.

"You thought so?"

"Yeah. I grew up around kids like that," he explained. "I got my ass kicked nearly every day at school or baseball practice."

Finally, AJ showed a spurt of interest. "Why?"

"Bullies don't need a reason. I was probably a little turd, though." He glanced sideways in time to see AJ's mouth soften, on the verge of smiling.

"What did you do about it?" he asked.

"Ran like a scalded dog. They still caught me, though. I was a puny little thing."

"You?"

"Yep. Just a tadpole, until my growth spurt started. Right around the time I turned fourteen, I started waking up at night hollering from the pain in my legs. 'Them's growing pains,' my big brother, Stoney, used to tell me. Turns out they were, and by the next year, I was more than six feet tall, and people stopped messing with me. They tended to back off, thinking they couldn't take me. Which was a lucky thing, because to this day, I don't know the first thing about fighting."

AJ fell silent, the fragile thread of connection broken. Bo hoped he'd speak up again, explain himself without prompting. Clearly, that wasn't going to happen. After a while, Bo said, "So why'd you do it, AJ? Why'd you take off like that?"

Silence.

"I can't hear you." Bo tried to keep the annoyance from his voice. "Talk to me. I'm trying to understand."

"I wanted to find some place where they could help me get back with my mom," said AJ.

"I want that, too, AJ, but skipping school and jumping on a train is no way to handle it. Jesus, why would you take off like that?"

"Because nothing's happening." His voice was low and unsteady.

Bo pulled into a loading zone and turned to him. "Listen, there are people who would like nothing better than to send your mom south of the border and out of the U.S. forever. They'll use any excuse to justify it. If you become a runaway, they'll claim you're a baby outlaw and they'll say, 'Why should we grant residency to a woman who is raising a delinquent?'"

"So every time a kid does something bad, they have the right to deport the mother?"

"Nope, if the mom's a U.S. citizen, we get to keep her. I didn't create this system but you need to abide by it."

"The system's not working. My mom didn't do anything wrong. She did her job, every day. She works harder than anybody I know. She paid her taxes, I know she did because she showed me one time."

"She's a good person," Bo said. "We know that. She doesn't deserve what happened to her, and that's why we're going to work so hard to help her. Just because you're not seeing any progress doesn't mean nothing's happening. Running away from me is probably the worst thing you can do."

The kid showed iron control over his emotions. He narrowed his eyes and turned to Bo. "I can think of worse."

Bo took a deep breath. Flexed his hands on the steering wheel. "I know you're bummed about your mom. But what are you going to do? You can do crazy stuff, like skip school and take the train to the city, which accomplishes nothing except maybe to prove to authorities that you're trouble. Or you can try to make the best of a bad situation."

"Easy for you to say."

The terror that had gripped Bo earlier was turning to ice crystals. "You think? Well, you're wrong. And if you think anything about this situation is easy for me, yeah, go ahead and tell yourself that. Just remember, I'm the last person you should be running away from. I'm the only one working on getting your mom back. Nobody's more committed to that than I am."

"Sure, so you can take off, too. That's all you care about."

"It's business," he explained. "It's my job, and I have to do it. And going to school is your job."

More silence. It was nearly dark now. In the falling light, Bo caught the gleam of a tear in AJ's eyes. It cut him like a knife, seeing the boy in pain like that. AJ had lost his mother. Now Bo was planning to leave him.

Or not.

He put the car in gear and pulled out into the stream of traffic. "Listen, maybe I was wrong, AJ. You gotta remember, I'm new to this…to being responsible for somebody. I don't need to go down to Virginia. Let me figure out a way around that."

"You just said it was your job."

"You're my job, too."

"I didn't ask for that," he said.

"Yeah, well, you got it. So I'm taking you home. And don't give me any lip about Avalon not being home, because it is. Right now, that's your home base."

Sixteen

"You're crazy," said Bagwell, practically yelling at Bo. "It's in your contract. You have to go to Fame School." They were at the Hilltop Tavern, drinking beer and shooting pool with Ray Tolley and Eddie Haven. It was boys' night out and the first time he'd left AJ since the New York incident. Dino was taking AJ out for pizza and a movie tonight.

Though Bo no longer tended bar at the Hilltop, it always felt like home to him. "I don't have to," he said, twisting a cube of chalk on the end of his pool cue. "And it's a pre-contract agreement with the Yankees, anyway. I've memorized practically every word. It says I'll pursue media training, and I will." He lined up a shot, rammed it home with lightning-quick accuracy. "I don't know what they have left to teach me. I've been trying for this practically all my life. I've dreamed about everything, every damn minute."

"You know what they say about dreams," Bagwell pointed out.

"No, what?"

"They're always better than the reality."

"Bullshit."

"There you go. That's why you're supposed to have rookie training. You have to learn not to swear, or chew with your mouth open, stuff like that."

"I can figure that out on my own," Bo insisted.

Bagwell snorted. "What, is there some kind of online course?" He paced back and forth near the pool table, clearly impatient to play the winner.

For the first time, Bo clearly understood why. He aimed again and missed. "I can't up and leave."

"Because of AJ?" asked Rayburn Tolley, lining up a corner shot.

"Yeah, exactly. I thought it would be simple. I'd take off, Dino would look after the kid. Turns out the kid's kind of freaked out. I'm afraid if I leave, he might run away again, and he might stay gone." He took a small sip of beer. "I can't risk it."

"You're an admirable fool, that's what you are," said Ray.

Bo shook his head. "Don't admire me."

Tolley took his shot, sinking his target. "Okay, I won't. No problem."

Bo grinned. "You're a real pal."

"What about taking AJ with you?" asked Eddie Haven. "I spent my whole life tagging after my parents, and it didn't kill me." Eddie came from a show-business family that had traveled constantly.

Ray—who had been Eddie's arresting officer in an old, old case—threw back his head and guffawed. "If you consider court-ordered community service 'okay,' then I guess you're doing just fine," he said.

"I'm not dragging AJ anywhere else," Bo said. "He's been uprooted enough."

"I have a solution," said Bagwell. "You can do a lot of the stuff they work on at Fame School, only you could do it here. With Kimberly van Dorn. She was a media trainer in L.A."

Bo had been thinking the same thing. He pictured himself spending hours and hours with her, being told what to do and how to do it. The hours and hours together he could handle. Being bossed around by her... "Not a good idea. Besides, I'm told this whole thing is about meeting people. That's the point, not which fork to use and how to order wine."

"Is not," Bagwell said simply. "There's plenty she could teach you."

Meanwhile, Ray lined up another shot, sank it.

Damn. Ray was really on his game tonight. He sank two more balls before he missed and handed the play back to Bo.

"Seriously," Bagwell added, "there are things you need to know before you start running with the big dogs. A guy can easily be led or manipulated into saying stuff." Bagwell knew what he was talking about. He had played exactly three stellar games with the Boston Red Sox before an injury had ended his major-league aspirations. He'd returned home to Avalon, where he went to work at his father's small-engine repair business and play for the Hornets in summer and in the Dominican Republic in winter.

"She'll drive me crazy. Why her?" Bo asked with a scowl. His turn again. He tapped the hole he wanted his ball to go into, and lined up his shot. He misjudged the angle and the ball hit one bumper, then wandered away, a failure.

"No need to play dumb," Bagwell said. "We'd all do exactly the same thing in your shoes."

Seventeen

Leaving the bank with her mother, Kim felt a sense of cautious optimism. Bo had been right; as a victim of pressure sales, her mother was entitled to recourse from the bank. Fancy that, Kim thought. Information from a guy they could trust. It had to be a first.

In consultation with a specialist at the bank, she and her mother had worked out a payment plan that would help Penelope extricate herself from the punishing, complicated loan, assuming they were very careful, and a little bit lucky.

"We should celebrate," Kim said.

"I'm on a strict budget now, and I intend to stick to it." Penelope snapped her pocketbook shut and headed for the car. "We need to stop at the grocery store on the way home and I'll prove it to you."

"We'll stick to the budget," Kim promised her. "We just need to figure out how to celebrate for very little money."

Penelope nodded. "I used to take you to the St. Regis for high tea, remember?"

"I remember my shoes pinching. And the harp music was boring."

"I never cared for it, either." Her mother stabbed the key into the ignition and started the car.

"Yet we went all those times. I thought it was so important to you."

"And I thought it was such fun for you. One of us should have spoken up."

"I'm speaking up now," Kim said. "No more boring teas."

"Hear, hear." Penelope pulled out of the bank parking lot. Even her driving felt smoother, more confident. Dino Carminucci had been giving her lessons. Penelope said he was a natural coach, but Kim suspected a deeper appeal. It was a bit of an adjustment, this idea that her mother might be dating.

"You went quiet, all of a sudden," Penelope said. "What are you thinking about?"

"You, dating. That's what you and Dino are doing, right? Dating?"

A pause. "We're enjoying each other's company. Very much. You're not troubled by that, are you?"

"No, of course not," Kim said quickly. "God knows, you deserve your happiness, Mom."

"I know you're angry about the things you've found out about your father. But I hope you'll remember, his way with finance was only one aspect of him. I didn't spend our thirty-five years together in a state of constant suffering. Nor did you grow up in misery. In many ways, we were a very happy family."

"Were we? I know it felt that way at the time, but now…there was no foundation, Mom. It was all a big pretense."

"We weren't pretending to be happy. We simply… were."

Kim's father had been demanding, judgmental. She could see that so clearly now. Yet pleasing him had brought her something she thought was happiness. To know how much she'd yearned for his approval, how much it had meant to her, all for an illusion—that was what made her angry.

"Mom, you're kidding, right?"

"I spent more than three decades of my life with your father. And for the most part, they were happy times. I suppose we had our ups and downs, same as everyone. When I look back through the years, I can see little signs along the way that something wasn't right. I ignored them. Or perhaps I was too preoccupied with all the work that went into maintaining appearances. I forgot to come up for air. I did love your father, but being left that way, with all his secrets coming to light after he was gone… Everything's so different for me with Dino. Not to compare him with your father, but the man's entire life is an open book. He has four adult children and an extemely bitter ex-wife. He's been very honest with me about his past. He was no saint. But I think he's wonderful."

"And I think he's a lucky guy, being with you," Kim said. She was happy enough for her mother, though Kim herself was buoyed by the knowledge that for once in her own life, happiness didn't depend on pleasing some man, or bending over backward to make him look good. What a novel idea.

Back in L.A., she used to think in terms of what would be good for Lloyd—from his needs in bed to his looks in front of a camera. It was humiliating to realize she had actually rationalized that way of life to herself. No more, she thought. Never again.

They stopped at Wegman's and, true to her word, Penelope didn't stray from her budget.

Although she never expected it of herself, Kim was getting used to small-town life. She was even getting used to Fairfield House. It was all a matter of adjusting her attitude and making sure she was modestly covered when she stepped out of her room. At first, her mother's enterprise had seemed the height of insanity, filling the house with unrelated strangers. Yet before long, Kim found a sense of community with the residents of the big, rambling house. Well, with most of the residents, anyway.

The jury was still out on one of them.

Not now, she reminded herself. She was not going to think about Bo Crutcher now. She shouldn't be thinking about him at all, but for some reason, her mind kept going there. Her earlier sense of cautious triumph frayed into an unsettled feeling. She wanted to move on to new things, but kept circling back to what she was best at—finding the upside of any situation. That was really what her career had been all about, and she was good at it. She ought to be able to give herself a positive spin—she was reconnecting with her mom in a way she never had before. Helping Penelope through a financial crisis. Finding the charm in small-town life.

Daphne McDaniel was getting back from work when Kim and her mother arrived home. The sight of her always lifted Kim's mood. In only a short while, Daphne had become a good friend. In other circumstances, she and Kim might have nothing to do with each other; on the surface they seemed to have nothing in common. It made Kim wonder how many other people she'd overlooked in the past.

"Can I help with the groceries?" Daphne offered.

"Thanks." Kim handed her a sack, and hefted two of them herself. The three went to the kitchen and began unloading. In one sack, she came across a pocket puzzle game, and handed it over to her mom. "Check it out," she said, and took out a balsa wood airplane she herself had bought. "We've both got AJ on our minds."

"That makes three of us." Daphne reached into her shoulder bag and produced a hand-sized ball made of rubber bands. "This has been two years in the making. I decided to bring it home for him."

Everyone in the house seemed determined to give AJ extra consideration. Running away had been an act of desperation, and the boy's sadness and his yearning for his mother touched them all. "We can give these to him when he gets home tonight," Penelope said. "Dino took him to get pizza for dinner. Bo and Early are out with friends, so it's just the three of us."

"Then you shouldn't go to any trouble," Daphne said. "I'm fine with cereal."

"Oh, no you're not, young lady," Penelope said. "I thought I'd make a salad with spinach and mandarin oranges. The sort of thing men don't care for."

"A girly salad," Kim said. "My favorite."

Daphne went to her room to get out of her work clothes, which usually meant trading the fishnets and Uggs for black jeans and Doc Martens. Kim finished with the groceries. She noticed her mother studying the cash-register receipt, pressing her lips into a firm line as she folded it up and put it away.

"Mom, I could help you. I've got some savings. I mean, I can't pay off your debts, but—" Kim said.

"That's not what I need from you, and you know it. Money is money, but you...just by being here, you're helping." Penelope sighed. "I feel so foolish. Sometimes I think that's the worst part of this—feeling foolish."

"Trust me, everybody's foolish about something. Look at me and my stupid job and even stupider taste in men."

Daphne returned, helping herself to a satsuma from the fruit bowl. "What men?" she asked.

"A guy in L.A. He was a client." Kim shuddered.

"Lloyd Johnson, right?" Daphne asked, leaning forward. "What was he like?"

"A self-absorbed man-child with symptoms of narcissism—that about sums him up. No idea what I was thinking. I feel like an idiot for believing it would work out."

"Aren't you supposed to do that?" Daphne asked. "I mean, if you start a relationship thinking it will never work, then that's kind of the kiss of death, right?"

"Yes, but this was one of those romances everyone knows is doomed from the start. Everybody except the couple directly involved. I mean, come on. Did anyone think Dennis Rodman and Carmen Electra would last more than five minutes?"

"Dennis and Carmen probably thought so," Penelope chimed in. "Do we really want to criticize people for believing in love?"

"No, for having poor judgment. Which I freely admit I had, for a long time. I mean, when things are happening fast in a big career like Lloyd's, you get swept away. It's like a wave, and you just go with it."

"I know what we need," Daphne declared, hurrying toward the stairs. "I'll be right back."

It was still hard for Kim to think about what had happened to her old life. She remembered the flashbulbs
going off as Lloyd walked the red carpet with the
sponsors' backdrops behind him. She could still hear
the shouted questions, feel the rush of excitement at all
the attention. She remembered standing off to the side
with Lloyd's other handlers, holding her breath as he responded to question after question the way she'd trained
him.

For the most part his performance was as crisp and
controlled as his left-handed layup, and as his career
flourished, so did their relationship. They were a team,
the two of them. They were invincible. There was no
stopping them.

Then came the night in question. Her mind flinched
from the memory. One day, she would have to face up to
what had happened—his tantrum, and the fact that she'd
willingly provoked him for the sake of deflating his temper,
saving his career. What sort of person did that? Where had
her self-respect gone?

"I'm sorry you got hurt," her mother said. "But I'm also
happy for you. I think the Lloyd fiasco will turn out to be
a blessing in disguise."

"This so-called blessing came disguised as a man I
thought I loved. A man who publicly dumped and fired me.
On camera." She shuddered, hoping her request that the
clip be deleted from YouTube would be honored. "Kind of
hard to see that as a blessing."

"Maybe you'll see this as a blessing." Daphne returned

with a brown paper sack, from which she took a few limes and a bottle of tequila.

"Excellent," said Kim. "Think of the money we'll save on therapy." She went to the cupboard and got a cutting board and knife, a shaker of salt and three shot glasses.

"Good heavens, I'm not doing tequila shots," her mother declared.

"You are, too," Kim insisted.

"You and Daphne enjoy," she said. "I'll clean up the mess afterward."

"You're not weaseling out of this," Kim said. She led the way into the sitting room and deftly poured three shots, her movements as neat and controlled as a bartender's.

Her mother recoiled. "I'll make myself sick."

"Not with this," Daphne assured her. "It's El Tesoro. Smooth as filtered water, you'll see."

"But it has a bite," Kim added, cutting lime wedges. "Watch and learn, Mother. Watch and learn." She demonstrated the time-honored ritual of tequila consumption—shake, lick, swallow, bite, grimacing with the lime's tartness. Finally, she leaned back, smiling as the fiery liquor spread.

Daphne followed suit, dispatching her shot with efficiency and expertise.

"Your turn, Mom," said Kim.

"But I promised you a girly salad—"

"We're not hungry," Daphne said.

"She's right," Kim added. "Humor us. Come on, Mom. It's a bonding experience."

"All right, but I'm not licking my hand. That's disgusting."

"Lick your damn hand. How else will you get the salt

to stick? And try to do everything in one fluid movement. The key is not to stop until you're through." Kim did another demo, then lined everything up for her mother.

Penelope pursed her lips. Then, working quickly, she licked the back of her hand and added a sprinkle of salt. She took a moment to compose herself. Finally, like a diver about to take the plunge, she tongued the salt, knocked back the tequila shot and chased it with the lime wedge. In compliance with instructions, she smacked her lips, then patted her mouth with a paper napkin.

"There. Are you satisfied?" she asked.

"It's a good start. You have to do two more," Kim said.

"Or three," Daphne added.

They set her up for another shot, and then another a few minutes later. She sank back on the sofa with a sigh. "I'm a new woman. It's nice to know I'm not too old to try something new," she declared. "My, but that was invigorating."

"We knew you'd think so." Kim poured three more shots and saluted Daphne with her glass. "To new perspectives," she declared.

"Better late than never," Penelope said, and clinked glasses with Kim.

"Agreed," Kim said.

"To trying something new," Daphne said.

"To no more pro athletes," Kim added, remembering all those shallow, spoiled bullies who expected the moon and then complained when someone handed it to them. Many of them harbored a sense of entitlement that led them to break laws and hearts with equal aplomb. And afterward, to claim they'd been victimized.

Sometimes, however, even intentions spoken aloud

were drowned out by something louder—common sense. Even in the midst of a round of tequila, Kim knew it wasn't enough to declare what she didn't want. She needed to figure out what she *did* want.

"Isn't it ironic," her mother said, "now that you've sworn off athletes, you live in a house full of them—Dino, Early and Bo."

"He is so gorgeous," Daphne declared, and they didn't need to ask who "he" was.

"Ask him out," Kim said with a casual wave of her hand. "As far as we know, he's unattached."

"Nah, not my type. He's a family man, and I'm not into kids."

Bo, a family man. Perspective was everything, Kim thought.

"Besides," Daphne added, "he likes you. It's so obvious."

"He barely knows me," Kim protested, ignoring the flutter in her stomach. Getting a guy to like her was no special trick. Through no fault of her own, she'd come endowed with red hair, big boobs and long legs. It didn't take much else to get some guy's attention, and that hadn't changed since junior high.

"He's totally into you. I predict a romantic fling."

Kim's face flushed. She had barely acknowledged the mutual attraction between her and Bo, and she didn't think anyone had noticed. *It's so obvious.* Kimberly tried not to feel intrigued by Daphne's suggestion. "What's the point of a romantic fling?"

"Geez, girl, it's only one of the best things in the world."

"Yes, but the definition of a fling is that it's quickly over and in the end, you're…"

"Flung?" her mother suggested.

"Exactly. A fling has an expiration date. And that's sad."

"Just because it's sad to see something end doesn't mean you shouldn't enjoy it," Daphne pointed out. "I'm right. You know I'm right."

They lost track of the time, getting sillier and forgetting dinner entirely. Bo and Early came home, fresh-faced, their color high from the cold. She tried not to acknowledge what the sight of Bo Crutcher did to her. Tried not to notice her pulse speeding up, her face warming with a blush. That was the tequila, surely.

"Hello, gentlemen," her mother said. Her attempt at sounding unaffected by the tequila gave both Kim and Daphne a fit of the giggles.

Bo's gaze flickered over the tequila setup. "Everything all right?" he asked. "Is AJ okay?"

"Of course," Kim was quick to assure him. "He and Dino had dinner out, then came home and played cribbage—"

"Played what?"

She laughed at the expression on his face. Was there anything more appealing than a man in a state of complete befuddlement? "It's a board game. And they've both gone to bed by now. And we've been celebrating."

"Yeah? What's the occasion?"

"I'm getting my financial house in order," her mother informed him. "And learning to do tequila shots. Oh, and Kimberley's new leaf, we mustn't forget that."

"What leaf?" asked Bo.

"My new one," she declared with an airy wave of her hand. "I've turned over a new leaf."

"How's that?"

"I'm going to reinvent my career with a better purpose. No more covering up for felons having tantrums in public. No more trying to garner sympathy for guys who just signed a multimillion-dollar contract. No more training guys who never finished their education to sound like Rhodes scholars." She and Daphne made another toast.

"Go girl," said Daphne.

"Here's to no more athletes," she reiterated. "No more loutish clients, no more making sows' ears into silk purses." She sipped her tequila. "I wonder how that phrase came into being. Who would ever look at a sow's ear and see a purse?"

"Judith Leiber," said Bo.

Bagwell frowned at Kim. "What have you got against athletes?"

She sent him a wry smile. "How much time do you have?"

"How much do you need?" Bo asked. He was so good-looking. When did he get to be so good-looking? Watching him and Early, she decided her troubles didn't stem from athletes per se. Or even men in general. She simply wanted a new life that didn't resemble her old life.

"None, because I'm done talking about all that."

"Good. I came to propose something to you," he said.

"I'm sorry, did you just say *propose?* You should know better than to throw that word around when a single woman is within earshot."

"Make that three single women," her mother reminded them.

"Sorry," Bo said easily. "Poor choice of words. So does that mean you're looking to get married?"

"I need to work on getting a date first." Kim refilled the shot glass.

"Well, then—"

She held up her hand like a shield. "A nice, safe, boring man who knows how to behave himself."

"Yeah, whatever. But I still have a proposition to make you."

"I don't like the sound of that."

"It's a win-win, I swear."

"That's right," Early said. "See, he figured out what he's going to do about Fame School."

"That's right. I'm going to hire someone to work with me right here, so I don't have to leave AJ."

"Oh, that's brilliant," her mother said, oblivious to the tension straining between them. "That sounds like a fine solution indeed."

Kim felt a queasy sensation in her gut. She swallowed hard. "You're going to ask me to do it, aren't you?"

"Come on, Kim," Bagwell urged her. "Make an exception for Crutch. He needs you."

Kim refused to acknowledge the surge of warmth she suddenly felt. "I've just spent the evening adjusting to my newfound freedom from my old life. And believe me, a man's need is not exactly the most powerful motivator in the world."

Bo crossed the room, took a seat beside her. "This can be about your needs, part of your new leaf."

"That won't work," she said.

"What won't work?"

"This earnest-and-charming thing you're doing. I won't fall for it."

"Look, I know we got off on the wrong foot."

"You think?"

"You dislike him?" Her mother gave her a quizzical look. "I had no idea you disliked him."

Kim kept glaring at Bo as she answered Penelope. "It's nothing personal."

"Nonsense," said her mother. "Dislike is always personal. You should have mentioned this before he came to stay with us."

"It wouldn't have mattered," she told her mother. "Living with us is the best solution for AJ. I think we can all agree, he's what's important here."

"And he's the reason I need you," said Bo, pressing his advantage. "Come on, Kim. What do you say?"

She thought of AJ, and how lost and lonely he looked, and how brave he had to be, separated from his mother. Because of AJ, she only really had one option.

"I need another tequila shot."

Eighteen

The next morning, Kim awakened with a pounding headache…and the kind of what-have-I-done? feeling she used to get back in her sorority days. She reminded herself that people who did tequila shots were expected to do stupid things and say things they didn't mean. And they were expected to regret them the next day.

Yet no matter how hard she tried, she couldn't figure out how to regret making the deal with Bo Crutcher. She scowled at herself in the mirror while furiously brushing her teeth. Then she spat into the sink, saying, "You swore off athletes. Now you're breaking a promise you made to yourself."

The woman in the mirror looked unrepentant. "I simply placed other people's needs above my own. And, no, I'm not talking about Bo Crutcher. I'm talking about my mother, who needs the extra income, and AJ, who needs his dad to stick around."

She raked her fingers through her hair. "And you're talking to yourself. When did that start?"

A knock at the door startled her. She grabbed a robe

but couldn't find the sash. Clutching it in the front, she opened the door.

"Check your e-mail," Bo said. He was fresh from the shower, and he hadn't yet buttoned his shirt. She wondered if that was by design.

The sight of his bare chest made her weak in the knees. "I always check my e-mail," she said, telling herself to snap out of it. "You don't have to barge in first thing in the morning to tell me."

"My agent's sending you a video interview so you can decide whether or not I need the media training."

You don't, she thought, desperately trying to keep from staring. *You just need to stand there...* She ducked her head to hide a smile. "I'll take a look." She glanced up at him, and unlike her, he was making no effort to avoid staring. His frank gaze made her suddenly and achingly aware of the scantiness of the robe. She cleared her throat. "Did you tell AJ about our deal?"

"Yeah, and he's fine with it. I mean, as good as he can be, considering. He needed to hear that I'm going to do what it takes in order to stick around for him."

"You make me sound like a last resort."

He checked out her bare legs. "You are nobody's last resort."

She knew she could read all kinds of meanings into that remark. "I want you to know, I agreed to do this for AJ's sake. No other reason. And for his sake, we're going to do a good job. By the end of the day, I intend to land an interview with *Baseball Monthly,* out of Cooperstown." She'd lain awake last night thinking about him, despite the tequila. The notion of a new project was like a fresh shot of espresso, and she'd gone into planning mode, mentally going through her media contacts and planning a strategy.

"No shit." He scratched his bare chest, then clasped his hands in his underarms, rocking back on his heels. "That's great, Kim. I appreciate it."

Eyes front, she reminded herself. "You're probably not going to like working with me. I intend to be like a drill sergeant, because time is short."

"Yeah? Well, you're wrong about one thing."

"What's that?"

"I'm going to like it. I'm going to like every minute of it."

"I'll see you downstairs, then," she said, shutting the door in his face. She dressed hurriedly and went downstairs. As she fixed herself a cup of coffee, she sang along with the radio.

"You're in a good mood," AJ remarked, coming into the kitchen.

"Am I? I guess I'm just glad to see you," she said.

That drew a reluctant smile from him. "Right."

"So your dad explained that he's going to be working with me, right? Media training and public relations—what I used to do in my former job. So this way, he won't have to go away."

"And that's why you're in such a good mood?"

Yes. "No," she said quickly. "But I think it's good news that he figured out a way to stick around for you."

AJ was quiet for a few minutes as he poured himself a bowl of cereal. Kim watched him surreptitiously, thinking about Daphne's comment last night about having a romantic fling with Bo. Right here, Kim thought, is the reason there couldn't be any fling—because she knew better than to play around when there was a fragile, frightened boy in the mix.

She watched him from the corner of her eye. She couldn't tell if he thought it was good news or not. He probably didn't understand what Bo was risking by skipping Fame School. More than media training and business skills development, he was going to miss out on the networking that was so crucial to a high-level career. Meeting the right people at the right time led to endorsements and alliances that could be invaluable.

She would make it her mission to find other networking opportunities. The *Baseball Monthly* interview would not be a stretch. A quick exchange of e-mails with someone she knew there, and it would be done. Under the influence or not, she was committed, and she intended to move forward quickly. There was an upcoming event she already had her eye on, a reception informally known as the Debutant Ball for new Yankees hopefuls, held at the Pierre in New York City. It was meant to bring the press and sponsors together with up-and-coming rookies. Invitations were extended only to the most promising of players—and she intended for Bo Crutcher to be one of those players.

In addition to the cereal, AJ loaded up on muffins, fruit, yogurt, juice and milk, putting everything on a tray to carry into the dining room.

"I'm always amazed at how much you eat," Kim observed. "Where are you putting it all?"

He shrugged. "I'm a kid. We eat a lot."

"I'd say so. I've never been around kids before," she confessed.

"It's not like we're an endangered species or anything."

"Up until recently, I was really busy with work. Of course, some would argue that my former clients acted like children." She thought for a moment. "But that would be an insult to the children."

That brought on a full-blown grin. "Right."

"I mean it. Some of my clients were terrible."

"Like who?"

"Well, there was this one, a tennis star, who was so notorious we couldn't even convince anyone to be his driver. Seems like getting someone to drive a client around would be simple, but not for this guy. He was twenty-six years old and he used to throw temper tantrums like a baby."

"So why'd people let him get away with it?"

"That's the trouble with a grown-up who's paying you to look after him. You can't just put him in the time-out corner when he misbehaves."

"Nobody puts Bo Crutcher in the corner." Bo arrived, wearing old jeans and a new sweatshirt, clean-shaven and looking ridiculously attractive.

Kim busied herself checking her PDA, not that there was anything on her agenda except the Bo Crutcher project.

"Hey, AJ," he said. "That's a line from an old movie— *Dirty Dancing.* 'Nobody puts Baby in the corner.' Ever seen it?"

"Doesn't sound like my kind of movie."

"It will be, one day," Bo said, holding open the dining room door for AJ and his breakfast. "Save me a seat at the table."

While Kim perused the breakfast offerings, Bo helped himself to coffee. He passed close behind Kim at the counter, so that their bodies brushed together. "Define *'misbe-have,'*" he said, leaning down to murmur in her ear.

"You're doing it right now," she said. "Don't be a jerk."

"I'd never."

"Seriously, we've got work to do. We need to review that filmed interview, see how you did and figure out what to focus on."

"Cool. I'll get my laptop."

"Good idea. We'll all watch it after breakfast."

Bagwell, Daphne and Dino filed in for breakfast. Penelope put on a fresh pot of coffee. Day by day, Kim was getting used to this house full of people—the chatter at breakfast, the clink of dishes and her mother's flair at the simple act of serving food. Lately Kim noticed Dino's attentions to her mother. Penelope's coffee cup was always full, her chair always held for her. This guy meant business, and he was going about it in the right way.

After breakfast, Bo set up the laptop on the dining room buffet. "So this is an interview from back in November, after tryouts," he said. "It's the kind of thing a player's supposed to do on a regular basis."

While the video was loading, AJ grabbed his backpack. "I better go," he said. "Almost time for the bus."

Interesting, Kim observed. He had a good ten minutes before the bus. He seemed to be in a hurry. Following the New York incident, AJ had turned into a bus-riding pro. Bo had promised that if he went AWOL again, he'd find himself being driven to and from school every day, something no middle-schooler wanted. Also, AJ was nobody's fool. He'd realized that his behavior could affect his mother's case. When the stakes were this high, everything mattered.

"That book report you wrote is still on the printer," Bo reminded him. "And do you have that signed permission slip for the field trip to West Point?"

"Yeah," AJ said, heading into the study for his homework. "See you later."

"You have a good day, now." Bo's gaze followed the boy out the door.

"You're getting pretty good at sounding like a parent," Bagwell observed.

"You think?" Bo smiled a little, but worry lingered in his eyes. Kim knew he phoned the school every morning to make sure AJ had arrived. In a short time, Bo had come a long way from the guy she'd encountered at the airport. That brutally cold morning, she never would have guessed he'd become someone she couldn't stop thinking about.

Reining in her thoughts, she turned up the volume on the laptop. The segment opened with canned sports-show music and the MLB logo, followed by a tight shot of the new stadium. Then the camera panned across the handful of players who had received precontract invitations to spring training. There were a lot of hoops to jump through to get on the coveted roster, and this was an early one. Blowing it at any stage could mean the end of a dream.

Lined up in front of two shared mics, the players took turns fielding questions. They all looked so young and green, all so clearly nervous in front of the unfortunate backdrop of a gray cinderblock wall, the table stark and unadorned in front of each man.

Kim couldn't take her eyes off Bo on the small screen.

It was like watching a train wreck in slow motion. None of his magnetism or natural charm came through. Instead, he resembled an ex-con defending himself, right down to the hair hanging lank around his face, which was disreputably marred by a five-o'clock shadow. His delivery alternated between forgettable and offensive. Asked about his background, he offered a toneless resumé of previous experience. And when asked about the incidence of a pitcher in his age range making it in the majors, he responded, "I reckon they're rare as <bleep> on a bullfrog."

"Hey," said Bagwell. "What'd they bleep out?"

"I think I said *'tits.'* Yeah, rare as tits on a bullfrog."

"You can't say things like that," Kim pointed out over Bagwell's guffaws. "Now, hush up and let me listen."

The rest of the interview was as excruciating as the first part, a disaster made of awkward silences, studied stiffness, inappropriate language and a veritable symphony of ambient noises—shuffling feet, throat-clearing, heavy breathing into the mic, sloshing water glasses.

I've got my work cut out for me, she thought.

When the interview ground to a halt, Bo's image stayed frozen on the computer screen. He wore the haunted expression of a man facing a firing squad. In the ensuing vacuum of silence at the end of the video, everyone around the table seemed to be at a loss for words.

Finally, Daphne passed around a plate of pastries from Sky River Bakery, helping herself to one. "Have one—better for your mental health than an hour of psychotherapy."

"But higher in calories," said Kim's mother, taking a bear claw.

"How'd I do?" Bo asked, clueless.

"Honestly?" Kim's appetite was gone. "You were like a prisoner under interrogation."

"C'mon, I wasn't that bad." He grabbed a powdered doughnut from the plate. "Was I?"

"Yes." Everyone around the table answered at once.

"Listen, don't be discouraged. It's a learning process. That's why there's fame school," Kim said, going into rah-rah coaching mode. "That's where I come in. It's training, like anything else. You have thirty seconds to make them remember you." She indicated the frozen screen. "All they're going to remember from that is being bored."

"Ouch," said Dino, wincing.

"I think they'll remember when he called Roger Clemens 'dumber than a bag of hammers,'" Daphne said.

"Well, he is," Bo insisted. "So's any other juicer. I hate that shit."

"Hate it all you want," Kim said, "but keep the interview about you. Honestly, you've got a lot to learn. That was, to put it mildly, a complete disaster."

He put on a fake announcer's voice. "Ladies and gentlemen, and it's Kimberly van Dorn out of the bullpen, warming up for what promises to be a great game."

"I'm not playing games."

"Whoa, look who woke up on the wrong side of bed this morning. You agreed to do this," he reminded her.

"For AJ's sake. Remember, that's how you talked me into doing this. I like AJ."

"What about me? Don't you like me, even a little bit?"

She sniffed, forbidding herself to think about the way her nerve endings fired every time she was around him.

"The jury is still out on you. Just don't start acting like one of my usual clients. You're not like them."

"Right. They're all rich and successful. And I'm not."

"But you aspire to be."

"I aspire to play ball. It's what I've always aspired to do." His eyes lit with passion. "The rest—money and fame—it may or may not happen. But if I'm in the game, then I'm happy."

She stared at him. "Oh, my God."

"Now what'd I do?" He held his hands with his palms up.

"I can see it in your face. You're really not concerned about being rich and famous. You genuinely love the sport."

"Well, excuse the crap out of me. Of course I love the sport. Why the hell else would I play year in and year out for no money, tending bar and doing odd jobs just to buy groceries? If this was about the money, I would have bought into a car dealership or gone to work on an oil rig in the South China Sea. But baseball for the money?" He threw back his head and offered up his signature Bo Crutcher laugh, showing the easy humor that was so conspicuously absent from his interview persona. When he realized he was the only one laughing, he quit. "What? How come you're looking at me like that?"

She couldn't help herself. When she was in the grip of inspiration, she tended to stare, mouth agape. "That's genius," she said.

"What?" He bit into the powdered doughnut, showering his chest with white flurries. "Me?"

She caught herself staring at his white lips. "Right. No, I mean, what you just said—that's who you are. You spoke from the heart and you told the truth, and that's going to endear you to people. Everyone will remember your sincerity."

"The baseball player who likes baseball? How is that different from any other player?" he asked.

"It's not the sentiment that's so different. A lot of athletes like their sport. It's your delivery I liked. Everyone's going to like it."

"Yeah?" He grabbed a napkin and brushed at the powdered sugar, which merely served to smear it on his navy blue sweatshirt. "Hey, Dino," he said, "I'm a genius. Kim here just said I'm a genius."

Dino eyed him briefly, focusing on the powdered sugar. "Uh-huh."

"The thing I always used to ask my clients to do is to tell their story," Kim said. "Unfortunately, a lot of them don't do it well. Or their story is boring. Some of them— too many—started training for their sport at such a young age that they never had a chance to decide for themselves whether or not they love the game."

"And Bo simply loves the game," her mother said, beaming. "That's lovely."

"It makes my job easier, having a client people are going to like. I've had my fill of clients I had to persuade the media to like."

"Cool," said Bo. "So I'm good to go?"

She shook her head. "Not even close."

"Fine, then just tell me what I need to do. It's your specialty, right? Turning a diamond in the rough into a polished gem."

She regarded him skeptically. "Assuming there's a precious stone under that exterior."

"Ha. You know it, sugar pie."

"New rule," she said. "Don't go around calling women names like sugar pie."

"If I called men names like that, people would think I'm queer."

"And don't say queer."

"Everybody says queer. It's even in the name of that show."

"It's a matter of context. And judgment. Just do yourself a favor and don't use that word."

"What should I use? Ho-mo-sexual?" He separated the word into obnoxious-sounding syllables.

"How about you avoid the subject altogether? People can go for long periods of time without debating sexual orientation." She assessed him with her eyes. "Unless this is a preoccupation of yours."

He snorted. "Right. You slay me, lady. You really do. First, you rag on me for being a Lothario. Which, by the way, I looked up. I'm nothing like that guy. He was banging anything in hoop skirts. And I'm not. I don't have that problem. At the moment, my biggest problem is you. And you're supposed to be helping me."

"I am, but I need some cooperation from you."

"You got it," he said, polishing off the doughnut. "Sugar pie."

Nineteen

Kim insisted on getting an early start each morning. By eight o'clock, she was either on the phone or at the computer, preparing her game plan for Bo Crutcher. And finally, for the first time since she'd fled from L.A., she felt anchored to something. She was in her element. It was pathetic, discovering how much she missed this part of her old life. She couldn't help herself—the work brought her an incredible sense of satisfaction. The pressure and challenge of it was exciting. Even the seeming impossibility of making someone like Bo Crutcher into a star was exhilarating.

She consulted the off-season schedule provided by Gus Carlyle, then glanced through the open door at her client, who was currently in the sitting room, teaching his son "Deep in the Heart of Texas" on his electric bass, killing time before the bus. Since Bo had decided to stay in Avalon, there had been a perceptible thawing in AJ's attitude. Every once in a while, the boy forgot his worries about his mother, and the bond between him and Bo had a chance to flourish.

Whenever she grew frustrated with her client, Kim reminded herself of this.

The schedule listed a program of upcoming physical training with a strength coach. That aspect of the program would be no problem. Despite all his complaining, Bo was a natural athlete who excelled at physical challenges. He was doing sixty throws a day at the indoor gym, and Kim couldn't wait to see him on the mound. The strength and grace of a talented pitcher was a thing of beauty; she had no worries about him in that regard. The real trouble would start when he had to step up for meetings with club management and the media. In addition to the upcoming gala reception for patrons, boosters and sponsors, they needed to prepare for New Player Week. He would require a press portfolio and media training right away.

She made some notes on the schedule and then joined them, pausing in the doorway for a moment. After the bass lesson, they'd moved on to ripping a phone book in half. Unguarded, they looked like father and son, although they probably didn't realize it. On the surface, the two were wildly dissimilar. AJ lacked Bo's lanky frame. The boy's Latino coloring contrasted with his father's blue eyes and Germanic features. Yet when AJ laughed and his eyes sparkled, it was Bo's spirit that shone from the boy's face. Bo was like a big kid around his son, with endless patience for silliness.

He was still grinning when he noticed her, and his smile widened. "Time to get to work," he said to AJ. "I gotta go learn how to be a big-league player."

"I don't see what's so hard about it," AJ said. "You said you've been pitching since Little League."

"The pitching I can handle. It's everything else I need help with. What's on the agenda now, coach?"

"An extreme makeover," Kim informed him.

He traded a glance with AJ. "I don't like the sound of that," he said.

"You're probably not going to like any of it," she warned him. She had a long list of things to do in order to prepare him for the gala reception in New York that would kick off New Player Week.

"Try me," he said.

"You need a publicity photo."

"I got one. It's up on the Hornets' Web site."

"That one looks like a mug shot."

"It kind of is. Ray Tolley, from my band, he's a cop. He took the picture."

"We'll need a new photo. Your new ones are going to look like fine art."

"You're the boss."

"We'll get a whole portfolio of shots, professionally done."

"Yeah, whatever."

"I'll book a studio in the city."

"No need."

"Look, we're doing this my way, or—"

"I'll go along with getting a new picture made, but we're using my photographer."

"You have a photographer?"

"Daisy Bellamy. My best friend Noah's stepdaughter. She can use the work."

"It's nice of you to think of your friend, but no. We need a pro. We need—"

"Hang on a second." He went to the rotunda and returned

with a coffee table book. It was one she recognized—*Food For Thought,* Jenny Majesky McKnight's memoir about the Sky River Bakery. He handed it to her. Now she noticed the line on the cover: Photographs by Daisy Bellamy. Paging through the glossy book, Kim was impressed by the quality of the photographs and the photographer's eye for composition.

"She's a pro, then."

"A college student, studying photography. But she shoots like a pro."

"Is she available?"

"We'll have to ask."

"Excellent. Give me her number, and I'll set everything up. In the meantime, we've got a lot of work to do." She enumerated the things they needed to cover—grooming, bio, message development, delivery, on-camera exercises and general issues of poise.

He listened, frowning. Then he said, "I'd rather have my teeth drilled."

"Actually, that's on the schedule," she said. "Not exactly drilling, but teeth whitening."

"Oh, man."

She glared at him. "We made a deal. You hired me to do a job and I intend to deliver. I've done this before, and there's a progression. Before the publicity photos, the first order of business is your teeth. It's one of the first and simplest parts of this process."

"I use that whitening toothpaste," he protested.

"Permanent whitening."

"Shoot."

"Who's your dentist? We need to make sure he can do the instant whitening technique."

"You're assuming I have a dentist."

Kim frowned. "You don't?"

"Just a reminder, up until November, I was making a pittance for playing baseball and tending bar for tips. I went to the dentist once for a toothache. What he did to fix it made the toothache seem mild, so I haven't been back since."

AJ hurried to the door and pulled on his snow boots. "Time for the bus," he said.

"This might turn out to be a long day," Bo warned him. "If I'm not here when you get back, Dino is in charge."

"Okay."

"I'll have my phone with me, although if she's serious about the dentist, I'll probably be in a dead faint."

"It's no one's favorite thing," she agreed. "Is it, AJ?" If she could get his support, this would go easier. Where AJ was concerned, Bo clearly wanted to do the right thing.

"I guess." AJ offered a vague shrug.

Oh, Lord. An alarming thought struck her. "What about you, AJ? When was your last visit to the dentist?"

He shrugged again. "Never been. Never had a toothache."

This was incredible to her. Everyone went to the dentist, didn't they? She considered the thousands of dollars that had gone into her mouth over the years, from regular checkups to the best orthodontics money could buy. She'd taken it all for granted.

"Well, there's good news for you both, then," she said.

They regarded each other with expressions of stark terror.

She offered a reassuring smile. "Think of it as a form of male bonding."

* * *

Agreeing to coach Bo Crutcher was like making a deal with the devil. Kim betrayed her own vow to get on with a different life, a different career. But in exchange, she would be helping AJ and also earning money—always a good thing after leaving a job without notice.

She was surprised to discover how important this project was to her. Perhaps it was because she had something to prove in the wake of the Lloyd Johnson fiasco. Yet one undeniable aspect of the business was that her success was inextricably tied to her client. And so was her failure. She tried to work with Bo on things that would make him seem polished and confident—fast. They went to Avalon's premier restaurant, the Apple Tree Inn, so she could help him with his skills in a social setting. Preparing for the evening, she'd dressed carefully in a form-fitting black jersey dress and burgundy patent leather high heels. The belongings she'd had in storage had arrived from L.A., yet this didn't feel like a step back into her old life. Everything about this felt new. She told herself she was simply trying to appear professional, but it was more than that. She wanted to look good—for Bo.

When he helped her off with her coat at the restaurant, the gleam in his eye told her she'd succeeded. "I'm starting to like this part of the training," he said. "Maybe we could skip dinner and—"

"No, you have to learn how to use the right fork, eat like a gentleman and say all the right things."

"Hard to see how this stuff matters," he said.

"Trust me, it matters."

"Baseball fans won't care which fork I use."

"News flash. You're not going to *have* any fans unless you get picked up. And sponsors do care about this stuff. Members of the media—whether they care or not, they're going to notice everything about you. You're not just playing baseball for the fun of it. And it's not just for the money, either. This is about your place in the sport, your image, and—" She stopped, pursed her lips. No point in getting into a philosophical debate with him.

The waiter arrived and she insisted that he order something he'd never tried before, which he did, gamely enough.

"You're being a good sport," she remarked.

"No, I just don't know what half this stuff is."

When their meal arrived, he scowled down at his plate.

"Is something wrong with your trout?"

He poked at it with his fork. "Looks like a mullet out of Galveston Bay."

"It's *truite au bleu,* and it's delicious."

"They couldn't be bothered to take the head off before serving it?" he asked.

"Watch and learn," she said, sitting back as the waiter neatly boned the fish and served it.

Bo sampled the fish. "Doesn't taste like much," he said. "A lot of lemon and butter, and that's about it."

"You know, it's all right to pretend you like something even when you don't."

"I thought you said I should be honest. You know, show my passion and my heart and all that."

"I said you should have judgment. There's a difference."

He leaned back in his chair, his posture deliberately loose, she suspected because he knew it would provoke her. He couldn't seem to resist teasing her. "How do I know when you're being honest, and when you're being diplomatic?"

"You're not stupid," she said. "I think you'll figure it out."

"I'll never figure you out. Now every time you say something to me, I'll wonder whether or not it's the truth."

That stung. "I've never lied to you. I never would."

"But you've been diplomatic with me."

"Is that some crime?"

He smiled. "No. But I do want complete honesty from you, Kim. And believe me, I can take anything you can dish out."

"Fine. I feel like dishing out some dancing lessons."

"I don't dance."

"Not yet, anyway. Now, get up and ask me to dance."

"I'm eating my trout."

"You don't like the trout."

"But—"

"Ask me, Crutcher."

To her surprise, he did so smoothly, holding his hand out with the palm turned up. "Hey, I've been known to watch *Dancing with the Stars,*" he explained.

She walked him through some basic dance steps. He kept trying to hold her close; she kept insisting he needed to hold a dance frame, which he claimed wasn't nearly as much fun. A natural athlete, he was a quick study, and after just a few tries, he was able to get around the dance floor.

"How am I doing, coach?" he asked, navigating around a middle-aged couple who seemed blissfully lost in each other.

"You're not humiliating yourself, so that's good." Kim watched the other couple a moment too long, and her heel wobbled through a turn.

She would have stumbled, except Bo caught her against him. "Whoa there. I got you," he said.

Kim let herself enjoy the feel of his arms around her for about three seconds. It felt…exquisite. She was startled but not surprised by his rock-solid musculature. Although he was tall and slender, graceful in everything he did, he was incredibly strong. She savored the sensation for a moment, then pulled back. Any longer than that, and she'd be hopelessly lost.

"That's the second time I've saved you from your high heels," he said.

The morning at the airport seemed so long ago. She'd learned so much about him, probing into his past as she prepared his publicity materials. His frankness in talking about his past was so unexpected, yet so compelling in its honesty, she couldn't help being moved. What had emerged was a picture of a man who had grown up rough, and emerged honest and hardworking, never afraid of a challenge. Her favorite kind of client.

At the end of the evening they returned to Fairfield House. Bo seemed quite pleased with himself.

The house was quiet at this hour. In the foyer, Bo took her hand and pulled her to him, lowering his head to hers.

"What in the world are you doing?" she demanded, batting him away.

"Kissing you good-night," he said, as if she were an idiot. "That's what people do at the end of a date."

She actually considered letting him. Kissing a person told you so much about him. Once her lips were joined intimately with a man's, she could let instinct do the rest. Kim wondered if she was strange in that way. There was something about a kiss, some nuance of taste or texture, the angle or pressure, that gave her more data than a background check. Mostly, kissing a man told her in an instant whether her attraction to him was justified or not. Usually, the answer was not.

But in the case of Bo Crutcher, she couldn't risk it. "News flash," she said to him. "Number one, this wasn't a date—"

"It felt like a date," he objected. "Honey, every time I'm with you feels like a date."

"I beg your pardon."

"Because I'm falling for you," he said. "Hard."

His words made her ache in places she had no business aching. "And number two, we are not *people*. We're a client and publicist."

"Who happen to be attracted to each other," he said.

"Speak for yourself."

"Fine, I will. The first time I saw you at the airport it was like being blinded by the sun. I'm not one to believe in signs," he added, "but when I showed up at this house and there you were, I figured it had to mean something. And I do believe in second chances. I have a feeling you do, too."

"You have no idea what I believe. I happen to think—"

He touched his fingers to her lips in a gesture that felt far too good. "Hush. I'm speaking for myself here. You should listen because I don't say stuff like this every day. You're a beautiful woman, Kim. I know you know that. But the world is full of beautiful women, which I don't object to at all. And I can look at them and think, yeah, they're beautiful, but the attraction's not there, not in any real way. Then there's you. For me, you're like the pull of the moon, I swear. I can't resist you and I wouldn't want to.

Instead, I want to kiss you until we can't stand it anymore and we need to be closer. And then I want to unbutton your blouse and—"

"Stop, okay? I get the message." She had an urge to fan herself. She hoped he didn't notice her furious blush.

"I love it when you blush," he said.

"Go away," she said peevishly, batting his hands again. "I'm not blushing. It's just hot in here."

"It is hot in here, and you're blushing, and it's all good."

She marshaled her defenses. "We're done here, Bo. You did a good job at the restaurant and we're going to put together a great media kit and it's all going to be good, just as you said. So good night. Sleep well, and remember we have plans with AJ tomorrow."

"Yeah," he said good-naturedly, yet she heard an edge to his voice. "But there's something you should remember, too. There's a lot more to us than client and publicist, and you know it. You know damn well I'm right."

At that, she mustered a bit of humor. "Now you sound like one of my clients."

"I am one of your clients. But I don't want to sound just like every other guy."

"Then quit claiming to be right all the time."

"Look at us," Bo said, stepping into the room with AJ in tow. They found Kim at the computer in the study. "We got million-dollar smiles."

After their final appointment at the dentist, Bo felt as if he could take on the world. He and AJ were both extremely lucky to have reasonably healthy teeth. Each had needed fillings but nothing extreme. Dr. Foley recommended an orthodontic assessment for AJ. The laser whitening for Bo created a transformation that was subtle but definitely noticeable.

"Those aren't million-dollar smiles," Kim said. "Those smiles are priceless."

"Hear that, AJ? We're priceless."

"That doesn't mean you're off the hook. We've got more work to do for your photo shoot."

Bo gave AJ a nudge. "It's going to pale in comparison to the dentist, I swear."

"Don't be a baby," she scolded. "I'm taking you to a stylist."

"What kind of stylist?"

"For your hair."

"Oh, you mean a haircut," he said. "I usually go to the barber for that. When I'm really broke, I just don't bother. That's how I ended up going for long hair. My girlfriend at the time said it was a good look for me."

"She was right. It is a good look for you," Kim agreed.

From the expression on her face, he suspected she was making a picture in her mind of his "girlfriend-at-the-time." She was probably assuming tight clothes and bleached hair. And she'd be right.

"You got a girlfriend now?" AJ asked.

Bo paused. The boy had never asked anything like this before. Bo thought about Kim, and how much he liked her, and how much more he wished she liked him. "Nope," he said. "The two of you are way more fun than a girlfriend, bud."

Kim smiled. "Hear that, AJ? We're fun."

"Except for when you're dragging me to a stylist."

"You need a stylist," she insisted.

"I thought you liked my long hair."

"We're keeping the long hair but we need to refine it."

He sent AJ a look. "What do you say? You want to come and get refined with me?"

"No, thanks. I think I'll hang out here."

"It can't be as bad as the dentist." He glanced at Kim, and had second thoughts. "Can it?"

The salon smelled of perfume and hair dye and God-knew-what. Bo never knew you had to sit so long in the chair. The barber was a gay guy named Goldi ("with an *i*") whose head was shaved, so there was no telling whether or not he actually knew what he was doing. Oh, and he wasn't a barber, but a stylist. He walked around the chair in slow circles, deep in contemplation. Bo felt like a slab of marble to Goldi's Michelangelo. It wasn't enough to get a haircut. He had to have a *style,* which meant the guy spent a good half hour studying Bo and consulting with Kim.

"I can see you're in good hands," she finally declared. "I'm going to check with the photographer and make sure eveything's all set for the shoot." She sent a questioning look at Goldi.

"Threeish," he said.

Bo checked the clock. Damn. That was two hours away. What could possibly take two hours?

He soon found out. The haircut was excruciatingly slow. Goldi concurred that they should preserve the "long look" but he was going to give it more "polish." This meant continued circling and snipping off bits the length of an eyelash. Bo set his jaw and glowered. He wished he hadn't drunk so much water at lunch because he had to piss like a racehorse.

The cut was only the beginning. With Goldi acting as art director, a couple of girls in pink smocks swooped in and painstakingly separated strands of his hair and painted them with a noxious substance. Then they carefully encased the locks in foil so he resembled a *Star Trek* extra. He was placed in a chair where—no lie—they lowered a plastic dome over his head and set it on Bake. Under the plastic dryer-dome, Bo sat there like an abductee and pondered what else his captors had in mind. He wondered when they were going to bring out the probe.

The fun never ended. His abductors also subjected him to a manicure, not just soaking and scrubbing his nails but submerging his hands in hot melted paraffin, which was oddly sensual, despite being just plain weird. The nail tech—who the hell knew there was such a thing as a nail tech?—filed and shaped his nails. Then, before he knew what was happening, she applied a coat of polish.

"Jesus," he said, snatching his hand off the table. "Are you kidding me? Get that stuff off me."

She grabbed his hand, slapped it down on the table. "Be still and let me finish."

"I don't want any damn nail polish."

"Kim said you'd probably be a baby about it."

"This is not being a baby. This is being a guy."

"Don't worry, it's a matte finish, not a gloss."

"Oh, well, then," he mocked, "that's different. Come on, we're not taking pictures of my hands."

"You don't know that. You're a pitcher. It's all about the hands."

So he spent the afternoon surrounded by bossy women, suffused in products that made him smell like a greenhouse. They lulled him into submission, painting something warm and liquid on his eyebrows. Then—yow!—they ripped the hair right out and said, "Just cleaning up the brow line." As if that made it okay. He tried to go away somewhere in his head, a zenlike technique usually reserved for his sport. People called it different things—the zone, the mechanism, the safe place. To Bo it was a level of consciousness that took him outside himself. He'd started doing this on his own when he was a kid, desperate to escape a life that felt scary. Coach Holmes, his mentor, had taught him to put the process to good use, helping him focus on both the art and the mechanics of a good pitch.

In the salon, it didn't help. He couldn't escape.

The processing under the dryer turned the foil-wrapped strands of his hair almost white. Bo nearly puked when he saw it after the rinse-out. Unconcerned, Goldi wielded his blow-dryer like a warrior priming a rifle, and attacked. Bo shut his eyes against the hot wind. After a while, Goldi set aside the dryer, looked Bo in the eye and said, "I need to finger-scrunch you" without a hint of irony.

"Go ahead, I can take it," Bo said, bracing himself. Finger-scrunching involved the application of a clear substance referred to as "product," followed by a humiliating shot of hair spray. Hair-fricking-spray. If anyone had told Bo that a major-league career involved hair spray, he would have known they were joking. Except it was true. Hair spray.

His ordeal ended with the ritual removal of the giant plastic gown.

A few minutes later, Kim returned. She stood in the doorway, her gorgeous mouth agape. "Oh. My. God," she said in a breathy voice, which he found incredibly sexy. "You look fantastic."

So okay. This was cool. He grinned, hooking his thumbs into his back pockets. "I've been finger-scrunched."

"You should have done it long ago." She flew across the salon with arms outstretched. But her hug of gratitude was not for Bo. She embraced Goldi, saying, "You're a genius. He looks like a superstar."

"Hey, where's my hug?" Bo demanded. "I had my cuticles pared for you."

"No, you did that for your career," she corrected him, then grabbed his hand and inspected it. "Marie, you're a genius, too," she told the nail tech. She looked up at Bo. "Your hand feels really good." Then she dropped it hastily. "Let's get going and hope it doesn't snow and ruin your 'do."

"Yeah, God forbid I ruin the 'do."

The photographer's studio was a converted empty space in a building up at Camp Kioga, clear on the extreme north end of the lake. Fortunately for the Z4, the roads were kept plowed and sanded, since Camp Kioga had recently become a four-season resort. Although it had begun life as a summer camp for families in the 1920s, these days, it was open year-round, a haven for people who enjoyed winter sports. The operation was run by a local couple, Connor and Olivia Davis. Olivia was a member of the tight-knit Bellamy clan, first cousin to Daisy Bellamy, who was doing Bo's publicity shots.

"Daisy's going to show us just how good she is," Bo assured Kim. "This is a big break for her."

"I don't mind giving her a break," Kim said. "Since

she's new, you might have to be patient with her. It could take all afternoon to get the shots we need."

"Hey, if I can sit through Goldi's salon, I can sit through a photo shoot."

"I won't forget you said that."

They passed under the arched sign. Wrought iron twig lettering spelled out, Camp Kioga, Est'd. 1924. "Everything looks so different," Kim remarked.

"It's all been renovated."

The original main pavilion now housed a restaurant. The deck had been expanded, and near the lake was a covered gazebo with a sizable hot tub with puffs of steam rising into the afternoon sky. Bo glanced over to see that Kim's face had turned thoughtful. "My parents sent me to summer camp here when I was little," she said. "I used to love it so much."

He tried to imagine what summer camp was like. For him, summers were a time for hustling, so he could earn enough to pay his Little League fees. He used to work for tips at the auto-detailing place, or go door-to-door, asking for odd jobs. A summer of just being a kid was unimaginable.

This made him wonder what AJ's summers were like. It was a good bet there weren't any trips to camp.

Daisy's studio was a big, mostly empty room in a building constructed in the old days of the camp. Surrounded by windows, the studio was filled with the white light of winter, streaming in through the windows and reflecting off the frozen lake. Daisy and her crew were busy getting ready. She had an array of lights set up on tripods, reflecting shields of all sizes and a variety of backdrops. Fans and props lay on a table near a laptop setup. The old wooden floor creaked as Bo and Kim stepped into the room.

The minute she spotted Bo, Daisy's jaw dropped. "Ho-lee cow," she said.

"Yeah, two hours of being fussed at in a salon, and I'm a natural beauty."

"I wouldn't go that far," Daisy said. "You're going to need hair and makeup first. Then we'll talk about natural beauty." She introduced them to Chantal, the wardrobe and makeup stylist, and Zach, her assistant.

Daisy was all pro, and Bo could sense Kim's confidence in her growing. After seeing the setup of cameras and lighting, the computer, electrical cords and reflectors, she relaxed and asked how she could help out.

Bo thought Daisy was kidding about the makeup. Then Chantal opened a huge tackle box full of the stuff—lipstick and brushes, pots of color, clippers and cotton balls and strange devices. He looked at Kim, who didn't say a word, just nodded at a stool.

"Oh, man," he said. But he cooperated. This was his career, after all. His future. He sat through the humiliating ritual, resigned to his fate. After the salon ordeal, nothing else that happened to him was apt to freak him out. He mentally retreated to his happy place again while Chantal brushed on face makeup called "foundation" and traced around his lips with a pencil. But as in the salon, his retreat didn't help much. When she came at his eyes with something pointy, he put his foot down.

"Uh-uh, no way," he declared.

"She's almost done," Kim said encouragingly. "Be still a few minutes longer."

"Forget it. You're not putting eyeliner on me. I'm done." All this stuff was starting to make his skin crawl. He peeled off the towel they'd put around him. "If I'm not pretty enough now, I never will be."

She surrendered with a little wave of her hand. "You're the client."

As the day progressed, he sensed a subtle shift in their relationship. He'd allowed himself to be transformed. He trusted her. And he could tell, by the way she looked at him when she didn't know he was watching, that she thought he was sexy. Damn, he hoped he was right about that.

Daisy stepped in and started lining up the shots, assisted by Zach. "You look amazing," she remarked.

"You think?" He grinned, relaxing a little now that sharp-object-girl had backed off.

Kim nodded in agreement. "I've always thought there was something weirdly attractive about a guy in a baseball uniform. Couldn't say why. Under any other circumstances, a guy would look like a dork in knickers and knee socks. But a baseball uniform…" She and Daisy nodded their approval. He could tell the two of them were going to get along fine. Both were determined to make him look larger-than-life. Like a baseball god, Kim said.

What a world, he thought. One day he was mopping beer off the floor of a dive bar. A few months later, he was being made into a god. The moment he slipped on the coveted gray-with-navy pinstripes, he felt like a different person. The uniform reminded him why he was doing all this in the first place.

"I am so ready to just play baseball," he muttered.

"You know there's more to this career than playing baseball."

"I had no idea how much more."

"The photos are critical," Kim said. "A great photo can really enhance a career, assuming the player has the talent to back it up."

"It should be all about talent."

"You know it's not," she said. "Image is everything. Remember Cal Shattuck? He was driving a meat truck in the off-season, and then they ran that iconic shot of him on the cover of *Vanity Fair*, and the next day, he was a star."

"I've seen that shot," Daisy said. "He was buck naked."

"The grapes were strategically placed," Chantal said.

"Yeah, don't get any ideas," Bo said.

"As if." Daisy shuddered. "Ew." Because of his connection with Noah, she had always regarded him as someone not of her generation. An older guy, one of her stepdad's friends.

At long last, Daisy declared it showtime. He quickly found out that posing for photographs was not for sissies. In fact, it amazed him that something so simple could be so much fuss and bother. You looked at a player on a baseball card or roster sheet and you never thought about the work that went into the shot. Models who did this for a living were nuts.

Everybody worked nonstop. They turned him every which way but loose, posing him like a double-jointed action figure. He was on the stool, off the stool. He was holding a bat, then a ball and mitt. Cap on, cap off. Then they tried some creative artsy stuff—Bo playing his bass. Brooding out the window at the snowy woods as though willing spring to come. Every time they paused to review the shots on the laptop, he stood back, discomfited by the dozens of images.

"These are not quite right," Kim said.

"Come on, I look good."

"She's right," Daisy said. "These are okay, but we can do better."

"You look…stiff," Kim said.

"You say that like it's a bad thing."

"You look scared of the camera, see? You look like someone who's having his picture taken."

"Okay, so I'm supposed to look like some guy who just happens to be sitting here?"

"Exactly. The best shot makes me forget it's a set-up."

"Here we go." Daisy advanced to some other frames. "You're better when you have the gear in your hands. Still not quite right, but better."

"There, that one's my favorite so far." Kim indicated a shot of him with his electric bass. "See how natural you look?"

Not really, but he nodded his head.

"This is good because you're a left-handed pitcher and the focus here is on your left hand. And you've got a look of concentration on your face."

"Some models get into their role by telling themselves stories in their heads," Daisy suggested. "It's a subtle thing, but it adds dimension."

They went back to work, and he tried telling himself a story. However, with Kim standing there, checking him out the whole time, the only story he could tell himself was X-rated. In his story, she was wearing leather and lace, and not very much of either. In his story, he held her pushed against a wall and did it fast and hard, and later, he laid her down on a cloud-soft mattress and made love to her so slowly and so tenderly that she wept.

"Oh," she said, moistening her lips. "Now, that's what I'm talking about."

"Yeah?" He chuckled softly. "I'm telling a story in my head."

"Keep doing that," she said. "It's working. You're taking me somewhere else, and it makes me want to come with you."

"In that case, the story's got a happy ending."

After a while, they exhausted all the props, including his twin amps, the wind machine and even articles of clothing, like his Under Armour shirt and spike-soled shoes. Daisy looked out the window. "There's a little bit of sun, but it's fading fast," she said. "I'd like to get a series of exterior shots. We've got to work quickly."

A glare from Kim convinced him not to bellyache about the cold. Daisy explained that the "golden hour," the deep amber of the lowering sun, was a gift this time of year. In winter, the sun didn't like to show itself, but when it did, the light was strong and intense, creating a natural drama everywhere the camera pointed.

"I love this idea," said Kim, bundling into her parka.

"The key is going to be for you to look totally cool but not cold," Daisy explained. She did a series of shots in front of the lake, saying she wanted him to look like he was dreaming of summer in the dead of winter.

"I'm dying here," he said, steeling himself to keep from shivering. "I am flat-lining."

"You look great," Daisy objected. "Let's hurry before your nose turns red. Let's go over here."

Despite the cold, Bo knew it was a one-of-a-kind back-drop. Meerskill Falls was a cascade that started high in the secret reaches of the hills and spilled down a steep gorge spanned by a footbridge. In winter, it turned into a wall of ice so thick and layered that it seemed to conceal a different world within its depths.

"This is genius, guys," said Zach, holding a reflector on Bo as he strode along in front of the frozen falls.

"Try it with these shades." Chantal tossed him a pair of sunglasses.

"We've only got a few more minutes of sunlight," Daisy said. "Knock yourself out. Do whatever you like."

"That would be running for the fire to thaw myself out."

"Baby," Kim teased.

He scooped up a snowball and lobbed a line drive at her.

"Hey!" She threw one back and he fielded it with ridiculous ease, his mitt so soft he barely broke it.

"You don't want to get in a snowball fight with me," he said.

"Ha. You don't scare me."

He packed a snowball, gave it a fine windup and pitched it straight at her. The ball exploded against her shoulder, right where he'd aimed it.

Her laughter taunted him to keep up the attack. She looked like a supermodel herself, laughing and completely in her element in the snow. She was the one who should be in pictures, not him.

As the late golden sunlight slanted across the snow, Daisy declared a wrap. "And guess what, the best shots of the day are going to be the ones I just took. It's so often the case that the best come last."

That was probably because the subject was so beaten down, he'd do anything to get the shoot over with. He was shivering by the time they got back inside. Mercifully, they let him scrub off the makeup and brush out the hair spray. After he put his street clothes back on, he found Daisy and Kim going through the shots on the laptop.

"These are just what we need," Kim said, stepping back so he could see the screen.

He winced. There was something painful about staring at shot after shot of himself, especially those that inadvertently revealed something. "Do I really look so pissed off all the time?" he asked.

"That's not anger," Daisy said.

"It's intensity," Kim agreed, clicking through the frames. "And here—that's yearning, and this one is smoldering."

Bo flushed. It was one of the fake-sweat shots. They had misted him with water and shot him with his jersey unbuttoned. "Yeah, that's me, smoldering."

"We've got some happy shots, too." Daisy showed him. "You look good when you laugh."

"Everybody looks good when they laugh."

She shook her head. "You'd be surprised."

The outdoor shots looked weird to him, but according to Kim, that was what made them good. The contrast between the baseball uniform and the arctic surroundings was striking. He looked as if he'd landed on another planet.

"It's stunning work." Kim pointed to a shot of him walking toward the camera with a purposeful stride, his long hair fanning out behind him, his eyes intensely blue. "That's my favorite."

The frozen waterfall created a dramatic backdrop, glittering in the setting sun. "Yeah, I love that," Daisy agreed. "And this one, where he's throwing a snowball like it's a winning pitch."

"Thanks, Daisy," Bo said.

"I appreciate the work," she said. "I'll have all the retouching done by the end of the week."

"You're just like your mom," he said. "Hardworking and talented."

At that, she laughed. "Sorry, I'm not used to being compared to my mom."

That surprised Bo. Daisy and Sophie were cut from the same cloth—fiercely smart and ambitious, determined to balance work and family.

"You've been great," Kim said to Daisy, then turned to Bo. "You were totally right about her. What a find."

"I'm surrounded by talented women," he said. "I just can't beat you girls off with a stick."

"Right." Daisy carefully stowed her camera equipment.

"You're going to see these photos everywhere," Kim said. "I'm sure of it."

Olivia Bellamy Davis, who ran the resort, arrived to see how the shoot had gone. Clicking through the frames on the laptop, she gave her stamp of approval. "You made him a star," she said to Daisy.

"No, I made him *look like* a star," Daisy clarified. "Kim is the one who has to make him a star."

"Hey, what am I?" Bo asked. "Chopped liver?"

All of them responded in unison: "Yes."

"Okay, I'll shut up." He made himself useful, helping Zach lug the gear to Daisy's van. A few minutes later, Kim and the others came out.

"Can you stay?" Olivia asked. "I can offer you a drink and a soak in the hot tub."

"Sounds tempting," Daisy said, "but I have to pick

Charlie up by six. He's been with his dad all afternoon."
She noticed Kim's expression and said, "Charlie's my son.
He's a year and a half old."

"I hope I get to meet him one day," Kim said. "I love kids."

Bo studied her face. She'd told him sometimes a diplomatic lie worked better than the truth. Ever since, he found
himself wondering about some of the things she said—like
I love kids.

As the van pulled away, Olivia turned to Bo and Kim.
"What about you two?"

"Sure," said Bo. Dino had taken AJ for pizza and bowl-
ing, so there was no hurry to get back.

Kim elbowed him in the ribs, hard.

"She'd love to," he added, pretending he hadn't felt it.

"Great," said Olivia, and led the way.

Fifteen minutes later, they found themselves in borrowed swimsuits in a big hot tub under a gazebo at the
lakeshore. Olivia was the ideal hostess, serving chilled
champagne and then—conveniently—disappearing.

"Nice place," Bo commented, tasting the champagne.
Honestly, he preferred beer, but he remembered what
Kim had taught him about being a good guest. He
floated in the comforting heat of the water and looked
around at the wilderness surrounding the camp, now
purple in the twilight. A few of the lakeside cabins were
occupied, and a good number of diners were at the restaurant in the distance, visible through the glowing windows. "I've never been here in the winter. Last summer,
when the place reopened, I came up to teach a baseball
clinic."

"When I was a kid, I used to mark off the days on my calendar until I could come here."

"I wish I'd known you back then," he said, picturing a girl with knobby knees and fiery red hair.

"No, you don't," she said. "I was a brat."

He leaned his head back against the edge of the tub, watching her through half-lidded eyes. "My favorite kind of girl."

"A brat?" Steam swirled up from the surface of the water surrounding her.

Setting aside the champagne glass, he slipped his arms around her, pulled her close and said, "You. You're my favorite kind."

"Bo—"

"Hush. Wait a second." He moved to the opposite side of the hot tub, bringing her with him and turning her so they were both facing the lake. "There, that's better."

"What's better? What are you doing?"

"I want it to be perfect the first time I kiss you."

"The first... Why?"

"Because it's important and I want to treat it that way. I want you to remember that the first time I kissed you, the moon was coming up over the lake, and it was so quiet we could hear the snow fall, that we were in the most beautiful spot on earth."

"But why?" she persisted, but the tremor in her voice told him she understood.

"Because you're different from other women. We're different, together. I've kissed women in cars and movie theaters and on their front porches, and under the bleachers after a game. Never in a place like this."

"I don't…know what to say to that."

"You're not meant to say anything. You're supposed to kiss me back, and then we'll hold each other and watch the moon rise. And for the rest of our lives, we'll remember our first kiss."

"Bo Crutcher," she said, relaxing against him. "You're a true romantic."

"I am," he agreed. "And you know why?"

"Why?"

"Because when it comes to you, I think mushy thoughts and I'm not embarrassed or anything."

"I'm not embarrassed, either," she said, her voice shaking in a way that touched his heart. "And you're right— this is the most beautiful place on earth, and I'm glad we're here. And—" She broke off.

"And what?"

"And I wish you would kiss me instead of just talking about it."

He touched her face, one hand cradling her cheek. "My thoughts exactly." He slid his other hand around behind her, pulling her against him and holding her so close he could feel the rhythm of her breathing. His heart was beating so hard, he was sure she could tell. He didn't care, though.

Their lips were close, almost touching. He whispered her name, and then settled his mouth over hers, drawing a light gasp from her. She put her arms around him, and he deepened the kiss, parting her lips, his tongue slow and languid. She tasted delicious, and her hair smelled like the snowy air, and it was the perfect moment Bo had been thinking about practically from the day he'd met her. He knew that as long as he lived, and no matter what else happened to him for the rest of his life, he would never forget this moment.

With a groan of reluctance, he ended the kiss, holding her for a moment and then pulling back.

She let out a sigh and rested her head on his shoulder. They sat for a long time together, neither of them speaking as they watched the moon over the lake, outlining the forested mountaintops in the distance. It was a scene of such quiet splendor that it felt almost holy.

"What's that smile?" he asked, gazing down at her.

"Just…everything. You were right about the kiss."

He smiled back. "Yeah?"

"I'll never forget it."

"Me, neither. I'm going to be thinking about that kiss for a long, long time. Like, forever. I probably won't be able to sleep tonight."

Bo had always thought he'd known what love felt like. He'd loved other women, but he'd never experienced this intensity. It was an expansive feeling in his chest, both sweet and searing, almost but not quite to the point of pain.

She caught him studying her. "You're not watching the moon," she said.

"I'm watching you."

He kissed her again and once again, soft and romantic, but also slow and sexy. The kind of kiss that made him wish there was nothing between them, nothing at all. Bo had made out with a lot of women through the years, but with Kim, each kiss felt like the first time—new and undiscovered, exciting. He could feel her body respond before common sense told her not to. He couldn't remember ever wanting to make love to a woman more than he did right at this moment. He sensed an answering need in her, but that was probably wishful thinking on his part, because after a lingering kiss, she pulled away.

"That was…nice," she said. "I'm not getting involved with you, though."

"Then why do you keep making out with me?" He moved toward her, slipped his arms around her from behind.

She sighed, reclining back against him. "This is why," she said quietly. "Because it feels so…" Her voice trailed away on another sigh as he bent his head to gently nip her shoulder.

"Come on, honey," he said. "Let's get involved, what do you say?"

Women were so damned easy to love. They had sweet voices. They were soft in all the right places and they smelled so good. And they tasted like… He groaned, leaned down and kissed her again, just at the top of her clavicle.

"It's a bad idea," she said. "That's why. And stop doing those things. I can't think when you act like this."

"That's the plan."

"It's not my plan." Yet it seemed genuinely hard for her to move away from him. "You're a client. I don't get involved with clients."

"What about Lloyd Johnson?"

When she pulled back, Bo could see the surprise on her face. "He's the reason I made that rule," she said.

In addition to what Kim had told Bo, he'd done some digging on his own. Johnson was NBA royalty, the whole package of talent, looks and marketability. According to the gossip blogs on the Internet, Lloyd and Kim had been serious right up until a nasty, public breakup. The commentators all pointed the finger right at Kim, accusing her of being controlling, manipulative and jealous. Of course, the commentators hadn't seen her in the morning after the big drama, in a skimpy evening gown and dark glasses at the airport.

"Listen," he said, "whatever Johnson did to you, whatever he was to you—I'm not him."

"Exactly. Because we're not getting involved. It's a new policy of mine. No personal involvement with a client. I'm not going to let you turn into another one of my bad choices."

"Fine, then. You're fired."

She let out a brief laugh. "Right. So you'd rather have me than a career."

He figured he could win her over if he said the romantic thing—*To hell with the career, it's you I want*—but he'd never been good at lying. He tugged her toward him and said, "I want it all—the career, the girl, the white picket fence…well, maybe no fence."

She slid away from him. "Right. You just want to get laid."

"Let's think about that a moment," he said. "Here I am with my golden highlights, in a hot tub with the hottest girl I've ever seen, a girl who by the way, kisses like a goddess and tastes like candy from heaven. And you assume I want to get laid."

"Tell me I'm wrong."

"Hell, you're so far from being wrong I can't even tell you. And in case you're wondering, we *are* involved. It *is* personal. I felt involved even when we were two strangers at the airport. So don't give me this 'I don't get involved with clients' shit. I'm not buying it."

"I'm not asking you to."

"Fine."

"Fine." She moved away from him in the water, settling on the opposite side of the tub. Droplets of water beaded in her hair and eyelashes, and she looked so pretty he had to remind himself not to groan aloud. She narrowed her eyes at him. "Quit staring at me."

"Sorry. No can do."

"Whatever. Stare all you like. I'm not changing my mind."

"Nope," he said, "that's my job—to change your mind."

"Don't waste your time." She laid her head back on the rounded edge of the tub and gazed up at the stars. "When I was little, I used to think the stars were holes in the sky and that their light belonged to another world, and we could only see a little bit of it, seeping through the holes, like the sun through a pinhole camera."

He reached out, tucked a stray lock of hair behind her ear. "Maybe that's just what they are."

"Right, that's me. A real rocket scientist."

"Rocket scientists. What the hell do they know?"

"Rockets, for one thing. And science."

"I thought the stars were a bunch of eyes, watching me," Bo said.

"We're a couple of geniuses." She made the first move, levering herself up and out of the tub. The steam rolled off her in waves, making her look even more like a creature from another world. A Titian-haired goddess—that was a phrase he learned from reading Penny's old books of poetry. Kim embodied a kind of otherworldly beauty that made his eyes ache, yet he couldn't look away. When she grabbed one of the big white robes and covered herself, Bo came as close to crying as he ever had in his adult life.

Twenty

Ever since the New York scare, Bo was hypervigilant when it came to AJ. He slept lightly, his senses attuned to his son in the alcove bed. If AJ so much as sighed in his sleep, Bo tended to spring awake. He kept telling himself to relax. AJ seemed resigned to his fate. According to his teachers, he was cooperative and quiet. He seemed to be settling in.

Although there had been no further running away or truancy, Bo couldn't help worrying. He sensed AJ wasn't settling in at all. He was guarded, wearing attitude like body armor and keeping his distance from people.

Bo knew what it was like to be a boy on fire, restless and watchful, thrumming with impatience. He knew how it felt when you yearned to make something happen, even if it meant doing something foolish. God knew, he'd been there himself, once upon a time.

Each morning, Bo stood at the front door of the house, watching until AJ boarded the school bus. Every afternoon, he stood in the same spot, waiting to see him get off and head home. Bo's stomach always knotted up until he saw the boy actually appear.

The sun was making a rare appearance this afternoon, turning the yard into a field of diamonds.

When Kim came into the vestibule, interrupting his afternoon vigil, Bo gladly welcomed the distraction. He found her extremely distracting. After the photo shoot, he'd theorized that the rush of emotions he got from kissing her might have been the result of unwinding after a long day. It wouldn't be the first time his heart lied to him. Yet instead of subsiding, his feelings for her escalated. With everything else on his plate, he hadn't yet figured out what to do about that.

"You're hovering," she said, joining him at the front window. "Ever since AJ went to New York, you've been hovering."

"Do you blame me?"

"No, it's understandable. Not helpful, but understandable."

"I feel bad for AJ," Bo said. "He still hates it here."

"Has he told you that?"

"No need. It's obvious. He writes letters to his mother, and we have no way of knowing if they ever get to her. That kills me, and I can only imagine what it's doing to him. He's not making friends, not really doing anything other than marking time. That's no way to live your life."

"And you know this because…?" she prompted.

"Because he's waiting around for something to happen… people spend their lives that way, and then they look back and wonder what the hell happened to all the time."

"Is this the voice of experience talking?"

"It's one of the reasons I pursued Independent League baseball instead of taking the traditional path in the minors. When you're waiting around to be tapped for a major-league team, you're so focused on the future that you miss what's happening right under your nose. I've seen ballplayers get so busy looking ahead to the next move that they forget where they are. That's the silver lining to my long wait for the Yankees. I quit focusing on getting there and figured out how to live my life in the here and now."

"I like that," she said quietly. "But how do you get him to think like that?"

"Good question." He turned away from the window, reminding himself AJ would get home when he got home. "I sure as hell don't want him to look back on this time in his life and see nothing but trouble. A boy deserves to be happy." He noticed the way she was watching him, her face thoughtful, her smile soft. Christ, where had this woman been all his life? And how could he get her to stay? "What?" he asked.

"You're a philosopher," she said. "Where'd that come from?"

"Dunno." He found himself remembering his mother. Almost up to the day she died, she had drifted from moment to moment, convinced she'd find the right man, the right job, the right life, if only she waited patiently enough. Even when he was little, he'd felt her looking beyond him, trying to see past him. He remembered yearning for more attention from her, but ultimately, she couldn't give him what he needed.

He pictured the way Kim was with AJ, hanging out with him, helping him with homework. *I love kids,* she'd told Daisy.

Unaware of his thoughts, she said, "How about making a fire in the living room? AJ might like that with his afternoon snack."

The living room had a big, old-fashioned fireplace with a marble mantel and a neat stack of split wood in a box on the hearth. He busied himself laying the fire. "I know I can't force the kid to like it here, and nothing's going to feel right to him until he's back with his mother. Still, I wish I could do something to make him feel more at home."

She handed him a box of kitchen matches. "Let's think of something fun for him to do this weekend. The weather is looking promising."

"Promising. Like the temperature could shoot up above freezing? I could take him to the video arcade. Or to a movie." He struck a match, touched it to the crumpled paper under the logs.

"Not that kind of fun. Kids can do that anywhere. He should do something new, something he can only do here."

He eyed her suspiciously. "What did you have in mind?"

"Snowboarding at Saddle Mountain."

He threw back his head and let out a belly laugh. "You crack me up, lady. You really do."

"I'm not kidding. Boys his age love snowboarding. *I* love snowboarding. I bet he'd do great."

"Fine, *you* take him up the mountain. I'll just stay home by the fire." He lit another match, then leaned down to blow on the small flame.

"No way. The whole point is for you to do something together. He's been without you long enough. So you're coming with us."

The tiny flame caught and flared, licking at the dry firewood. "I'm an athlete. What if I blow out a knee? Hurt my shoulder?"

"Don't be a baby. You'll be fine."

"We're supposed to be working on my image."

"I thought you wanted to show AJ how great it is to live here."

"What's great about sliding down a mountain?" He shuddered at the thought.

"We're taking him snowboarding."

"I'll fall on my butt and freeze to death," Bo grumbled. The log caught, crackling brightly.

At that moment, AJ came into the room, his backpack dragging at one shoulder, his jacket hanging open. "Cool," he said. "That's something I'd like to see."

"Smart-ass," Bo said.

Kim smacked his arm. "Watch your mouth." She turned to AJ. "We didn't hear you come in. How was school?" She held up her hand. "No, don't answer that. Bo and I were talking about finding some fun things for you to do while you're here. We're going up to Saddle Mountain for some snowboarding. You up for that?"

Excitement flashed in his eyes, but he masked it quickly. "I guess."

She sent Bo a smug smile. "You're outvoted."

Bo felt ambushed by Kim and AJ. They rushed around, borrowing gear from Noah Shepherd, who had plenty to share and no sympathy at all for Bo's aversion to snow and cold. In Noah's sloping yard, Bo and AJ learned the rudiments of snowboarding, which only added to Bo's apprehension and AJ's excitement. On Saturday, he leaped out of bed, making enough noise to rouse Bo even before the sun, and by nine in the morning, they were among the first to arrive at the ski resort.

There was something called a chairlift that scooped up the skiers and snowboarders and transported them, against all laws of physics, up the side of a frozen mountain. Bo felt as if he was being lifted up to be dropped into a volcano. Saddle Mountain, which looked so quaint and picturesque when viewed through the window, now appeared as forbidding as the frozen mountains of Middle Earth, in *Lord of the Rings.*

Bo turned to his two companions, who were chattering away with excitement and looking around at the scenery. They acted as though this was a kiddie ride at Disney World.

"We're going to die," he said. "You know that, don't you?"

"Quit being a baby," Kim scolded. "You're not going to die. I won't let you die."

She looked crazy beautiful, even in the unfamiliar getup of a snowboarder. AJ looked pretty cool, too, in an outfit and equipment borrowed from Max Bellamy. As for Bo, he felt a deep distrust of this whole process. There was nothing natural about it. For the chairlift ride, they each had one foot fastened to a snowboard, the other dangling free. Kim promised when they reached the top, they would fasten the other boot in place, which made him even more apprehensive. But he kept his mouth shut because of the expression on AJ's face. For the first time since his arrival in Avalon, the kid looked animated, his eyes sparkling with anticipation.

"It's a beautiful view, isn't it?" Kim said, as AJ twisted around to check out the valley below.

"Yeah, it's like we're flying," he said.

"When the day is clear like this, you can see all the way across the lake. That's the main part of town there." She pointed out the toy village clustered at one end of a vast field of white. "That's the square, and you can see Blanchard Park. There's a puff of smoke coming out of the skating house. That's where people go to warm up and rent ice skates."

Do not promise him ice-skating. Glaring at her over the boy's head, Bo tried to telegraph the message to her with his eyes.

"Ice-skating is really fun," she went on, either oblivious to or willfully ignoring Bo's glare of warning. "Your dad and I will take you skating soon, maybe tomorrow."

"Cool," said AJ.

"You think you'd like that?"

"I doubt he would," Bo said.

"I'd definitely like to try," AJ said.

"You bet," said Kim.

"No way," said Bo.

"Come on," she said, "it's really fun."

"That's what you said about snowboarding, and so far, I'm not having fun."

"You haven't even tried it," AJ insisted.

"I'll be glad when this is over."

"It's gonna be great," AJ insisted.

Kim sent Bo a look of triumph, then resumed her guided tour. "At the very far end of the lake is Camp Kioga. Meerskill Falls is open for ice climbing this year."

"Ice climbing?" AJ perked up yet again.

Oh, geez, thought Bo. *Ice climbing?*

"When a waterfall freezes, it creates a thick wall of ice.

That's where we did the photo shoot. I'm told it's a great way to climb, fun and challenging. I've always wanted to try it."

"Yeah, me, too."

They both regarded Bo expectantly.

"Sure," he said. "I can think of no better way to injure myself right before my first major-league season."

"The town has a winter carnival," Kim went on. "I've never been here for it, but I'm told it's a big event."

"I was here for it last year," Bo volunteered.

"What was it like?" asked AJ.

"Hell—heck—I stayed inside where it was warm," said Bo. "They have ice-hockey tournaments, stuff like that. Oh, and there's this insane race—an Iron Man triathlon. Noah does it every year. It involves snowshoeing, dogsledding and cross-country skiing." Bo shuddered.

"Dogsledding?" AJ's eyes lit up. "You mean, like in the Iditarod?"

Kim nodded. "Mush, and all that. I bet Noah would take you and your dad."

"Forget it," Bo said.

"Excellent," AJ said.

"Man, for a kid who doesn't like sports, you're sure interested in trying a lot of them," Bo remarked.

"So can we go dogsledding with Noah?"

"We'll see."

"Heads up," Kim said, lifting the safety bar. "We're near the top. Now, remember what I showed you about getting off the lift. Just step off and slide away from the chair. Ready?"

No, thought Bo.

"Yes," AJ said, leaning forward.

"Here we go." Kim put her arms around AJ and helped him glide smoothly off the chair lift.

Bo fell on his ass. "Hey," he wailed. "This sucks."

"You'll be fine." Kim extended her hand to him. "Get up and let's get our boards on."

A few minutes later, they had fastened their booted feet onto the snowboards, and they stood together at the top of the slope. It was marked with a green sign.

"Green means this is the easiest way down," Kim explained.

Bo regarded the long, forbidding incline with gut-clenching dread. "The way I see it, the easiest way down is with those guys." He gestured at a toboggan being towed behind a snowmobile.

"That's the ski patrol bringing an injured person off the mountain," Kim said. "You don't want to leave like that."

Bo still wanted to leave. Yet one glimpse of AJ's face reminded him to keep his mouth shut. The boy's eyes shone. There was no other word to capture that bright, intense glow of interest. Maybe Kim was onto something here. Here was a chance to connect with AJ, give him something to like about this place. And maybe even about his father.

"I've never stood on top of a mountain before," AJ said. "It's like being on top of the world."

Kim took a cell-phone picture of him. "You *are* on top of the world. Come on, guys. Let's go snowboarding."

All around them, skiers and snowboarders zipped past, seeming to coast down the hill. Bo and AJ spent more time on their butts than on their boards. There was a silver lining, though. In order to help Bo get up on his board, Kim spent a lot of time clutching him around the waist, trying to hold him upright. Eventually, they reached the bottom. Bo yearned to call it quits, but it was no use—she made them ride the lift back up and do it all over again. And again.

AJ picked up the basics fairly quickly. "Hey, check it out," he yelled on the third or fourth run, easing down the hill like a surfer in slow motion. "Hey, it's working."

"How come he picked it up so fast?" Bo demanded, frustrated.

"He's got a lower center of gravity. That helps," Kim said.

"Yeah? What's going to help me?"

"I will." She grabbed his waist, coaching him until he managed to keep his balance. She was stronger than she looked, manhandling him into position. She coaxed and guided him down the hill, showing a patience and forbearance he hadn't known she possessed.

"Hold me tighter," he said as they made their way to the bottom. "I don't want to fall."

It was too late, though. He was already falling. The snowy surface raced up to meet him, gathering speed. He and Kim went down together, hitting the ground in an explosion of fresh snow.

AJ didn't exactly laugh aloud, but he couldn't keep the amusement from his eyes. "You look like the abominable snowman," he called, laughter flowing behind him as he glided down the hill.

"I've been trying to make him smile for days," Bo said. "Turns out all it took was wiping out in a snowbank." He felt a lump of snow slither down his neck. "This is humiliating."

"But worth it," she said, offering her hand to help him up.

"Why? Because I get to grab you?"

She rolled her eyes. "No. Look."

At the bottom of the hill, AJ was talking to some kids his age. Bo forgot his misery for a moment as he watched them laughing together. *Laughing.* Bo didn't think there was anything sweeter in life than seeing your kid laugh. Friends could make all the difference.

The boys were still hanging out when Bo wobbled to a halt near AJ. "I made it down again," he said. "All in one piece. But you beat me by a mile."

"Uh, yeah." AJ's smile disappeared. Clearly, he wasn't sure what to do in the situation.

Bo took off his goggles. "Bo Crutcher," he said, greeting the kids. "And this is Miss Kimberly van Dorn."

The boys introduced themselves. Bo couldn't tell whether they were more impressed by the fact that they were talking to Bo Crutcher or by the fact that Kim was a world-class looker. One guy, Vinny Romano, declared himself a die-hard Hornets fan. "I went to every single home game last summer," he said. "You had an awesome season."

"Thanks," said Bo.

"I came to your pitching clinic," said another boy, whose name was Tad.

"You did," Bo confirmed. "I remember you. You're a lefty like me. AJ's a southpaw, too." At the moment, he felt like giving these boys a generous tip, because they made him look good in front of AJ.

"These guys were going to take me up the other chair-lift," AJ said, gesturing at the longer lift. "And then over to the half-pipe, where you can do tricks and stuff."

Bo was dying to say no to that. Kim gave him a look.

It was remarkable how much she could convey in a single look.

"I'll be careful," AJ promised. "I'll keep my helmet on."

"Meet us at the lodge when the lifts close," Kim said. "We'll be by the fire, relaxing."

"In fact, we were just headed there now," Bo said.

"We're not." Kim bullied him toward the chairlift again. "We've got two more hours before they shut down the lifts."

He tried not to groan aloud. "Okay, see you," he told AJ. "Be careful."

As AJ and the boys headed for the last line, Bo heard one of them say, "That's your dad? Man, you're lucky."

Kim gave Bo a nudge. "Hear that? His friends think he's lucky."

"I wonder what AJ thinks."

"He's warming up to you," she said. "Especially after today. I can tell."

She worked him like a ranch dog for the rest of the afternoon. She was the most relentless of coaches, pushing him, yelling at him, praising him, scolding him. After each fall, he made a big show of rising to his feet, making certain he grabbed her and held fast for longer than was necessary. Damn. She felt so good in his arms, he was almost grateful for the outing. Almost.

Eventually, he was able to ride down the slope without mishap. He couldn't keep the grin off his face. "I feel like I just pitched a shutout."

"Good for you." She high-fived him, but refused to let him rest on his laurels. "Let's try the other chair."

"Let's try a cold beer by the fire." He gestured at the

lodge, so friendly-looking, with its glowing windows and puffing chimney.

"Ha. You're on a roll, Crutcher. I'm not letting up on you now."

"Media training and now this. What other tricks do you have up your sleeve?"

"Let's see, ice-skating, tobogganing, snowshoeing…"

"Forget I asked." He gritted his teeth and endured another chairlift ascent, longer and steeper than the other. This side of the mountain had more challenging runs.

"You want to see me dead," Bo accused.

"I've never lost a client yet. Not to snowboarding, anyway." She gave him no time to worry or talk himself out of taking on the intermediate slopes. Besides, there was this invisible but huge element in play—his pride. With dogged determination, he forced himself to conquer the hill. And somewhere between the bone-jarring wipeouts and soul-numbing cold, he actually learned how to ride a snowboard, and it started to be fun in a way he hadn't experienced in a long time.

"Look at you." Kim clapped her mittens in excitement. "You're snowboarding."

He dared to try a little more speed. In his mind, he was like the Silver Surfer in comic books—confident, agile, effortlessly graceful.

"AJ's over at the half-pipe," said Kim. "Let's show him what you've learned."

They found the boys taking turns on the engineered slope. It was a gully carved out of the snow, designed to facilitate airborne turns.

"Watch this!" AJ called out when he spotted them. With

his friends calling encouragement, he surfed the half-pipe, taking a spill or two, but managing a couple of clean, sharp turns. He wobbled as he landed, but stayed upright.

Bo felt a crazy kind of pride. "That's my boy," he said.

"Yes, it is," she agreed.

"My turn." Before he lost his nerve, he went to the edge and teetered there.

"Go for it," AJ called, his voice echoing through the pipe. "Come on, you can do it."

Bo took a deep breath and watched Kim demonstrate. She made it look effortless and fun, looping back and forth, from one side of the U-shaped trench to the other. To Bo, there were few things more attractive than a woman who was good at sports. Growing up, his crushes had always been for woman athletes—Gabriela Sabatini, Jackie Joyner-Kersee. Kim easily qualified for membership in their club, because she was fearless and good at what she did. Best of all, she was close enough to touch.

Taking a deep breath, he pushed himself over the edge and down the slope of the half-pipe. Instantly he knew he had miscalculated his aim. Instead of gliding down one bank and up the opposite side, he slid down the middle of the pipe, gathering speed by the nanosecond. Vaguely, he could hear warnings being shouted, although he couldn't make out the words.

He was going faster than he'd ever gone without the benefit of an internal combustion engine. If he crashed now, he would break every bone in his body. He needed to figure out how to slow himself down. In desperation, he tried the weight-shift move Kim had shown him and, amazingly, he turned, diverting his relentless downhill run. Now he was headed up the steep side of the pipe. The steepness would slow him down like a runaway truck lane off a freeway.

Except it didn't work that way. Crazily, he gathered speed with centrifugal force, violating the laws of physics so many times, he ought to be arrested.

He heard the roar of voices as he cleared the lip of the pipe. Saw a patchwork of blue and white, the sky and snow, and beneath him, he felt absolutely nothing. He was weightless, flying. Ascending to heaven.

Okay, he thought. *This is the part where I'm supposed to wake up and realize it was all a dream.* Instead, from a terrifying height, he dropped like a bird shot from the sky. *Boom.*

A mushroom cloud of snow erupted all around him.

Moments later, AJ, Kim and the two boys gathered. "Are you okay?" AJ demanded, his voice edged with concern. "Dad! Are you all right?"

For a few seconds, Bo lay still. He wasn't injured, but savoring the sound of AJ calling him Dad.

"Hey, Dad." AJ nudged him. "You okay?"

"Fine," Bo said, grinning. "Just peachy."

"Cool," AJ said. "You were awesome."

Bo rubbed the snow from his goggles and focused on Kim. "*Now* can I go inside, coach?"

"Lemme help you up." AJ extended his hand.

So this was new. For the sake of this boy, Bo had done something way out of his comfort zone. A startling thought struck him—this was something a father did, every day. Bo had never experienced it firsthand. His concept of a father came not from what he had, but from what he lacked.

It came from AJ himself. It didn't matter that he'd practically done himself in, that he was sitting half frozen in a snowbank. It didn't matter that he was dying to be indoors, by the fire, nursing a beer. He looked at AJ and thought, that smile is worth everything.

Twenty-One

After dinner, Kim found Bo in front of the fire with his hands clasped behind his head and a wide, somewhat sleepy grin on his face. As she stood unobserved in the doorway, she felt a surge of lust.

I'm an idiot, she thought.

But there was no denying the truth. Athletes were her weakness. And this particular type—long-haired, long-limbed and bad for her—had been her downfall.

Taking care to erase all evidence of attraction from her face, she stepped into the room and perched on the arm of the settee. "You certainly look happy with yourself."

"This is what they call in Texas a shit-eatin' grin," he explained. "And, lady, I earned it today." He picked up the stereo remote and turned on some music. Vintage Neil Young drifted from the speakers. Bo was a fan of the pedal slide guitar, something she'd never given much thought to until he'd introduced it to her. "I ache in every part of my body," he said, "is how I earned it. I ache in places I didn't know I had."

She caught herself thinking about his "places." She had no business thinking of such things, but couldn't help herself. "Snowboarding will do that to a person."

He poured two small glasses of peppermint schnapps and handed her one. "To you, for making me face my fear."

She sipped the fiery clear drink. "Apart from the whining, you did all right."

"How about you? Are you feeling all right?" he asked.

"Perfect," she said. She watched the flames dancing in the grate, pleasantly mesmerized. "A day on the slopes always leaves me feeling perfect. How's AJ?"

"Dead asleep. You saw him at dinner," Bo said. "He practically fell asleep in his lasagna. He could barely drag himself up the stairs. Almost didn't make it to bed, and he was asleep before his head hit the pillow. But it's a good kind of tired. He sure had fun today."

"That was the whole idea, right?"

"It worked out even better than you promised. It was good to see him hanging out with kids his age."

"He's so great, Bo. You must be proud of him."

"I am, although I can't take any credit for it. That goes to Yolanda."

Kim stayed quiet. He rarely mentioned her by name.

"I can tell she's been a good mother," he added. "Raised him well. She sure as hell doesn't deserve what's happening to her."

Kim wondered what it was like to have such an intimate connection to someone, to make a child, and then... nothing. "I know she'll be grateful to know you're taking good care of AJ."

"I guess. No idea what she's like anymore."

"But you did love her," Kim said, though the statement was a question.

"We were kids," he said, "but, yeah. In a way teenagers are in love."

"Was she your first...you know?"

"You're sure curious tonight," he said.

She was. She wanted to know everything about him. "Well?"

"Okay, she wasn't my first," he said. "But it was the first time it was my idea. And that's all you'll get out of me about that, so don't even ask."

"Fine, then don't ask me, either."

"I won't, because what matters to me is you, right now." He laughed softly. "I never thought I'd be thanking somebody for dragging me up a mountain and forcing me down on a snowboard, but thank you. It's the happiest I've ever seen AJ."

"You're welcome."

He angled his glass in her direction. "I'd raise a toast to you, but I can't lift my arm."

"Is that going to affect your pitching?" She laughed at his expression. "And does whining ever help?"

"Hey, I'm wounded."

She couldn't help herself; she examined him from stem to stern. "Where?"

"Everywhere. But especially my...neck and shoulders. Yeah, if you could just massage the kinks out—"

"I could, but I won't."

"Come on. You do me, and then I'll do you. And, yes, I know how that sounds."

"I'm not sore at all," she said.

"But I am, and I need help. Come on, have a heart."

"You're a big baby, you know that?" Yet she got up and stood behind him, gently kneading the large, powerful muscles of his neck and shoulders. Her excuse was that maybe this close contact would satisfy her stupid craving to be near him, to touch him. She could get it out of her system—yet she knew the thought was a lie the moment it occurred to her.

He let out a blissful sigh. "You have me pegged," he agreed. "A big baby."

The feel of him under her hands only made her wish things she shouldn't be wishing. "I can't believe snowboarding gave you aching shoulders," she said.

"There are parts of me that ache worse," he said, tipping back his head to look at her. "But it would be ungentlemanly for me to ask for a massage there."

She swayed slightly toward him and hoped he didn't notice. He'd taken a shower after they got home, and he smelled wonderful. "I didn't realize you cared about being gentlemanly."

"Normally, I don't." Then he added, as though it were the most obvious thing in the world, "And then I met you, and now it matters a lot."

She let go of him and stepped away, taking a seat at the opposite end of the sofa from him. This had to be a new form of flirting—promising a woman he would improve himself for her sake.

"So I'm ready when you are," he continued.

She nearly choked on her schnapps. "Ready for what?"

"Aren't you supposed to teach me to be a gentleman for the media?"

All right, she'd been wrong. He wasn't flirting or looking to improve himself to impress her. This was a career
move. Of course it was—as it should be.

"Not tonight." She drew her knees up to her chest, looped
her arms around them. Yet even in the protective tucked
position, she couldn't stop herself from staring at his mouth.

"What can you teach me tonight?" He stared right back.

"I thought you were tired," she said. "I thought you
were sore."

"I'm better now. Your massage cured me. I'm just…damn,
Kimberly…" He moved in close, cornering her on her end of
the sofa, gently trapping her. On one side she could feel the
glow of warmth from the fire. On the other was Bo, a wall of
solid heat. He was making a mockery of her vow to resist him.

She tried. She really did, curling her hands into fists and
pushing against his chest. But after the hot tub at Camp
Kioga, it was even harder to keep her distance. Somehow,
it only seemed to draw him closer, a gesture of resistance
that turned into a kiss.

She rationalized the impulse. Perhaps this time she
wouldn't be so swept away, as she'd been after the photo
shoot. Perhaps she'd discover her interest was misplaced.
It wouldn't be the first time she'd been taken in by a pretty
face and great hair. Here was a guy with an agenda, a guy
who had too much going on in his life, who had a whole
host of priorities stacked above her. How good could it be?

As it turned out, this was not just any kiss. This was her
favorite   kind.   The   I've-been-wanting-you-since-the-
moment-I-saw-you kiss. Making out in the hot tub had only
been a prelude. He was tender and generous, yet at the same
time completely honest, in a nonverbal way, about what he

was feeling. He held her close and kissed her and told her with every inch of his body exactly how he wanted her.

Kim felt dizzy with the sheer, raw need she felt. It was a powerful contrast to the usual warm attraction she'd had for former boyfriends—even Lloyd, whose memory spun away on a wisp of thought. All of those past desires were burned to ash when she kissed Bo Crutcher. She'd thought the first time had been a fluke, that she'd felt turned on by the moonlit setting and the champagne, and the completion of a fine day of work at something she loved.

Now she couldn't deny that there was a lot more going on. This was so wholly unexpected that she pulled back with a gasp, torn between bolting for the door and asking him for more. The latter impulse nearly won out. Her limbs felt warm and heavy, and all she wanted was to melt against him. Drawing on her last reserves of willpower, she tried to pull away.

"Not so fast," Bo whispered, keeping his arms around her. "I've been wanting to do this again ever since that time in the hot tub. And I got to say, honey, I am not disappointed."

She tried to deny the warm affection she heard in his voice. "This is such a bad idea. How many reasons do I need to give you?"

"None, because none of them would make a bit of difference for me," he said easily. "And I lied earlier. There is something I'm disappointed in."

She extricated herself from his embrace and sat back, arms folded in a shield across her chest. Now he was talking like the kind of man she had sworn off. Self-absorbed. Critical—hypercritical—of others. Particularly of her.

"You're disappointed in me," she said.

"In us," he corrected her.

"I don't know what you mean."

He smiled, then gently unfolded her arms. He leaned forward to press a kiss to her mouth, the light play of his lips on hers slowly dismantling her resistance. He tasted and felt so good that her toes curled inside her woolen socks.

"Honey, what I mean is, don't get me wrong. I like making out with you. But I'm disappointed, because what I really want is to make love to you."

Kim didn't move a muscle, but she knew she was inches from a mad impulse to rip off her clothes, right then and there. She tried to take offense. "That's rude."

"Rude to want you, or rude to say so?"

"Both." She realized she was still clinging to him. She let him go. Instantly, she grabbed him again. This was insane, but she couldn't help herself. "We'll go to my room. And you're not spending the night. And we're not telling a soul."

"Those are your ground rules?"

"Yes." She jutted her chin up in defiance.

He offered a low, murmuring laugh. "Yeah? Well, I got a few rules of my own."

Good, she thought. He was going to spoil everything by being a jerk. And then she wouldn't be attracted to him anymore, and that way, no one would get hurt.

"What kind of rules?" she asked.

"Rule number one is, you let me know how you want me to make love to you. I mean that. I want to know what you like, and you have to tell me without getting all bashful about it. Or, if you can't help feeling bashful, you could try to let me know like this. Hand signals." He demonstrated, his hands slipping up under her sweater.

She was so stunned, she neither spoke nor moved.

"Rule number two is, you have to let this be all about you. No worrying about reciprocation, nothing like that. Because believe me, if I'm making love to you, I'm already getting exactly what I want." With studied gentleness, he slid his hand down and unbuttoned the waistband of her jeans.

"And rule number three is, no faking orgasms. I can't stand that. I don't take shortcuts and I'm not in a hurry. Which leads me to rule number four." He bent low and whispered, his breath warm in her ear.

Prior to this whispered suggestion, which made her blush to the roots of her hair, she'd believed she had a shot at resisting him. Now, however, she was a goner. She didn't even remember leaving the room and taking his hand, leading the way upstairs to her bedroom. She barely heard the gentle creak of springs as they fell together onto the bed.

Then he kissed her in earnest, and she didn't think at all. The day spent out in the cold, in vigorous physical activity, suddenly took its toll. Coupled with the narcotic effect of the peppermint schnapps, she felt amazingly relaxed. Their bodies seemed to fit perfectly together. He was big and warm, and seemed happy enough to lie still for a while and hold her. Just as he'd promised, he made no hurried demands, just showed a curiously sweet affection.

"What's this sweater?" he asked, toying with the front of it.

She watched his hands steal upward, over her rib cage. "Your excuse to feel me up."

"No, I mean, yeah, I intend to feel you up. But this sweater. What's it made of? It's really soft."

"Angora."

"Nice. Makes you feel like a giant plush toy I won in a shooting gallery."

She was trying to decide what to make of the remark, but it only made her laugh. "I've never been called a giant plush toy before."

"It's meant as a compliment. Everybody loves a plush toy. I like your green eyes, too. They remind me of my favorite flavor of Jelly Bellies." He started kissing her again, and she let him, thinking perhaps the newness would wear off and she would not feel so desperate with wanting him.

Yet an extraordinary thing was happening to her. Something she'd never expected or felt before, ever. It wasn't mere lust but something else, a sense of comfort and safety, which made no sense at all. The feeling persisted even when he lay back and pulled her into the curve of his body so that they fit together as precisely as pieces of a 3-D puzzle.

He touched his lips to her temple. "This is nice."

"Mmm, it is," she agreed.

"Today was nice," he added. "Even though I nearly broke every bone in my body, I kind of like snowboarding."

She was enjoying the vibration of his deep voice as she rested her cheek on his chest. "After all that whining, you liked it?"

"I liked trying something new with AJ," he said. "And with you. I like you. A lot."

She sighed, smiling as she closed her eyes. She lay still for a few minutes, riding the gentle rise and fall of his chest and listening to the settling sounds of the old house at night. A warm breath of heat blew gently from the furnace register.

"You probably hear this stuff all the time," he said.

"I swear, no one's ever told me my eyes are like green Jelly Bellies."

"You know what I mean."

She did. And she knew if she lived to be a hundred, she would never feel this way again. It was a curious thing to know, considering she wasn't all that old, yet she deeply felt the truth of it in a hidden place inside her. The thought made her sad, because she wanted so much more than a fling with him. She wanted forever, and they couldn't have that.

"I like you, too," she confessed, her voice an intimate whisper in the darkness. "That came as a surprise to me. I mean, I didn't expect to like you. I thought you'd be like so many of my former clients, self-absorbed and well, frankly, a jerk. And instead, you turned out to be sort of a good guy. I think. You're kind, and you are trying hard with AJ. You make me laugh and…" She paused, weighing her words, wondering if she should own up to this. He was so quiet, such a good listener. "I like the way you kiss me," she confided. "No, that's a lie. I actually love the way you kiss me. I think—against my better judgment—I might have a crush on you."

She was grateful for the darkness and for the deep silence of the night, hiding her blush and cushioning her whisper. It made the heartfelt admission come easier. She was amazed at what she heard herself revealing to him, yet now that she'd started down that road, she couldn't stop herself.

"I'm supposed to be training you to deal with your career, and here you are teaching me something. Or at least reminding me of something. Namely, that not every single guy I meet is an insensitive jerk."

She smiled in the dark, the beat of his heart strong and

deep against her cheek. He smelled so good, and knew just how to hold her to make her feel safe and cherished. Everything about him felt good.

"You're an amazingly good listener," she added. "I hope I'm not making you too uncomfortable, baring my soul like this."

He kept quiet, except for his gentle breathing and the steady pulse of his heart. Kim bit her lip and squeezed her eyes shut. Oh, Lord. He was giving her the silent treatment. She'd said too much. She'd been too honest. And clearly, it was freaking him out. He was speechless. Perhaps speechless with horror.

"I've said too much, too soon," she admitted. "It's probably too much information, and it just might be the schnapps. Okay?"

Silence.

"Bo?"

More silence.

Reluctant though she was to shift from her position of warm comfort, she braced herself on one arm and half sat up. "Bo? Did you even hear a word I said?"

Amber light from a streetlamp slanted through the window. Kim could just make out his features.

He was sound asleep.

"Oh, for heaven's sake," she muttered. "That was the best conversation I've ever had with a man, and you've been dead asleep. No wonder you're so easy to talk to."

He didn't react. In sleep, his face looked completely relaxed and unguarded. Boyish and vulnerable. The crush she had on him didn't go away. It intensified.

Very gently, she laid her head back down on his chest.

"I am in such trouble," she whispered, drawing the quilt up over them both.

Bo dreamed he'd had his arm amputated. His left arm. His pitching arm. And in the dream, it just wasn't that big a deal. So this was not some athlete-losing-his-gift dream. It was something else. What, he wasn't sure.

He awakened slowly, hugging his soft pillow closer as though to keep himself in the grip of an incredibly relaxing moment. No bed had ever felt so warm or soft or—

A breathy female sigh drifted from the pillow, snuffing out the amputated-arm dream. A moment later, he was wide-eyed, fully awake.

Dang. He'd fallen asleep. How the hell had that happened? He finally got Kimberly van Dorn in bed with him, and he'd fallen asleep immediately. He couldn't even blame it on the drinking, not this time. They'd each had a glass of schnapps, not a sip more.

His left arm—his pitching arm—was leaden, completely numb.

He gently lifted his head from the pillow and saw the reason. Kim lay sleeping in the crook of his arm, her cheek against his chest and her hand splayed over the flat of his stomach.

Well now, he thought. This was a first for him. He'd never slept with a woman without *sleeping* with her.

Now here was Kimberly, fast asleep in his arms. She'd been thoroughly kissed by him, but that was all. Not a damned thing more.

He couldn't believe it. That was just purely wrong. No way around it. She'd given him his chance, and he'd—good

Lord almighty—fallen asleep. And with Kimberly, of all people. The one woman he wanted to stick around. Generally, the women in his life were temporary wayfarers. There would usually be wine, a few laughs and the sex, of course. But inevitably, they would figure some things out about him. And then, of course, they would leave. He hadn't blown a chance like this since…

He found himself remembering a certain day in April when he was fourteen years old. He had been home alone as usual that day. His mom was at her job—that year she was selling Mary Kay cosmetics, and she traveled around the suburbs with a tackle box of samples in the trunk of her car. Stoney had been off somewhere with his latest sugar mama. That was what Stoney called the women he dated who were older than him, women who cheerfully gave him money and let him drive their Cadillacs or HumVees anytime he wanted.

That long-ago April day, his mom's friend, Shasta Jamison, stopped by, the way she sometimes did. Shasta and Trudy went way back, or so they said, but when Bo asked what that meant, they just said, "We've known each other forever."

Shasta was pretty in a weary, too-many-cigarettes way, with yellow hair and a good figure. She always seemed a little sad to Bo. A little lonely. She sometimes had a suspicious-looking bruise on her face, and maybe she moved slowly because her ribs were sore. She was a fool for love, that was the way Bo's mother put it. She tended to go out with guys who roughed her up.

That day she had on a long-sleeved sweatshirt even though it was hot and muggy outside. The skintight sweatshirt was unzipped to show off a red bikini top stretched taut across her amazing boobs. They glowed softly with a suntan, creating a deep cleavage that made his mouth water.

Reminding himself not to stare, he turned down the music and said, "My mom's not here. I don't know when she'll be back."

"Oh. I got time," Shasta said. "I'll just wait for her."

"Um, okay. It might be a while."

"Don't mind me," she said. "Just go on with what you were doing."

Right, like he could do that. He'd been reading a book on sports psychology about Nolan Ryan and listening to the Talking Heads turned up loud. It would be rude to do that with Shasta around.

"I wasn't doing anything." His gaze slipped, and he quickly corrected himself, hoping she hadn't noticed.

She noticed. She slid the zipper of her sweatshirt down another inch or two. "It's okay for you to look," she said, taking a step closer to him. "I don't mind."

She was trouble. He didn't have to be a genius to realize that. Even so, he couldn't keep himself from staring at her. She liked it, too, letting him know by trailing her hand down her arm and then back up, briefly touching her lower lip.

"It's okay to touch, too." She moved in even closer.

"Ma'am, I—"

"Don't *ma'am* me. It makes me feel old. I don't like feeling old."

"Yes, m—yes, okay." His voice was husky, yet due to nerves, it squeaked on the ends of his words.

She smiled and rested her hand on his chest, then went

up on tiptoe to kiss his cheek. He caught the cindery scent of cigarettes smoked hours ago, mingling with the flavor of a more recent breath mint. The smell of her, combined with the feathery action of her lips moving across his cheek, was so sexy his knees almost buckled.

"So tall," she murmured. "You've grown so tall."

As though she could read his mind, she chuckled and gave him a gentle shove toward his bedroom. It was small but he kept his side neat because he hated losing stuff. He had his Nolan Ryan and Randy Johnson posters on the wall, and his Little League trophies lined up on a shelf over the bed.

Shasta kissed him full on the mouth, her tongue startling in its quickness as it darted invitingly past his lips. Bo caught on fire, every nerve ending flaring up with a need he'd never felt before. Light-fingered, her hands traced the shape of his shoulders and headed downward, circling the waistband of his jeans, undoing the top button. Sirens went off in his head, drowning out everything. His hands, clumsy with excitement, tried to figure out what to do. He found the front zipper of her sweatshirt and oh-so-slowly coaxed it downward until the shirt fell open, exposing the low-cut top.

Bo had spent many an hour picturing what it would be like the first time. This was nothing like the experience he'd conjured up in his imagination. This was...overwhelming, the biggest thing that had ever happened to him and that included catching a home-run ball at the Astrodome when he was twelve. He couldn't believe she was going to let him do it. She was an angel, a goddess, a dream come true.

His hands shook as he slipped them around her and up to her shoulders, feeling her impossibly soft skin. He was close to losing it and making a fool of himself, and he clutched her upper arms to steady himself. She gasped and winced—with pain, not pleasure.

Misgivings sloshed over him like a bucket of ice water. He took a step back, breathing hard. "Aw, jeez, did I hurt you?"

"What?" She regarded him through half-lidded eyes. "No, honey, it's nothing."

As gently as he could, he took hold of her hand, angled her arm toward the light slanting in through a gap in the drapes. On the softest part of her upper arm was a stark bruise in the shape of a very large hand.

"Who hurt you?" Bo asked her.

She offered a short, dismissive laugh. "It's not important. Let's just get back to what we were doing."

There was a part of Bo—a very specific, out-of-control part that wanted to do exactly that. But something had quieted the sirens in his head and turned his brain back on.

"Ma'am," he said, "we can't be doing this."

She stared at him. To his horror, tears pooled in her eyes, threatening to spill over. Suddenly she looked old to him, and tired, and just so sad and desperate, needing something from him, not just sex but comfort and understanding and a hundred other things he didn't have it in him to give.

"What the hell are you talking about?" she asked. "You know you want to do it. You're dying to do it. I haven't felt a hard-on like that since I was in high school."

His face and ears caught fire. "Ms. Jamison, you and I both know this is wrong."

"There's nothing wrong with two people sharing a little something," she said. "Don't you know that? Don't you understand?"

He felt scared of her desperation. "Not wrong in that way. I mean wrong because it's not going to fix that." He indicated the bruise on her arm.

"You stupid little shit," she burst out. "What the hell do you know about anything?" Her tone was harsh, cutting like a knife.

"Ma'am, I'm sorry. I don't mean any disrespect—"

"Then shut your mouth right now." She snatched her shirt off the bed, stuffed her bruised arms into the sleeves. She was crying openly now, her face contorted. "You're an idiot, you know that? You blew off a perfectly nice afternoon. And believe me, I won't offer again, ever."

He didn't know what else to say. He was an idiot; every horny cell in his body was telling him so. He couldn't, though, he just couldn't have sex with Ms. Jamison, not with her being so sad and hurt. It wouldn't be right, no matter what she said.

Bo learned something that day. He learned that, incredible as it seemed, having sex was not the answer to every problem. Which was totally weird because it was all he thought about. Listening to her car door slam, then the angry revving of the engine, he felt sorry for her. He knew he couldn't help her, and that depressed him.

Feeling the woman curled against him now, he still wondered what he'd taken from that day. What if he'd done something different? Taken what she'd offered?

Given her…what? He'd been a fourteen-year-old with a boner. He didn't have anything to give her.

That had been half a lifetime ago, but sometimes—like now—he wondered if he'd learned anything at all about women. Did he have anything to offer Kimberly? Or should he get out now, before it was too late?

It was dark still. A digital clock across the room read 5:47 a.m., its green digits floating unanchored in the darkness. AJ would still be asleep. Bo could sneak into his own bed where he belonged.

Except it felt so damn good right where he was. He lay unmoving for a few minutes, loath to awaken her and reluctant to disturb the nest of warmth created by their comfortably entwined bodies. She was so soft, and she smelled so good… The temptation to start kissing her again, to finish what he'd started last night, burned through him like a forest fire.

AJ, he reminded himself. He didn't want the kid to wake up and find him gone. Bo shifted slowly and carefully, drawing his chest and shoulders out from under Kim, attempting to replace them with pillows. Inevitably, she stirred, then woke up.

It was ridiculously gratifying that her first impulse upon waking was to curl her fist into his shirt, as though to hold him close.

He could tell the moment she remembered their position. She stiffened and softly gasped, sitting up in the bed.

"Hey," he said.

"Hey."

"I, uh, sorry to wake you. I didn't mean to. I was just going to head upstairs. You know, before AJ wakes up."

"Of course. I mean, that's the best thing." Faint light through the window limned her silhouette. She reached up, ran a hand through her hair, mussing it in a way he found incredibly sexy.

"That's what I thought, too. Yeah, so…" He stood up, stuck his feet into his Chuckies, the only article of clothing he'd removed the previous night. "So I'd better go."

"Yes, all right." There was a pause. "Bo?"

"Yeah?"

"Do you remember falling asleep last night?"

He cleared his throat. "Barely. I was out like a light. Swear to God, that's never happened to me before. Snow-boarding tired my ass out."

"So you fell asleep right away."

"Yeah." Now what? Did he apologize? He was sorry as hell he hadn't made love to her, but he didn't think that was the kind of sorry she wanted to hear. Probably better to treat the situation as though it had never happened.

"Then you didn't really hear the conversation," she said quietly.

"Conversation?"

"One-sided. I was just thinking aloud," she said.

Uh-oh. He couldn't imagine what she'd said. Apparently he'd missed his chance. "I'm all ears now."

She shook her head. "It doesn't matter. It's not important."

A chill slid over him. *It's not important.* "In my experience, when a woman says something's not important, then that means it's important."

"Are you being insulting on purpose, or does this come naturally?" she asked.

"I'm not being insulting."

"If I feel insulted, then you are. That's how it works."

Damn, but she was a mule-headed, difficult woman. Why in blazes did she have to be so difficult?

"Just so you know," he said, "that was a first for me. Normally when I sleep with a woman, we do a lot more than sleep."

"Just so you know," she countered, mocking him, "I don't actually care about your track record with other women."

"Sorry." He cleared his throat. "I, uh, I better get on upstairs," he said, pretty sure his thoughts would scare her if he said what was on his mind. "You know, in case AJ wakes up."

"Of course."

"I'll see you later, then."

"You will," she agreed.

There were a lot of things he wanted to say to her. He wanted to say he actually liked sleeping with her. Yeah, he would have loved to have sex with her, but barring that, the sleeping gave him a feeling of intimacy he'd never had with a woman before. As he stood by the bed and studied her, a graceful tangle of shadows in the half light, a truth hit him out of the blue—he could fall in love with this woman. Hard. Maybe he was already heading in that direction. Whether or not this was a good thing remained to be seen.

Twenty-Two

Kim didn't want to wait for Bo to get back from pitching practice at the gym, so she drove there to find him with a pile of mail and messages on the seat beside her. Lately, each day brought more to do in preparation for spring training. This was the way she used to feel when she was first getting started—filled with anticipation, looking forward to each new day. Now there was more. There was Bo himself, who drove her crazy. She couldn't stop thinking about him. He'd been at the gym for two hours, and she already missed him. The mail and messages were only an excuse.

The photos from the winter shoot at Camp Kioga turned out better than anyone had hoped. Expertly rendered by Daisy and then packaged for the press by Kim, they formed the centerpiece of the new-player press kit. The materials generated keen interest from a variety of outlets. Ultimately, Kim granted a temporary exclusive to the publication that offered the biggest spread and widest exposure for Bo—the Sunday magazine of the *New York Times,* including the cover, with reporting by one of the team's favorite journalists, Natalie Sweet.

The shots created an instant sensation and a storm of buzz. Overnight, everyone wanted to know who Bo Crutcher was and where he'd been all their lives. The article was perfect, a pictorial, which meant the text would be kept to a minimum while the pictures told the story.

The cover shot ran with the predictable but always-compelling headline, "The Iceman Cometh" and featured the most unusual photo of all, a shot of him pitching a snowball in front of the frozen waterfall. The article played up his plainspoken manner, his lifelong affinity for the sport and his extensive knowledge of the art and craft of being a left-handed pitcher. No mention was made of the fact that calling him up was merely a strategy move to position the team for a trade in midseason. Kim had made certain that this was not the most interesting thing about him, and it worked. The overall effect of the article was a classy, artistic treatment of a fascinating subject.

The first sign that the publicity was having the desired impact was that Bo's mobile phone and e-mail inbox nearly exploded.

She found him in his usual spot at a handball court that had been fitted with a net so he could lob his sixty pitches a day. With his back to the door, he didn't see her there, and she waited a few minutes, just watching him. And he was an eyeful, in shorts and a ripped T-shirt, a bandanna around his head. He pitched with a grace and athleticism that took her breath away. The intensity and concentration made him seem like a different person, someone with facets she hadn't begun to explore.

Pushing away an untimely fantasy, she cleared her throat. "Mail call," she said. "I just checked the post-office box in town."

He turned and gave her what she was coming to think of as his trademark grin, the one that had the potential to win him legions of fans. "I was just finishing up." He grabbed a towel, and they sat on a bench together and went through it. She tried not to be distracted by his sweaty smell, which she found maddeningly sexy.

For the most part, the mail was flattering and gratifying. Some was a little weird.

"Another blind proposal from some woman," he said.

"That one's presented quite...creatively," she said, pointing to the large envelope he'd just opened.

"Definitely a first," he said, indicating the proposal written on a pair of panties. "Did you know this was going to happen?"

"Well, I didn't plan the panty proposal. We wanted to create a media sensation," she said. "And guess what? It worked."

"Worked...how? Sorry to be dense." He slung the towel around his neck. "I'm kind of shell-shocked by all the attention."

She handed him a message from his agent. Gus Carlisle had been in the loop from the start, and heartily approved of Kim's work so far. "Congratulations, Iceman. You're going to the press reception at the Pierre. It's invitation-only, and you don't get invited unless they're dead serious about you."

"I've waited my whole life for someone to be dead serious about me," he said.

Although she knew the statement was meant to be light-hearted, it brought a lump to her throat. "The wait is over," she said, trying to keep her voice steady. Kim loved this part of her job—watching someone's dream come true. At that same time, she'd seen guys like this before, athletes with raw talent, who shifted from obscurity to notoriety overnight. Not all of them handled it well.

Looking through some of the press materials, he came across her CV. "You have a degree in broadcast journalism," he said.

"You seem surprised."

"From USC."

"That's right."

"Why aren't you broadcasting anything?"

"I am, in a way. When I train a client for the media."

"No, I mean *you*. In front of the camera or microphone at least. Doing, I don't know, sportscasting or color commentary. Don't tell me you never thought of it."

"I did some of that as an intern. Loved it, but I needed to make a living, and the PR firm offered me that."

"And now…?"

"Now my mother needs me. I can't go beating the bushes for some local affiliate in Timbuktu, competing with college interns."

"Sounds like an excuse to me."

She snatched the CV away from him. "Shut up and finish opening your mail."

"I got a better idea." He picked her up and swung her around, and planted a long and unabashed kiss on her mouth. When he let her go, she looked around to make sure no one was watching. They were keeping their as-yet-undefined relationship a secret. Not because there was anything wrong with it but because it was new, and fragile, like something that could blow away under the barest breath of scrutiny.

Avalon's annual Winter Carnival culminated with a celebration at the fire hall. It was a fund-raiser, featuring local groups performing in a battle of the bands, dancing, food and wine. Kim went with her mother, Daphne and Dino. As she surrendered her coat to the coat check in the foyer, a lurch of apprehension took Kim by surprise.

"What is it?" her mother asked, handing over her wool jacket. In a new dress the color of a valentine, she looked particularly pretty this evening, flushed and bright-eyed. She really did seem to be thriving on her new life in this small town.

"Nothing," Kim said. "It's just... I take that back. It's not nothing. It's everything. It all matters so much," she confessed. "I never expected that. I thought I'd come here and lick my wounds and then move on, but it hasn't happened like that."

Her mother touched her hand. "It happened the way it's supposed to. And I'm very glad about that, Kimberly."

Kim felt grateful for her mother's quiet, steady support. It had been there all her life, but until recently, she hadn't understood how vital it was. Bo Crutcher had not been her only project this winter. She had also made a commitment to her mother. They were closer than ever now, with a new level of intimacy and understanding that made Kim feel both brave and vulnerable at the same time. She decided to level with her mother.

"I haven't been to any kind of party since my last night in L.A.," she said. "I know this is completely different, but I just had a moment there."

"An extremely unpleasant moment, judging by the expression on your face," said Penelope. She threaded her arm through Kim's. "Don't worry. I'll be your wing-man, dear."

They walked into the party, side-by-side. At one end was a raised dais with a banner backdrop bearing a bold logo: O'Donnell Industries. The owner of the Hornets was the party's sponsor, and it was instantly apparent that her mother was right—this was not like the kind of parties Kim used to attend. People were not posing and jockeying for position. It was almost a relaxed atmosphere. The old-fashioned hall had an enormous fireplace that lit the room with a warm glow. There were long tables laden with food, urns of coffee and hot spiced wine.

AJ was with some of his new friends from school. Kim recognized Vinny Romano, and Tad. They were hanging around the food table, elbowing each other and helping themselves to munchies. She caught his eye and gave him a wave. That smile of his was going to break hearts one day, just like his—

"Hey, Kim, over here," Daphne said. "Come and meet my sisters."

Emily, Taylor and Martha McDaniel were, respectively, aged nine, ten and eleven. "We miss you at home, Daffy," said Emily, the youngest. "When're you coming back?"

"Hard to say, Em. I don't really have a plan."

"Dad wishes you'd come home, too," Martha pointed out.

"Then Dad should say something." Daphne added, half

to herself, "He won't, though." Then she brightened up. "But hey. We're together tonight, and it's going to be tons of fun."

"Yeah," Emily agreed.

"Kim's new, so you'll have to introduce her to people. Kim's working with Bo Crutcher, that guy from the Hornets. She's helping him become a famous baseball star."

"Dad's gonna teach us to watch baseball," Taylor said.

"It's pretty easy," Kim told her. "I used to be obsessed with baseball when I was your age. Come to think of it, I still am."

"You're nuts," Daphne declared. "Pretty much all sports fans are. I mean, why invest all that emotion in a team? It's a sure way to get your heart broken."

"There are lots of ways to get your heart broken," Kim pointed out. She turned to the sisters. "Tell you what. Once spring training starts, I'll watch some preseason games with you and we'll be fans together, okay?"

All three sisters nodded vigorously. Daphne sent them off to wait for the battle of the bands to start. Kim was surprised and gratified to discover how many people she recognized and how quickly she'd come to know them. Daisy Bellamy came rushing over when she spotted Kim.

"I was hoping you'd be here," she said, beaming. "Hi, Mrs. van Dorn."

"Hello, Daisy. And congratulations on your photographs. You had a very, very impressive layout in the magazine."

"That was Kim's doing," Daisy said.

"It wouldn't have happened without the photos. We're a team, all of us," Kim said. She loved seeing Daisy's excitement and pleasure. Kim knew the feeling of finding the sweet spot in a career. She hadn't felt it herself in a long time, but she still remembered feeling that way as an intern, working in broadcasting, following a sportscaster around a sweat-fogged locker room, analyzing plays. "Is your cousin Olivia here? I wanted to thank her again for that incredible location shoot."

"She was planning to come," Daisy said, "but she went to see her sister Jenny at the hospital in Kingston. Jenny and Rourke had a little girl last night."

They raised a toast to the new arrival, then Kim turned expectantly to Daisy's date. She felt a peculiar affinity for him—a redhead like her. He had laughing eyes, and he regarded Daisy with unabashed adoration.

"This is Logan O'Donnell," Daisy said. "Charlie's dad."

Oh. Maybe, then, they weren't a couple at all. That was pretty clear from Daisy's tone and choice of words. And even clearer from the not-quite-ineffable sadness that passed between them. It must be incredibly hard, sharing a child while leading separate lives. For the first time, Kim came close to understanding why AJ's mother had kept him away from Bo.

"I should have known by the red hair," she said. "You have a beautiful little boy." Kim wasn't exaggerating. She'd seen Charlie a few times while meeting with Daisy about the photo shoot. Charlie was a gorgeous baby, and he was almost unbearably sweet, the kind of child that made women Kim's age yearn for one of her own. She indicated the banner behind the dais. "Is O'Donnell Industries your company?" she asked.

"My father's." He started to go on, but an announcement blared from amplifiers onstage.

"Ladies and gentlemen. Here's the next entry in the battle of the bands—Avalon's own home-grown musical group, Inner Child."

The crowd erupted as the lights came up. The appearance of the band onstage banished the last of Kim's misgivings about the evening. She must have let her anticipation show, because her mother gave her a gentle push toward the front of the room.

"Go ahead," she said in Kim's ear. "I know you've been looking forward to hearing them."

Kim nodded and moved toward the stage. She greeted people along the way, surprised to realize so many faces were now familiar to her. She had found something unexpected here in this place—a sense of community. A feeling of caring pervaded the gathering. The people here genuinely wished each other well. She found Sophie Bellamy-Shepherd there, beaming proudly up at Noah, the band's drummer.

"My first time to hear them perform as a group," Kim said to Sophie.

"I think you'll be impressed."

AJ was already in the front of the hall, standing with a group of kids below the edge of the raised stage. Kim and Sophie watched them as the group came out, tuning up and doing a few quick riffs. "How's he doing?" Sophie asked.

"He's holding a lot in," Kim said. Emotion welled in her chest as she watched AJ. At the moment, his face shone with anticipation, his gaze riveted on Bo. "He seems okay, but he needs his mother, Sophie. There's no denying it. It's like the light inside him gets dimmer every day, no matter how hard Bo tries to keep his spirits up. This is fun for him, but tomorrow, he'll wake up and miss his mother more than ever."

"His mother must be heartbroken, too," Sophie said. "Before moving to Avalon, I lived apart from my kids, and it was the hardest thing I ever did. I wish I could say this will all be resolved right away, but the system moves so slowly, it's just excruciating. The emergency writ of appeal is bogged down in court, though, which makes me wonder which part of *'emergency'* they don't understand."

Lately, Kim had studied the situation, and now understood what a quagmire the immigration system was in. It was one of those things she'd never thought about much, until now. Until it touched the life of a boy she cared about. "In the past, I've had clients dealing with immigration issues," she said. "Not to sound like a skeptic, but professional athletes seem to have an easier time with the INS than working people."

"Yes, it's kind of hard not to notice that."

"I did have one client who came close to being deported, a baseball player from the Dominican Republic. Pico—I haven't thought about him in years."

"What happened to him?" Sophie asked.

"I worked with him when I was an intern with my last firm. Raul de Gallo—he was on the Dodgers' farm-league team. His teammates nicknamed him Pico de Gallo, due to his height. He showed a lot of promise, but the immigration suit was such a distraction that it affected his game. Then, just before he was about to be deported, the decision was reversed."

"Do you recall why?"

"Something about his mother, I think. Turns out she was born in the U.S. Virgin Islands, which made her eligible for naturalization. That's how I remember it, anyway."

"We've got someone looking into Yolanda Martinez's family background. The records are a whole new nightmare."

"I won't give up hope," Kim said.

"They're about to start." Sophie gestured toward the stage.

Kim found herself as riveted as AJ appeared to be. The unlikely group was made up of Bo on bass, Noah on drums, a local cop named Rayburn Tolley on keyboards, and the lead singer and guitar player, Eddie Haven. Bo claimed Eddie was the true musician among them, and he proved it with a crisp delivery of Green Day's "When I Come Around."

The biggest surprise was Bo Crutcher. He looked like a natural in tattered jeans, a black T-shirt and a bandanna around his head. His big hands held the bass with assuredness, and his face was a picture of concentration as he played. She'd been thinking a lot about those hands lately—the way they felt when he touched her, their irresistible combination of strength and tenderness. She'd been writing about those hands, too, in her press materials for him. A pitcher's hands were precision instruments, part of the fine alchemy of the pitch, with an instinctive way of holding the ball, fingers caressing the curving seams into perfect position, breaking with it at exactly the right time, letting go at the moment of greatest power. Now she watched his fingers on the strings of the bass with the same delicacy.

Kim found herself beaming at him, particularly when AJ and some of his friends went wild, dancing to the music.

At the end of the set, she leaned over to Sophie during the applause. "I wasn't sure what to expect. And you're right. I'm pleasantly surprised."

Sophie nodded. "They probably won't win any Grammy awards, but they're fun to watch."

The group's next number was a slow, beautiful song that was so romantic, she felt an ache in her throat. "What's this song?" she asked Sophie. "It's amazing."

"Something original by Eddie," she said. "Good, isn't he?"

"Uh-huh." Yet her attention strayed from the light-haired guitar player to Bo, whose face was intense with concentration, not unlike his expression when he threw a pitch.

They finished the set and Sophie went to find Noah. Kim felt a momentary twinge of envy, watching Noah's affectionate hug. Although hardly in the market for a husband, she wished she had someone to go to at the odd moment, just like that. To know that no matter where you were in a crowd, there was always someone you could seek out and be comfortable with.

Her mother came up beside her and squeezed her hand. "I'm seeing your heart in your eyes."

"You're not." Then, with a rueful smile, Kim admitted, "Maybe you are. I'm thinking it has something to do with an athlete's intense concentration, whether he's pitching a baseball or playing music. Why is that so hard for me to resist?"

"*I'm* thinking it has something to do with Bo Crutcher, specifically," her mother declared.

"If so, I'm not doing anything about it. The irony of my line of work is that doing a good job with a client means he moves on. His success dealing with the media means he doesn't need me anymore, and that's the way it's supposed to work. The mistake I made with Lloyd Johnson was holding on. I should have let go. I won't be making that mistake again."

"That only works if your relationship is strictly professional. If it's personal, then this is only the beginning."

"Beginning of what?" asked Dino. "Did you tell her about us?"

Penelope gasped. "No, but I suppose you just did."

Kim regarded them both with dawning understanding. "Mom?"

Her mother's eyes shone. "Dino asked me to marry him."

"And she said yes," he added, slipping his arm around her waist.

Kim's eyes teared up. "Oh, Mom. Sorry, I need a minute. I mean, I knew the two of you... Sorry," she said again. "It's not every day a person learns her mother is getting married."

"I was planning to tell you tonight. I know it seems sudden, but I'm very, very sure of this, and if I've learned anything, it's that life is short and putting off love makes no sense at all."

Kim looked from her mom to Dino and back again. Love and happiness surrounded them like an aura. The flickering colored lights in the hall illuminated her mother's face, and Kim saw someone who was more than her mother—a beautiful woman, flushed with excitement. Lit by love.

Without warning, she burst into tears and embraced them both. "This is the best news. I'm so happy for you both."

"Then dry your eyes and let's dance," Dino insisted.

They headed off to dance to the next band's rendition of Deep Purple's "Smoke on the Water." Up near the stage, she spotted Bo and AJ together. She noticed something new in the way the boy regarded Bo, a deeper admiration and affection than she'd seen before. Watching the two of them, she felt a fresh wave of emotion. How far they had come, in such a short time. Right before her eyes, the two of them had turned from strangers to father and son, and it was the sweetest of miracles. Yes, she could tell herself she was simply feeling tender over the news about her mother, but it was more than that.

Without meaning to—in fact, resisting all the way—she'd fallen in love with them both. With Bo, who was working so hard to do right by his son, and with AJ, still lost and missing his mother, even as he tried to fit into a strange new world. She hadn't gone looking for this but couldn't escape it, a feeling in the pit of her stomach, both happy and sad. Bo Crutcher had the power to break her heart, yet for the first time in her life, she didn't worry about that. She just wanted to be with him in the worst way, and the fallout didn't scare her.

As if he felt her watching him, Bo looked up and their gazes met. Was her heart still in her eyes? Could he see that? He came over to her and said, "AJ's been invited to sleep over at his friend's house. I said it was okay."

"I assume you know the friend, right? And his family?"

"Kid named Tad Lehigh. I know his aunt Maureen, who's the town librarian. And I just talked to his mother, and they've already left. I wrote down their phone number." His hand caught hers, fingers caressing the inside of her wrist. The music changed to a not-terrible rendition of Aerosmith's "I Don't Wanna Miss a Thing." He leaned down to speak into her ear, and she felt as though there was no one else in the room—in the world—but him. "So how about a dance?"

It wasn't a question, not really. And it wasn't really dancing, either. He moved with the grace of a natural athlete, though, and kept hold of her hands, pulling her up against him. *That's it,* she thought. *I'm a goner.*

She lifted herself up on tiptoe and said, "My mother's marrying Dino," she said. "I just found out."

"That's great," he said easily. "They're terrific together."

She watched her mother with Dino, who twirled her as if they were dancing on a cruise ship. "It's a bit surreal, seeing my own mother fall in love."

"Nah, it's the real thing. Look at those two. Dino's one of the finest men I've ever known. Dance closer," he added, giving her no choice as he pressed her against him.

The feeling in the pit of her stomach intensified. "I liked your band's performance," she said. "You guys are not half bad."

"Meaning we're more than half good?"

"Exactly." She smiled, feeling a wave of affection. "Why the bass guitar?"

"My older brother brought one home when I was a kid. Learned to play by ear, listening to old CDs."

"You have a good ear, then." She lifted her arms, laced her fingers behind his neck.

"Maybe. Eddie's the one, though. Eddie Haven's guitar playing can elevate anything. If we win, it'll be because of him." Bo smiled down at her. "At the moment, I feel like I already won something."

"You have," she said. They danced in each other's arms, and it came to her again, the feeling of the world falling away. They were in a room full of people, and it felt like they were all alone.

"Yeah? You look happy tonight," he remarked, his breath warm in her ear.

"I *am* happy tonight."

"I could make you happier."

She shivered, pressed herself closer. "I'll just bet you could, Bo Crutcher."

"And you'd be right," he said, and pulled her toward the exit.

They didn't even wait to see if his band won the battle, raising a nice sum for charity. She put her common sense in Park and rode home with him in a car that felt more like California than the Catskills. The dark and empty house welcomed them with a blast of heat from the furnace. At the bottom of the steps, he swept her up in his arms.

"Hey," she protested.

"I've always wanted to do this."

"You'll hurt yourself."

"Not a chance," he said. "What hurts is putting this off any longer." He made a slow and steady climb to her room on the second floor. Keeping his arms around her, he set her down, and they both took off their coats. "I promise I'll stay awake this time." Then he bent and kissed her, with a lingering heat she felt all the way to her toes. He pressed her up against the wall and kissed her again.

Suddenly it was all very real to her, what she was feeling, what they were doing, what they were about to do. Second thoughts crowded into her head. She was afraid, vulnerable. A memory of Lloyd flickered to life, but she snuffed it out. Then she banished it completely by looking into Bo's eyes and seeing nothing there but tenderness.

Still…she pushed her fists to his chest and gave a shove, but somehow, it came off as an invitation, not an objection. He took her wrists and gently held them against the wall above her head, bending to kiss her a third time. She knew if she raised a sincere objection, he'd let go. But she didn't want him to let go. The things she'd felt at the fire hall only grew stronger with each passing moment.

When he lifted his mouth from hers, she looked up at him and said, "This isn't supposed to happen."

"Being my girlfriend is not the end of the world."

"Perhaps not. But it's going to end badly and people are going to get hurt. Not just any people, you and me. Unless we stop it right here, right now."

"Not going to happen. Come on, if being with me is the worst thing that's ever happened to you, then you're one lucky lady."

"I'm not saying it's the worst thing. When it's over— well, that might be the worst thing."

"Then we'd better make sure it doesn't end."

Everything was so simple for this man. So simple and so possible. She wished she had a little of his optimism. "How are we going to do that?"

"We can start by making love tonight. Right now."

His hand slipped down, found the hem of her dress and moved slowly upward, teasing and caressing. Still kissing her again, he did something simultaneously with his hand and tongue that completely shut down her brain. He lifted his mouth from hers, and she had one more chance to pro-test, but she didn't. She couldn't, because he whispered a suggestion in her ear that set a torch to her blood. Objections meant nothing. So what if this guy was every bad decision she'd ever made, personified? He had magic hands, and the things he whispered to her made her desperate.

"All right," she said, tipping back her head while he kissed her throat. She was filled with the giddy relief of surrender. And it *was* relief, because until this moment, she hadn't known whether or not she still knew how to trust a man. "All right…" She uttered no other coherent words for the rest of the night.

He slid her dress to the floor and she stepped out of her shoes. Impatient with lust, she peeled off his shirt and jeans, and her fingers raced over him, tracing his smooth skin and hard muscles, drawing him against her. She was mesmerized by everything about him—his amazing physique and the way he tasted, the sound of his breathing and the sigh of her name on his lips. They sank onto the bed, their limbs tangling. There were a thousand more kisses, and laughter between the gasps and sighs of pleasure, and Kim let herself get lost in him, in a place that felt safe and fulfilling, a place she never wanted to leave.

She didn't let herself think about what would happen afterward. Maybe one day the memories would be as sharp and painful as a physical ache, but right here, right now, she wanted it all, his kisses and his laughter and the long, heated hours in bed with him. Regrets might come later, but for now, he was everything she'd ever wanted.

Over the next few days, Kim somehow managed to stumble through work, but she lived for the night, when she could be alone with Bo, and they could explore the searing passion that only seemed to grow stronger each time they were together. After everyone in the house was asleep, he would come to her room, and the secret, dark hours belonged to them. Sexual satisfaction was one thing, but this was something more, a singular sensation of emotion she'd never felt before, not with this intensity, this certainty. One night, when the house was completely quiet, she lay with her head on his bare chest and listened to the beating of his heart, and a sense of utter clarity took hold. The feelings swept over her in a wave.

"Hey now," he said, no doubt feeling the damp heat of her tears. "What's the matter?"

"Everything," she said. She thought about not telling him, but could think of no reason to hold back, not anymore. "Bo, I love you."

He didn't move a muscle, but she felt his heart trip into overdrive. "I'm glad you said it."

"It's not…the first time," she felt compelled to admit.

"Not for me, either. I reckon we've both had plenty of practice."

She laughed. "That's one way of looking at it."

"What I'm saying is, I don't mind if it's not your first time. What I hope, what I'm asking you, Miss Kimberly van Dorn, is that I want it to be your last time."

His words were so unexpected that her eyes filled with tears. "You mean that, don't you?"

"Hell, yeah, I mean it. You know, I first fell a little bit in love with you when I saw you at the airport, before I even knew your name. Just the sight of you hit me hard."

"What do you mean, you fell a little bit in love?"

"Come on, Red. You know what that feels like."

"No, I don't. Describe it to me."

"You just want to hear me talk about love."

"Guilty as charged. I want to hear you talk about it as though it means something."

"It means everything. So listen, because I'm not so good at all this emotional stuff."

"I think you're better at it than you know."

"Okay. When I first saw you, it was like I went blind to everything else. You were all I saw. I started trying to find things that match the color of your eyes—like a leaf or a watermelon-flavored Jelly Belly. Don't laugh—you said you wanted to know."

"I'm not laughing. And I do want to know. Bo—"

His phone rang—Sophie's ring tone. *It must be love,* Kim thought. *I've memorized his ring tones.*

He put her aside and sat up, already groping for his clothes.

She glanced at the time displayed on the glowing digital clock on the nightstand. This could not be good. She flicked on a lamp.

"Yeah, Sophie," he said. "What is it?"

Kim saw his bare back stiffen as though he'd been stabbed. He turned to her as he rang off. His face had gone completely pale.

"It's Yolanda," he said. "She's been deported."

Twenty-Three

It was even worse than they'd feared. Rumors were rampant in the detention center, and Yolanda had heard that her detention in the U.S. could last for years. She'd panicked and opted for immediate voluntary deportation. She believed that would allow her to apply for reentry. By the time her lawyer in Texas discovered what she'd done, she was already gone.

Lacking documentation for Mexican citizenship, Yolanda was placed in a detention center on the other side of the border. Now she had to wait until her case could be reviewed by the Instituto Nacional de Migración. There was no option for re-entry, not now.

Bo broke the news to AJ as gently as he could. The two of them were in a field near the house, building a snowman. It was totally unlike Bo to voluntarily subject himself to the cold like this, but he did it for AJ's sake. After the snowboarding, AJ had developed an insatiable appetite for new adventures, particularly those that took place outdoors, in the snow, in subzero temperatures.

Bo explained about the new development as they rolled a boulder-sized snowball around the field. "I'm so sorry, buddy," he said.

"How can she be deported and still be in detention?" he asked, ramming his shoulder into the ever-growing snowball, like a football player with a practice dummy.

"It's only until they find her birth records, and those of her parents," Bo said. It was more complicated than that, but he didn't want to throw too much at AJ all at once.

"Can I call her? I really need to talk to her."

"The center only has a few public pay phones. You have to have a calling card. The problem is, the cards have to be purchased at a store."

AJ's face turned hard. "And they won't let her go to the store because she's a detainee."

"It sucks, I know. The advocate in Texas is doing everything he can to reverse the deportation." According to a report from Sophie's associate, women had to wait days for an open phone. There was no privacy while they made their calls and they had to scream to be heard. Bo didn't tell AJ any of this, knowing it would only upset him more.

The snowball was nearly too big to roll. They positioned themselves side by side, shoving their hands under it to give it one final turn. "On the other hand," Bo said, "there's an upside. The center in Aguacaliente in Mexico has placed a limit to the length of her stay, so the records search can be expedited. You know what *expedited* means?"

"I know what everything means." AJ dropped to his knees and started rolling another snowball.

"I hear you, buddy. I do." Bo helped him with the rest

of the snowman. The whole time he was working with AJ, Bo forgot to be cold. He forgot he hated winter. He forgot everything, just watching his boy. Well, almost everything. He couldn't forget the fact that Kim was sitting by the fire, watching them through the window.

She was the one bright spot in all of this. Against all odds, they were falling in love. He was done holding back his feelings for her. He was officially crazy about her. He wanted nothing more than to spend every minute with her, but they both understood that AJ had to come first.

"Ready?" he asked.

"Yep."

It took the two of them to hoist the midsection into place. "You're pretty strong," Bo remarked.

"For my size," AJ said.

"I didn't say that."

"But you meant it."

"I meant exactly what I said. You're strong. And that's good." He added the bowling-ball-size head to the snowman.

AJ didn't say anything else, but it seemed to Bo he stood a little taller. That was good, because after the news about Yolanda, it was more important than ever to make AJ feel confident. And safe.

"He needs arms," AJ said.

"What's that?"

"Arms," AJ repeated. "He needs them."

"He looks fine without arms."

"You're just saying that because you want to go inside and get warm."

"Yeah, I'm kind of funny that way. I like being warm."

AJ shook his head. "Arms."

Bo heaved a frosty sigh as they trekked across the yard in search of low hanging branches. He found a couple, which they stuck in the sides of the snowman to create serviceable arms.

"Done," he declared, stepping back to regard their handiwork.

"Not quite." AJ put a Hornets baseball cap on the snowman's head, and a snowball in the twig fingers of his left hand. "There. Now he looks like something."

And so did AJ. He looked brave and sad all at once, and his doggedness at trying to keep his chin up broke Bo's heart. Where did he get that strength?

"High five," said Bo.

"Good times," AJ replied.

"Now can we go inside?"

"Whiner."

Kim called the campaign to help Bo's son "Operation AJ," and for that, Bo loved her all the more. She and everyone else at Fairfield House wanted to help the boy with his fears and insecurities. He was like an accident victim, missing a limb, but that didn't stop Kim from believing she could make things better. And sometimes it worked. Sometimes she and Bo were able to surprise and delight him, to bring a smile to his face. Unlike Bo, AJ had no aversion whatsoever to the snow, and he raced home from school each day to take part in snowshoe expeditions, making snow angels in the yard and snowmobiling in the Catskills Wilderness.

"So I was thinking this might be a good day for ice-skating on Willow Lake. When the weather's clear and

cold like this, conditions are ideal," she said one afternoon. "What do you say?"

"I'll pass," Bo said.

AJ was perched on a kitchen stool, devouring his favorite afternoon snack—Cheetos. "I'd like to try."

"It's the bomb, AJ. You'll love it." She sent Bo a look
of triumph, and within a short time, had everything orga-
nized. She even called Noah and Sophie Shepherd to invite
them along. By now, Bo knew resistance was futile.

The lake was swarming with skaters, the sledding hill
alive as kids dragged their sleds and saucers up and then sped
down, hurrying before twilight fell. A few tourists braved
the cold to photograph the town's winter centerpiece, a
house-sized ice sculpture in the shape of a colonial fort.

Kim fitted AJ with rental skates and led him out onto
the ice. Her patient, protective way with the boy drew him
out and gave him confidence, and before long, he was
wobbling across the ice, laughing with Kim. Bo stood at
the edge of the skating area, watching the two of them. If
he squinted his eyes and opened his heart, he could imagine
them as his family.

"Never thought I'd see you out here," Noah remarked,
joining him. "You used to be allergic to winter."

"Still am," Bo said, abashed by his own sentimental
thoughts. "Good thing I don't want any more kids, because
I'm freezing my nuts off. I'll be sterile after today."

"Your boy sure loves the winter."

"Yeah, who knew? But he's not doing so hot. Since we
heard his mom was deported, he's... I can hear him tossing
and turning at night. He looks pale to me, with dark circles
under his eyes. I won't lie to you, Noah. I'm worried."

Noah didn't make light of Bo's concern. A gifted vet, he had a natural compassion for wounded creatures. However, when he spoke, it was as a father. "After Buddy and Aissa first came to us," he said, referring to his children from Africa, "they had issues. Especially Buddy—he was five, which is old enough to remember too much."

Bo was surprised. From his perspective, the Shepherds seemed like the all-American blended family. "What do you mean, issues?"

"All the violence," Noah said. "The loss. They're haunted by it. I'm not saying AJ's experience was anything like my kids', but that kind of separation, of loss, it cuts deep."

Good God, thought Bo. Noah was right. AJ was showing symptoms of trauma. "What do you think I should do?"

"You're doing it. Being here for him, helping him."

As they watched, AJ tentatively joined a group of kids his age and Kim skated off on her own with the grace of an ice dancer.

"How's everything else going?" Noah inquired. "The media training and stuff."

"I had no idea how much of baseball was not about baseball. Oh, and I have the hots for my teacher."

"I figured as much." Noah didn't seem at all surprised. "Don't worry about it. It always happens that way in Pygmalion stories."

Bo scowled. "Pig—what?"

"From mythology. A guy called Pygmalion sculpted the ideal woman out of stone. Nowadays, it's shorthand for getting a makeover. You had your makeover. Now you're her ideal man. And no offense, bud, but it's about time."

He thought about the shopping trips, the visit to the barber—correction, *stylist*—the lessons in manners, elocution, dealing with sponsors and media. "You talk like something was wrong with me before."

"Oh, sorry, bro. You were perfect before."

"I'm not claiming I was, but geez. She's turning me into something…" Someone she can stand to be around, he thought.

"You like her, then," Noah said. "Now you have to decide what to do about it."

"I know what I want to do about it, but I'm not her type," Bo said. "We're *Lady and the Tramp*."

"Thanks to my kids, I know how that one ends," Noah said. "They have a litter of pups and live happily ever after."

"Right. Like that's going to happen."

"Keep up the attitude and it won't."

"It's just that I've never seen it."

Noah spread his arms. "You're looking at it."

He had a point. A year ago, Noah Shepherd had been as unattached as Bo, rattling around in a big house all by himself. Now he was married with a family, and happier than Bo had ever known him to be. This was something Bo could never picture for himself, though. Noah was one of those guys who was good through and through. In contrast, Bo was a total screwup.

"We slept together," he admitted.

"How was it?"

"The first time, very…restful. We slept, nothing else."

"Get out of town."

"It's true. After that…not restful at all." Bo couldn't suppress a grin.

"Hey, Bo, get your skates on," AJ shouted from the lake. "I'll race you."

"I need a beer," Bo said, switching gears.

Noah laughed. "Sure, that'd be good."

Resigned to his fate, Bo picked up his rental skates. Sophie and Kim joined them on a bench beside the lake. Kim's cheeks were bright with color, her eyes dancing with laughter. She looked classy and athletic. And sexy as hell.

"I'm done," Sophie told Noah. "Your turn. Two against one is too much for an old lady."

"Hey, no fair playing the old-lady card," Noah said.

"Daddy, come on, let's go, Daddy," his kids shouted.

"I don't have to play it," she said. "I am it." She shooed him away to skate with his kids, then headed off to get some hot chocolate. She was a good bit older than Noah, and Bo suspected she was more sensitive about it than she let on. She shouldn't be. The two of them made a great couple.

Kim turned to Bo. "Your turn. Skates."

He shot her a look, but bent to take off his boots.

She patted his arm. "This means a lot to AJ."

"That's the idea." He finished tying his laces and watched AJ for a few seconds. "It sucks, what's happening to him, but I kind of like having him around. I mean, I'm not saying I'm father of the year or anything like that, but we get along, you know? Even through the hard stuff with his mother."

"You sound surprised."

"I didn't expect... I mean, I don't know the first thing about being a father."

"Somebody, somewhere, taught you how to love a child."

"That's AJ. He takes me out of myself, you know?

Out of my own head. I got to tell you, I'm learning a lot from the kid."

She laughed. "Good to know. Now, go learn how to skate."

"I know how to skate." He stood and headed for the ice, wobbling a little. He hoped like hell he wouldn't fall on his ass.

Twenty-Four

Since learning his mom had been deported and was in some women's detention center in Mexico, AJ saw the world differently. Everything was gray to him—gray winter skies, dirty gray snow on the streets, a gray he never saw in the hot Texas sun. Sure, there were moments when Bo tried to distract him and succeeded sometimes, but every moment was weighted with the knowledge that his mother was in trouble and he had no way of getting her out.

Each day, he approached the bus stop like a condemned man to the gallows. Even though running away had been a stupid thing to do, and even though he was forcing himself to get used to Avalon, he still felt the same way—he wanted to be anywhere but here. Yet, realizing anything he did could affect his mother's status, he was scared into being on his best behavior. He was going to have to figure out some other way to be with his mom again, but he hadn't quite worked out what that was yet. In the meantime, he moved from day to day, crossing out each square on a small pocket calendar he kept in his backpack.

The middle school was an old-fashioned brick-and-concrete monolith rising out of a snow-covered expanse marked by bare trees and bike racks buried so deep, only the top rail was visible. To AJ, it resembled another planet, like the ice planet Hoth in *Star Wars*. Inside, the building was a maze of hallways jammed with loudly slamming lockers, and kids who seemed so different from AJ, they might as well have been space aliens. Hissing radiators filled the classrooms with steam, exuding a damp, uncomfortable heat.

AJ sat, subdued, through interminable classes and lectures by teachers who droned on and on in their Yankee accents. Every chance he got, he escaped to the computer lab to log on to the Internet. He kept hoping he would find a way, someone out there in cyberspace, to help him and his mom.

Back home, he used to wish for his own computer, but of course, there was no money for one. And even if there was, there would be no money for Internet service. He'd made do with school and library computers, but he'd never really needed one the way he did now. That was the difference—he needed to figure out how to save his mom. He thought about trying to stay in touch with some of his friends by e-mail and IM, but they weren't much for writing or talking on the phone, even. Back in Texas, he and his *cholos* tended to hang out. That didn't usually involve much talking or typing on the computer.

Bo let AJ use his MacBook anytime he wanted, but AJ had tried that, and ended up being stalked by the Avalon police. Here at school, he was probably just as easily tracked, but he felt somehow less exposed.

This afternoon he ducked into the computer lab, only to find every terminal busy with kids wearing headsets and acting all studious, even though most of them were probably playing games or trying to get past the school's firewalls into chat rooms. Some girl was hogging his favorite computer, the one in the carrel on the end, surrounded like a three-sided fortress. The girl was pudgy and had frizzy hair. She was in the eighth grade, and her name was Chelsea Nash. He recognized her because she helped out around Dr. Shepherd's veterinary hospital. AJ had seen her hosing down the dog runs, working around the barn, wheeling barrows of horse manure to a big steaming pile that rose out of the snow like Mount Vesuvius built of turds.

She was friends with Max Bellamy, Mrs. Bellamy-Shepherd's son. Here was something AJ had noticed about being in a town this small. Everybody was connected to everybody else, eventually.

Not AJ. He didn't belong here. Didn't want to belong. What was the point? If he started feeling too much at home here, he might lose sight of the fact that his mother was far away and in danger of never seeing him again. That was the scariest part of all. He was already losing little bits and pieces of her and had to work to bring her back into focus. He shut his eyes, trying to picture her hand, tucking a curl of hair behind her ear and the flash of her eyes as she smiled at him. He listened deep in his mind for her voice, calling his name. The need to be with his mom was like the need to breathe, and his chest felt tight all the time, his stomach in knots.

He decided to kill time by getting his homework out of the way. He had Spanish, which was a no-brainer for him, and English vocabulary, which, unfortunately, wasn't. The teacher had this word-of-the-day thing going, and she believed the way to learn a word was to study its roots and put it to use. Today's word was *churlish.* The root word was *churl.* According to the textbook, *churlish* meant rude and boorish, having a bad disposition; surly. Its root came from an old word for peasant. The rude and boorish type. AJ wasn't quite sure what boorish meant, so he looked that up, too. "Ill-mannered, coarse and contemptible in behavior or appearance..."

He drummed his pencil on the edge of the table, trying to decide how to use the word in a sentence. *The churlish boy was sick of waiting around for his turn on the computer,* he thought. He got up and paced restlessly. *Being ignored by the other kids made him feel churlish.*

Lately, AJ was learning a lot of big words, like detention. Deportation. Expulsion.

"You waiting for this computer?" asked Chelsea Nash, taking off her headset. "You're circling like a buzzard. I can't stand that. Pisses me off."

She had a way with words, that was for sure. He indicated the sign that noted a thirty-minute time limit on the terminal.

"Whatever," she said, gathering up her backpack. "I missed the bus today, so I had to call my grandfather to pick me up. I think he forgot."

AJ shrugged. "Call him again."

"My grandparents won't let me have a cell phone," she said. "They won't even have Internet in the house. Pisses me off."

AJ handed over his mobile phone. "You can borrow mine." Ever since the New York incident, Bo made him carry a cell phone wherever he went.

"Thanks." She made the call, and sure enough, her

grandfather had forgotten. She exhaled an exasperated breath as she handed back the phone. "Now it'll take him like an hour to get here, because he drives really slow. Especially when the roads are bad. We had another six inches of snow on Lakeshore Road last night."

She sure did talk a lot, AJ observed as he took his seat. She acted as though she'd known him forever.

"I'm Chelsea, by the way," the girl said.

"I know. I mean, I've seen you at the animal hospital," said AJ.

"Oh. You know Dr. Shepherd?"

"Mrs. Bellamy-Shepherd is doing some legal work for my dad." AJ hoped she didn't get too nosy.

"Who's your dad?"

Great. She was going to be nosy.

"His name's Bo Crutcher." More and more, it was starting to feel normal, calling Bo his dad. Anyway, that was the simplest explanation, so he stuck with it.

"Oh! I love Bo Crutcher!" Her face lit up and she looked almost pretty, in a chubby way. "I mean, he's a really good guy. He's always helping out with fund-raisers and stuff, on account of he's semifamous."

Only in a town like this would a guy like Bo be considered semifamous. Of course, if he really did make it with the Yankees, he'd be legitimately famous. "What do you mean, helping?"

"Like last year at the Wildlife Shelter Auction, he donated private baseball coaching to the highest bidder, and people went crazy, bidding on it. And when his band won the battle of the bands the other day, it was a benefit for juvenile diabetes. That kind of thing. Everybody thinks your dad is a totally good guy," Chelsea concluded. "So did you move here to live with him for good?"

"No," AJ said swiftly. "Just until…just for a while."

"Yeah, trust me, I know what 'a while' means. My parents left me with my grandparents for 'a while' and it's been years."

Nothing like a word of encouragement from a stranger. A talkative stranger. She told him her grandparents were really strict and old-fashioned. But she didn't say much about her parents, like why they had left her and where they were.

She changed the subject back to him, her features sharpening with curiosity. "You're new, aren't you? What's your name?"

"It's AJ. AJ Martinez."

"What's the AJ stand for?"

She had to ask. He didn't even know this girl. Why should he tell her anything? Because it didn't matter. He didn't care what she thought. "I go by AJ for a reason," he muttered.

"Is it something really dorky or out-there? Like Ajax, or Apollo Jehosephat, or Able Janitor…"

He tried not to laugh.

She slid a notepad across the table toward him. "Here, write your name on this piece of paper. I'll take one look at it, then destroy the evidence."

Geez, this girl was relentless. He wrote his two given names on a piece of paper and slipped it to her. Of course she couldn't keep her mouth shut, despite her promise.

"Angel?" she said, her voice a sharp exclamation that made heads turn. Noticing, she switched to a whisper. "Your name is Angel?"

"It's pronounced *Angel,*" he muttered, not that the Spanish *g* made it any better. "*Angel Jacinto.* And we had a deal."

"Right," she said. "Ahn-*hell.* Sorry, AJ." She ripped the scrap of paper into tiny bits of confetti. "I actually like how it sounds in Spanish. Are you fluent in Spanish?"

He nodded. AJ had grown up never sensing any boundaries between English and Spanish. Thoughts and words flowed freely across the divide, and until he started school, he hadn't realized he was speaking two different languages. In school, he'd been taught that English was the way to get ahead, but Spanish always echoed through his mind, somehow more expressive, more meaningful. It was the language of his dreams.

"That's lucky," Chelsea said. "Are you taking Spanish?"

Another nod. His teacher, Sr. Diaz, was from Puerto Rico. His Spanish sounded different from the language AJ was used to, but it was the one class he knew he'd ace without studying.

It was funny how Chelsea deemed him lucky. He didn't feel so lucky. He felt like a fish out of water, even in Spanish class. And she didn't seem to realize a lot of people in this country, even in Texas, considered his knowledge of Spanish a reason to hate him.

Chelsea turned out to be as good a listener as she was a talker. Without really planning what he was going to say, or knowing why he needed to talk, AJ told her what had happened to his mother. It was really the first time he'd told anybody, blow-by-blow, about that day.

He'd gotten up as usual. He could hear Mama in the kitchen, singing "Livin' la Vida Loca" along with Ricky Martin on the radio, a tune that suited her unselfconscious, happy voice. His mom was young and pretty, and she dressed for work like a kid, in jeans and sneakers. At her job at the rice-packaging factory, she had a locker where she changed into a coverall and hairnet. Since Bruno had left, she worked overtime whenever she could, but the mornings before school always belonged to AJ.

They'd had breakfast together that day as usual. She quizzed him on his spelling words because there was always a test on Friday. His mom had never finished school. She claimed helping him with homework helped her improve her English. This made homework seem important. He got all his words right except *disinterred.* She made him spell it three times and use it in a sentence: *The cats disinterred a fish carcass and had a smelly feast.*

It was a completely normal morning, and AJ probably would've forgotten all the details, except it turned out to be their last day together. He'd gone to school like normal, moved and jostled through classes, lunch, recess, study hall the way he always did. The nightmare had started last period. Mrs. Alvarez came and got him out of science class. The teacher's aide explained that there'd been a raid on the packaging factory where his mother worked. She'd been handed over to ICE—Immigration and Customs Enforcement—and detained.

AJ had never really thought about the word *detained.* He quickly learned that in his mom's case it essentially meant she'd been sucked off the face of the earth.

Mrs. Alvarez hadn't seemed concerned at first. She'd been sure there would be someone to look after AJ. Nearly everyone had relatives or someone with the church. AJ was the exception. He was the only child of an only child.

His grandma lived in the valley, on the Mexican side. Bruno, his former stepdad, had been out of the picture since he'd left them high and dry. Which was how AJ ended up flying through the night to be with Bo Crutcher, the father he'd never met.

"That's completely freaky," Chelsea said. "And totally unfair. She didn't do anything wrong."

Too bad Chelsea's opinion didn't matter.

Without being invited, she dragged a chair over to the terminal and started searching the Internet. She was like a dog with a bone, typing in phrases like *"immigration law"* and *"naturalized citizen"* and trying to figure out why his mom could be living like a regular person one day, and an outlaw the next. Mainly, like AJ, she wanted to figure out how his mom might be allowed to stay in the U.S.

"Let's write a letter to your congressman. Who is it?"

"No clue."

"Well, geez, let's find out." Chelsea was pretty good at all this, and within a short time, they had sent a note via the Web sites of a Texas representative and a senator. For good measure, they sent the same message to the assemblymen from New York, too.

"Says here a medical situation would warrant special permission," Chelsea continued, "if it's a condition only a special doctor in the U.S. can deal with." They both leaned toward the monitor and stared at before and after pictures of conjoined twins. The family came from a remote atoll in the Pacific, and a famous surgeon at Vanderbilt had separated the babies.

"Doesn't look like anything that could help my mom," AJ said, feeling relieved when Chelsea closed that particular Web site. Although the story had a happy ending, he was weirded out by the photos.

"Can she prove she's in danger in her country?" Chelsea asked. "What about seeking temporary asylum?"

Asylum. It had been on last week's vocabulary list. A place where crazy people are kept. *The lunatics are in charge of the asylum.*

"That won't work," he said.

"Then how about this? Bingo." She printed out a page and handed it over. "Give that to Bo."

AJ scanned the page. "Oh, sure. So he's going to marry her just so she can be in the U.S."

"It could work."

"Or not."

"Have you talked about it with Bo?"

AJ had a hard time talking to Bo about anything. Every once in a while, they connected. Like when they built the snowman together. And then there was that moment, when Bo had come to the city to get him, when AJ had felt a deep connection, safe in his arms. It had felt so good and so safe, that long hug. During moments like that, AJ could feel himself starting to like Bo. *Really* like him. But enough to talk about stuff like this?

He forced himself to step back, and to remember that he didn't want to get attached to Bo. It was crazy to get attached to somebody you were trying to get away from, someone you never planned on seeing again.

On the other hand, what if crazy Chelsea was right? What if this could actually happen? AJ would have a real, actual family. Two parents and him. The thought made his stomach hurt, he wanted it so bad.

"He'd think I lost my marbles."

"Why?" Chelsea demanded. "You said your mom's single, right? Bo is single. They could—"

"That's dumb. Just because they're single doesn't mean they should be together. They haven't seen each other in thirteen years." He ducked his head so she wouldn't see his face, because without even trying, she had found AJ's most secret dream—having a mom and dad.

"Well, I bet they were totally in love when they um, you know," Chelsea said. "Maybe they'll fall in love again."

"You're completely nuts."

"Have you figured out a better idea? Has your lawyer?"

She was nuts, but she had a point.

"I bet it's more complicated than that," he said. "They don't just let people get married so one of them can stay in this country."

"I've heard of worse reasons for getting married," she said.

Twenty-Five

"We're not in Kansas anymore," Bo said, looking around the suite at the Pierre Hotel. He and AJ were on the 34th floor, with a view of Central Park. They had ridden up on an elevator operated by an actual elevator man. The old-fashioned rooms overflowed with luxury—fancy furniture, amenities they didn't know they needed, like little linen mats beside the beds, so their bare feet didn't have to touch the carpet. There was a room service menu filled with stuff he couldn't pronounce, but no minibar, because this hotel was too classy for a minibar. The bellman who had delivered the bags said if they wanted ice or a little jar of peanuts, they just had to pick up the phone and someone would bring whatever they wanted.

This was all Kim's doing. The reception at the hotel to-night, staged for media and sponsors, was going to be key to moving up the career ladder. Amid the hot, young rookies and early-round draft picks, Bo was an unlikely candidate, but Kim had made sure he was front and center. You become a star by acting like a star, she'd said.

She had also said she loved him. She loved him. He'd never realized how bad he wanted to hear that phrase until it came from Kimberly van Dorn's mouth. The moment she said the words, he felt as though he could suddenly fly.

Yet AJ kept him grounded. Bo had insisted on bringing him along, hoping it might distract the boy from worrying about his mother. But it hadn't, really. Bo could see it in his face—the tension and despair, even though Bo had vowed he wouldn't rest until he brought her back.

"Get it?" he said. "Not in Kansas anymore—that's from *The Wizard of Oz*."

"Ha-ha." AJ stood at the tall, heavily draped window, gazing down at the stark, bare trees of Central Park. "I've seen it."

There was a knock at the door. A housekeeper came to deliver extra towels. "Here you are, sir," she murmured, a Spanish accent thick in her voice.

Just for a moment, AJ locked eyes with the woman. She was small, and wore her hair pulled back. Her uniform was embroidered with the name Juanita. In that brief instant of connection, Bo could sense a recognition between them, two strangers bound by the deep ties of language. The woman offered a quick smile but ducked her head in deference. As she left the room, Bo gave her a twenty-dollar bill.

"Thank you, sir," she murmured, quietly shutting the door behind her.

Bo could see everything in AJ's face—yearning, frustration, fury. The housekeeper was simply a reminder. It must be hard for AJ to see Bo getting everything he wanted while Yolanda was suffering in some detention center across the border.

"I know you're worried about your mom, but she's going to be all right," Bo said. "Mexico's a free country."

"She's not free to come and see her own son."

"We're working on that, AJ. Your mother's changed status is a setback. You've got to believe it's one we can deal with."

AJ swung around to face him. His eyes were puffy from tears he refused to shed. His small frame was backlit by the pale light through the window. The kid hadn't been eating well, and now Bo saw his thinness starkly outlined. For the first time, Bo realized with a lurch of panic that AJ's physical health was threatened. And there was no cure for a broken heart.

The boy took refuge in anger. "How do I even know you've been trying to help her?"

"I've been trying to help your mother since day one, and you know it. I just hired a private investigator, because Sophie wants to get more information about your mom's family background."

AJ narrowed his eyes. "Anything to get rid of me, right?"

"Don't be a little shit," Bo snapped, panic giving way to anger. "Your mom's back in Mexico and I know that sucks for you, but copping an attitude won't help a thing. Believe me, nothing will stop me from trying to bring your mom back."

"You can't wait for me to leave," AJ persisted.

"If that was so, I wouldn't have invited you to the city for the weekend. I would've left you behind in Avalon."

"Why should I believe anything you say?"

"Because I love you, dammit."

AJ looked as if Bo had hit him. "You love me."

"Hell, yes, I love you. You're my boy. My flesh and blood. And you're an awesome kid, and after you're back with your mom, I still want to see you, no matter what she says."

"So when did you decide this? All of a sudden you want to love me."

"It wasn't all of a sudden. Ever since you were born I've *wanted* to love you, but your mom was in charge. Even though she had her reasons, it didn't stop me from wishing we could be like father and son, at least some of the time. It's a terrible thing, the way we were brought together, but I'm glad I'm getting to spend time with you. Anyway, yeah. I always *wanted* to love you. I'm trying to do it right." He didn't know how else to explain it. Getting to know AJ was like falling in love—not in a romantic way, of course. But it was a kind of anticipation, something he felt in his heart. He couldn't wait to get up in the morning—couldn't wait to see what the day would bring. Couldn't wait to see his son's face.

The boy was quiet for a long time. Bo braced himself, hoping he hadn't crossed a line with that speech, which revealed more of his heart than he'd intended.

Finally, AJ said, "Okay."

"Christ, you're a pain in the ass sometimes."

"Yeah, well, so're you."

AJ had turned Bo into someone he barely recognized and never expected to be—a father. A better man than he'd been before AJ came into his life. He couldn't claim to be good at it, but he was clear on what he felt for this boy. "I'm not going to quit helping your mom. Say you believe that."

AJ stared at him for a long time. Bo sensed all kinds of things going on in the boy's head, but all AJ said was, "I believe it." He still looked unhappy, though.

"Would you rather I hadn't brought you to the city for the weekend?" Bo challenged him. "Would you rather have missed out on this?" He encompassed the fancy suite with a gesture.

"No," AJ admitted. "It's cool."

"And just so you know," he told AJ, "all this wouldn't seem nearly as cool if you weren't here with me." Bo meant it from the bottom of his heart. If there was one thing he'd learned from being with Kim, it was the power of saying what you meant, loud and clear.

"Okay." The boy was still guarded.

"So, what do you say? I better get dressed for high society. And you can get busy picking out what you want to order from room service and what movies you want to watch while I'm at the reception." He finally coaxed a smile from AJ by finding an upbeat radio station that was playing "Superfreak," and dressing in time to the music. He slapped on aftershave in exaggerated fashion, then tossed the bottle to AJ, who cringed a little as he daubed some on.

"I hope I don't blow it tonight," Bo said.

"You won't blow it."

"The reception's going to be full of VIPs."

"Quit freaking."

Kim had told Bo what to wear. He knew better than to argue with her taste. He held up a sport coat that had cost him more than his first car. The song on the radio faded, and a commercial came on, so he turned down the volume. He felt AJ watching him, and sensed a shift in the boy's mood. "What?"

"You could fix everything, you know," he said in a voice that was almost too quiet to hear.

Bo paused in the middle of knotting his tie. "What do you mean, fix everything?"

"My mom, is what I mean. You could fix it."

"If I knew how, I'd fix it."

"There's a way." AJ paused, took a deep breath. "You could marry her."

"Sorry, bud. What's that?" Bo hoped he'd heard wrong. But the curl of dread in his gut told him otherwise.

"If you married my mother, she'd be allowed to live in this country legally. I swear, it can work. People do it all the time."

The way it came out, all in a rush, indicated to Bo that the boy had been thinking about the idea for a while, probably trying to figure out how to broach the topic.

"Aw, AJ." Bo's heart ached for the kid. He'd probably built up this big scenario in his mind, picturing the three of them together as a family. Bo was familiar with his father fantasies. He'd had them himself as a kid. "That kind of thing isn't going to work. The system's set up to keep people from doing it."

"It's a free country," AJ said. "You're allowed to marry anybody you want, right?"

"The authorities have ways to figure out which marriages are sincere and which took place just to cheat the system."

"You know how to be sincere," AJ insisted. "You've been studying it, I've seen you. Kim taught you how to be sincere."

"It's not the same. That's media training, not... Sorry, AJ. I get where you're coming from, but it's not going to happen."

"You liked her once, didn't you?"

The stark question hung in the air. "Your mother, you mean?"

"Yes. You liked her once. You liked her enough to make

me. Maybe you could like her enough to bring her back, and stick around long enough for her to change her status. It wouldn't be hard. I looked it up on the Internet, and the forms are even on the Immigration and Naturalization Web site. You just fill them out and send them in. I know it can be done."

"You can't believe everything you read on the Internet."

"What about what you said before?" Desperation edged AJ's voice now. "You said you'd do anything for me."

"I should have qualified it—I'll do anything legal and ethical."

"This *is* legal. I need to be with my mom. Tell me you'll at least think about it." AJ sank down on one of the beds and grabbed a pillow. The massive bed made him look tiny and bereft.

Bo went down on one knee in front of him, touched his shoulder. "Your mom's lucky to have you, AJ, she really is. And the two of you are going to be together soon, that's a promise."

"Does that mean you'll do it? You'll get married to her?"

"It means I'll keep working as hard as I know how to find a solution to this."

"I found the solution."

"You found a rumor on the Web. I'll ask Sophie about it, okay? That's what I'll do."

AJ crushed the pillow against his chest. "You're gonna wrinkle your pants."

Bo stood up, brushed a kiss on the boy's head, and the gesture felt as natural as if he'd been doing it forever. He wished he could inhale all of the kid's pain and carry it away somewhere.

Then his mobile phone chirped—a text message from

Kim: Showtime. He was quickly finding out that one of the hardest things about being a parent was being pulled in different directions from moment to moment. He stuck the phone in his pocket. "I have to head downstairs, buddy. You go ahead and order room service and a pay-per-view movie, anything you want. I'll be in the ballroom. You call me if you need anything, anything at all."

"I'm not hungry," AJ muttered. "You know what I need."

Bo grazed the boy's cheek lightly with his knuckles, hiding his terror that his son was fading away before his eyes. "I'll see you later, okay?"

AJ nodded, hunching his shoulders, diminished. His gaze went to the photograph in the plastic sleeve, which lay on the nightstand. He brought the photo of his mother everywhere he went. It killed Bo that AJ only had the one photo.

"We'll figure this out," Bo said. "You're gonna be all right." The words felt empty and false. He studied his son's face, and saw the truth there: AJ was *not* all right. His heart was broken. He wasn't going to be all right until he was reunited with his mother.

Here was something Bo hadn't understood until AJ came into his life—that the hardest thing about being a father was seeing your kid hurting, and knowing you'd do anything to make it stop. And not being able to stop the hurt? Well, that was pure frustration. The boy's suffering would go on and on unless...

Bo's stomach was in knots as he made his way down the hall to the elevators. On the way, he phoned Sophie to ask if it was possible, what AJ suggested. "I know it sounds crazy, but I have to know, is it true? If I marry her, can she come back to the States?"

"Yes, but it's a very involved process…" She mentioned a residency requirement, a provisional visa and a two-year period to make certain the marriage was legitimate. Obviously, she'd already studied this possibility.

"Why didn't you say anything to me before?" he asked.

"It didn't seem like a good option for you. Bo—"

"But it's an option," he said.

"Yes, but—"

That was all he needed to hear. A yes from Sophie.

"Look into it for me. I'll call you later," he said, ringing off as the elevator arrived.

He stepped on board, nodding a greeting to a diminutive Filipino man whose name badge identified him as Timbô. "Evening," Bo said, trying to shift gears. He had to do a good job at this reception for AJ's sake, as well as his own.

"Good evening, sir," the attendant said. The elevator descended a couple of floors, and when the doors parted, there was Kim.

She looked like something out of a dream. Her long, fitted gown reminded Bo of the first time he'd ever laid eyes on her. She'd seemed so out of reach that day, yet now here she was, making him feel like the luckiest guy on earth. And just like that, he shifted gears. Knowing she was here made everything possible. "You look amazing," he said, bending to kiss her cheek, catching a waft of fragrance.

"Likewise," she replied. Then she addressed Timbô. "Did your phone call work?" she asked him.

"Yes, madam. My wife and I talked for one hour," Timbô said with a happy smile, stepping aside so they could exit to the lobby. "Have a good evening, Miss van Dorn."

"You're a marriage counselor, too?" Bo asked her.

"They've been apart for a year," she explained. "I showed him how to make an overseas phone call using a free service on the Internet. It's just too sad, thinking about them being apart so long."

Bo flashed on what that would be like—loving someone, but separated, unable to see or touch her. He wished they were alone instead of in a crowded hotel. There was so much he wanted to tell her. So much that he loved her for. He loved her because she did things that were hard, things she didn't want to do, for all the right reasons. He loved her because she had not just made him into a professional athlete. Like AJ, she'd made him into a better man. He even loved her for the fact that she noticed elevator attendants when most people gave them no more attention than a standing ashtray.

Yet tonight, maybe for the first time, he realized love might not be enough to keep them together. His situation with AJ and Yolanda had grown complicated, even more so after AJ had planted the seed of his idea. If the kid was really onto something, it would change everything between Bo and Kim. He thought about what it would mean, really mean, to marry a virtual stranger who had kept his son from him for twelve years. Then he thought about what it would mean to live without Kim, the woman who had finally taught him to love without fear and with a full heart.

For the sake of AJ, Bo would do what he had to, but he couldn't help counting the cost.

"Hey, don't look so serious," she chided him, taking his arm as they passed the lobby toward the ballroom. "It's your big night. You're going to knock them dead."

"I'll give it my best shot, coach."

* * *

The evening was a triumph in the professional sense. Nobody, not even Kim, seemed to notice that Bo was in turmoil, his mind a million miles away, his heart already hurting over what he had to do for AJ's sake. Kim had taught him well. You show people only what you want them to see, tell them only what you want them to hear. Time passed in a blur of handshakes, polite exchanges, hearty assurances of future meetings. After an hour or two, he had a pocket full of contacts—stars of the game, people from national TV, others who repped fine cars, booze, shaving products and all kinds of things that had nothing to do with baseball and everything to do with image. He was grateful to have Kim around. Just her presence gave him confidence. She worked the room like the pro she was, and seemed to enjoy every minute of it.

For the first time, he saw her in her element, completely at ease with guys who were named after founding fathers or investment firms, not country-western ballads. More forcefully than ever, Bo understood that not only did they come from different worlds, they *belonged* in different worlds.

She made a valiant attempt to make Bo seem like he belonged, too, introducing him to sportcasters and marketing experts.

"You've got quite a fan in this lady here," said Stu Westfield, a producer with ESPN. "To hear her tell it, you're going to be the second coming, bringing a balance of freshness, strength and experience to the mound."

"Sounds better than just saying I'm old," Bo admitted.

Westfield guffawed and shook his hand, then Kim's. "You're as good as you are good-looking," he told her, "and

I mean that in the best possible way. You ever do any on-air reporting? Color commentary?"

"Not since my college intern days. I worked for Vin Scully," she said, earning raised eyebrows, for Scully was a broadcasting legend in calling ball games.

Westfield tucked her business card into his pocket. "Who's your agent?"

She laughed. "I don't have an agent."

"Then I'll call you directly," he said, giving them both a wave before both Kim and Bo were invited to chat with Joe Girardi, the team's manager, followed by a handful of potential sponsors.

"You were fantastic," Kim said as they left the reception. "I'm proud of you."

Powerful words. He couldn't believe the way they made him feel. Insane with love and gratitude, but at the same time, sick in the pit of his stomach, because he'd been hiding something all evening. AJ's desperate suggestion had cracked open a door, and Bo knew what he had to do.

Unaware, Kim seemed to float down the carpeted hallway. "They'll never forget you," she told him. "I won't let them. You're on your way."

"You got that right," he murmured, his stomach in knots.

In the elevator, she sighed and pressed herself back against him, while the operator stared straight ahead. When it stopped at her floor, she tugged on Bo's hand, towing him along behind her as she exited the elevator. Then she stopped, lifted herself up on tiptoe and whispered in his ear. "I was just thinking, maybe we should go to my room and—"

Using all his self-control, Bo held her gently by the

shoulders and took a step away. "Honey, you know there's nothing I'd like better. I need to get back to AJ, though."

Her face fell. "I just thought…"

He knew what she thought. Boy, did he ever. But until he figured out exactly what to do, he needed to put some distance between him and this woman he loved so completely. He couldn't think straight around her.

"Anyway, I should go." He leaned down and gently kissed her mouth.

She tilted her head to one side, studying him with a keen expression. She knew him too well, and he could tell she knew something was up. "See you in the morning, then. We can sleep in. Take the afternoon train back to Avalon."

"Sure, sounds good." Without thinking, without being able to resist, he cupped her cheek in his hand.

She reached up and covered his hand with hers. "Last chance. You sure you don't want to come in for a nightcap?"

What he wanted was to come in for the entire night. For a lifetime.

"Like I said, I better check on AJ."

There was no way to adequately explain to Kim what he intended to do. There was a reason Bo Crutcher had never broken a promise. It was because he never made one.

Something was wrong. Kim knew it. She watched Bo walking toward the elevator, as grim and resolute as a man on his way to a firing squad. "Just a second," she said.

His shoulders stiffened; then he turned back to face her. "I should go—"

"Not before we talk. We'll go to my room—for privacy." She suddenly felt embarrassed for coming on to him earlier. His head was somewhere else, and she should have sensed that. Something had shifted, it was obvious now, and she could feel the weight of it, pressing on her. She unlocked the door and walked straight through the room, out to the balcony. It would be too distracting to talk to him with the big, cushy bed just sitting there, looking so inviting.

The night air bit at her, and she welcomed its sting on her cheeks; it completely counteracted the effects of the champagne she'd drunk at the reception. From this vantage point, she could see couples bundling into the horse-and-carriage rides in lamp-lit Central Park. It seemed terribly romantic, but she didn't let herself dwell on romance. Not now.

"What's going on?" she asked him.

"I'm taking AJ to Texas," Bo said quietly.

It meant something that he didn't bother to equivocate, just let her have it. She swallowed the lump in her throat, the one that had been building since he'd acted so strange in the elevator. Yet there was a note of regret in his voice, in the way he carried himself, the set of his jaw, that caused her to brace herself. She couldn't speak, though. There was nothing for her to say. She waited.

"It's something I have to do," he continued. "For AJ. I got a few weeks before training starts in Florida, and I...just have to do more for Yolanda. AJ—he's fading away before my eyes, and it's killing him. It's killing *me*. He has to be with his mother."

She'd never seen Bo like this, so intensely serious. "How will that work? Are you saying you're taking him to Mexico?"

He raised his hands as if to touch her, then took a step back, lowering his arms. Why wouldn't he touch her? It was all she could think about, his arms, holding her, hands caressing her. Yet now he seemed curiously distant.

"Is everything all right?" she asked. "You're scaring me."

"Sorry," he said. "I don't mean to act all weird. Bringing Yolanda back for good—that's the only thing I can think of that will save AJ."

"You've been trying to do that since day one. What are you talking about?"

"I'm going to marry his mother." He wore a look of absolute conviction, which was only underscored by the pain in his eyes.

The world tilted. Kim wanted to pretend she hadn't heard. But she couldn't. She suddenly knew exactly what the plan was.

"I checked with Sophie," he said. "It'll work. But there are rules."

"What kind of rules?"

"Forms to fill out—a visa petition, a hardship waiver. And…a two-year cohabitation condition. It's to make sure this is a bona fide marriage, not just a fast lane to a green card." He paused, waiting. "Talk to me, Kim. What's going through your mind?"

A hundred things—What about me, about us? How much does our love matter? She didn't ask those things, though, because ultimately, the thing that mattered most was AJ.

"I understand," she said at last. And she did, on one level. On another, she was devastated. Her heart was stunned. She couldn't quite feel it in her chest. Yet she knew when the numbness passed, she would feel it shatter.

"Then you understand what it means for us."

She was barely able to keep herself together. She was

shivering, not just from the cold but because everything was changing, and there wasn't a thing she could do to stop it. "There's no 'us.' There can't be," she said.

He nodded, his eyes dark with pain. "I do love you, Kimberly. More than words can say. But I won't ask you to wait for me. I *can't* ask it of you. I won't. You deserve better."

He was right, absolutely, even though everything about this felt wrong. Still, she didn't argue or try to change his mind. The old Kimberly would have had a fit, insisted on finding a better way, a way that kept her needs in the forefront. She wasn't that person anymore. This was bigger than herself, her desires. AJ's need was greater than her own. Yes, she could see how far the boy had come. He'd improved in school, learned new sports, made new friends. But when she looked into his eyes, even when he was smiling, she saw an emptiness there, one that had grown even more pronounced since the news of his mother's deportation. If there was a chance to save this boy, then Bo had to take it.

"I'm so sorry, honey." He studied her through pain-filled eyes. "Please say you'll forgive me one day."

She felt a flash of anger, quick and hot, but it passed in an instant. None of this was his fault. He was only trying to do what was best for his son. And they had all known from the start that what AJ needed most was his mother.

"There's nothing to say," she told him. *Don't cry,* she warned herself. *Don't make this harder than it already is.*

"Kim, I'm sorry—"

"You don't need to be. I'm proud of you for doing whatever it takes to help AJ."

"I'm just trying to do right by my boy. I, uh…there's something else."

She waited again, knowing from the expression on his face that it wasn't going to be more happy news.

"Under the circumstances, it's probably better if we don't work together."

The irony was hard to miss. This wasn't the first time she had been dumped and fired in the same conversation. Yet the circumstances could not be more different. With Lloyd, there had been ugliness and malice. With Bo, there was mutual concern for a child and the knowledge that there was only one choice to be made. She floated in a strange moment of suspension between the world before her and what might have been.

Let it go, she told herself. *Let it go.*

She couldn't speak, but managed to nod her assent.

"I have to go now," he said. "Lots to do." He offered a smile that was tinged with sadness. "I love you, Kim. I wish…" He paused, started again. "I'm so damned sorry."

She nodded again, found her voice. "You should go," she said. "Don't let me keep you."

Twenty-Six

Patches of snow clung stubbornly in the shadowy places of the yard, and high in the hilltops above Willow Lake. Yet where the sun shone, grass and daffodils and tulips burst through in a riot of color.

Six weeks after saying goodbye to Bo Crutcher, Kim still felt the deep hurt of losing him and AJ both. Together, they'd taken hold of her heart in a way she'd never thought possible. After she'd practically been destroyed in L.A., Bo made her believe in love again. But it was a funny thing about love. As much as it hurt now that he was gone, she had no regrets about letting him into her life. In a few short weeks, she had managed to love him with a depth and honesty that changed her in some fundamental way. In that sense, something good had come of it. She was better for having loved him, which made the empty ache almost bearable. Almost.

She could still picture a large, assured male hand, covering hers or feel the brush of his lips against her mouth. She could still hear the sound of his laughter, warm in her ear, and the memory brought on a bittersweet smile. She wondered where he was now, what he was doing.

No, she didn't. When he left, he'd left for good, and that was the way it had to be. No contact. No phone calls or e-mail. Nothing. Kim knew her only chance of emotional survival would be to make a clean break with one swift, sure blow and no hope of reopening the wound. She refused to let herself dream of getting back together with Bo. They'd both agreed it wouldn't work, not if he was going to create the family AJ needed—and one that would hold up to official scrutiny. She'd told Bo not to call her or send her e-mail. He needed to move ahead and do what he had to do for AJ.

After the reception, there had been hurried arrangements—passports and a swift departure for Texas. Now the third story of the house sat empty, abandoned, as though they'd never lived there, never filled the house with their voices and laughter.

According to the stack of picking-up-the-pieces self-help books she'd read, she was supposed to move on, too. By now, she should be emotionally ready, open to meeting new people, finding a new love. But she couldn't. She just couldn't. Bo had ruined all other men for her. Every time a man smiled at her, she thought about Bo's smile. When a guy flirted with her, she remembered Bo's voice, his easy laugh and the way his eyes lit when she walked into a room. There was no way someone else could compete with those memories. With Bo, she'd learned to fling herself into love in a way she never had before. Now she had to decide if it was worth the hurt.

What she could do was stay busy. At least one good thing

had come from the night at the Pierre. True to his word, Stu Westfield, the producer, had contacted her about a job— not in media training or PR, but on the other side of the mic. He wanted her to work with the play-by-play announcer for the Yankees, providing live color commentary. She hadn't given Stu an answer yet. It would be a dream job for her, but she wondered what it would be like, being in the same world as Bo Crutcher. It didn't seem possible.

Still, she couldn't bring herself to dismiss the opportunity out of hand. In the meantime, she had put her skills to use on behalf of *Casa de Esperanza,* which needed funding for its shelter for unaccompanied youths—American-born children, whose parents had been deported. She worked with advocates and volunteers, prepping them to take their case to the media. Because even though AJ was going to get his happy ending, there were too many others who lived in the shadow world of lost children.

Closer to home, she took unexpected pleasure in helping to plan her mother's wedding. When Kim commented on how quickly it was all happening, her mother said, "I've waited a long time for a man like this. It's either do it now or live in sin and embarrass you even worse."

She set the countertop TV on ESPN, still her favorite channel, to keep her company while she polished the silverware for the upcoming wedding. A quick news wrap-up caught her attention. In the NBA semifinals, Lloyd Johnson committed a hard foul in the paint and started a brawl, abetted by his archrival, Marshall Walters. Sidelined and fined a fortune, Johnson found himself with a broken nose and bearing the brunt of the blame for giving away a shot at the championship. Kim felt nothing but a passing interest. Lloyd was simply becoming more like himself, and she was glad she wasn't around to deal with the fallout.

A few minutes later, there was a recap of early-season baseball games, which she listened to with far more interest. She could easily picture herself in the broadcast booth, and the temptation to accept the job offer grew stronger. The Braves had defeated the Cardinals in a 9-0 rout. Cincinnati fell to Boston, and there was a puff piece on the identical twin brothers, each on opposing teams. After a commercial break, the latest Yankees win was covered, and the 90-second player spotlight that followed it galvanized Kim. "Once considered an unlikely prospect for this club, Bo Crutcher started his major-league journey as a batting practice pitcher. That only lasted a week, when a starting pitcher was sidelined by injury. Crutcher stepped in, and he stepped up, with a strong start to the season. A long, tall lefty with a deceptively smooth overhand delivery, his curveball is already getting a reputation—it just might be unhittable…."

Kim rubbed harder with the polishing cloth as her agitation morphed into energy. She and Bo had agreed not to contact each other. For AJ's sake, he needed to make a go at being a family, making a clean break with Kim. Seeing him now merely flayed an open wound, but she couldn't help herself. She couldn't take her eyes off the screen. The camera loved him. The press loved him. The fans loved him. And why not? Why should the rest of the world be any different from Kim? She couldn't help herself and neither could anyone else. She wondered what his life was like now. Had he and Yolanda gotten a place in New

Rochelle or Larchmont, perhaps? Had their two years of cohabitation started? Did AJ finally have the family he'd dreamed about?

She shook off the thought and focused on the broadcast. Bo looked as though he'd been born to play this game. The long-limbed grace of his windup and delivery inspired the announcer to declare that he was poetry in motion. It was wonderful to watch him play baseball, in the way it was wonderful to watch a gifted dancer. The sight of him made her heart skip a beat.

The report cut to the game's end, with a clip from the clubhouse. Kim couldn't suppress a smile when he said something straight out of her playbook: "I got one job to do—make it so the team has a chance to win. It worked today." He sounded as genuine and natural as he was in person.

"You're a lot scarier on the mound," the interviewer noted. "Is that where the nickname Iceman came from?"

"I'm not trying to be scary. Just doing my job."

"What about your personal life? Wife? Girlfriend? Family—"

Bo offered his trademark grin, the one Kim had once explained would never fail him, so long as he let the smile reach his eyes. "My friend, there's a reason it's called private life. And hey, thanks for coming out today. See y'all around the ballpark." He effectively ended the interview without seeming to be rude.

At least she knew he was doing all right, and there was some measure of satisfaction in that. By the time she'd left L.A., her ideals had been muted. She'd learned to lie and spin for the sake of the client. The refreshing thing about

Bo was that he was completely genuine, with a good story, and she was proud to have helped him shape it. She tried to feel a sense of accomplishment, but it was thin, and fleeting.

Kim reached across the counter and snapped off the TV. It was time to stop lying to herself. She wasn't okay. Not even close.

The morning of the wedding dawned cool and blustery, yet the air was sweet with the promise of spring. The cake had just been delivered by the Sky River Bakery and Kim found herself alone in the kitchen, admiring the colorful fondant icing that coordinated strangely with the color scheme of the house.

She fixed a cup of tea and sipped it, hoping the day would warm up enough so she could wear the party dress she'd picked out for the event. She could hear the sounds of people elsewhere in the house, getting ready for the big day. The rented tables and chairs had already been set up, and friends and neighbors were bringing the food, potluck style. Bo's former band—with a new bass player named Brandi—would be playing the music.

And just like that, her thoughts circled around to Bo Crutcher again. Maybe a time would come when she would wake up and her mind wouldn't go there, but today wasn't the day.

She heard the thud of a car door slamming and glanced at the clock. Another delivery? Or—

The kitchen door opened and a whirlwind burst in.

Kim dropped her mug into the sink, unable to believe her eyes. "What are you doing here?" she asked, already feeling the tears well up.

"Surprise!" AJ was grinning from ear to ear. "I bet you're surprised to see me."

She flew across the room and hugged him, loving the sturdy feel of him in her arms, the grassy boyish scent of him. She'd missed him more than she'd thought possible. More than... She stepped back. He looked like a different child, bigger, stronger, more vibrant and assured, his eyes sparkling with an inner light she'd never seen before. "I can't believe it! What's going on?"

"We came to Avalon to live," he said. "My mom and I— it was Bo's idea. He fixed everything. Everything!"

"Oh..." Despite her joy at seeing AJ again, her heart plummeted. She'd only just begun to believe she would survive what had happened, and now this. What was Bo thinking, bringing the woman he'd married to live in this town? Did he really mean to torture her like this?

"He said he'd go crazy missing me if we stayed in Texas." AJ's smile turned shy. "And I'd miss him. Really bad."

"How about you, pretty lady?" Bo asked, walking through the door, his tall frame seeming to fill the entire room. "Did you miss me, too?"

Kim stood transfixed, feeling as though all the air had been sucked out of her. She clutched the back of a chair, needing to steady herself.

"I didn't mean to startle you," Bo said. "Dino wouldn't hear of me missing his wedding. Besides, we've got a lot to talk about." He made a gesture with his head, and AJ responded instantly, scampering out the door.

"He looks wonderful," Kim said, finally finding her voice. "I've never seen him so happy."

Bo nodded. "He needed his mom. You and I were right

about him needing her more than anything. And, Kim, about that—"

"Yes, about that." She was trying not to freak out, but he looked incredible, standing just a few feet away. She found herself staring at his arms, his hands, his mouth. Oh, she was so not over him. "I can understand you wanting him to live closer to New York. But here, Bo?" Her voice broke on a note of anguish. She couldn't imagine what it was going to be like, meeting Yolanda, both women knowing what they knew and pretending not to.

"I couldn't do it," he said, "couldn't leave him down in Texas, where I'd never get to see him. I just met my son, just learned to love him, and I wouldn't have been able to stand having him so far away."

She stepped back. If he touched her, she'd be lost. "Bo, you shouldn't have come here—"

"I need to explain about Yolanda," he said, coming closer. "Just listen, okay? I didn't marry her."

The words resonated through her, but still, she thought she'd heard him wrong. "You…didn't…"

"Didn't have to. Now, don't get me wrong—I would have, if that was what it took to keep her in the States. I would have done that for AJ's sake."

A cold knot formed in her stomach. "Are you…going to?"

He stuck his hands in the pockets of his jacket. It was a Yankees jacket, still bright with newness. "See, when I went down to Texas, the lawyers' investigators told me they'd found some irregularities in Yolanda's family records, and we needed to do more research into her family background."

"What kind of research?"

"The birth records for her parents were the key. Yolanda always thought they were both born in Mexico, but, well, that was just an assumption. Her mother was born in Nuevo Laredo—that's in Mexico, just like she thought. But her father—Hector Martinez, who passed away—turns out he was born in Laredo, on the U.S. side, although he grew up in Mexico. Took forever to locate the records, but we did. And because of that, Yolanda qualifies for an expedited temporary visa, and she can apply for naturalization."

"It's...that's amazing, Bo. Why didn't you call me?" She braced herself for some other unexpected blow.

"Honey, I wanted to tell you what was going on, but we agreed, I wouldn't call. Things kept changing on a daily basis, and I didn't want to jerk you around or make you a promise I'd have to break. It was like being lost in a maze, all the paperwork and regulations. I couldn't declare victory until Yolanda was officially back in the States. And now, finally, she is. I wish you could've seen AJ," he added. "I wish you'd seen the look on his face when he saw his mom again." He paused, a faraway expression on his face. "I can hardly describe it, Kim. It was like watching a light turn on inside him, and he's been lit up ever since."

"She's going to be living...here. In Avalon."

"That's right. She's staying at the Inn at Willow Lake for the time being. I couldn't stand being away from my son," Bo said. "Almost as much as I can't stand being away from you."

Her heart stumbled. Did he know how much this was hurting her? What was he thinking? "Let's not do this again," she said, folding her arms across her middle and edging back a little more. She was just on the verge of figuring out how to go on without him, and now he was back, finding his way to her heart again. She blurted out the only coherent thought that occurred to her—"I'm still in my bathrobe."

"And I'm still in love with you." He gently cupped his hands around her shoulders. As if he could feel the objections welling up in her, he touched his finger to her lips. "Let me finish. I never wanted to leave you," he said, "but it was my decision. I had to do it for AJ's sake. That's not the case anymore, and when I figured that out, I got scared."

"You? Scared of what?" She searched his face, wondering how she'd survived even a day without him.

"That we weren't meant to be together. That night at the Pierre, watching you work the room, I lost my confidence in us. You almost had me convinced we were too different, that we come from places too far apart. But guess what? None of that matters. I'm perfect for you. Maybe we did a lot of things wrong, but we were right about the one thing that matters. I love you, Kim. I always will."

She felt a tear escape. "I love you, too, but—"

"No buts, and I'm still not finished. I need to ask you something."

Kim didn't breathe, didn't take her eyes off his face. "I'm all ears."

He laughed gently, took both her hands in his. "Okay. Here goes—what are you doing for the rest of your life? See, I got these big plans, but nothing's going to work without you. Because you're the main reason for all my big plans—to make a home with you, love you for the rest of my life, that kind of thing. Plus, I come with a free bonus kid, and he's the best kid in the world."

Kim imagined being with Bo—a man who had become her best friend, her lover, the keeper of all her hopes and dreams—and she was afraid to be this happy. Afraid to trust that she deserved it, or that it could last. "You know, when I got up this morning, I wasn't expecting…whatever this is."

"Aw, honey." His hand darted into his pocket again, this time emerging with a tiny jewel box. "What part of *Will you marry me* do you not understand?"

The diamond winked at her from its velvet cushion.

"Say yes," Bo urged her. "Come on, you're killing me."

She threw her arms around him and whispered yes into his ear so many times, she lost count. Then when she looked up at him, a world of possibility bloomed in her heart. Everything lay before her. Everything was going to happen. Starting now.

* * * * *

Turn the page for a preview of Susan Wiggs's
JUST BREATHE

After a solid year of visits to the clinic, Sarah was starting to find the decor annoying. Maybe the experts here thought that earth tones had a soothing effect on anxious, aspiring parents. Or perhaps that the cheery burble of a wall fountain might cause an infertile woman to spontaneously drop an egg like an overly productive laying hen. Or even that the soft shimmer of brass chimes could induce a wandering sperm to find its way home like a heat-seeking missile.

Forty-five minutes, flat on her back with her hips elevated, was starting to feel like forever. It was no longer standard procedure to wait after insemination, but many women, Sarah included, were superstitious. They needed all the help they could get, even from gravity itself.

There was a quiet tap on the door, then she heard it swish open.

"How are we doing?" asked Frank, the nurse practitioner. Frank had a shaved head and a soul patch, a single earring and a tattoo. At six foot two, he looked a bit incongruous in pastel-pink surgical scrubs with little bunnies on them. Mr. Clean showing his nurturing side.

"Hoping that it's a 'we' this time," she said, propping her hands behind her head.

He smiled, offering a look so filled with compassion and hope that Sarah wanted to cry. "Any cramps?"

"No more than usual." She lay quietly on the cushioned, sterile-draped exam table while he checked her temperature and recorded the time.

She turned her head to the side. From this perspective, she could see her belongings neatly lined up on the shelf in the adjacent dressing room: her cinnamon-colored handbag from Smythson of Bond Street, designer clothes on padded hangers, butter-soft Manolo boots set carefully against the wall. Her mobile phone, programmed to dial her husband with one touch, or even a voice command.

Looking at all this abundance, she saw the trappings of a woman who was cared for. Provided for. Perhaps even—no, definitely—spoiled. Yet instead of feeling pampered and special, she simply felt…old. Like middle-aged, instead of still in her twenties, the youngest client at Fertility Solutions. Most women her age were still living with their boyfriends in garrets furnished with milk crates and unpainted planks. She shouldn't envy them, but sometimes she couldn't help herself.

For no good reason, she felt defensive and vaguely guilty for going through the expensive therapies. "It's not me," she wanted to explain to perfect strangers. "There's not a thing wrong with my fertility."

When she and Jack decided to seek help in getting pregnant, she went on Clomid just to give Mother Nature a hand. At first it seemed crazy to treat her perfectly healthy body as if there were something wrong with it, but by now she was used to the meds, the cramps, the transvaginal ultrasounds, the blood tests…and the crushing disappointment each time the results came up negative.

"Yo, snap out of it," Frank told her. "Going into a funk is bad karma. In my totally scientific opinion."

"I'm not in a funk." She sat up and offered him a smile. "I'm fine, really. It's just that this is the first time Jack couldn't make the appointment. So if this works, I'll have to explain to my child one day that his daddy wasn't present at his conception. What do I tell him, that Uncle Frank did the honors?"

"Yeah, that'd be good."

Sarah told herself Jack's absence wasn't his fault. It wasn't anyone's fault. By the time the ultrasound revealed a maturing ovarian follicle and she'd given herself the HCD injection, they had thirty-six hours to inseminate. Unfortunately, Jack had already scheduled a late-afternoon meeting at the work site. He couldn't get out of it. The client was coming from out of town, he said.

"So are you still trying the old-fashioned way?" Frank asked.

She flushed. Jack's erections were few and far between, and lately he'd all but given up. "That's not going so hot."

"Bring him tomorrow," Frank said. "I've got you down for 8:00 a.m." There would be a second IUI while the window of fertility was still open. He handed her a reminder card and left her alone to put herself back together.

Her yearning for a child had turned into a hunger that was physically painful, one that intensified as the fruitless months marched past. This was her twelfth visit. A year ago, she never thought she'd reach this milestone, let alone face it by herself. The whole business had become depressingly routine—the self-injections, the invasion of the speculum, the twinge and burn of the inseminating catheter. After all this time, Jack's absence should be no big deal, she reminded herself as she got dressed. Still, for Sarah it was easy to remember that at the center of all the science and technology was something very human and elemental—the desire for a baby. Lately she had a hard time even looking at mothers with babies. The sight of them turned yearning into a physical ache.

Jack had begun to resent "duty sex" for the sake of procreation. There had been a time when he'd looked at her in a way that made her feel like a goddess, but that was before he'd gotten sick. It was hard to be interested in sex, Jack often said these days, after getting your gonads irradiated. Not to mention the surgical removal of one of the guys. Jack and Sarah had made a pact. If he survived, they would have a baby. Lots of babies. They had joked about his single testicle; they'd given it a name—the Uni-ball—and lavished it with attention. Once his chemo was finished, the doctors had said he had a good chance of regaining fertility. Unfortunately, fertility had not been restored. Or sexual function, for that matter. Not on a predictable level, anyway.

The nightmare had come to light at 11:27 a.m. on a Tuesday morning. Sarah clearly remembered staring at the time on the screen of her computer, trying to remember to breathe. The expression on Jack's face had her in tears even before he said the words that would change the course of their lives: "It's cancer."

After the tears, she had vowed to get her husband through this illness. For his sake, she had perfected The Smile, the one she summoned when chemo landed him in a puking, quivering heap on the floor. The you-can-do-it-champ, I'm-behind-you-all-the-way smile.

This morning, she had tried to sustain that can-do attitude as she told her husband goodbye. "You smell delicious." She inhaled the fragrance of Karl Lagerfeld's finest, which she'd given him last June. She'd secretly bought it, along with a box of chocolate cigars, for Father's Day, thinking there might be something to celebrate. When it turned out there wasn't, she had given him the Lagerfeld anyway, just to be nice. She'd eaten the chocolate herself.

She noticed, too, that he was wearing perfectly creased trousers, one of his fitted shirts from the Custom Shop and an Hermès tie. "Important clients?" she asked.

"What?" He frowned. "Yeah. We're meeting about the marketing plans for the development."

"Well," she said, "have a good day, then. And wish me luck."

"What?" he said again, shrugging into his Burberry coat.

She shook her head, kissed his cheek. "I've got a hot date with your army of seventeen million motile sperm," she said.

"Ah, shit. I really can't change this meeting."

"I'll be all right." Kissing him goodbye one more time, she suppressed a twinge of resentment at his testy, distracted air. It was understandable, after all. She was one of the reasons he spent so much time working. Lord knew, her own earnings as a comic-strip artist couldn't finance anything, certainly not fertility treatment. Particularly in a place like this.

Now that Jack was cancer-free, she intended to focus on the comic strip, expanding her syndication. People thought it was simple, drawing a comic strip six days a week. Some believed she could draw a whole month's worth in one day, and then slack off the rest of the time. They had no idea how difficult and consuming self-syndication was, particularly at the beginning of a career.

The very worst of Chicago weather flayed the windshield when her car emerged from the parking lot. The city had its own peculiar brand of slush that seemed to fling itself off Lake Michigan, sullying vehicles, slapping at pedestrians and sending them scurrying for cover. Sarah would never get used to this weather, no matter how long she lived here. When she had first arrived in the city, a wide-eyed University of Chicago freshman from a tiny beach village in northern California, she thought she'd encountered the storm of the century. She'd had no idea that this was normal for Chicago.

She had always planned to leave the moment she graduated. She hadn't pictured raising a family here. But that was life for you. Filled with surprises. But Jack Daly had been a surprise, as well.

"I'll build you your dream house," he had promised her when they got engaged. "You'll learn to love the city, you'll see."

She loved him. The jury was still out on Chicago.

Her front tire sank into a pothole. The jolt sent an eruption of mud-colored slush across the windshield, and she heard an ominous thud from the backseat. A glance in the mirror revealed that the fax machine had done a swan dive to the floor. "Lovely," she muttered. "Just swell." She pressed the wiper-fluid wand, but the ducts sputtered out only an impotent trickle. The warning light blinked *Empty*.

Traffic crawled in a miserable stream northward. Stuck at a stoplight for the third cycle, Sarah thumped the steering wheel with the heel of her hand. "I don't have to sit in traffic," she said. "I'm self-employed. I might even be pregnant."

She wondered what Shirl would do in this situation.

Shirl was Sarah's alter ego in her comic strip, "Just Breathe." A sharper, more confident, thinner version of her creator, Shirl was audacious; she had a screw-you attitude and an impulsive nature.

"What would Shirl do?" Sarah asked aloud. The answer came to her in an instant: get pizza.

The very thought flung such a craving on her that she laughed. A craving. Maybe she was already showing signs of pregnancy.

Twenty minutes later, the car filled with the fragrance of fresh-baked pizza covered in all of Jack's favorite toppings, she turned off the state highway and wended her way to a suburb where he was developing a community of luxury homes. She slowed down as she drove through the figured concrete gates that would one day be operated by key-card only. The tasteful sign at the entrance said it all: Shamrock Downs. A Private Equestrian Community. This was where millionaires would come to live with their pampered horses.

In the late-afternoon gloom, she saw that all the work crews had gone for the day, driven away by the rain. There was a Subaru Forester parked at the barn, but no one in sight. The foreman's trailer looked abandoned, too. Maybe she had missed Jack and he was heading home. Perhaps he'd had an attack of conscience and had left his meeting early to be with her at the clinic, but had gotten stuck in traffic. There were no messages on her mobile, but that didn't mean anything. She hated cell phones. They never worked when you needed them to and tended to ring when you wanted peace and quiet.

The unfinished houses looked eerie, their skeletal timbers black against the rain-drenched sky. Equipment was parked haphazardly, like giant, hastily abandoned toys in a sodden sandbox. Half-full Dumpsters littered the barren landscape. The people who moved to this neighborhood would never realize it had started out looking like a battle zone. But Jack was a magician. He could start with a sterile prairie or a reclaimed waste-disposal site and turn it into Pleasantville. By spring, he would turn this place into a pristine, bucolic utopia, with children playing on the lawns, foals gamboling in the paddocks, women with ponytails and no makeup and thigh-hugging riding pants heading for the barn.

Darkness deepened by the minute. The pizza would be cold soon.

Then she spotted Jack's car. The custom-restored GTO was the ultimate muscle machine, even though legally, it belonged to her. When he was ill, she'd bought it to cheer him up. Now that he was well, the car remained his prize possession. He only drove it on special occasions. His meeting with the client must have been an important one.

The black-and-red car crouched like an exotic beast in the driveway of one of the model houses. In its nearly finished state, the home resembled a hunting lodge. On steroids. Everything Jack built was bigger than it had to be—wraparound deck, entryway, four-car garage, water feature. The yard was still a mud pit, with great holes carved out for the fully grown trees that would be installed. *Installed* was Jack's word. Sarah would have said planted. The trees looked pathetic, like fallen victims, lying limp on their sides with their withered root-balls encased in burlap.

Balancing the Coke on the pizza box, she opened her push-button umbrella and got out. A gust of wind tugged at the ribs of her umbrella, turning it inside out. Icy rain battered her face and slid down inside her collar.

That's it, she thought. I'm making Jack take me home to California for a vacation. Her hometown of Glenmuir, in Marin County, had never been his favorite place. He favored the white sand beaches of Florida, but Sarah was starting to feel it was her turn to choose their destination.

The past year and a half had been all about Jack—his needs, his recovery, his wishes. Now that the ordeal was behind them, she let her own needs rise up to the surface. It felt a tad selfish but damned good all the same. She wanted to have a baby. A vacation away from soggy Chicago. She wanted to savor each worry-free day, something she hadn't been able to do in a very long time.

No locks had been installed yet on the prehung doors of the huge, unfinished home.

She smiled as she pushed open the front door and sighed with relief. What could be cozier than sitting in front of the fire on a rainy afternoon, eating pizza? Quite possibly, this house was the only warm, dry place in the neighborhood.

"It's me," she called, stepping out of her boots so as not to muddy the newly finished hardwood floors. There was no reply, just the tinny sound of a radio playing some-where upstairs.

Sarah felt a twinge of discomfort in her belly. Cramping was a side effect of IUI, and Sarah didn't mind. The fact that there was pain lent an appropriate sense of gravitas to her mission. It was a physical reminder of her commitment and determination to start a family.

Shaking off the raindrops, she padded in stocking feet to the stairs. She'd never been here before, but she was fa-miliar with the layout of the house. Though it wasn't obvious to most people, Jack worked with only a few floor plans. The massive size and luxurious materials aside, he built what he unapologetically called "cookie-cutter mansions." She had once asked him if he ever got bored, building essentially the same house over and over again. He had laughed aloud at the question.

"What's boring about netting a cool million on a tract home?" he had countered.

He liked making money. He was good at it. And she was lucky, because so far, she was terrible at it. Each year when they filed their income tax return, he would look at the revenues from her comic strip, offer her a generous smile and joke, "I always wanted to be a patron of the arts."

At the top of the stairs, she turned toward the sound of the radio, her raincoat brushing against the machine-turned banister. "Achy Breaky Heart" was playing, and she winced. Jack had terrible taste in music. So bad, in fact, it was actually endearing.

The door to the master suite was ajar, and the friendly glow of the fire glimmered across the freshly carpeted floors. She hesitated, sensing…something.

A warning, beating like an extra pulse in her ears.

She stepped into the room, her feet sinking into the deep pile of the carpet as her eyes adjusted to the soft, golden light. The diffused, kindly glow of the lifetime-guaranteed Briarwood gas logs flickered over two naked bodies entwined on a bed of thick woolen blankets spread in front of the hearth.

Sarah experienced a moment of complete and utter confusion. Her vision clouded and she felt light-headed and nauseous. There was some mistake here. She had walked into the wrong house. Into the wrong life. She fought against the panicky, random thoughts playing Ping-Pong in her head. For a second or two she simply stood immobile, assaulted by shock, forgetting to breathe.

After endless seconds, they noticed her and sat up, gathering blankets to cover themselves. The song on the radio switched to something equally appalling—"Butterfly Kisses."

Finally, Sarah found her voice and spoke the only coherent thought in her head: "I brought you a pizza. And a Coke. Extra ice, the way you like it."

She didn't throw the pizza or spill the drinks. She set everything carefully on the built-in media console next to the radio. She was as discreet and efficient as a room-service waiter.

Then she turned and left.

Jack called her name.

Sarah skimmed down the stairs with the speed and grace of Cinderella at the stroke of midnight. Shoving her feet into her boots barely slowed her down. In seconds, she was outside with her broken umbrella, heading for the car.

She started the engine just as Jack burst outside. He wore his good pants—the ones with the creases she had admired this morning—and nothing else. She could see his mouth working, forming her name: *Sarah.* She put the headlamps on bright and turned the car, feeling a satisfying crunch as the rear bumper of the Lexus toppled the custom river-rock mailbox. Her high beams washed across the front of the house, illuminating the porch timbers and fine wooden window casements, the Andersen glass and the grand front entranceway.

For a moment, Jack appeared pinned by the glare, a prize buck frozen in the headlights.

What would Shirl do? Sarah asked herself. She gripped the steering wheel, threw the car into gear and floored the accelerator.